NICK SETCHFIELD

THE SPIDER DANCE

TITAN BOOKS

The Spider Dance
Print edition ISBN: 9781785657115
E-book edition ISBN: 9781785657122

Published by Titan Books
A division of Titan Publishing Group Ltd
144 Southwark Street, London SE1 0UP

First edition: July 2019
1 2 3 4 5 6 7 8 9 10

A CIP catalogue record for this title is available from the British Library.

Printed and bound by CPI Group (UK) Ltd, Croydon CR0 4YY.

For Mum

1

JUNE 1965

There was a human heart in a locker at St Pancras station.

Christopher Winter came to collect it on a Thursday afternoon in early summer. London felt listless; cranes idled on the heat-blurred horizon, ready to peck at the new tower blocks sprouting to the north of the city. There was no wind and the weathervane that topped the gothic spire of the grand Victorian building did not tilt or turn.

The heart cared little for London and even less for the living.

Winter strode through the redbrick arch on Euston Road, into the main concourse, scattering sickly-grey pigeons. The birds took to the roof, settling on its wrought-iron ribs. The station clock hung like a glass moon above the locomotives. It was almost five.

The heart had outlasted centuries. The heart could wait forever.

Destination boards clattered, place names spinning in the slats. St Albans. Kettering. Melton Mowbray. There was the promise of more exotic departures too: Liverpool, Manchester, Edinburgh Waverley.

The heart had known many lands.

Winter kept walking, past the walls of diesel-blackened bricks. It was hot inside and this gutter-stained cathedral smelt of soot and engine oil. Soon, he suspected, they would take a wrecking ball to St Pancras. Build something new, streamlined and modern, fit for the times.

The left luggage lockers were ahead of him, bookended by posters for Pall Mall cigarettes and cheap breaks on the Spanish coast. He located his locker and inspected the edges of the door for signs of disturbance. The pinch of gum he had wedged in the crack was intact, his pencil-tip indentations preserved. Standard operational practice in the field. He rather missed it.

A Salvation Army band had gathered outside the ticket office. They began to play 'The Well is Deep', the sound of the brass incongruously mournful on such a sultry afternoon. Winter let his gaze skim the concourse, his face blank. Good. He was unobserved.

He took a small key from his shirt pocket. It was wet from the sweat that had seeped into the nylon. The serrated silver slid into the lock. The key turned.

The package was there, just as he had left it. It had arrived in the post two days before, tied with sturdy bows of string and plastered with colourful Ecuadorian stamps. Where to store it? Not at his damp-riddled room in Battersea, that was for sure. His landlady had the infiltration skills of the KGB's finest. No, far safer to keep it here, concealed behind this anonymous wall of lockers, safe among the suitcases and the hat boxes and the pills and the guns and all the other secrets London banked when no one was looking.

He pulled the parcel from its aluminium nest. It was Karina who had addressed the label, her handwriting as sleek and contained as he remembered her physical presence (those upward slashes, so like the movement of a blade...). She had sourced the heart for him, drawing on her network of contacts who traded in the unobtainable. It was a favour. He tried not to think of it as a final gift.

Winter placed the parcel under his arm and closed the locker door. As he stepped away one of the station's rat-catchers passed behind him. The man had an inky bottle of poison in his hand and a small but belligerent dog on a leash. The terrier snarled, springing at Winter's legs and leaving two grimy paw prints on the knees of his suit. The man pulled the dog back with a jerk of the strap. The animal whined, straining to reach the package, half curious, half anxious. It continued to stare as the rat-catcher hauled it towards the goods yard. 'Get away, boy! Daft thing, you are!'

Winter strode out of the station, the clipped tones of the tannoy fading behind him. He flagged down a black cab at the kerbside.

'Camden Town. Betting shop on Chalk Farm Road.'

He eased himself onto the seat behind the driver, the

parcel balanced on his lap. Stealing a look in the rear-view mirror he saw the spires of St Pancras retreat, the late afternoon sunlight striking the sandstone bricks. Picking up speed, the taxi trundled north along the Euston Road, the traffic a drowsy hum outside the windows.

Sat there in the back of the cab Winter imagined he could hear the faintest throb of a heartbeat. A muffled but insistent drumming, coming from inside the parcel. Tiny, determined, impossible. Once he would have crushed such a thought. He knew better now. He knew that magic was the hidden pulse of this world.

Winter extracted a pack of Woodbines from his jacket pocket. He placed one between his lips, poking the tip into the flame of his gunmetal lighter. He clearly wasn't about to make conversation and so the driver spun the radio dial. On Radio London Sandie Shaw was singing about waiting a long, long time for love.

The heart had the patience of a dead thing.

Tommy the Face admired himself in the nicotine-clouded mirror that hung in the hot, boxy room behind the betting shop. His new three-button Anthony Sinclair suit was perfect. The lines were lean, the cut trim, the fit modishly tapered. He particularly savoured the way the fine Italian wool clung to his own sharp and flawless angles. Inspecting his sleek, snow-blond fringe he idly adjusted his cuffs, allowing a glimpse of coral cufflink at the edge of each sleeve. He was, he knew, the business.

Tommy saw Winter's reflection enter the room. 'Alright, Frosty?'

As ever there was a detectable hint of needle in the young man's voice. Winter had known him for two months now, ever since the Southwark job, and they tolerated each other's company like wary cats.

'Just call me Winter, Tommy. Christopher if you must.'

Tommy smirked, returning to the lure of his reflection. 'Your call, mate. Just being friendly.' And then he turned, smiling just a little too much. 'Tell me, what do you reckon to the suit? It's a corker, right? I reckon I'll slay the birds up West in this.'

Winter gave him a weary, dead-eyed look. 'If I had an opinion on your suit I'd kill myself.'

There was a grunt of a laugh from the armchair, where a doleful, balding man in his late fifties was slicing a pomegranate with a switchblade. This was Albert White, more commonly known as Sparkling.

Tommy nodded, his smile dropping at the edges. 'Is that so? Well, that's no surprise, buttercup. Look at the bloody threads you're wearing.'

He stepped closer and smoothed the lapels of Winter's rumpled seersucker suit. 'I can't tell if this is a fashion statement or a suicide note.'

Sparkling grunted again then fell back into his customary lugubrious silence. Gathering pomegranate seeds on the edge of the blade he flicked them at a bin full of betting slips.

'I mean, who are you?' baited Tommy, as if spoiling

for a fight in this cramped, windowless room. 'You turn up one day, no references, no rep. Just a blank little bastard from nowhere.'

He moved an inch closer, making his wiry, well-tailored frame as intimidating as he could. 'Who's to say you're not undercover filth?'

Winter's bright green eyes matched Tommy's gaze. 'Get out of my face, son. Or you won't be so pretty for much longer.'

'Is that a threat?'

'More a statistical probability.'

Tommy pushed it. 'Based on?'

'Years of research,' said Winter, evenly.

Tommy weighed his response. And then he flashed his cocky, livewire grin. 'Well, at least we know your suit's criminal.' He turned to Sparkling, expecting a laugh. Sparkling had a mouthful of pomegranate.

Winter sat down on a baggy, cigarette-scorched leather sofa. He tossed a copy of *The Sporting Life* to the carpet, where it joined an empty bottle of Johnnie Walker and a scattering of playing cards. Next to him was another man, thick-set but matinee handsome in an entirely oblivious way, as if perpetually surprised by his own good looks. Winter had never heard his real name but knew that he was Italian. Naturally he was known to the others as Spanish. That was the private logic of the world he now found himself in.

'It is not a bad suit, really, Signor Winter,' said Spanish, with a clumsy sweetness. 'I've seen people buried in worse.'

Winter smiled. 'Thank you, Spanish. I appreciate the sentiment.'

Ten minutes passed in an itchy silence. Tommy continued to preen like a mod Narcissus in the mirror while Winter found himself examining every last detail of the stamps stuck to the package. If the heartbeat had ever been there it was gone now. Finally the door opened and a pre-emptive fug of cigar smoke and peppery aftershave declared the arrival of Jack Creadley.

The room changed in his presence. There was a sullen charisma to the man that assumed and won respect. Winter estimated Creadley must have been in his early sixties – the black hair was neatly clipped and parted with pomade, the face pocked like animal hide – but he carried the ghost of his younger self, the lad who had flashed knives in Thameside dockyards, the boy who had earned the wide, pale scar at his throat, curved like a smile.

'Checked the merchandise?' he asked, indicating the parcel on Winter's lap.

'Of course,' said Winter, tetchily. And then, more gently, because Creadley had the temper of a landmine, 'It's exactly what they're looking for.'

Creadley exhaled cigar smoke between his teeth. 'Good. I hate to disappoint a client. Especially one with real money. Alright, Winter. You're staying on the payroll.'

He turned to address the room. 'The trade's at four am. We leave at three. Get some food down your gullets. No booze. And I mean no booze. If there's booze I slice you.' He nodded to a small trestle table in the corner. It was stacked with firearms. 'Let's be professional about it.'

And with that commandment Jack Creadley left the room. Sparkling sighed and reached for the copy of *The Sporting Life* that Winter had flung to the floor. 'Nine bleedin' hours.'

Tommy consulted his watch, hitching his shirt-cuff so that the elegant dial was fully exposed, the light from the room's lone, bare bulb bouncing off the glass. He stepped nearer to the sofa, making a concerted attempt to snag Winter's attention.

'Like the watch? It's new.'

Winter peered at Tommy's wrist. 'You know,' he said, with a dark little smile, 'I don't think that's how you spell Cartier...'

The North Circular had a profound emptiness at three in the morning. There were other people on the road, to be sure – black cabs, transit vans, the occasional greaser on a twin-cylinder Triton – but to Winter they were all complicit, part of an unspoken fraternity in these dead hours. Ghost traffic, anonymous and slippery.

He sat in the back of Jack Creadley's Jaguar saloon, wedged like a kid between Sparkling and Spanish, the package on his lap. Tommy the Face was driving. Creadley was in the passenger seat upfront, a fresh cigar on the go. No one spoke but the bass growl of the Jag's engine thrummed through the upholstery.

As they powered along the dual carriageway Winter

considered just how many bodies might be buried in the tarmac beneath them. Creadley had doubtlessly put some of those bodies there himself. Snitches, competitors, former business partners. Perhaps the man who had slashed his throat. Christ, the company Winter was keeping these days. He turned to the window, peering past Spanish, trying to tune out his own disquiet.

He needed a job. This was a job. It was that simple.

The road took them past garage forecourts and transport cafés, sleeping industrial estates and unlit factories, the bright hub of London retreating as the asphalt snaked toward Watford and beyond. Winter watched as the roadside landscape became bleaker, more derelict, husks of buildings consumed by countryside. These were the abandoned edges, the outermost margins of the capital, where an alliance of rot and wild shrubs claimed the city for itself.

Maybe it was the hour but this part of London felt liminal, a shadowy threshold between the lawful world and everything that lay outside it. No wonder a man like Creadley favoured such a location. *Home turf*, thought Winter.

Creadley glanced in the wing mirror. He was convinced they had been tailed ever since they left Camden. A gangster's instinct. 'We shaken it?'

'Nothing there,' Tommy reassured him. 'We're clean, I told you.'

'We better be, son. Keep an eye out.'

The Jaguar took a side road, following a half-obscured

15

signpost for Scratch Hill Junction. Ahead of them lay a deserted car park, its concrete walls choked by briars. A wasteground now, it sat beneath a brambled railway cutting, close to the black maw of a foot tunnel. Beyond the embankment rose a viaduct, spanning a straggly width of river.

The saloon edged into the car park, its headlamps dimming as it crawled to a stop. The men got out, buttoning jackets, smoothing the outlines of guns. The breeze was surprisingly warm ahead of the dawn. There was already a chorus of blackbirds in the trees.

'We'll wait for them inside,' said Creadley. 'Let's see them arrive.'

They walked in lockstep to the shell of the station. It had been bombed in the war, clipped by the tail end of a raid on a local munitions factory. The remaining structure was officially condemned but the money or the will had never been there to demolish it. And so Scratch Hill had been left to decay, saving a not inconsiderable amount of paperwork. Over the years the land had gradually clawed the area back. Nature was vengeful, but she was patient, too.

Inside, wartime propaganda posters peeled from the walls. *Dig For Victory. Hitler Will Send No Warning. Keep It To Yourself – War's Not A Family Matter.* Someone had taken a Stanley knife to the last one, blinding the eyes of the handsome, apple-cheeked brood until only jagged white shreds remained.

The men moved into the shadows of the waiting

room, fragments of timber and glass splintering beneath their shoes.

'I'm not happy with any of this,' said Sparkling, his voice a dry whisper. 'What do they want with this thing? It's obscene...'

Creadley was patient. 'It's fine. It's a trade. Just a bit of unusual merchandise, that's all.'

'We've never dealt with these people before,' Sparkling persisted. 'They're a breed apart, by the sounds of it.'

'They're clients, same as anyone. If they try to stiff us, they'll soon know about it, believe me.'

The thought of imminent violence – as close as Jack Creadley came to a personal guarantee – seemed to mollify Sparkling. He lapsed into a glum silence, staring out through the shards of glass that hung like icicles in the window frames.

At a little after four a glare of headlights swept the room. A fin-tailed Mercedes-Benz slid into the car park, a milky smear of moonlight on its gleaming black bodywork. As the engine died the driver's door opened and a man in a chauffeur's cap and breeches exited the vehicle. He glanced impassively at the ruined building then strode to the rear door of the Mercedes, opening it with a slick twist of the handle.

A woman climbed out of the car. She was dressed in a crisp, dark business suit and wore her silver-blonde hair in an ornately braided bun. There was a sinuous elegance to her, noted Winter, almost like Shrimpton or one of those other bony wonders who were forever in the fashion pages of the Sunday supplements. She looked, in truth, like the last person who belonged in this place.

The woman strode towards the station entrance, the driver a discreet number of paces behind. There was a trim black attaché case in her hand, swinging on a leather handle.

The pair entered the waiting room, prompting Creadley and his men to step from the shadows. The two parties exchanged nods. There were no introductions, no pleasantries, but the edges of the woman's mouth danced as Tommy emerged from the gloom. She put a hand to the young gangster's face and let it glide across his cheek, the motion unmistakably sensual.

'Such an exquisite boy.' The accent was impossible to place but the words rippled like silk.

Tommy gave a forgivably smug grin, relishing the attention. And then the smile became a grimace, as if the woman had just trailed thorns across his face. Curious, Winter peered at Tommy's skin but it was unmarked.

He let his gaze skip to Spanish, who was stood next to Tommy. There was a fine sweat on the Italian's forehead. He didn't meet Winter's eyes.

'Let's see the money,' said Creadley, prioritising.

'Of course.' She unlocked the latches of the case and raised the lid, revealing tight clumps of banknotes, stacked against baize lining. 'Ten thousand, as we agreed. Now you show us the heart.'

Creadley gave the nod. Winter took a step forward, the parcel in his hand. The woman regarded him, a glitter

18

of fascination in her pupils. They had expanded to almost eclipse her irises but Winter had the feeling they were hungry for more than just light. It was as though they were absorbing everything in the room, every potential stimulus. Her eyes were cool but they craved.

She raised her hand again, her lean, almond-nailed fingers eager for Winter's skin. He caught her by the wrist and gave a polite shake of his head. She let her hand fall, disappointed but amused.

Winter delved into Karina's parcel. His hand emerged holding a small, plump bundle of wax paper. He cradled it in his palm, almost tenderly, and began to peel away the semi-translucent layers, as if unwrapping a butcher's cut. There, in the centre, was a leathery, blood-blackened heart, the mound of veins and tissue shrivelled by age but recognisably human. Perched on Winter's hand it began to beat in the stillness of the room.

'This is Frontenac's heart?' the woman challenged, watching as it throbbed, the ventricles quivering almost imperceptibly in the half-light.

Winter nodded. 'Guaranteed.'

'What do you want with it?' asked Sparkling White, an ill-concealed note of disgust in his voice. Tonight was beyond both his experience and his understanding. This deal clearly didn't sit well with him.

The woman kept her gaze on the heart. 'We just want to keep it safe. Such a precious object.' She almost purred, a kitten with a wounded bird.

'No more talk,' said Creadley. 'We trade now.'

19

Winter prepared to exchange, motioning for the woman to hand him the money. She moved the attaché case closer, keeping her right arm parallel to his. For a moment they were synched in perfect mutual distrust.

There was a sudden flurry of dust on Winter's face. It had come from directly above him.

He stared up, blinking the soot from his eyes. Something had disturbed the rafters of the old station. There was a shape there – but barely there, almost indistinguishable from the darkness that hid the rotted joists. A coiled, compact mass of shadow, as if the dark had contorted itself into something solid.

The darkness uncurled and dropped from the rafters as a man.

Winter barely had time to register a midnight-blue suit and wormy white skin before the heart was snatched from his hand.

As one the gangsters pulled their guns. Sparkling was the first to fire and Sparkling was the first to die, his throat ripped by a slash of nails. Blood hit the wall, spattering the propaganda posters. The coppery arc of fluid stained the torn white eyes.

Spanish waved his gun, protesting the death. 'No! This is not what we agreed! No killing! We agreed no killing!'

The figure in the dark blue suit turned to confront the young Italian. He had a pale, bald head, embroidered with veins. The skin was dragged taut across the bone, hugging the skull like a sheath. There was a scent in the room like spoilt fruit.

20

'What do you mean we agreed?' demanded Creadley, fighting to process what he'd just heard, let alone what he'd seen. 'Who did you agree with?'

Spanish battled the tremor in his throat. 'Mr Creadley... I... Boss...'

Now Creadley swung his gun at Spanish. 'You cut your own deal? You sold us out to this bastard? You did this to me, you cheeky little sod?' His knuckle tightened around the trigger. There was fury in his face.

A bullet thumped into Spanish's chest. He staggered, knock-kneed, to the wall, a surge of blood on his lips. Then he sank to the ground, his eyes dead.

Creadley switched his aim to the figure in the blue suit. The blade-like nails sliced the hand from his wrist, severing the flesh in a swift, feral motion. Creadley's hand smacked the floor, a slab of meat now, still clasping the butt of the gun, a signet ring gleaming. He barely had time to stare at the wet stump in his sleeve before the nails came again, shredding his face to rags.

In the chaos the woman and her chauffeur had fled the room. Winter could see them racing to the Mercedes outside. They had abandoned the attaché case, spilling its upper tier of banknotes in the dust of the station floor.

The man in the midnight-blue suit turned to face Winter and Tommy, the stolen heart in his hand. Winter stared at the intruder, taking in the bloodless skin and the curiously upswept ears with their jagged little tips. The eyes were robbed of colour, pale as quartz. It gave him the look of some blind fish in a lightless ocean trench.

What was left of Jack Creadley wailed in the corner of the waiting room.

The man who had taken the heart turned and ran.

'Come on,' said Winter, urging a clearly reluctant Tommy to follow him.

'Right bastard night, this is,' muttered Tommy, Creadley's blood decorating his Turnbull & Asser shirt.

They set off in pursuit, hearing the Mercedes tear out of the car park with a furious rasp of tyres. The man in the blue suit had already reached the mouth of the old foot tunnel. They saw him disappear inside, his thin frame quickly taken by the darkness. Winter and Tommy sprinted towards the archway.

The entrance to the tunnel stank of dead water. Winter took the lighter from his pocket and cracked a flame, exposing the slimy ceramic tiles that lined the pitch-black hollow. It was a feeble attempt at illumination – the shadows in front of them were still a thick, forbidding wall – but it was all they had.

They pushed ahead, into the tunnel, kicking through dank troughs of water, the tiny flame dancing and dwindling in Winter's hand. It felt as though they were carving their way into solid night. There was no sign of the man they were chasing, no sound of footfalls in the tunnel's depths. The smell of putrefaction almost made them gag.

And then there he was, caught in the oily shadows cast by the lighter. He stood directly ahead of them, motionless, the heart still clutched in his fist. Gobs of moisture fell from the ceiling, striking his skull and running the length of his face.

Winter and Tommy stumbled to a stop, their own breathing all they could hear in the echoing length of the tunnel.

The figure regarded them with those colourless eyes.

Tommy flashed his cocksure grin. 'Nice tailoring, gorgeous.'

For a moment the man made no response. And then the edges of his mouth parted, the lips peeling to expose a chain of teeth. The incisors were the size of nails. It was a smile, of a kind.

Winter levelled his Mauser. But he didn't shoot.

Something was massing in the deep, wet shadows of the tunnel. Something that was gathering strength in the dark.

The sounds came ahead of the shapes, echoing along the cracked tiled walls. A scratching and a thrashing and a shrill, half-crazed screech.

A flood of sewer rats burst from the darkness.

They swarmed upon the walls and surged through the potholes, their bodies tangling together, skinny tails whipping each other's matted hides. There was another noise now: a sustained, incessant chittering, like hunger itself.

Winter and Tommy ran. They turned on their heels and raced to the entrance, thrashing through water, skidding on the slick tiles. Breaking back into the night they made for the car park. The mass of rats pursued them, scrambling through the withered undergrowth, fast and ravenous.

Tommy was the first to reach the Jag. He tore the keys from his pocket and cursed as he missed the lock on his first attempt. Then he hauled the door open and threw it shut behind him.

Winter slammed the passenger door, sealing them inside. 'Start the car!'

Tommy stabbed the key into the ignition. No response.

The windscreen darkened. The rats were upon it, their countless teeth and tiny, almost ludicrously human hands squeezed against the glass.

Again the engine failed to fire. 'Shit!' cried Tommy, again and again. He had the voice of a boy now.

Something thumped the roof. And then came another thump, and another, and another, harder and louder, the weight of the things accumulating by the second. The windows of the car were running with the vermin. Now the only light came from the dim glow of the dashboard.

The Jag's engine finally turned over. Tommy thrust the gear lever into first. Releasing the handbrake he floored the throttle.

A series of fine cracks suddenly filled the windscreen. Beyond it was a shifting mass of darkness.

The car was gaining speed but Tommy was driving blind, swerving erratically in a bid to shake the rats. He accelerated, stamped on the brake, accelerated again, trying to throw them free. The protest of the tyres merged with the squeal of the creatures.

The windscreen was fracturing. Winter took a look behind him. The rear window was black with rats.

No choice now.

Winter twisted the door handle. Flinging the door wide he hurled himself out as Tommy accelerated again. Tarmac slammed against his body, tearing his hands as he tumbled. He rolled, fighting to steady himself.

The Jaguar slammed into the wall of the car park, its bodywork crumpling on impact. Winter heard a shattering of glass. And then a scream, a scream that was quickly engulfed, then gone. The rats had found Tommy's mouth.

The ruptured fuel tank exploded. The Jag ignited with a hot bloom of flame, lighting up the car park and the ring of ash trees beyond it.

Winter pulled himself to his feet, shielding his eyes from the fireball. Through the haze of heat he could see the man in the blue suit, emerging from the other end of the foot tunnel. He was on the hillside now, making for the viaduct, his thin body outlined against the early London light.

Winter took a brass knuckle-duster from his jacket pocket and squeezed his bloodied fingers through its thick, scuffed rings. In his other hand he gripped the Mauser. He sprinted across the car park and scrambled up the wooded embankment, following the fox path through the brambles, thorns snagging his suit.

On the crown of the hill the full span of the viaduct lay revealed. The abandoned bridge straddled the river on a row of semi-circular arches, squatting above the water like an infinitely patient spider. Winter estimated the ribbon of rail track had to be two hundred yards long, perhaps sixty feet high. The once-proud Victorian structure was crumbling now, shorn by the Luftwaffe strike in the war.

Winter ran along the maintenance walkway, clattering down the plates and rivets. He took a rash shot. It was a waste of a bullet, lost to the sky.

Another running shot. Another miss. The bullet rebounded, embedding itself in brickwork.

Winter raced along the rusted tracks, closing in.

The man in the blue suit tilted his tapered ears as Winter approached, hunting sound. He stopped running and began to turn. The motion was unhurried, utterly confident.

Winter smashed the knuckle-duster into his face. Then he punched him again, harder still, straight across the mouth. The brass took the impact that would have cracked his own bones.

The man reeled, Frontenac's heart still clutched against his chest. With an irritated swipe of his free hand he knocked the Mauser from Winter's fist. The pistol spun away to the ground.

This part of the bridge had been half razed by the Blitz. The rails ended in scorch-blackened prongs, torn forks of metal that framed a gaping hole in the tracks. Directly below was the dirty-dark water, swilling over weeds and boulders. The wall, too, was gone, blown away on the right-hand side, leaving a vertiginous drop.

The man in the blue suit snatched at Winter's jacket, hauling him to the very edge of the breach. Brickwork broke beneath their shoes, tumbling through the gap to the river.

Winter was half treading air, fighting to hook his heels on the broken spurs of the rails.

He grabbed his opponent's wrist, using him for leverage as much as blocking a potential blow. As he struggled to keep his balance he saw the man's nails glint in the grey light. The hand was opening, the fingers flexing as they unfurled.

At first Winter thought the man must be injured; blood was leaking from his palm, running from a half-moon scored in the skin. It was almost a stigmata.

And then the skin broke like a wound. Twin rows of teeth emerged from the fissure.

It was a mouth, yawning out of the flesh.

It reached for his face, the tiny teeth shiny with blood and spittle. Winter thrust his head away but the hand was closing against his throat.

Suddenly his opponent twisted, spasmed. Winter felt a shock of impact pass into his own body. He recognised it at once: the emphatic wrench of a gunshot. He flinched, wondering if the bullet had found him too.

The man tottered, his colourless eyes narrowing with anger. He spat a single syllable, a word that Winter didn't recognise. Then he lurched towards the shattered wall and dropped from the bridge, the heart held tight in his fist.

He had chosen to fall.

Winter reached the wall in time to see the figure hit the river. It smacked into the greasy water, sending ever-widening ripples to the banks. The body began to drift, claimed by the current. The heart remained in the man's hand, cradled triumphantly against his chest as he floated deeper into this unloved tributary of the Thames.

Winter exhaled. It was a pained breath. 'Next time you might want to try a head shot. It's a little more satisfying all round.'

The girl faced him across the bridge. She was in her early twenties, dressed in a short, belted raincoat, her chestnut hair cropped urchin-style. The Webley & Scott revolver in her hand undercut her waif-like appearance.

'Well,' she said, 'they did warn me you were a wanker.'

Winter bent to retrieve his gun. 'I'm grateful. Who are you?'

There was a trace of north-west London in her voice as she replied. And something proud, too, just on the edge of defensive. 'Libby Cracknell. British Intelligence.'

Winter slid the gun into his shoulder holster. 'Not interested.'

She scrunched her nose as she considered this. 'Not how it works, mate.'

'I know how it bloody works.' Winter looked away. The sky had brightened over the hills, the first streaks of blue emerging from the crush of grey. Another good day was promised.

'Sir Crispin wants you,' she said, simply. 'At least hear him out. What have you got to lose, Mr Winter?'

Winter gave a hot sigh. 'Right now, damn all.'

He returned his eyes to the river. Something nagged at him. A detail he'd clearly registered but his conscious mind had missed. He stared at the dark rush of water, replaying the man's plummet from the bridge.

It was then that it came to him, as obvious as it was inexplicable.

The figure had fallen without a shadow.

2

The two-seater convertible sped through a waking London, a blur of British Racing Green.

Winter watched the city pass, an elbow propped on the passenger door of the compact MGB. It was just after five in the morning and the streets already had a dawn rhythm. Traders were setting up stalls of fish and fruit as the last partygoers swayed home, bow ties askew, bra straps adrift. The air was cool, the early light a hazy blue.

London had changed in the last year. It was as if the city had started to thaw, no longer the bomb-punished capital that had endured the flinty, penny-pinching years after the war. People were trading soot, tweed and ration books for the clean, plastic promise of tomorrow. There was colour and confidence now. You heard it on the radio and you glimpsed it in the street. Yes, the loss of empire was an open wound, but the future was rushing in regardless.

Winter wasn't convinced there was a place for him in this brash new London. He rather suspected it belonged to the young.

He turned to Libby Cracknell, watching as she ran another red light, a peaked, checkerboard-patterned cap pulled low across her fringe. They had just passed Regent's Park.

'How did you find me?'

Something impish played on her lips. 'I found you three months ago.'

She stole a look at him, the tip of her tongue playing against her teeth. The car's engine surged again, the needle dancing as it swung into Hampstead Road.

'Three months?' Winter was sceptical.

'I've been your guardian angel, Mr Winter. Been looking out for you. Saved your life once or twice. Sir Crispin really wants to keep you alive. Sentimental attachment, I suppose.'

Another, even cheekier smile. Her eyes were bright as busker's coins in the sun.

'That's impossible,' said Winter, flatly.

'That shoot-out in Silvertown? Who do you think had your back?'

Winter's mind flashed to a night in May. A fleeting armistice with the Krays had ended in an exchange of gunfire. Winter remembered the punch of the guns, bullets splintering the beams of a dockside warehouse. Two of Creadley's men had died. A week later the Krays had sent wreaths to their funerals, a territorial warning in orchids.

'Someone had a gun on me,' said Winter, the moment still vivid. 'I never had a chance to reload.'

Libby nodded. 'I know. I took care of it.'

'I assumed it was a ricochet.'

'Like I told you. Guardian angel. And I reckon you need one.'

'So you were the one following us from Camden. Creadley's instinct was right.'

Libby seemed genuinely put out by this. 'Shit. He noticed? I thought I was better than that.'

The MGB growled as it gained speed, leaving an idling milk float far behind.

'You're a field agent, then? That's unusual.'

'Plenty of field agents last time I looked.'

'You know what I mean. You're a woman. Hell of a leap for you.'

'Yeah? Well, maybe I earned it, mate.'

They motored through the leafy squares of Bloomsbury. Winter had imagined they were heading to the service's new headquarters in Lambeth but it was clear the girl had another destination in mind.

'How much do you know about me?' he asked, equally curious and suspicious.

'You have the biggest file I've ever seen. They let me read the first page.'

Winter smiled, almost to himself. 'I doubt you'd believe the rest.'

'Oh, I read it all, mate,' said Libby, breezily. 'Broke in to the Boneyard one night. Sometimes life's too short for security clearances. Mind you, by the sound of it you've had quite a life, haven't you?'

Winter said nothing. The sports car purred into

Maple Street. Libby eased it into a parking space – she was spoilt for choice – and they slid to a halt among the brick-fronted townhouses.

'Well, there it is,' she said, as the engine dwindled. 'The eighth wonder of London.'

The Post Office Tower stood like a dream the morning couldn't quite shake. It rose to the clouds, coiled in steel and glass, its upper section bristling with transmitter dishes and meteorological sensors. A corona of sunlight framed the aerial-studded mast. It was the first time Winter had seen the building since it had been completed the year before. It looked like a monument to tomorrow, sunk into the heart of Fitzrovia.

'We're going inside?'

'Of course. He's waiting for us.'

Libby left the car and walked to the parking meter, plucking shillings from her purse. Winter spotted a discarded bundle of fish and chips beneath the driver's seat, its cold contents wrapped in pages of the *Daily Mirror*. The vinegar-stained face of Charles de Gaulle stared back at him.

He was about to follow her. And then he paused as he reached for the door handle.

'So who told you I was a wanker?'

The lift climbed the floors, the numbered squares on the metal plate illuminating in sequence, clocking up the highest numerals Winter had ever seen in an elevator. He felt his stomach shift as they reached the final floor, the lift docking with a murmur of hydraulics.

The red doors whispered apart. A man in an old Etonian tie was waiting, his frame filling the doorway. Winter was patted down, his gun and knuckle-duster taken. Then the man discovered the discreet knife strapped against Winter's left calf. He took that too, piling the weapons in his hand.

'This way, sir.' The manner was brisk but courteous. He had been trained well.

Winter followed him in, stepping on to plush blue carpet. The wide, circular room filled the entire floor, ringed by tall windows that commanded a giddying view of the capital, stretching like a train-set village to the horizon. Even the dome of St Paul's was dwarfed by this technological monolith. Light flooded in, giving the room a gauzy, almost unreal quality, like something half seen or half remembered.

Libby strolled to one of the panoramic windows and looked out to Parliament Hill. She pulled an apple from the pocket of her raincoat.

There was a beechwood desk in the centre of the room. The man in the Eton tie placed the pile of weapons upon it. And then he stood to one side, his fists behind his back.

Sir Crispin Faulkner lifted the knuckle-duster from his desk. He turned the tarnished brass in his hand, regarding it with undisguised distaste.

'I did wonder what would become of you, Winter. I never dreamt you'd end up as a common thug.'

'I think only my pension arrangements have changed, sir.'

Winter immediately regretted the word 'sir'. It was ingrained.

The head of British Intelligence ignored the barb, turning his attention to Winter's gun. He lifted it up, pinching the barrel between his fingers as if unwilling to make any more contact with the weapon than he needed to. 'And this. Mauser HSc 7.65mm. Shabby choice. It's a Nazi pistol, for God's sake. Belonged to some prisoner of war, no doubt. Black market was flooded with them in '45.'

'It does its job.'

Faulkner wrinkled his eyes, unimpressed. 'And just what sort of job might that be? Bank raid? Protection racket? Smash and grab? Or is Jack Creadley a more upstanding citizen than I give him credit for? I'd hate to stain a decent man's reputation.'

'He's dead,' said Winter, bluntly. 'And I didn't have much choice. It's not as if references are easy to come by when you've signed the Official Secrets Act.'

Faulkner returned the pistol to the desk, using a thumb to nudge it away. 'We would have taken you back, you know. You're an asset.'

Winter kept his words measured. 'You used me. That's what you do with assets, isn't it? All those bloody lies I lived for you. My wife. My home. Everything. You knew the truth about who I was all that time, and you kept it from me.' He felt a sudden flare of contempt that he couldn't suppress. 'Why the hell would I come back to you?'

'You were Malcolm's project. Another example of his rather unorthodox approach to national security. I must say I almost miss his expertise in such matters.'

'Project?' Winter reached across the desk but the man with the Eton tie already had a gun on him. Winter grudgingly raised his hands. Libby watched from the window. She took another bite of her apple.

Faulkner hadn't even flinched. He was like a grey flannel battleship behind the desk. 'Your grievance against the service is noted.'

'That's not an apology.'

'Her Majesty's government isn't in the business of apology.' Then something softened in Faulkner's eyes. 'But, yes, personally speaking, I'm sorry, Tobias. You deserved better.'

A muscle moved beneath Winter's cheek. Tobias Hart. The man he had been. A magus, a warlock, a disciple of the darkest magic. That part of his soul had been stripped from him, consigned to Hell. It had died in 1947, in the burning Namib desert. British Intelligence had taken what was left, the shell of the man, the husk. They had constructed a new identity, created a new life. He barely remembered being Hart but the name was like a naked nerve.

He spoke softly, assuredly. 'My name is Christopher Winter.'

Faulkner nodded, not unsympathetic. 'Your prerogative, of course.'

Winter gestured to the skyline. 'I presumed I'd be

taken to Lambeth. Not the most conspicuous bloody building in London.'

'This is Location 23. Officially it's still a state secret.'

Winter kept his face straight. 'Right. So you've disguised it as a tourist attraction. That's truly ingenious.'

'This building is a communications hub, the most powerful in Britain. But it doesn't just transmit television or connect trunk calls. It listens. It listens to everything. Of course we're part of it. Not that the press know that, of course, but we'll maintain our presence here when it opens to the public. And besides, I can't imagine you're in any hurry to be reunited with your colleagues at Century House, given your circumstances.'

'They're not my colleagues. Not anymore.'

'Well, technically you never resigned.'

Winter considered this. 'Technically, sir, I never shoved it up your arse. But we have time.'

Again Faulkner didn't deign to register the jibe. 'You were involved with a Russian Intelligence agent during Operation Magus.'

'Involved? Leading choice of word.'

'Karina Lazarova. Naturally she's of considerable interest to us.'

'She infiltrated the Russians. She wasn't one of them.'

'We're aware that her loyalties were fluid, to say the least. She was reported to be in London some eighteen months ago. We were very near to seizing her. And then she vanished. She must have known how close we were.'

Winter gave a dry smile. 'For the best, I imagine. Saved your boys some grief.'

'Our most recent intelligence placed her in the Dominican Republic, employed as a bodyguard to Colonel Caamaño in that coup against the junta, before the Americans muscled in. But that was two months ago. I take it you're not aware of her present whereabouts?'

'I'd just follow the bodies, if I were you.'

'Did she compromise you emotionally?' asked Faulkner, with a sudden bluntness. 'In the field, I mean?'

Winter paused. 'It was a purely practical relationship. We made the best of our circumstances.'

'Of course. And I'm sure the end of that relationship had no bearing whatsoever on your subsequent descent into London's gutters.'

Winter bristled. 'Do piss off.'

'Still, in the end you proved a tad easier to locate than she did.'

'Just tell me why I'm here.'

Faulkner opened a drawer. A manila folder hit the desk, its contents ribboned shut and stamped CLEARANCE – AMETHYST. Each file in the Boneyard was assigned a precious stone, denoting its place in the hierarchy of secrets. Amethyst was reasonably high-tier intelligence.

Faulkner took a letter knife and slit the red ribbon. He spread the contents of the file before him, spinning a glossy black-and-white photograph so that Winter could view it.

'Recognise her?'

Winter appraised the eight by ten. The woman in the

39

picture had a sleek black bob, almost brutally geometric. There was a wide, unmistakably sensual span to her mouth, the lips full but set in a stern, confident line. The image itself was flat and washed-out. Clearly a harsh lighting source had been used. Winter suspected it was a mugshot of some kind, a police photo or a portrait for a government dossier.

And yet the woman's pupils were enlarged, defying the flashbulb that should have made them shrink.

He stared at the picture, engaged by those wide, kohl-shadowed eyes. For a moment a memory seemed to stir like dust. And then it was gone.

'She's vaguely familiar, I admit. But I can't place her. Who is she?'

'Alessandra Moltini. Italian extraction, as far as we can ascertain. Currently in Budapest. Employed by the state. Works honeytraps, and pretty irresistible bait by all accounts. She's compromised a fair number of foreign officials over the past few years, including some of our own men. Photographs, blackmail, the usual filthy snare. Now she wants out.'

'She wants to defect?'

Faulkner nodded, briskly. 'Needless to say, we could use her knowledge to establish an accurate register of exactly who the party is manipulating. Use those people to our advantage. Start to feed back some disinformation, find the faultlines. Sabotage the whole infrastructure. Make it work for us.'

Winter absorbed this in silence. Only one question occurred to him. 'What the hell has this got to do with me?'

Faulkner tapped the photograph. 'I want you to get her out.'

'This is a simple extraction job. Anyone can do it. Cracknell can do it. She's good enough. Give her a promotion.'

Libby gave an ironic little smile from her position by the window. And then she continued to munch her apple.

Faulkner regarded Winter with his imperturbable blue eyes. 'She's asked for you by name.'

It was a clear play for his curiosity. But Winter resisted. 'I don't know this woman. Never met her, not that I recall. I certainly don't owe her any favours. I owe you even less.'

'I'm not asking you for a favour, Winter.'

'Well, it was your best option, Sir Crispin. I'm all out of patriotic duty.'

He turned and began to walk to the lift. No need to get involved with any of this, he told himself. There would be other opportunities available to him: he had the skills and he had the experience. He could carve his own fortune any time, far from a government payroll. The shadow war against the Reds was no longer his war.

'She didn't ask for Christopher Winter,' Faulkner said, without raising his voice. 'She asked for Tobias Hart.'

Winter paused. The fish hook had landed, expertly cast by the old bastard.

It was an unlikely place for a psychological evaluation. Banks of instruments stood against the walls. Needles shivered in gauges while meters spoke the private language of voltage, electrical counters ticking behind glass. In the corners were bunches of brightly coloured wire, lashed together with crocodile clips. The small, windowless room felt like an untidy science experiment, caught mid-tinker.

And then there was the hum. You felt it as much as you heard it. The steady, contained drone of the tower, its power ever present.

Winter took the stiff-backed chair propped in front of the solitary desk. He suspected it had been requisitioned from the GPO, just like the room itself.

'How are you?' asked Dr Bhamra, resting her glasses on her greying hair. There was a cup of Assam tea in front of her, a filter-tip cigarette glowing on the rim of the china saucer.

'Is that officially a question?'

She smiled. 'You can take it as you wish.'

'Then I'm fine. Thank you for asking.'

She raised a fountain pen and scored a single word on a waiting sheet of paper. Winter was practised in reading upside down. It was a necessary skill in the field. Bhamra's writing was scratchy but he was fairly certain the word she had chosen was *defensive*.

'Spot on, I'd say.'

She kept the sheet exactly where it was. 'I'm glad you agree.' And then she wrote another word. This time it looked like *ego-syntonic*. At least it wasn't *wanker*, thought Winter.

'I've been asked to evaluate you,' she said, dispassionately. 'I'm not here to parry with you and I'm not here to judge. I'm here to assess whether you're fit for purpose. Understood?'

Winter nodded. 'Understood. It's been a while since I've had to do one of these.'

Bhamra reached for the stack of cards placed next to her teacup. She turned the top card over, revealing a splotch of black ink.

'So tell me, Christopher. What does this remind you of?'

Winter made a show of studying the mess of ink. 'It reminds me very strongly of a Rorschach test.'

Bhamra reached for her cigarette and took a drag. 'Humour tends to be an act of avoidance or displacement,' she said, letting the smoke issue between her teeth. 'It's not particularly helpful in this situation. But do go on.'

Winter stared at the ink, trying to find some pattern, some shape, any comment he could make to move this conversation closer to its endpoint.

'God knows. A house?'

The fountain pen raced across the paper. 'And by house do you mean home?' pressed Bhamra. 'Do you feel separated from it? Or is it a reassuring image for you?'

'It's a load of bloody ink.'

'Go with your gut feeling. Go with whatever you don't want to tell me.'

'Separated.'

'And would you consider the service your home?'

Winter grunted. 'At the moment home is a bedsit in

43

Battersea. I imagine the ink reminds me of the damp. Honestly, the state of the walls is shocking.'

Bhamra replaced her cigarette on the saucer's rim. 'The Rorschach test is a little misunderstood. Hermann Rorschach originally created it as a tool to aid in the diagnosis of schizophrenia.'

'I'm not schizophrenic.' *Defensive.*

'I wasn't suggesting you were. Schizophrenia is characterised by fractures in cognitive functioning. I've read your file. What you've experienced appears to be closer to dissociative identity disorder. Two distinct personality states. It's fascinating.'

'Well, I'm glad I'm giving you some professional pleasure, at least.' God, he ached to be out of this room.

Bhamra turned another card. This time the riot of ink instantly snapped into focus, coalescing in his imagination.

'That's an entry wound,' he said, without hesitation. 'That's how the flesh ruptures, given the typical passage of a bullet through tissue. I imagine normal people see butterfly wings, don't they?'

Bhamra sipped her tea and smiled. 'You'd be surprised.'

She wrote his answer in the file then let the fountain pen hover. 'Tell me. This parallel personality you've experienced. This Tobias Hart...'

'He's gone,' said Winter, emphatically. 'That's not who I am anymore. My name is Christopher Winter.'

'Of course,' Bhamra assured him, the pen moving again. Another word on the page. Winter was sure it said *denial.*

'Do you feel as though you have a relationship to

him? Do you access his memories, his thoughts?'

'Glimpses. Now and again. No more than that.'

'And do you feel as though these thoughts, these memories, belong to you in any sense? Or are you simply observing them, detached?'

'I've told you. He's gone.'

Winter shifted in his chair. The room was hot and its insistent hum was starting to scrape at his nerves. He gestured to the table. 'Give me another card.'

She did so, lifting it from the pile and placing it neatly in front of him. Winter stared at the black symmetrical blooms, trying to fathom some meaning, some symbol. This time nothing leapt out at him. For a moment he caught an echo of the kohl-shadowed eyes he had seen in the photograph on Faulkner's desk. But they were soon gone, as if snatched back and buried by the ink.

'What do you see?' Bhamra prompted.

Winter squinted. 'Nothing. There's nothing there. No pattern to it at all.'

'Keep looking. I'm sure something will come to you.'

Winter fought to impose some order on the formless mass. The sooner he did so the sooner he would walk from this room. The collusion of ink continued to resist him. And then he spotted something: the blot wasn't symmetrical after all. The left-hand bloom was larger and denser. Considerably so, in fact. How had he not noticed that? Surely the two halves had been identical, perfect mirrors of one another?

The more he stared at the ink the more it had a sense

of movement. The splatters curled on the white card, almost like tiny, spiralling tendrils. They crept to the edges, unfurling, extending. Winter couldn't take his eyes away. The black chaos had become mesmerising. It coiled and it writhed and it slipped through infinite possibilities. The world, it told him, was fluid. It could be taken and it could be moulded, reshaped like spilt mercury. It was easy. He'd done it before. What was he afraid of?

Winter took the card and turned it face down on the desk. His breathing had quickened.

'What did you see?' asked Bhamra, her pen poised above the open file. 'Was it something that you recognised? Something you knew?'

Winter hesitated. And then he spoke a single word, as if wanting it gone from his mouth.

'Magic,' he told her.

3

Tram cars clattered through the smoky heart of Budapest's western bank. Drab little Trabants kept pace, bouncing on the cobbles while infinitely more graceful Soviet Volgas slid by, ferrying party officials behind tinted glass. It was a warm, parched evening, typical of a long Hungarian summer, and the air had turned to an amber haze of exhaust fumes and dwindling sunlight.

Winter made his way along the terraces beneath the steep green Buda Hills, his tie hanging below his collar, a concession to the heat. He walked at a brisk pace. It was almost eight and he had an appointment to keep in Szentháromság tér.

A Trident from Gatwick had brought him to Ferihegy airport the night before. His credentials were impeccable, forged by an SIS craftsman proud to be known as Bullshit Evans. But as he handed over the artfully aged and battered passport Winter had felt the familiar sensation of time expanding, the seconds crawling as the calm eyes behind the desk scrutinised every detail of his bogus identity. It was a moment you could never be comfortable with.

Anthony Robert St John Prestwick. Born in Epsom, 12 November 1917. Married to Jill. Darling, dog-crazed Jill, Winter imagined. A photocopier salesman by trade. Something unhappy in his eyes, perhaps, but a decent stick just the same. He'd be dead of a gin-soaked liver in ten years, tops. Poor darling, dog-crazed Jill. She'd never quite get over it.

The border official had glanced between Winter and the glum black-and-white photograph before turning his gaze to the visa. Finally satisfied, he'd reached for a ledger and flicked through its fat stack of pages, the nibbled stump of a pencil in his hand. He had neatly recorded the Englishman's details, the lead scratching along the lined paper. And then he had stamped the passport, leaving a blotch of purple ink.

A stiff-lipped smile, a final look. *'Halad.'* Proceed.

Winter had nodded, careful not to look too grateful, and Anthony Robert St John Prestwick had stepped behind the Iron Curtain, heading for baggage reclaim.

His cover had compelled him to spend the day at a photocopier salesman's conference in the Erzsébetváros district, listening to insights on recent advances in liquid toner technology. By the end of the morning session he had considered extracting the contents of his skull with rusted pliers.

Lunch had been a little more bearable: sweet cherry brandies, a plate of pork and cabbage, the trading of crisp new business cards whose number, if ever rung, would cue a cool but sympathetic female voice, explaining that Prestwick Copy Solutions had succumbed to a regrettably sudden bankruptcy. The afternoon had been devoted to the commercial possibilities of dye sublimation in Eastern Bloc countries. Winter had pondered the possibilities of setting his head on fire.

Now he was in the Old Town, a mazy medieval enclave fighting a rearguard action against the bleak socialist housing that ringed the city. Budapest was nothing if not resilient, Winter knew. It had withstood Mongol invasion, Turkish occupation and a world war that had nearly razed it to the earth. The Soviets held it as a satellite state – they had crushed the uprising in '56, rolling tanks into the bloodied streets – but for all they imposed their statues of heroic workers they were, Winter suspected, only ever borrowing the city from history.

He strode into Szentháromság tér, the aroma of fried batter and garlic on the breeze, drifting from a street vendor's stall. The right side of the square was dominated by Matthias Church, its diamond-patterned roof glittering as it caught the last of the day's light. A carved crow crowned the gothic spire. In the church's shadow was a bench, and on the bench was a man shuffling a set of playing cards. Winter went and sat next to him, disturbing a cobalt-blue butterfly that had settled on the wooden arm. They were everywhere in Budapest.

'I believe you dropped a card.'

The man barely acknowledged him. He continued to sort the cards, plying them between his fingers. Even on the bench he cut a long, rangy figure, dressed in brown suede lace-ups and a matted tweed blazer that gave him the look of an out-of-season lecturer. His eyebrows curled like millipedes, as thick as his moustache.

'Are you sure?' The voice was British, and it had the sour, dull tone of someone reading from a script. 'The Hungarian deck only contains thirty-two cards. The suits are different, too, of course. Leaves, bells, acorns and hearts. You might be mistaken.'

Winter followed the protocol with an equal lack of enthusiasm, plucking a single picture card from his chest pocket. It showed a female monarch. 'Queen. And country.'

The man inspected the card, accepted it and added it to the deck. And then he smiled, surprisingly warmly. 'Not quite the winning hand it used to be, old man.'

'We do what we can.'

A firm hand was offered. 'Bernard Gately. Been here six years. I write for *The Economist*. Well, that's the day job. You know the rest.'

'Decent cover.'

Gately nodded. 'It gets me around. Lets me ask questions. We don't push it, though. London likes to use me sparingly. The odd eavesdrop, the occasional wiretap. Running extractions every now and then, like tonight. I keep my hand in. But subtly, you know. Nothing too showy.'

'Understood. I won't drag you into the spotlight.'

'I'd appreciate that. To be honest the journalism's rather better paid.'

'You're a true patriot, Bernard.'

'We do what we can.'

They scoured the square as they talked, sifting the crowd for the presence of state security. Both men knew that any cover, however solid, however embedded, had to exist in a permanent state of potential compromise. It was your default position in the field. Keep sharp, expect the worst, be ready to move at a moment's notice.

The butterfly spun like a spill of paint in the air.

'So where do I find the woman?' asked Winter.

'The Maria Theresa Hotel in Pest. That's her hunting ground. She'll be there tonight. But she'll have company. For a while.'

'And she's expecting me?'

'Yes, of course. I briefed her yesterday. But don't expect her to acknowledge you, not at first. She'll need to work. Turn a trick or two for the Ministry of Internal Affairs. And they'll be watching her. Choose your moment carefully. She's rather prized.'

The butterfly wheeled past a group of young secretaries in headscarves, sharing cigarettes in the cool shadow of the old town hall. They were chattering animatedly in Magyar.

'Why does she want to defect? Ideological reasons?'

Gately snorted. 'Is it ever? Oh, sure, maybe when it comes to our lot. The Burgesses and Macleans have the ghost of Karl Marx whispering in their ears. To each according to their needs, all that noble collectivist shit. It's the higher ground to them, the East. But when someone jumps to the West they're not thinking of the moral superiority of the capitalist system. They just want to get away from the state. They never seem to realise we'll also be watching them, every day of their lives. We just have nicer manners and better tea.'

He squinted, his eyes retreating beneath the thick brows. 'Things might change here one day. Kádár's a progressive at heart. But Moscow put him in. And they'll only tolerate so much progress before they bring the tanks back.'

The butterfly landed on an ornate stone column that stood in front of the bench. The tall white pillar was decorated with saints and cherubs, rising to an intricately carved depiction of the Holy Trinity. The figures that ringed the base of the monument were altogether less sanctified. They had been immortalised in a state of terror, all ragged clothes and screaming mouths.

Gately followed Winter's eyes. 'They're plague victims. The pandemic came to Buda in 1691. Devastated the city.'

'So it's a memorial?'

Gately shook his head. 'No. They built it as a defence. And then the plague returned in 1709. People were convinced God had abandoned them. That thought must have been even more terrifying than the plague. Now what have they got? Statues of Marx and Engels. I trust they're keeping the proletariat plague-free.'

'Where do we rendezvous?' asked Winter, practically.

'Keleti station. Tomorrow morning. Ten am sharp. We'll get the pair of you on the Salzburg train. I'll have the papers prepared for her. Pick-up in Austria. London will handle it from there. She knows you already, doesn't she?'

Winter hesitated, shaping an answer. 'She certainly says we're acquainted.'

Gately frowned, puzzled by Winter's choice of words. 'So you've met her, then?'

'It's just a little complicated.'

'She referred to you by another name. Tobias Hart. Previous operational cover, I take it?'

Winter held Gately's gaze. 'Like I said, it's a little complicated.'

His contact shrugged, sensing he shouldn't push the conversation any further. 'Whatever you say. Above my clearance, I take it. Wouldn't be the first time with you London boys. But I'll tell you one thing, Winter. Be careful with this woman. She may be more than she appears. To be honest I've heard some rather unsettling things about her.'

'Tell me what you know.'

Gately had kept his voice low throughout but it was barely a murmur now. 'Oh, just bar talk, old man, nothing I can file. But some people reckon she's mixed up in more than just honeytraps. There have been some deeply suspicious deaths in this city over the last few years. Discreet political assassinations, opponents and agitators found dead in their beds, that kind of thing. Her name's been linked to them. Nothing official, you understand, no hard proof, but too often to be coincidence.'

Winter gave a tight smile as he rose from the bench.

'It's never coincidence, Bernard. Coincidence is what happens to civilians.'

The Széchenyi Chain Bridge united Buda with Pest, its cast-iron span straddling the Danube. The river rolled beneath it, the axis of the city, pouring from the Black Forest in Baden-Württemberg to the Black Sea on the distant Romanian coast. The churn of water had a peaty smell, as if the heart of the German forest still clung to it.

Flanked by traffic, Winter crossed the century-old suspension bridge, heading for Pest on the eastern bank. The sun had retreated behind the Buda Hills, leaving the sky the colour of a rose. There were coal barges on the river, bobbing brightly in the dusk. The evening wind had a sweet, powdery quality, stealing the scent of paprika from the hillside.

Why had he come to Budapest? He was still turning that question over in his head. Part of him wanted the sense of purpose an assignment gave him. So much of his life had been built on the familiar certainties of briefing, infiltration, implementation, escape. He had the rhythm of a mission in his bones. And he missed it.

But it was more than that. Tobias Hart was a scab that kept itching. Karina had urged him to box away his past but it intrigued him, that black void in his memory. Who had he been? Who had he hurt? How much pain had he brought to this world – and how thin was the line that divided them, the young warlock and the veteran spy? If this woman, this Alessandra Moltini, had known him as Hart then Winter might get some answers.

For a moment he saw the Rorschach test on Bhamra's desk, the ink seething on the paper, its possibilities infinite, seductive. He glanced down at the Danube. The water looked dark and limitless beneath an early moon. Magic could shape this world. Hart had known that. Maybe curiosity had led him to that understanding.

Winter strode past the stone lions that guarded the Pest-side approach to the bridge. A trolleybus soon rattled him along the embankment, into the grand boulevards of bicycles and fountains, their broad sweep lit by a march of street lamps. This half of the city was crumbling handsomely, its buildings full of a *fin-de-siècle* swagger for all their decay. Gargoyles roosted above the gutterings, keeping watch on the passing trams.

The Maria Theresa Hotel stood in Belváros, the innermost part of Pest. It was a baroque, six-storey townhouse, elegant as a cake, bulging with balconies. Winter pushed his way through the oak-and-glass doors, into a reception area that smelt of coffee and beeswax. He made his way to the bar and ordered a small glass of Hungarian red.

An hour passed, Winter sipping his wine and pecking at a bowlful of spiced nuts. He had his back to the hub of the bar, a position he had chosen carefully. There was a bevelled mirror bolted to the wall in front of him, one that gave a strategic view of the other patrons. He studied their reflections. Businessmen or management, mainly, most of them middle-aged, their throats plump and pink, bulging over stiff shirt collars. There might have been a minor politician or two, maybe a low-ranking state official, nursing a sickly fruit brandy.

It was the perfect hunting ground for the Ministry of Internal Affairs. This was where honeytraps were sprung, among well-placed, vulnerable men pushing guilty coins into the hotel payphone to tell their wives that no, they wouldn't be home, because work had piled up tonight so unexpectedly. They would return in the early hours, check for lipstick in the shaving mirror, dab on cologne to cover the unfamiliar perfume that had seeped into their skin. And then they would creep into dark, loveless bedrooms, knowing their wives were only pretending to be asleep.

Within a week the envelope would arrive. It would come to the office, not the home, and it would contain frames of film, neatly snipped, the clumsy, hurried sex caught behind a mirror or through a light fitting or a ventilation grille. There would be instructions, of course. Nothing as blunt as blackmail. Just a reminder that obedience was owed to the state. And one day information would be required, or an act of loyalty requested. Perhaps an eye would have to be kept on a potential dissident, or some disappointing export figures would need massaging. It was leverage, simple as that.

Winter knew there was a dark science to the whole operation. Both East and West had departments dedicated to the fine art of the honeytrap. Libido strategists, they were called – well, there were other, filthier names, naturally. They would profile the target, discover what turned them on, note it in forensic detail: leather or fur, boots or stilettos, the cane or the kiss. Maybe the scent worn by that pretty young teacher, forty years ago. Fetishes, triggers, erotic faultlines. They would take this information and construct the perfect irresistible bait.

Winter's eyes went to the mirror. Alessandra Moltini had entered the bar.

4

Winter knew who she was the moment he saw her. The woman prised her way through the crowd, slipping between the men, her movements sinuous and assured. She must have dyed her hair or chosen a short blonde wig but the wide mouth and confident dark eyes were unmistakable. The photo in Faulkner's file had captured her perfectly: disdain offset by something sensuous, something hungry. She was dressed in a starkly cut grey suit and an ivory silk blouse, her hands hidden by stiff leather gloves. An opal locket danced at her throat. A low-key glamour, just right for a public seduction.

For a moment their eyes connected in the mirror. Winter caught something black and fathomless in her gaze. He quickly looked away. He knew this woman. He had no memory of her but he knew this woman.

She took a seat, close to a slight, sandy-haired man in his early fifties, sitting alone. Clearly this was the intended target. The man waited a moment to look at her. A glance and then his eyes fell and he gazed a little too intently at his drink. The woman unpeeled her gloves, smoothed them flat and placed them on the table next to his. One leg slid over the other, revealing a shimmer of seamed nylon and a sharp heel. She had an almost geometric poise, every angle calculated, balanced. The man stole another look, letting their eyes lock briefly.

Winter took another sip of red, watching the mirror. The woman removed a slim black cigarette case from her handbag, the polished onyx gleaming in the light of the bar. She then made a play of searching for her lighter. The man offered his. She let him attend to her cigarette, nudging its tip against the flame until she exhaled the first languorous curl of smoke. It was textbook stuff, as ritualised as Japanese theatre.

They made conversation, their bodies edging closer as they leaned forward in their chairs. The man ordered drinks and a showy choice of champagne arrived. Soon they were oblivious to the rest of the bar. Winter watched as the woman expertly echoed the man's body language, subtly mimicking his posture. He did the same, more unconsciously. At one point their heads fell together in laughter and she touched the nape of his neck, scoring a nail through the close-cropped hair above his collar.

Eventually they stood up, the man steadying himself as he drew his jacket together. He collected the champagne bottle then put a proprietorial arm around the woman's waist and walked her out of the bar. Part of him obviously wanted to leave unnoticed; part of him needed the other men to see.

Winter abandoned his wine and followed the pair, keeping a cautious distance. He saw them disappear up the thickly carpeted stairs that led from reception. They would be heading to the third floor. She was room 304; Winter had been installed in 303.

He was about to take the stairs when he found someone standing in his way. A squat, buzz-cut man in a gold-buttoned blue waistcoat. A laminated badge identified him as hotel staff but there was an implicit aggression about him, something vicious burning just beneath the skin.

'I'm sorry, sir.' The apology had a surly edge. There was no smile.

Winter said nothing, waiting for him to step aside. After a moment the man did so and headed down the corridor that led to the buffet room. Winter watched him walk away, evaluating his physique, assessing the probability of concealed weapons. State security, no doubt, keeping tabs on the whole honeytrap operation. Not entirely unexpected – and Winter had no reason to suspect his cover had been compromised – but it was another variable to factor in.

He climbed the stairs, passing sombre portraits of Hungarian monarchs, peering down from dingy, cream-painted walls. There were cracks in the plaster, fine as veins. Like most of Pest this hotel's glory had begun to rot.

He turned into the third floor. The door to room 304 was firmly closed. Winter heard laughter from inside. He hovered for a moment, nodding blandly to a passing maid, then unlocked the door to his own room. A snap of the light switch illuminated the modest but aspirational furnishings. A crisply made bed, a square armchair, an antique table.

He sat on the edge of the bed and quietly unbuckled his watch strap. His head felt heavy on his shoulders. Over the years he had learnt to hate rooms like this. Something about their anonymity, their neat emptiness, always got to him, made him feel adrift. Tonight it was worse. Tonight he couldn't even feel that familiar numb ache for home, because home was now a room in Battersea with sour milk in the fridge.

He indulged a smile as he wound his watch. This had to be an improvement on that, at least.

Waiting there, hunched in his suit, Winter became aware of a steady, rhythmic vibration thudding through the wall. It was accompanied by a quickening squeal of bedsprings. He sighed, turning the watch in his hand, seeing the seconds tick from every angle. It was moments like this when surveillance felt more like voyeurism.

The pace of the thrusts increased, the headboard smacking the wall in the room next door. He could hear the interplay of grunts and moans, the pair of them struggling to synchronise as they made love. Made love? No, it sounded more ragged, more urgent than that, a purely physical act, torn from the moment. Winter imagined the softly whirring camera behind the mirror or the grille, recording every sweat-slick detail while the men from the state looked on. It was reassuring to know there were even seedier ways to serve your country.

And then there was a scream.

Winter couldn't tell if it was the woman who had screamed or the man, but it cut through the wall and it cut through his nerves. It was an anguished, animalistic sound, turning guttural as it died.

The light in his room flared and dimmed.

Another scream, even louder than the last.

Winter sprang from the bed. He threw the door open and stepped outside. The wall-lamps were flickering, casting a stutter of light and shadow the length of the empty corridor.

He stood by the door to 304. As he did so a third scream came. This one ended in sobs. Winter kicked to the left of the keyhole, targeting the weakest part of the lock. He kicked it again, the wood splintering beneath the impact of his heel.

And then he stepped back, set his muscles and barrelled forward, sensing the door loosen on its hinges as he slammed against it. He made a second attempt, channelling all of his strength into his right shoulder. This time the door gave way.

The air in the room had a brittle, jagged edge, as if it was threaded with electricity.

The pair were on the bed, in a mess of sheets and half-discarded clothes. The man's head lolled over the edge of the mattress, eyes fixed on the ceiling, his face frozen, caught between ecstasy and pain. His hands curled and shuddered as if snatching at something just out of reach.

The woman was on top, stockinged thighs straddling the man's waist as her skirt rode up around her. She had her hands on his bare chest, the fingers embedded in the flesh, pressing hard against the ribs. Her skin seemed to be lit from within, a bright, translucent pink, mapping her veins with its glow.

She looked directly at Winter, saliva running from her lips.

Her eyes were golden.

There were no whites, no irises, no pupils. Just solid shells of gold, opaque and gleaming.

The light in the room continued to quiver, the lamps buzzing in irritation as the voltage danced. It made a tableau of the bed.

And then, as the light steadied, the woman's eyes changed. The golden shells shrank, retreated, swallowed by the pupils. Moments later her eyes were dark again.

'Hart, I'm feeding!' said Alessandra Moltini.

Her voice had a low rasp, older than her face suggested. There was anger there but something fond, too. The glow had faded from her hands.

Winter was speechless. He was about to step towards the bed when he felt a sudden impact against his spine. Someone had leapt on his back.

An arm locked around his throat and began to tighten its grip against his windpipe. He glimpsed a black sleeve. The arm was surprisingly slender given the pressure it was exerting. Winter spluttered, feeling the breath being muscled out of him.

As he staggered he tilted his weight. With a grunt he managed to heave his assailant over his shoulder, hurling them into a small wooden table that promptly collapsed.

A furious, cold-eyed young woman glared up at him. It was the maid, the one he had passed in the corridor; the one he hadn't given so much as a first thought, let alone a second. She had to be part of the state operation, staking out the room.

Grimacing, the pinafored woman pulled herself up. She seized a floor lamp with both hands and hurled it at Winter's head. He sidestepped and the lamp hit the wall, its bulb shattering.

The maid spotted the bottle from the bar, abandoned beside the bed. Grabbing it by the neck she smashed it against the wall, showering the sideboard with champagne and glass. Now she had a proper weapon. She inched closer to Winter, swiping at him with the broken bottle.

Winter raised a fist in defence. The glass scraped his knuckles and claimed blood. Instinctively he reached for his gun. But it was in his room, waiting in his case. He glanced at Alessandra, still crouched over the bare-chested man on the bed. She was watching the fight with a thrill of hunger in her eyes.

The bottle sliced past him again. Winter saw a ceramic ashtray on the bedside table. He snatched it and sent it spinning into the maid's teeth. Now it was his turn to draw blood. She simply wiped her lip and kept coming, thrusting the bottle at him, scoring it through the air.

Winter's eyes swept the room, hunting for another weapon. There was a Bakelite phone on the sideboard. He ripped the heavy black handset from its cradle and swung it by the severed cord.

The woman dodged it. Smiling now, she closed in.

Winter backed deeper into the room, aware he was running out of options. The maid matched him, the bottle poised as if ready to take his eyes.

He stepped past a heavy oak wardrobe. One of its doors was ajar. For a moment the wardrobe was between him and the maid.

Winter flung the door. There was a thick smack of wood against bone.

The maid dropped to the floor, concussed.

'Were you enjoying that?' asked Alessandra, her tone playful.

Winter stepped over the maid's body, confirming she was unconscious. 'Did it look like I was enjoying it?' Irritated, he wiped his knuckles on his trousers, smearing the fabric with blood. The wound had begun to throb.

'I imagined you were playing with the girl. You could have killed her at any moment, Hart, we both know that. All you had to do was cast a blood hex or summon a shadow scythe or...'

Winter cut through whatever she was saying. He indicated the man on the bed, still spreadeagled beneath her thighs, a look of agonised rapture on his face. 'What the hell have you done to him?'

Alessandra grazed her nails across the man's chest,

snagging the sparse, sandy hairs. 'Why, I've used him, darling.'

Her nonchalance rankled Winter almost as much as her familiar use of darling. He had encountered creatures like this before. 'What are you? Some kind of bloody demon?'

'What are you?' she shot back. 'Some kind of bloody amnesiac?'

Winter stared into the mirror that faced the bed. There was doubtlessly a camera on the other side of the glass, capturing all of this. They would have his face now. And there would be men, too, alerting their colleagues.

'We don't have time. We have to get out of this hotel. Right now.'

She began to button her blouse. Winter glimpsed pale, heavy breasts rising beneath the silk. He took his eyes from her, conscious of a sudden dryness in his mouth.

'Move,' he urged. 'She won't be alone.'

Alessandra slid from the bed and snatched her jacket from the tumble of clothes on the floor. They entered the corridor, checked it both ways, then made for the lifts. Winter chose to abandon his gun in his room. Every second was crucial now.

The lifts were tucked to the side of the stairs, a pair of bronze doors decorated with peacocks. An illuminated panel lay between them, indicating the floors of the hotel. Ground level had just lit up. Winter could hear the grind of metal from inside the shaft, the gears crawling in oil as the cage rose. Someone was on their way.

'Come on,' he said, turning to the stairs instead.

The man in the blue waistcoat was scrambling up the final flight.

Winter spun, making to run. And then he swivelled at the waist, launching a foot at the man's throat. The kick connected. The state security agent tumbled down the stairs.

The bell chimed as the lift arrived on the third floor.

'Go!' cried Winter, pushing Alessandra in front of him.

They were already running as the lift doors opened, slamming through fire doors and racing down the next hallway. Winter calculated options as they ran, remembering what he could of the hotel's layout. Six floors, arranged around a central stairwell. There had to be a fire escape, even in a building of this age. It was the best chance to get them out unseen. A street level exit would be too conspicuous – and state security would undoubtedly have the main entrance under surveillance.

They heard the fire doors smash apart behind them. Somebody was sprinting in pursuit, pounding down the carpet. A third agent. Christ, they were cautious.

A bullet studded into the wall, hacking through plaster.

Winter swerved, throwing Alessandra to the side. Whoever had taken that shot was an idiot – a gun fired at a shallow angle in a corridor like this could easily provoke a ricochet.

'What's wrong with you?' demanded Alessandra, hotly. 'Cast a shadow scythe, for God's sake! Deal with them!'

Winter ignored her, focused on keeping them both

alive. Zigzagging, they hurled themselves through another set of fire doors. The reinforced glass puckered as a second bullet embedded itself.

There was a double-sash window ahead. Beyond it was the grilled lattice of a fire escape, framing the Budapest skyline. An emergency ladder waited, connecting the platform outside to one by a fourth-floor exit directly above.

Winter heaved the window open. He hastened Alessandra through and she began to climb, her heels ringing on the steel rungs. Winter followed her, threading the cold metal through his hands. Glancing down, he saw their pursuer emerge through the open window. He was looking for them on the platform below.

Winter stealthily dropped a couple of rungs. And then he kicked the gun from the man's hand. The weapon clattered into the dark.

The agent turned, seizing Winter by the left leg, intending to drag him from the ladder. Winter broke his grip and booted him in the teeth. The man fell back, clutching his bloodied mouth.

Winter carried on climbing. But then two arms wrapped themselves around his ankles. His opponent was balanced on the lowest rungs now, exerting all his strength in a bid to rip him from the ladder.

Winter clung to the handholds. His calf muscles bulged, resisting the lockhold. Straining, he managed to work a leg loose. He clipped the sole of his shoe against the man's chin, knocking him back by a matter of inches.

Collecting momentum, he swung his foot and drove his heel hard into the Hungarian's face.

The man tumbled backwards, his balance lost. His spine smacked against the edge of the platform and he fell, flailing, to an alleyway four storeys below. Winter turned his head but still heard the wet crunch as the body hit the tarmac.

Alessandra's hand was waiting for him. It coiled around his wrist and helped him to the next platform. Winter took it gratefully, but he shuddered at her touch. It felt like his skin had been grazed by tiny blazing needles. He remembered how her hand had glowed in the hotel room. What was she?

They climbed the remaining ladders, passing the windows of the fifth and sixth floors. Finally they reached a terrace beneath the grand arches of the hotel's roof. The sky seemed huge above the city, the stars mirroring the lights that pricked the streets and glittered on the bridges flung across the Danube. Winter could see the dome of Buda Castle to the west, the sacred Crown of Saint Stephen high and vigilant above the gloomy hills.

He stepped past a chimney to the edge of the parapet, where the guttering curled over the side of the Maria Theresa Hotel. All the buildings in this boulevard were packed tight, rising in each other's shadows like weeds competing for sunlight.

Below the hotel was another terrace. The building it belonged to was unlit, and looked as if it had been dark for some considerable time. Its ornate balconies were shattered, a headless stone gargoyle left to guard the drains. Artillery scars, Winter imagined, from the siege of '45. One jump and they could reach the roof, find a path to the backstreets, disappear.

'I've never seen you fight like that,' said Alessandra. It was a simple statement but her tone made it accusatory. 'So much bone and sweat and muscle. It's not your style at all. Not the man I remember.'

Winter could feel her eyes on him, searching behind his skin.

'I'm not the man you remember.'

'*Sì*. That's obvious, Hart. What's happened to you? Your gifts?'

Winter broke eye contact. 'We'll do this later. I need to get you out of Budapest. You know that's why I'm here.'

Something mischievous played around her mouth, breaking the intensity of her gaze. 'I know that's why you think you're here.'

He was about to challenge her on what she meant by that when he saw a slice of light on the ground. A service door had opened on the far side of the terrace. The man in the blue waistcoat was strolling out of it, the one he had kicked down the hotel stairs. There was a Makarov semi-automatic pistol in his hand.

Winter took the bullet a second before he heard the shot.

It tore into his chest, shredding skin, skimming bone.

For a moment he felt nothing. It was as if his body was simply noting the bullet's arrival.

And then it came, the numbing, consuming punch. Winter swayed, one arm wheeling for balance, the other pressed to his chest. His hand covered the wound, trying to plug it. He felt a warm insistence of blood pumping against his palm.

The world tilted, the stars and the city blurring. Winter buckled and fell, hitting the terrace.

He sensed Alessandra cradling him, lifting his head from the tarmac.

The man with the gun was almost upon them, his breathing still ragged from the kick he had taken to the throat. Winter fought to keep focus as the figure loomed. The outline of the man rippled and warped as Winter's eyes watered. He glanced at Alessandra and then moved his gaze to his left ankle.

He slid the heel of his right shoe against the trouser leg, hitching up the fabric.

She saw the knife strapped to his calf. With a nod she eased it from the sheath and hid it in her hand.

And then she spun at the waist, slashing upwards, targeting the man's ribs. She corkscrewed the mean little blade, twisting it into his side until the blue waistcoat purpled with blood.

Winter lay there, curling into himself as he watched the man stagger and crash. Now their bodies lay parallel on the ground.

Alessandra withdrew the knife and tossed it away. She crouched over the fallen state security agent, easing her thighs across his chest. The man was clearly in agony but she smoothed her hands over him as if savouring each spasm of pain, stealing it into herself. As her nails traced down to the knife wound her skin began to shimmer.

The Hungarian screamed and there was an unmistakable shudder of pleasure in the sound.

Winter saw the world darken, the stars receding in his peripheral vision, turning the sky into something black and crushing. One last image lingered as he lost consciousness.

Alessandra's eyes, bright and blind as gold.

5

Adrenalin never truly took pain away. At best it dulled it, made it easier to manage. When that hormonal surge eventually subsided the pain would still be waiting, twice as unforgiving for being denied.

Winter felt as though someone had lit a bonfire in his ribcage. The numb ache in his chest had become molten, burning in his veins, in his muscles, inescapable.

'Easy,' said Alessandra, kneeling in front of him. Her face was indistinct, half in shadow. Either they were in a barely lit room or his vision was almost gone.

He must have slipped away again. It was so easy to give in. The darkness had a steady, tidal rhythm. It kept coming for him. *Go under,* it whispered. *Succumb.*

How had they found this place? All he had were sensory impressions, nothing more. They came back to him in flashes: Alessandra holding him on the roof terrace, the scent of Guerlain L'Heure Bleue strangely familiar on her skin; the jump to the building below that had knocked the breath from him and made his chest blaze; the door that Alessandra had smashed, sending glass tinkling into the dark.

'Try to make your breathing smaller,' she told him now. 'Little breaths, that's right.'

Winter did as she instructed, concentrating on keeping his chest from heaving, because it hurt like blue hell when it heaved. His right hand still clutched the entry wound, a crust of dried blood on his fingers.

Alessandra tore her wig away and plucked grips from her hair, placing them between her teeth. It made her look oddly theatrical, but then this was a theatre, Winter realised, albeit a derelict one. There were curling posters on the walls. One had turn-of-the-century showgirls high-kicking in a frilly chorus line. Another, in a sharper, more modern style, displayed a burly tenor caught mid aria.

Three tall, gilt-edged mirrors surrounded them, their silvered surfaces grey with dust. Brushes and pencils lay on a nearby bureau table, abandoned. This must have been a dressing room, Winter imagined, trying to focus on anything other than the pain crippling his body. It still had a waxy, greasy smell, mingling with the scent of must and rotten wood.

He could feel a breeze on his skin. Glancing up he saw that part of the ceiling had gone, the plaster ripped apart, another souvenir of the great siege. The first spits of rain were coming through, hitting the exposed floorboards.

Alessandra shook out her black bob. And then she began to unfasten the buttons of Winter's shirt, flipping his tie to one side.

He held her wrist. 'No. Leave it.'

'Don't be stupid, Hart.'

'There's nothing you can do.'

'I can look at it, can't I? What are you, embarrassed?'

Winter sighed, letting his arm fall to the floor. He had no energy for arguing. His chest rose and fell as she unbuttoned him.

'Just be careful, alright?'

Alessandra reached the last button and spread the sticky halves of the shirt either side of his chest.

Winter heard a sudden catch in her throat.

'What in God's name are these?' she asked, softly.

He knew what she had seen. The scar tissue of John Dee's runes, still vivid in his flesh. Karina had carved the Enochian symbols into his chest in that ruined basilica in Bavaria, nearly two years ago now. Some mornings they still bled. There were times he suspected they would never entirely heal.

'Collateral damage,' he said. 'Let's leave it at that.'

She stared at the markings, concerned but clearly fascinated. 'Why would anyone do this to you?'

'Because there was no other choice.' Winter coughed, and blood came through his teeth.

She spotted a ribbon of discoloured skin above his belt. 'There's another one here. This one's older, more faded. It looks like a knife wound. Someone else tried to kill you, I suppose?'

'Yes. There's a precedent. Maybe I just have one of those faces.'

Alessandra smiled. It was a private smile. 'I always liked your face, Hart. But some days I wanted to kill you too.'

77

Her mouth tightened as she saw the extent of the injury. The bullet had punched through his torso, leaving a raw crater the size of a small coin. The wound itself sat on a swollen whorl of skin, the heart of the rupture thick and black with blood. It flexed as he breathed.

'Turn over,' she told him.

Winter rolled on his side as best he could, the movement sending fresh spasms of pain through his chest. He stared at the far wall, concentrating on a tattered bill poster that showed an impeccably moustached man juggling flaming torches.

'There's no exit wound,' said Alessandra, examining his back. 'It's still inside you.'

Winter made himself turn again, scowling with the effort. This was bad. The bullet might be lodged in his pleural cavity, possibly even embedded in lung tissue. There was a strong chance of haemorrhage, let alone infection. The wound was open and sucking in air, too. That could trigger total lung collapse.

He was lucky he'd been shot by a Makarov pistol. At least 9mm bullets remained intact, didn't rip through arterial thoroughfares in a burst of shrapnel. Of course, there were more appealing definitions of luck.

'We need to get you to a hospital.'

Winter shook his head sharply. 'No chance. State security has my face now. I'll be dead in their hands anyway. They'll torture me first.'

'For God's sake, you can't just stay here like this.'

He took his eyes from her, staring up at the shattered

ceiling. 'If I'm captured then you're captured,' he told her, measuredly. 'I screwed up, that's all. But it's alright. They'll send somebody else. Some other asset. You'll get to the West.'

'I don't need to get to the West.'

'Well, then. I'm glad it was all for nothing.'

Alessandra was legitimately angry with him now. 'You're going to die here, Hart. You're going to die here in this dead place. And you're going to make me watch it.'

He met her gaze again. 'My name,' he insisted, quietly and firmly, 'is Christopher Winter.'

Alessandra's eyes looked older than her face, older than the darkness that framed her.

'You can use magic.'

It didn't sound like a suggestion. It sounded like a provocation. A dare.

'You've done it before,' she urged. 'I saw you do it. I was there, in Tangiers. In the souk. You took a bullet then too. The Persian assassin. You cast a hex of restoration and—'

'Not me. Another man. A long time ago.'

She grunted dismissively. 'You're the same man, you obstinate bastard, whatever name you call yourself.'

'That man would have taken me to Hell. I'm nothing that he was. Nothing!'

Winter started to cough again. The bare wound widened, even as his chest felt tighter still.

'You were powerful,' said Alessandra, practically under her breath.

He gave a brittle smile. 'I was lost. Believe me.'

Alessandra lapsed into silence, her frustration cooling as she considered this. 'What happened to you?' she finally asked him. 'Tell me the truth.'

The rain drummed on the floorboards, building now.

'I died,' said Winter, reaching for the simplest words he could find. 'Just for a moment, but I died. And I came back. But he was gone. Tobias Hart. All his memories. All his gifts. Whatever part of me he was. My soul, my spirit, whatever you call it, was cut in two, and he was gone. So don't ask me to use magic, because I wouldn't begin to know how. Not even to save my life.'

Alessandra lifted his hand from the floor. She slipped her long fingers between his. Her skin prickled like a murmur of static.

'Magic doesn't live in memory,' she stated, calmly. 'It lives in blood. In the bones. It sinks into you and roots itself. You told me that when we met, just before we made love for the first time.'

'That's one hell of a seduction.'

'You were once a very charming man.'

Her fingers tightened around his. He felt the touch of metal. A ring, cold and hard, pressing against his skin.

'Let your body remember,' Alessandra urged. 'I'll help you.'

Winter saw how huge her pupils were in the dark. They consumed her irises, so deeply black they were almost luminous. He had seen eyes like that before, he realised. The woman at Scratch Hill Junction, the one who had come to trade money for Frontenac's heart. Suddenly he felt a rush of questions, in spite of the killing pain.

'I couldn't save myself from a knife wound. What makes this so different?'

'Usually it demands a considerable blood sacrifice to a higher entity. Luckily for you, I'm not that needy. And the only blood you're sacrificing right now is your own.'

Winter searched her gaze. 'What are you? You're not human, I know that.'

'It never bothered you. Not back then.' There was something defiant in her voice as she said that.

'I've met demons before.'

'Demons,' she echoed, coldly. 'There's no nuance to that word. I could just as easily call you an animal. That's how most of us see you. But then your fellow animals don't claim moral superiority over us. That distinguishes your kind, at least.'

'So you are a demon.'

Winter felt the edge of the ring cut into his skin, a prick of pain that registered despite the agony in his chest.

'Once you could have listed the Houses of the Unbound Sun,' she told him, dismayed at everything he had forgotten. 'The grand dynasties of the Dusklands. The Burning Saints and the Children of the Great Defiance. You knew our names and our truths.'

'All gone,' said Winter, his breathing rapid now, the copper tang of blood on his tongue. 'Tell me. What are you?'

Alessandra's mouth curled with hauteur. 'According to your myths I'm a succubus. I've always found that such an ungainly word. I'm a daughter of Lilith, the Firstborn

Woman. The bloodline of the Archangel Samael is within me. My queen is Na'amah of the Silken Thirst. I'm not some common demon, Mr Winter.'

Her fingers twisted around his. There were filaments of gold in her eyes. 'I'm an Erovore.'

Winter was dragging air into his throat more urgently than before. His chest felt like a snare around his lungs, tightening by the minute. Flashes of white dotted his vision, like static corrupting a television signal.

He had often wondered how he would face death again. Of course there was every chance the next bullet you took would be your last, brisk and anonymous. That was just the law of averages. But he never imagined it would come quite so soon, or feel quite so arbitrary, so incidental.

Alessandra's pale face blurred and doubled, then resolved itself as he concentrated on her.

She had offered him life. She had offered him magic. The two were indivisible, it seemed. And magic scared him. It had been in his veins before, so powerful, so intoxicating, and part of him hated the thought of tasting it again.

But he didn't want to die, he realised. Not tonight, not like this, in some forgotten room, on a dead-end mission that had meant nothing. There had to be another death out there, years from now. A better, smarter death. One with at least a scrap of meaning.

He pressed the bones of his hand against her. 'Tell me how I can live.'

She smiled and drew the hand close. Winter's knuckles brushed the silk of her blouse, the firm warmth of her breast. Their wrists were parallel. He could feel her pulse against his, steady through the skin. Briefly they beat out of step. And then they synchronised, keeping the primal rhythm of blood.

'Search your body,' she told him, her voice barely louder than the rain. 'Flesh is memory. Bone is memory. Blood is memory.'

Winter repeated the words, his eyelids flickering. He sensed her lean in, her breath on his face. The powdery scent of Guerlain perfume blended with the sweet, leathery trace of Sobranie cigarettes, still in her hair. He knew this woman. He had known her for so very long.

Alessandra's mouth found his throat. Her lips closed around his flesh, her tongue darting wetly against him. For a second he experienced a flare of memory. It came like electricity torn from darkness: the two of them, joined naked, the scent of sweat and incense, a hot sun through a high Moorish window. Then it was gone, stamping an afterimage in his mind's eye and a shiver of recognition in his body.

'Flesh is memory,' he said again, reciting her words like a mantra, his voice cracking with the effort. 'Bone is memory. Blood is memory.'

The rain was hitting the tall mirrors that stood watch around them. It trailed down their surfaces, scoring through the dust, revealing slivers of reflected light. But the glass was darkening. The rain had become the colour and consistency of ink. It was turning the mirrors black.

Alessandra moved her mouth lower. She placed

kisses across his chest, her tongue playing over the scars. Winter experienced another grenade-burst of memory: cold forest air, a grey-blue dusk, a ring of pines, the first stars. The two of them were in the snow, the heat of their bodies turning it to slush. Alessandra's legs were locked around his back and she was urging him closer inside her, murmuring as her pleasure built. He glimpsed her eyes. They were gold, sightless.

'Be with me,' she told him, and Winter didn't know if that was a memory too.

The black liquid dripped from the mirrors, pooling beneath them. And then it slid across the floorboards, seeking Winter's hand. It sank into his pores, found his veins, chased its way through the maze of arteries and capillaries, nerves and synapses. Soon it was swilling inside him, heady and dark.

It was so easy. He remembered that now. Magic was ink. You wrote the world with it.

Alessandra guided his other hand to where the bullet had pierced him.

'Flesh is memory,' she chanted, softly. 'Bone is memory. Blood is memory.'

She pressed their hands together against the wound. Blood swam from the gash, smearing their knuckles. Winter sensed a tremor of some unknowable energy, building between their palms, radiating through their bones. Whatever it was it began to calm the relentless burning.

Something trickled against his fingers. It was wet but it had a different texture to the blood. Harder, more granular.

He lifted his hand and saw a dull silver fluid, oozing from the hole in his chest. It took him a moment to realise what it was. The 9mm bullet, rippling out of him like mercury.

'My God,' he sighed, struggling to process all this.

There was a brittle crack of glass. The mirrors had splintered into cobweb patterns. Light bled from the fissures, white and blinding. It filled the room, every abandoned corner. And then, just as quickly, it faded.

Alessandra returned his hand to the wound. Her skin was glowing now, lit by her veins. They looked like fairy lights inside her.

Winter could feel his torn flesh reuniting. With the bullet expelled the tissue was knitting itself back together. The pain steadily receded, replaced by a wave of pleasure. If this energy was demonic he surrendered to it regardless. Magic was ink, he told himself again. You wrote the world with it. No, you rewrote the world with it.

Still clutching his hand, Alessandra rose and sat astride him. Winter felt the pressure of her body but to his surprise there was no discomfort, no protest from his ribs. Her eyes had turned to gold again, blank and gleaming, and as he heard her breathing deepen he knew she was feeding on him, taking his pleasure for her own. She squeezed his chest between her thighs and began to slide against him.

The downpour was fierce now, pelting through the break in the roof. It streamed down their skin and saturated their clothes. It had a summer warmth, in spite of the hour.

Alessandra leaned in again, rain running from her lips.

'All magic is seduction,' she said, and Winter believed her.

6

Winter pushed the coins into the slot and heard them tumble through the innards of the payphone.

There was a state propaganda picture glued to the kiosk wall, just above the cradle for the receiver. It showed a worker's fist breaking through the soil to meet the hand of a soldier. In Uralic alphabet it declared 'Forward Through Cooperation'. Someone had scrawled '1956' across the worker's knuckles, then beneath it *aratás*, the Hungarian word for harvest. The graffiti was blood red. Winter picked at the gummy edge of the placard.

'Hello?' said the muzzy voice at the other end of the line. It was two am and Bernard Gately had obviously been woken by the call.

Winter dutifully recited his half of the clearance protocol, a line of poetry by Sir Francis Bacon. It felt as ludicrous as ever in this context. 'The man of life upright, whose guiltless heart is free...'

The line hummed, awaiting Gately's response. Winter glanced out of the grimy kiosk window. Alessandra was standing on the empty boulevard, one arm across her chest, a cigarette pinched between her fingers. She met Winter's eyes and exhaled a casual drift of smoke. The rain had gone but the street glistened like black marble behind her.

Gately remembered the words. 'From all dishonest deeds, or thought of vanity. Hello, Winter. What do you need?'

Winter wedged the handset closer, analysing the sound of the connection. He could hear faint fluctuations in the background hum. Sonic artefacts, probably, glitches in the cables, but you could never be entirely sure. The state always had its ears pressed to the city.

'Hello?' said Gately, a little rattily now.

'This is a secure line?'

'Of course it is.'

A standard wiretap tended to produce a tiny but detectable echo, riding just behind a voice. Gately sounded clean, but there was reverberation in the signal that made it hard to be sure.

'When was the line swept?'

'Two days ago. Junction box too.'

Winter spoke quickly. 'My cover's gone. The mission's compromised. They know I'm here.'

'What happened?'

'I made an intervention. It was problematic.'

'What the hell did you do?'

'Read the report when I bloody well write it.'

'Are you injured? Is the woman?'

Winter's eyes fell to his shirt. The blood had dried

88

to a sprawl of a stain that his tightly buttoned jacket couldn't quite conceal. It was the only remnant of the wound. That and a lingering sense that he'd reawakened something dangerous, unwanted, inside him.

'I'm fine. She's fine. I'm still going to get her out. But there's something else. This is more than a defection. She has some kind of agenda beyond that.'

Gately paused and static chittered on the line. 'What agenda? What does she mean?'

'I'm just about to find out.'

'Where are you?'

Again the insect whisper of static. 'Look, we need to forget the rendezvous. I'll get her to the West as arranged but it's too much of a risk for you. They've got my face on film. They'll be scouring the city for me, every station, every border. We can't be seen together.'

'I'll be careful. For God's sake, Winter, I'm always careful.'

There was a barely suppressed petulance in Gately's voice. Winter recognised the sound of a second-tier operative craving a little more adrenalin in his life.

'No. You need to dead-drop the tickets and the papers. Do it now. I'll pick them up in the morning.'

'But, Winter…'

'Do what I say. Fallback protocol.'

Gately sighed, then grunted his acceptance of the situation. 'Alright. I'll let London know. You were given a potential drop point, I take it?'

'Of course. Part of the mission brief.'

'So where are you?'

Winter hesitated. For a second he saw the kiosk and Gately's apartment as two points on a vast copper-wire web, quivering through the city. A web of cable that infiltrated bricks and stitched itself between buildings. A tremor on a single, humming strand would alert the spider at its heart.

Time to end this conversation.

'Thank you, Bernard.' Winter replaced the phone on the cradle. A coin clattered into the refund tray beneath the dial.

'Is there a problem?' asked Alessandra as he stepped from the kiosk.

'I don't know. But you had an awful lot of chaperones at the hotel tonight. Three of them, at least. That's either overkill or an ambush.'

'You think they were expecting you?'

'Not sure. If it was an ambush then we've been compromised from the beginning. Maybe before I even got to Budapest.'

Winter lit a Woodbine and exhaled. Tonight was a mess.

They left Pest and crossed Liberty Bridge to the Buda Hills. The city was quiet at this hour but the dark slopes of the western bank had a deeper silence. Gellért Hill lay ahead of them, a bluff crag of dolomite rock that reared over the Danube, crowned with dense vegetation.

Winter spotted turrets beneath the wild bushes. It seemed to be some kind of castle or hillside fortress.

Alessandra led the way along the embankment road. They moved quickly and hugged the roadside shadows as the river smacked its concrete banks behind them. The occasional passing car found them in its headlights but they kept walking, their faces turned from the road. Eventually they crossed into an unlit side street that clung beneath the hill.

A prefabricated cabin stood against the base of the rock, electric light bleeding through its sides. Some kind of workman's refuge, Winter guessed, given a concrete mixer was parked a little way down the road. There was a thick padlocked chain slung across the door.

Alessandra reached for the opal locket at her throat and neatly prised it apart. A small silver key spilled into her palm. She inserted the key into the lock and turned it, catching the weight of the falling chain in her other hand.

The door opened, and a waiting man acknowledged their arrival with a curt nod. He was dressed in drab, earth-spattered overalls and his lean, cautious features were sharpened by the bare bulb that hung from the cabin's ceiling.

'János,' said Alessandra, greeting him just as briskly in return. 'This is Tobias.'

'Not my name,' insisted Winter under his breath. He was frankly tired of pointing this out.

She turned to him, her expression suddenly cold. 'Listen to me. This is going to be hard enough as it is but these people are here to meet Tobias Hart. That's who you are tonight. Otherwise they'll kill you. Do you understand?'

János looked between them, his eyes suspicious. 'This is the man you said you would bring?' He had switched the conversation to Hungarian but Winter had a working knowledge of the language.

Alessandra nodded. 'He has a cover. He's being cautious.'

János said something else then, but Winter struggled to make sense of it. It was a phrase in Hungarian he had never heard before. A nonsense phrase. It sounded like 'the king of tiny wings is waiting...'

Keeping Winter in his eyeline, János took a torch from the table tucked inside the cabin's entrance. Motioning them forward, he drew back a heavy sheet of tarpaulin, exposing a broad black fissure in the rock.

'Follow me,' he said, speaking English now.

They stepped through the crack, feeling the air cool as they entered a limestone tunnel. János's torchlight bobbed ahead of them, illuminating gnarled rock walls sweating with moisture. A footworn path led them deeper into what was obviously a natural cave system. Winter remembered that the hills of Buda were riddled with hollows, some of which reached as far as the city's cellars. He watched as insects chased the torch's glow.

The route was long and mazy. At points the trail made them edge past jagged outcrops of rock. At other times they bent nearly double to squeeze under low limestone overhangs. The only sound was their breathing and the intermittent ping of water. Winter sensed they were walking through the heart of the hill itself.

His eye was caught by something as they followed the path. A succession of crude white crosses, chalked on the rock walls. And there was a word, too, also etched in chalk, the letters streaking as the limestone wept. *Megváltás*. It took him a moment to place it. *Salvation*. Winter wondered if it was an act of worship or a plea for protection.

Presently the tunnel broadened, giving way to a crudely furnished anteroom. Lights were strung from wooden beams, lashed to a generator. A haze of moths hovered around the dim bulbs, their wings magnified by the shadows.

'Alessandra. At last.'

A woman was waiting for them. She was in her fifties, short and sturdily built, dressed in a rollneck sweater and jeans. Her hair was dotted with grey and a stubby cigarette hung from her mouth. She had worn, determined features, the kind that had been earned by conflict.

Alessandra turned to Winter. 'This is Judit Majoras. She's in command here.'

'Command?' he asked. 'Is this a military operation?'

The woman appraised him, as wary as János. And then she removed her cigarette and offered a firm, dry handshake.

'Mr Hart. I've led the Hungarian resistance for over twenty years. It may not be a military operation as the British judge it, but then who could ever live up to your nation's glorious standards?'

93

'Well, I hate to break it to you but I hear the war's over.'

Majoras didn't smile. 'Enemies change. Ideologies change. Resistance is what endures. We resisted Szálasi and the national socialists. Now we resist the communists. It's what our country demands of us. You British need to go back a long way to know what occupation feels like in your soul.'

'I'm not here for a revolution. I was sent to get this woman to the West.'

'Your priorities are changing. Get used to it.'

Majoras picked a tattered manila folder from a desk and handed it to Winter. 'Take a look at this. I imagine it'll be familiar.'

Winter opened the file and flicked through a sheaf of documents. It was a blur of Hungarian, endless tightly typed pages, many of them stamped in assorted shades of governmental ink. Then he found the photographs, black-and-white glossies slid between the sheets of A4.

'My God.'

He had seen autopsy pictures before. They were always hard to take, however detached you tried to be. These were worse than most. The starkly lit bodies were closer to skeletons than corpses, the flesh crumbling like fruit to reveal bone and sinew. The limbs were oddly elongated, the long, spindling fingers reaching almost to the knees.

There was something else. Each body had a hole smashed in its ribcage. Their hearts had gone.

'What am I looking at? Are these post-mortem reports?'

'You know what they are,' said Majoras, impatiently. 'You collaborated with the Russians during the war. You were part of Operation Paragon, the Allied mission that recovered the body of Prince Bernhard from Kriegstein Castle.'

Winter frowned, genuinely puzzled. 'Prince Bernhard?'

'You're looking at him,' said Alessandra, indicating the top photograph. 'He's not quite the catch he was in the eighteenth century.'

Winter stared at the image, uneased by the eyes. They had the familiar agonised blankness of all corpses. Somehow photochemical film seemed to preserve the moment a soul was torn from a body. You saw it in battlefield shots, the ones they kept out of the papers.

'What's happened to his heart?'

'Oh, the undead rarely remain intact,' said Majoras, dryly. 'God knows the research would be so much easier if they were. But you know this. Your part in the war is a matter of record. Special Operations Executive officer Tobias Hart. Twice decorated for gallantry. But never quite a hero. I believe they tried to burn your file shortly after VE Day.'

Winter continued to examine the photographs. These weren't post-mortems. They were lab reports. Someone had taken a scalpel to these cadavers in the name of science. Had he really been part of it, twenty years ago? Once again he had a sense of being taunted by another man's life, just beyond the reach of his memory.

Shattered ribs. Stolen hearts. In that moment he

could hear the low, rhythmic pulse of the package he had collected from that locker in St Pancras.

He turned to the next picture. It was a flimsy dental X-ray, the skull frozen in monochrome, faintly spectral. Winter studied the mouth. The canines were long and pronounced, curling like tusks from the gums. They swept down, scraping the lower jaw. He had an inkling of what these bodies were now.

'The undead? Are you telling me these are vampires? That these things also exist?'

Majoras exhaled, her patience gone. 'Enough,' she declared, crushing her half-smoked cigarette in an ashtray. 'I need your knowledge, not this performance.'

Winter looked to Alessandra. 'You should have warned her. I can't be expected to remember any of this.'

Alessandra gave a pained look to Majoras. 'He says he's suffered extreme trauma. His memory is lost. I don't think he can help us.'

'No one forgets what this warlock bastard has been through.'

'Believe me,' said Winter, 'I can't give you what you need. I have nothing to do with these corpses. Now let me do what I've been hired for. Let me bring this woman to the West.'

Majoras listened to his words, the lines around her mouth deepening with disdain.

'Perhaps your memory will improve once you meet our honoured guest.'

She led them to a roughly tooled door at the far end

of the chamber. There was a thick key in the lock and it turned with a scrape of rusted iron. Majoras waited for Winter to walk through, watching his expression change as he saw what the door had been hiding.

7

They were in a church. A church of living rock.

Candles filled the hollows in the limestone walls, casting a milky, quivering light across the makeshift nave. Other recesses held sacred ornaments, hardwood saints and a pale alabaster Madonna. There were even stained-glass windows knocked into the rock itself, the moon gleaming through the faces of Jesus.

The cave reared over this strange little chapel, its dank, pitted walls dwarfing the statue of Christ's crucifixion that hung above the altar. There was a hush and a stillness here. The banks of limestone felt porous with history.

'What is this place?' asked Winter.

'Saint István's Cave,' said Alessandra, matter-of-factly, as candlelight shuddered around them. 'The home of a hermit saint. The monks of the Pauline order consecrated it in the twenties.'

Majoras nodded. 'When the communists took our country they raided this church. The brothers were arrested, the entrance to the cave sealed with concrete. The monastery's superior was condemned to death by the State Protection Authority. 1951, would you believe. Even this half of the century gives us Christian martyrs. Perhaps one day he'll get to be a saint too. I'm sure that'll be a considerable comfort.'

'I take it you're not a religious woman,' Winter observed.

'The war burned my faith from me, Mr Hart. But this place is useful.'

Winter felt a sudden disturbance in the stillness of the cave. Something swept past him, close enough to skim his skin. An agitation of tiny dusk-grey wings, moving as one. It was a rush of moths, chasing into the church from the tunnel. They settled on the statue of Jesus.

'Oszkár,' called Majoras, her voice breaking the calm of the chapel. 'I've brought someone to meet you.'

The shadow of the crucifix fell on a high-backed wooden chair, set directly in front of the altar. As Winter stepped deeper into the cavern he saw that there was a figure in the chair, sat with its back to him. A man, completely motionless. He had a military-issue haircut, the sides sheared close to the skull, and there was a threadbare bandage looped around his head, stained with old, dark blood.

A length of plastic connected the man to a pouch of liquid mounted on a trolley. The fluid was a watery red in the candlelight. It seeped its way through the tube, slowing and stopping then starting again, as if the man were sipping it into his system.

Winter walked around the chair, his steps measured and cautious. The figure was wearing a grimy blue uniform, the jacket buttoned to the throat. There was a red-and-white armband on the left sleeve. It bore the pointed insignia of the Arrow Cross Party, Hungary's very own Nazis. A militia man. A soldier.

The other sleeve had been rolled to the elbow. The tube punctured the forearm, delivering the thin red liquid directly to the veins.

The man's hands were strapped to the chair, his wrists bound with barbed wire. Winter was intrigued to see garlands of holly threaded between the coils of metal, the leaves intertwining with the twists. The hands themselves were chalky and covered in cracks. There was some kind of break in the flesh on the right hand, just below the knuckles, as if the skin there had simply crumbled. It looked like the shattered hand of a porcelain doll.

The surgical bandage twisted around the man's face, leaving him blind. A matching pair of small gold crucifixes had been stitched into the cloth, one upon each eye. Below the bandage part of the face had also collapsed, leaving the left cheek a sunken hole. If the man was even breathing it was impossible to tell.

Winter was almost convinced he was looking at a cadaver, just like the ones in the photos. But then the right hand rose and began to tap the arm of the chair.

Tap. Tap. Tap.

The finger repeatedly struck the wood. At first the taps seemed random, disjointed. And then the nail found a rhythm and followed it.

Tap-tap. Tap-tap. Tap-tap. Tap-tap.

'Do you not recognise your own heartbeat? The soft drumming of your mortality?'

The tapping had synchronised with the thud of Winter's heart.

Tap-tap. Tap-tap.

The man in the chair smiled beneath the bandage. 'You have some splendidly rare antigens in your blood, whoever you are. But you've gone and spoiled them, haven't you?'

The upper lip drew back, trembling. There was a glimpse of broken teeth.

'Yes, you've allowed contamination. There's another presence in your blood. A darkness. A toxicity. What were you thinking?'

If the words unnerved him Winter was determined not to show it. 'You sound quite the connoisseur, Oszkár.'

'Oh, I'm just a humble expert, I assure you.' The man in the chair laughed and it sounded like cloth tearing.

Tap-tap. Tap-tap.

Only the chair cast a shadow.

Alessandra came and stood next to Winter. Sensing her presence, the captive tilted his head, the crucifixes stamped to his eyes glinting in the candlelight.

'Oh, but of course. This explains it. A succubus. A daughter of Lilith, the first, forgotten wife. What a damned bloodline you demons have, and so freely shared with the living.'

The bandaged gaze stayed upon her. It felt as though the buried eyes were boring through the gauze and the crosses.

'Tell me, does it still hurt that your mother was cast out of Eden for not knowing her place as Adam's vassal? Eve proved to be far more obliging.'

Alessandra took the taunt with a smile. 'I imagine you must have a mother, Oszkár. But like you she must have been dug up.'

Again there was the parched laugh. The fluid shifted in the tube, drawn into the veins.

'Who is this man?' asked Winter, turning to Majoras.

'This little snot is Oszkár Várkonyi. An officer of the Arrow Cross. A fascist and a revenant. I can never quite decide which is worse. We found him in the great siege of 1944, gone to ground in the eastern suburbs, drinking the blood of Budapest's wounded.'

'I could hardly drink the blood of the dead,' hissed Várkonyi. 'Please, grant me some standards.'

Impassively, Majoras reached for the tube and squeezed it in her fist. The plastic bulged as the flow of liquid was staunched. Várkonyi spluttered, his hands flexing beneath the straps that bound him.

'This is all you have, you graveyard vermin. And if I choose, you don't even have that.'

Winter indicated the bag of fluid. 'What is that stuff? Blood?'

'It's a synthetic substitute, close enough to keep him... well, hardly alive, given the bastard's undead, but enough to ensure that his body remains functioning. It's a weak proxy, though, not one of the high-grade surrogates. You can see the effect it's had on his body. The breakages

103

in the skin where the tissue's deteriorated. It's really a fascinating case study.'

'Be kind…' Várkonyi was pleading with her now, his voice rising, unnervingly childlike. 'Please. I'm sorry. Let me taste the sweetness again.'

Majoras made a play of considering the request. Finally she released her grip on the tube. Várkonyi sighed in relief as the liquid trickled its way back into him.

'They depend on blood for so much of their power. It's more than a biological thirst, it seems. At their full might these creatures can summon a pestilence. Rats, crows, bats, even wolves. Deprived of blood the best this filth can manage is moths. Proud of your little army, aren't you, Oszkár?'

Winter glanced at the statue of Christ. The fuzz of insects covered the cross, their wings flittering anxiously. 'Why are you keeping this man here? Some kind of specimen for your research, I take it?'

Majoras shook her head. 'I wouldn't dignify him with a scalpel. We keep him here to prevent others from learning what they can. Even in 1944 the Russians were hunting for his kind. A body dragged from the grave is one thing, but to have one of these beasts sat breathing in front of you… well, it's a gift, isn't it?'

There was a fundamental cruelty to this setup that bothered Winter. 'My God. He's been your prisoner for over twenty years.'

'We had to keep moving him through churches in the city, drag him onto holy ground. It burns what soul remains inside him, keeps him weak and in pain. When the communists sealed this cave it gave us the perfect place to hide him, away from their eyes. But yes, it's a commitment. Resistance is commitment.'

Winter wasn't convinced. 'Whatever he's done, and whatever your cause, he deserves better than this. There's no dignity here.'

The Hungarian regarded him with a sour look. 'Is this empathy, Mr Winter?'

'Not really. Surprised you don't just kill him.'

'And then we'd be left guarding his corpse. Because inevitably he's going to rise from death. Try to understand, these things don't die easily.'

Sated by the liquid, Várkonyi spoke again, his voice as brittle as old leaves. 'I think you should listen to this gentleman. You've already entered into an alliance with this ballroom harlot of a demon. What makes my needs so different from hers?'

Alessandra seized Várkonyi by the roots of his hair, wrenching his bandaged head towards her. The movement was sudden and furious, enough to take Winter by surprise.

'You're an infestation, like all your kind.'

'Predators,' Várkonyi retorted, short of breath but determined to correct her. 'We are part of the natural order. We thirst to live. That's more than your kind ever do.'

Alessandra tilted the man's head until the veins bulged in his throat. 'You are no better than animal scum.'

Winter flinched at the word *animal*. She had used it

earlier tonight, and aimed it at him.

'We drink blood,' spat Várkonyi, the twin crucifixes staring up at her, defiant. 'And our hearts burn with its warmth, brighter than you can imagine. What do you steal from this world, girl? The pleasure of flesh, would you call it? That's the sweet thrill of blood too. The joy in the veins. No wonder your kind crave it. You are cold, empty things. How jealous you must be of the living. They have a fraction of your time in this world but they know how to taste it. We both want the gifts of their bodies. I simply choose to bite, not screw.'

Alessandra reached for Várkonyi's face with her other hand. She prised his mouth apart, her fingers forcing back the upper lip until she'd fully exposed his teeth.

'Go on,' she jeered. 'Take a bite, then. Take a bite with your big mouth, little soldier.'

Winter recoiled. Várkonyi's teeth had been sawn down to rutted stumps. Now they were no more than vestigial fragments of enamel, embedded like broken pebbles in the gums. His captors must have done this to him. Perhaps they'd taken his eyes, too.

'Alessandra,' he cautioned, touching her arm.

She turned, a flash of something vicious in her dark eyes. 'Spare him?' she asked, incredulous.

Winter nodded. 'Please. There's no need.'

She removed her hand. Várkonyi let his head slump, a curl of amusement on his lips.

'So brave, demon. Taunting a captive man. What confidence you have. One day you will face my kind without their shackles. Let's see how your confidence serves you then.'

'Vampires and Erovores,' said Majoras, her tone resigned. 'Old enemies. Older than this world, I think.'

'Operation Paragon,' said Winter. 'You're telling me I was part of it?'

Majoras nodded, finally – reluctantly – accepting Winter's plea of amnesia. 'A joint initiative between British and Russian Intelligence, before this Cold War came and set your nations at each other's throats. You weren't just part of it, Hart. You were integral. You headed the missions that scoured Europe for the undead.'

'What the hell did we want with these creatures? We were fighting a war...'

'The vampire is a phenomenal species,' conceded Majoras, momentarily putting her hate aside. 'Death is a minor setback to them. Their bodies have a way to defy it. A capacity to reanimate themselves, time and time again. Imagine that power on the battlefield, to say nothing of their unholy strength and agility.'

'You wanted their secrets,' added Alessandra, a trace of condescension in her voice. 'Because your science believes anything can be dissected, even the damnation of the undead.'

'It's not damnation,' muttered Várkonyi. 'It's a birthright.'

Winter mulled what he had just heard as candlelight guttered on the cavern's walls.

'We wanted to fight the war with these things? Is that what you're asking me to believe?'

'Not as such,' said Majoras. 'You didn't want to create more of their kind. They were human once, after all. We share our essential biological code with them. Your scientists wanted to isolate the deviation in the DNA, graft it into the human body. Make soldiers who could afford to die, and die again.'

Winter understood. And he felt cold at the implications. 'Recyclable casualties of war. The ultimate acceptable losses.'

'And then you won the war,' Majoras continued. 'And made a new enemy of your former ally. Operation Paragon was officially abandoned as a dead end. At least on the British side. The communists are rather more tenacious.'

'It's ongoing?'

'We intercepted signal intelligence from Belarus station ten days ago, rerouted from Moscow. They already have a team in the Carpathians, ransacking crypts. I imagine it won't be long before they're in Hungary.'

'Imagine that, Oszkár,' teased Alessandra. 'Leaving your body to science when you can never actually die…'

'They'll come for your kind next,' Várkonyi countered. 'They already know what you are.'

Majoras hushed them and continued talking to Winter. 'If the Soviet Bloc finally unlocks the secrets of undead biology then it will hold a clear advantage. The communists will be empowered to escalate this Cold War to the real thing. That's why I summoned you here, Hart. We're racing against them now.'

'What did you think I could do?' asked Winter.

'You led the missions. You were a specialist. You knew where these things were buried. The Russians are chasing rumours, peasant whispers. You had facts, not folklore. With your knowledge we could get to the bodies before they do.'

'Whatever I might have known... it's all gone. I'm sorry.'

Majoras sighed, some of her earlier fire gone now. She gestured to Alessandra. 'Then do the job you came for. Get this woman to the West. Let her tell British Intelligence what we've learned here in Budapest. There will be other men who worked on Operation Paragon. Find them. Find them soon.'

She turned to lead them out of the limestone church. Alessandra gave a contemptuous parting smile to Várkonyi and then followed her. The flames of the closest candles gusted at their departure.

Winter stood where he was, watching as the sac of pale red liquid bubbled above the blinded soldier.

'I appreciate your compassion,' rasped Várkonyi. 'Your blood is tainted, but you have a good heart.'

Winter made to go. As he did so Várkonyi's nail began to rap the arm of the chair. The sharp, staccato taps reverberated against the rock walls. And then, just like before, the finger found a rhythm. As if locking on target, thought Winter.

Tap-tap. Tap-tap. Tap-tap. Tap-tap.

His own heartbeat, echoing again.

8

It was already light when they left Gellért Hill, the sky poised between grey and blue.

Winter hadn't slept for over a day. His eyes ached and he could feel his senses blunting. Usually he would fix this with a sharpening amphetamine hit but his allocated pills had been left at the hotel, along with his gun. No doubt state security had taken his possessions. Now they would be sifting through them, scrutinising labels and serial numbers in a bid to know just who had walked into their country as Anthony Robert St John Prestwick.

Sometimes he wondered if Christopher Winter was just another shell of an identity, fundamentally no different to a Prestwick or a Hastings or a Swinstead or one of a hundred meticulously constructed covers he had used over the years. Another name, another life, just one he had chosen to believe in. It was a thought he quashed as quickly as he could each time it whispered. This was who he was now. He owned this name.

But here among the twisting shadows of Budapest – in the company of Alessandra – the line that divided him from his past, from Tobias Hart, felt altogether hazier. Standing in that cave, hearing Judit Majoras talk about Operation Paragon, his buried years had seemed closer than ever. Something unresolved was stirring, determined to find its way back into the present.

God, he itched to be in London now. Home soil, he knew, would help him shake this feeling. A cup of sugary Lipton tea in his Battersea bedsit could keep the world away.

Budapest seemed to prickle with eyes this morning. Every archway, every window, was a potential surveillance point, every commuter queuing for an early tram an agent of the state until proved otherwise. Winter felt conspicuous and wanted to be out of this city as soon as he could. He kept his movements small and contained as he threaded through the waking streets, his pace brisk but not quite quick enough to attract attention. Alessandra followed him rather less subtly, still dressed for a seduction. Her glamour was part of her, somehow. She inhabited it like a skin.

'I'm pretty sure I encountered something like Várkonyi in London,' he told her at last. 'Just before I got this assignment.'

'The undead are everywhere. They're hardly indigenous to Eastern Europe.'

'You think it's a coincidence?'

She gave a sharp smile. 'They're predators; they go where the blood is. This entire planet is a banquet to them. So many regional flavours, so many vintages.'

112

'This thing was after a heart. A human heart. I was told that it was very old and very valuable. I saw those photographs back in the hill. Those creatures' hearts were missing. That's coincidence too, I take it?'

Alessandra's smile had faded. 'Maybe not.'

'And there's something else. I'm equally certain I met one of your kind, too, the same night. They were also after the heart. I think there's a bigger picture here, one that you're not sharing. So tell me. What's going on?'

Alessandra paused, considering her next words. 'First we get out of Hungary. Then we talk. You're right. There's much you should know.'

It was scarcely an answer. But Winter could tell from her face it was all she would grant him for now.

The conversation ended, they made their way to Toldy Ferenc, a quiet residential street close to the pale turrets of the Fisherman's Bastion. There they located a concrete-fronted apartment building, the agreed site for Gately's dead-drop. It was utterly nondescript, so camouflaged by drabness it barely registered in anyone's eyeline. Winter walked into the ammonia-scented hallway and, using a key that London had provided for just such a situation, opened a letterbox marked in the name of Kautzsky, Apartment 12.

He sorted through a stash of post. Utility bills mainly, but there was a postcard from some humdrum Caspian resort, a hand-tinted photo of a trawler on the front, a scrawl of Hungarian on the back. A British operative must have sent it, maybe a sleeper agent, doing a favour for

Queen and country. Anything to maintain the integrity of this address and keep the imaginary Kautzsky alive. The state watched everything, even postcards.

'Is it there?' asked Alessandra, just as eager as Winter to slip the city.

Winter glanced across the hallway. A boiler-suited janitor was mopping the communal area, sloshing suds across the tiles. The man was young, no more than thirty, but had a hearing aid clipped to his ear. Winter watched him a moment longer then returned his attention to the post.

'Yeah, this has to be it.'

He tore open a beige envelope, addressed in black type. It was stamped with the shield of a local charitable trust, one that was just as fictitious as Kautzsky. Inside was a glossy black-and-white pamphlet, urging a donation. Wedged between the glum portraits of orphans was a pair of train tickets and documentation providing a new identity for Alessandra.

'Gately didn't let us down,' said Winter. 'Come on, let's go.'

He unbuttoned his jacket to pocket the tickets and the papers. The janitor eyed him from across the hall, taking in Winter's blood-smeared shirtfront. Winter stared back. The man looked away again and continued to push his mop, the thick strands of yarn foaming across the floor.

Winter tilted an ear. He was sure he had heard something, just for a second. The crackle of a voice, a metallic whisper, leaking from the cleaner's hearing aid.

He strained to catch it again but a vehicle had begun to reverse in front of the building, its engine sluggishly loud. Winter turned to the door and saw a newly arrived refuse truck through the glass.

'Let's move,' he told Alessandra.

They pushed through the door and out into the narrow street. At the edge of the pavement a man in oilskin trousers and a black labourer's jacket was shaking a bin into the back of the truck. The steel teeth of the compactor turned, gnashing through the waste. A scent of refuse drifted from the hulking vehicle, hot and nauseously sweet.

Winter and Alessandra crossed the cobbles. They walked calmly but there was an edge of threat in the thin, bright sunshine. Winter sensed it immediately. It was tangible, like air tensing before lightning. The truck nudged its way along the gutter, keeping pace with them, its motor grinding.

Aluminium clattered on concrete. The man in the oilskin trousers had slammed the bin to the kerbside.

Winter studied the wing mirrors of the parked cars. Each sun-struck reflection gave him a new and clearer view of the figure behind them. The man was walking now, ignoring the bins that had been placed for collection, his concentration fixed on Winter's back. One mirror exposed a dull glint beneath his jacket. The next confirmed it as the handle of a gun, snug in a shoulder strap.

Winter felt the acute lack of his own gun. The ankle knife was also gone, discarded on the rooftop of the Maria

Theresa. His eyes flicked to Alessandra, the briefest of glances telling her that they should keep their pace up.

The truck continued to crawl, its thick wheels turning on the cobbles. A cyclist passed them, soon lost to another street.

Winter slid a hand into his jacket pocket. His fingers found the brass chill of his knuckle-duster. His other hand made a play of patting the left-side pocket then pulled out a packet of Woodbines. He flipped it open, the movement drawing the stalking man's attention as his right hand wriggled into the metal rings.

Winter leapt on to the bonnet of a Škoda estate, stamped across the car's roof and launched himself at his pursuer. He had surprise and momentum on his side and the pair of them smashed into the road.

Twisting, the man tried to slam a hand against Winter's face. Winter countered with a clout of brass, hearing cartilage crack as his fist connected with the man's nose. He hit him again, a whip of a punch. The man's eyes were momentarily blinded by his own blood.

The truck had stopped, its engine cutting. The driver flung open the cabin door and jumped down to the pavement. Alessandra strode towards him, smiling with purpose, entirely confident.

Winter and his opponent grappled on the hard cobbles, their bodies rolling through petrol spills. The man was well-muscled and in seconds he had managed to wrestle an advantage. He balled both fists and hammered Winter either side of the head.

Winter reeled, numbed by the double blow against his skull. Then he took a steel-toed boot in the ribcage, the velocity of the kick thrusting him back onto his feet. He staggered, fighting for balance, the street lurching, a drunken churn of architecture and sky.

A matter of feet away the driver faced down Alessandra. His expression was wary. He was clearly perturbed by her smile. Impulsively he snatched her wrists and wrested her towards him. Her smile only widened.

Winter backed against the door of a building. His adversary advanced, blinking blood as he cleared his vision. He was reaching for his gun, sliding the weapon from its leather holster.

Winter was upon him, exerting all his strength to straighten the gun arm. Gaining leverage he gripped the man by the bicep then contorted the forearm to an ugly, unendurable angle. With a grunt he shifted his body weight, accentuating the pressure. A final twist and the bone snapped like coral.

Howling, the man collapsed to his knees, the pistol smacking across the cobbles. Winter strolled over to retrieve it. Grasping the barrel he swung the gun and cold-cocked his opponent.

Alessandra stared into the driver's eyes as he held her. Her black gaze was measureless. She set her face against his, provocatively close. Her mouth fell against the man's throat and her tongue darted across his skin, lapping at the pulse points.

The driver gave a small, involuntary sigh, his eyes

quivering. In moments his body had surrendered, shuddering with pleasure.

Alessandra easily shook his hold now. Freeing her wrists she cradled the man's face, her lean fingers glimmering in the morning sunlight. She sunk her nails into his cheeks and he gave up a noise that began as a swoon and finished as a scream.

'Leave him.'

Winter was behind her. There were people in the street now, keeping a watchful distance behind the cars. Any moment one of them would surely summon the police.

The succubus ignored him, savouring every ecstatic, terrified tremor of her victim's body.

'Alessandra…' He placed a hand on her shoulder.

She spun with a snap of black hair. Her eyes glared gold and her expression was savage. She was a demon. Winter knew that. But until now this knowledge hadn't turned his blood cold.

Her eyes faded to black again. She acknowledged him with a nod, mopping her mouth with the back of her hand. Then she pushed the whimpering man to the ground, leaving him rocking on his knees.

Winter turned the gun in his hand. A FÉG PA-63 semi-automatic. Hungarian security forces issue. Two-tone, black and chrome. Built for the alleyway, not the battlefield. He already knew the first shot he would fire with it.

Securing the pistol in his holster he began to walk away from the crowd and the empty truck and the two men, one still shaking, the other unconscious on the cobbles. Alessandra kept pace beside him. A moment later they broke into a trot, stirring a clump of gulls that had strayed into the city from the river. By the end of the street they were running.

'Bernard! It's me.'

Winter rapped the door again, more insistently this time. The sound of his knuckles rang along the landing of the dark-walled apartment building in the Belváros district.

Finally there came a shuffle of footsteps from inside the second-floor flat. Winter pressed his eye to the peephole above the brass numerals, trying to peer into the hallway. He saw Bernard Gately's eye, looming dimly in the convex glass.

'Open the door, Bernard.'

The door parted an inch, the silver latch chain dangling in the gap. Gately's breath was all high-tar cigarettes and black Hungarian coffee.

'Winter?' The word rose in surprise.

'There's been a complication. You have to let us in.'

Gately's voice fell to a whisper. 'I thought I wasn't meant to be seen with you...'

Winter heard a faint sibilance on the word *seen*. The man on the other side of the door was nervous. 'We're already compromised. Let us in.'

The chain slid and dropped. Gately reluctantly drew the door open. He looked from Winter to Alessandra then cast a glance along the corridor before letting the pair of them in. 'Alright,' he sighed. 'But you're breaking protocol. I want that noted.'

'Duly,' said Winter, dryly.

They entered the living room. It was a scholarly clutter of books and pens and half-drained cups. A window was open to the city and a nicotine-faded net curtain fluttered in the sunlight. Distractedly, Gately turned from his visitors and began to tidy a stash of *The Economist* that had spilt across the coffee table.

'So what happened? I set up the dead drop just like…'

The sentence died in his mouth. He found a gun pressed to the nape of his neck.

'You certainly set us up, Bernard.'

Winter pushed the tip of the barrel deeper into the soft flesh above the collar.

Gately started to shake his head then stopped, as if afraid of provoking the gun. He kept his voice calm and his eyes on the wall. 'You're mistaken.'

'They knew the location. They were waiting for us. I'd say that qualifies as an ambush, Bernard, wouldn't you? Coincidence is what happens to civilians, remember.'

'I swear I had nothing to do with it.'

Winter disengaged the safety catch, ensuring Gately registered the sound before he spoke. 'The dead drop was bait. You told them exactly where to find us. I take it the money's better on their side? Almost as good as journalism?'

A muscle tremored in Gately's cheek, just below the eye. 'What can I say to convince you?'

'I'm already convinced.'

'So why even threaten me with that bloody gun? I'm going to keep telling you I had nothing to do with it. And then I imagine you'll get bored and you'll kill me.'

Winter withdrew the gun and spun Gately around by the shoulder. The man's forehead was beading with sweat. 'I take it you have a car, Bernard?'

The blue Fiat 1100 saloon hugged the back roads, sunlight playing on its chrome trim. Bernard Gately was at the wheel, profoundly aware of the gun pointed at him from the passenger seat. No one in the car had spoken for the last twenty minutes. Alessandra winched down one of the rear windows, as much to disperse the crush of silence as the summer heat.

They had left the hub of Budapest behind and were now climbing into countryside, heading west past the paprika fields. The roads were shoddier this far from the city, the hot tarmac cracked and neglected. There was precious little traffic and only the occasional tumbledown farmhouse signified life.

Gately had been instructed to take them towards Tatabánya. Now, as they passed a gated track, Winter told him to stop the car instead. He did so wordlessly, without eye contact, his face giving no reaction. Winter took the keys from his hand as he was about to pocket them. Only then did the two men exchange a glance.

The gate opened with a grind of weatherworn

metal. The three of them followed the track, their shoes kicking up clouds of dusty soil. Soon they were at the top of a parched slope, standing on grass that had been burnt from the earth in patches.

'You're going to kill me, I know,' said Gately, perspiring freely now in his unseasonal tweed blazer. He was attempting to sound defiant but there was a catch in his throat that undid his bravado.

Winter levelled the pistol. 'Be quiet.'

A wasp darted past on the thinnest of breezes. The trees in the distance were static as a painting, their branches motionless. If there was a still, quiet centre to the world, this was it.

Gately made to raise his hands. Then he thought better of it and let his arms fall to his sides. The tic beneath his left eye had returned.

'Look, I'm not in this for ideology,' he blurted, the prospect of a bullet finally prompting a confession. 'I'm no friend of Marx. They gave me money. You can understand that, can't you?'

Winter didn't blink. 'Betrayal's a free market, Bernard. You're just an old-fashioned capitalist, right?'

'Moscow's already marked you. Do you want to know why?'

Winter kept the gun steady in his hand. 'Don't overestimate my curiosity.'

Gately kept talking, bartering for his life now. 'I was fully briefed. You were mixed up in something during the war. A joint operation that went sour, right?'

'So I've heard.'

'Well, there's more to it. You killed one of our own. Someone on the British side, for God's sake.'

Alessandra looked to Winter. His face gave nothing away.

'So don't talk to me about betrayal. They told me what you did. And they know about the house in Venice, too. Il Portone. They're on their way.'

Each word was a last, wretched bargaining chip. Winter knew that.

'My past is dead,' he stated. 'Turn around.'

A sound rose in Gately's throat as he turned. There were rags of cloud in the morning sky. Shrikes circled the sprawl of fields.

'Tatabánya's that way,' said Winter. 'I'd start walking if I were you.'

Gately tilted his head, the edge of his spectacles flaring as the glass caught the sun. He took a moment to absorb what Winter had said. And then, seizing the opportunity, he began to walk.

'Bernard...'

Gately stopped mid-stride and turned to face him.

Winter put a bullet between his eyes.

By noon the Fiat had brought them to Sopron, a medieval miniature of a city at the edge of Hungary's western border. The little municipality lay in the green foothills of the Alps, close enough to breathe the air of Austria.

Here, close to the shimmering expanse of Lake Fertö, it was easy to forget the miles of high-voltage fence that ringed the country like an electric snare.

Winter eased the car into the northern end of the main square, letting it idle in the long shadow of the Firewatch Tower, the tallest building in Sopron. He leaned into the dashboard, resting his chin on the tortoiseshell wheel. The sun was unpleasantly warm through the windscreen.

Alessandra had found a bag of black cherries in the glove compartment. She bit into another one, her teeth slicing through the skin. 'I assume you do actually have a plan?'

'Not yet.' Winter's voice was detached, his mind otherwise engaged.

'We can't cross the border by train? We're so close to Mattersburg here.'

'No chance. They'll be searching every carriage in the country for us.'

'By road, then?'

Winter grimaced. 'Your new identity papers are worse than useless. That name they gave you will be red-flagged at all the border crossings.'

Alessandra spat the cherry stone through the window. 'So how do you propose we actually get out of this country?'

Winter stared directly ahead, into the heart of the square. A man in a high-collared grey jacket was standing in front of a white Trabant. A leather strap crossed his chest, clipped to a belt that held a baggy leather holster.

He wore a peaked cap, its enamelled red star the symbol of the Hungarian police.

'Like this.'

Winter was already out of the car. Alessandra tossed the bag of cherries to the seat and followed him across the square.

The policeman acknowledged them with a smile, ready to dispense a little local knowledge to a couple of tourists from Budapest. He was young, still with a smattering of acne on his chin.

Winter smiled back, equally brightly. 'Hello,' he said. 'I'm Christopher Winter. I'm a fugitive British Intelligence agent. This is Alessandra Moltini. She's a traitor to the state and trying to defect to the West. Would you care to arrest us?'

The policeman stared at him, nonplussed. He was on the verge of a grin.

'I mean, if it's not too much trouble...' added Winter. 'Hate to be a bother.'

The officer allowed himself the grin.

'Check your briefing,' Winter urged him, indicating the clipboard he had spotted through the window of the white Trabant. 'We're very much hot property. In fact I believe this could be a career-making move for you.'

The young man's eyes were wary now. He glanced, uncertain, at the telex he had left above the dashboard of his police car, the one that had arrived a matter of hours before, informing him of two fugitives, presently on the run.

'I know,' said Winter, persuasively. 'How much good fortune can one man have? It's barely even midday.'

'Promotion,' added Alessandra, her dark eyes twinkling. 'Definitely a promotion.'

For a moment the three of them stood in a profoundly awkward silence. And then the policeman gingerly unclipped his holster. Winter nodded, encouragingly, watching as the young officer leant inside the Trabant and plucked the two-way radio. There was a confused, static-filled conversation with a superior and then Winter and Alessandra found themselves waved inside the car at gunpoint.

The Trabant exited the square with a growl of its two-stroke engine and a cough of blue exhaust. Winter sat in the passenger seat while Alessandra bounced in the cramped rear. She was sat directly behind the young policeman, close enough to lean in and kiss a breath into his ear.

He shouted at her to remain still, but her hands were at the nape of his neck, teasing the skin with delicate, languid strokes. Concentrating on the road he tried to shrug her away but she coaxed a shimmer of sweat to the surface. Soon the pulse in his throat was drumming against her fingers. Winter glanced at the rear-view mirror and saw a telltale flash of gold.

Ten minutes later the policeman lay in a wooded lane, gagged with a seamed stocking and bound with his own handcuffs. Winter was wearing the man's uniform, the cuffs riding a little too high on his wrists. He adjusted the peaked cap.

'You'd better get down,' he told Alessandra.

She curled into the back seat, pressing her face against Winter's abandoned suit.

Winter searched the dashboard, eventually locating the switch that summoned the car's siren. The beacon on the roof began to twirl, throwing glimmers of blue light against the trees. As the siren howled the branches gave up a panicked flap of birds.

It wasn't far to the checkpoint. Winter could already see the soldier waiting in the wooden hut, the men with rifles standing by their dogs, the spiked wire crowning the walls either side of a zigzag barricade.

He kept the needle steady at thirty, coaxing a fair clip from the dismal box of a car. The distance to the checkpoint narrowed beneath the Trabant's wheels.

There was only one way to play this, Winter knew. Absolute belief. He fixed his eyes on the guard in the hut and gave a sharp, comradely nod.

The soldier found himself with seconds to make a decision. Persuaded by the impatient shriek of the siren he hit the button that opened the gate.

The barricade shuddered and rose. Winter threw the man a salute as the Trabant sailed through.

Alessandra sat up as Austria swept past them in a green rush of freedom. 'How far to Salzburg?' she demanded.

Winter shifted into fourth gear. 'Not as far as Venice, that's for sure.'

9

The Boeing 727 banked over the green–glass waters of the Adriatic, commencing its descent to Marco Polo airport. Winter leaned into the cabin window, peering past the sunlit scratches on the Perspex. The Venetian Lagoon was beneath them, the low tide exposing a brackish expanse of marshland.

The wing tilted, its shadow passing over waves and sandbanks. Now the city was revealed. The six *sestieri* of Venice, glittering and sinuous, an ornamental maze of palaces, churches and quaysides carved by the Grand Canal. From the air the city's original grandeur was intact, the slow decay of the past centuries simply a vicious rumour.

Winter saw the redbrick palazzos come into view, their marble veneers shining in the early evening sun. Up close, he knew, they would be crumbling, victims of saltwater erosion. For now they were the memories of the buildings they had been. This was a dying city, a drowning city, and Winter already sensed it welcomed ghosts.

Had he been here before? Not as Christopher Winter, certainly. But there was something terribly familiar in

129

the twisting pattern of canals and alleyways below. For a moment he saw Venice as a vast magical symbol, the serpentine slash of water that divided its six districts a sigil waiting to be unlocked.

Winter blinked the image away. He kept having thoughts like that, thoughts he was sure had belonged to Tobias Hart. Sometimes it felt as if his skull was somebody else's attic and he was sweeping a torch through its eaves. Memories drifted like dust in the light, impossible to catch.

Maybe that was why he had come to this city. He had told Bernard Gately that his past was dead but those were big words he didn't entirely believe. No, he needed to know more about his time with Operation Paragon. That void in his head bothered him. It was a black hole into which all sorts of potential guilts were tumbling. 'You killed one of our own,' Gately had said. Was that true? He had to know.

Winter took his eyes from the window. The more he thought he had buried Tobias Hart the greater the itch to exhume the bastard.

Alessandra was in the seat next to him, the latest issue of *LIFE* spread glossily on her lap. London already knew they wouldn't be keeping the rendezvous in Salzburg. Yesterday Winter had made contact via a relay station secreted above a candle shop in Vienna. He had informed Century House that they were heading to Venice in the interests of national security – he had relished that line; it was so hard to argue with. The Soviets had reactivated Operation Paragon. He was pursuing the intelligence trail. They would hear from him in due course. That was the beauty of a one-way transmission: he sent the facts, someone exploded later, an agreeably long distance away.

He watched as Alessandra turned the pages of the magazine, pausing at a full-page advert for Dial Soap. The black-and-white photograph showed a woman's face in tight, ecstatic close-up. She was showering, her perfect teeth bared as the water pummelled her. Alessandra traced her fingers over the image, as if trying to absorb some of that sensual pleasure through the ink.

Winter realised he hadn't seen her sleep, not once in the past two days. He had snatched a handful of hours on a couch in Vienna; stirring in the night he'd found her standing by the window, staring out across the city's lights. She'd still been there when he'd surfaced at dawn. She could pass for human but there were times when it seemed like camouflage.

What he had witnessed in that hotel room in Pest still perturbed him. The sight of Alessandra perched upon that man, her hands embedded in his flesh as he lay there, mute and shuddering. It reminded Winter of something he had once spotted on a pavement in London: a wasp mounting a butterfly, its stinger skewering the underbelly of its prey. For a moment the insects had seemed to be one, a chimera of a creature. There was an intimate cruelty to that coupling, just as he had seen in the room.

That morning, on the bus to Vienna International, he had asked her outright.

'What do you do to people?'

'I told you, we feed. Your ecstasies are our sustenance.'

'But you're willing to hurt them.'

'It needn't hurt. All we do is open a vein to the senses. It can be a mutual pleasure, if we're careful. I didn't hurt you, did I?'

'Gately told me you'd taken lives in Budapest. Political assassinations. You didn't just work honeytraps.'

She had met his eyes then. 'Sometimes the state insisted I be less than careful.'

Winter felt the 727 plunge.

'So how well do you know this contact of yours?' he asked, a communal fug of cigarette smoke still skulking in the cabin as the plane dropped altitude.

Alessandra continued to flip through the magazine, the parade of images boring her now. 'Gideon? I haven't seen him in years. Not since I found I couldn't get out of Hungary.'

'What makes you so sure he'll be in Venice?'

Alessandra smiled, and Winter thought he detected a hint of private amusement there. 'It's not as if he has much choice.'

He chose not to follow that up, not yet. 'And you think he can help?'

She folded the magazine and tucked it below the seat in front of her. 'If anyone in Venice can help us, he can.'

Like all field agents, Winter had once had a working knowledge of key informants in the major European cities. It was a network of tipsters and snitches, some acting out of loyalty to the Crown, others bleeding information for money or leaking secrets in exchange for the British government turning a blind eye to their other, less patriotic activities. All of them operated in a state of twilight but their names were known in London. The Whisper Index, SIS called it.

'Gideon Jukes. I've never heard of him. So either he's very, very discreet... or I imagine he's dead by now.'

The jet's undercarriage unfurled, juddering against the onrush of air.

'Oh, he's definitely dead,' said Alessandra, matter-of-factly. 'I killed him myself.'

Venice was possessed by water. It permeated the city, infiltrating bricks, staining stone. It hung in the salt haze of the air and it slapped against the mossy quaysides, the rhythm of the waves calm but determined, content to wage a long war against the terraces and trattorias.

It was dusk now and the streets were lit by gas lamps, casting the canal's shadows across the walls. The undulation of the water made the city itself seem shifting, insubstantial. Church bells rippled as the evening cooled, the mosquitoes swarming in the grey light.

Winter and Alessandra crossed a succession of rust-withered bridges to the Dorsoduro district. It was a warren of shabby, half-shuttered houses with damp little alleys that ended at odd angles, hinting at adjoining streets instead of revealing them outright. Winter imagined those streets had formed like water, spilling through cracks to find a path.

The café they were looking for was situated between two terracotta-tiled houses, the light through its window the brightest point in the alley. There were people inside, a handful, no more, sat at lopsided wooden tables, picking at plates of prosciutto and olives. The place was dead, the chalkboard menu outside still offering yesterday's specials. Winter glanced at the name on the cracked plaster of the frontage. *Café Casanova*. No, he couldn't quite see the old rake tucking into the bruschetta.

Alessandra entered first. The solitary, under-occupied waiter turned to meet her, his fine-boned features breaking into a smile of recognition. Winter saw that he had the exact black eyes that she did.

'Alessandra! My God, how long…?'

She put a hand to his cheek. '*Ciao*, Franco. How are you?'

'Never busier,' he smiled, with a charming flash of teeth.

'Still the greatest gigolo in Venice?'

He gave a mock bow, a grease-spattered tablecloth slung over his arm. 'The greatest gigolo in Europe, the ladies insist.'

He was one of her kind, Winter realised, trying to recall the word for the male equivalent. It was there in Hart's attic. An incubus. That was it. Another bloody demon, for all his easy smile and patter.

'What brings you here?' asked Franco, his eyes on

Winter though he was speaking to Alessandra. 'It can't be the house red.'

'Business,' she replied. 'Always business. You know how it is.'

Franco nodded, clearly at ease with her evasiveness. '*La sala privata?*'

'*Naturalmente*, Franco.'

He laid a bill on one of the tables, winked at a clearly smitten woman in her sixties, then turned and led them out of the main dining area, past the steam and clatter of the kitchen. Here the dark timber walls were decorated with framed portraits of Sinatra and Gina Lollobrigida, hung at a tipsy angle but smiling just the same.

Franco opened a heavy, silver-handled door and ushered them into a private function suite. It was a larger space than Winter was expecting: nine sets of tables and chairs arranged around a softly lit room. What struck him immediately was the sheer amount of glass in the space. Not just the octagonal mirror that dominated the back wall or the polished wine glasses gleaming on the tables but the array of vases that filled every corner, set upon stools, placed in alcoves. Some of the vases were tall and lean, others swollen, engorged. Some were fluted, some were intricately patterned, a few were perfectly plain. They were all exquisite examples of the glass-blower's art. The room looked ready to shatter at any moment.

'And to drink?' asked Franco, taking a pencil and a pad from the zippered pouch at his waist.

'Ombretta,' said Alessandra, taking a seat.

Winter wiped a fine layer of dust from the menu. 'Whiskey and ginger. Thank you.'

Franco almost contained his disdain. 'A very British choice, sir.' He bowed again and left the room, jingling with an evening's worth of tips.

Winter pushed the menu away and looked around him. The vases caught the light from the wall-mounted lamps, cutting it into countless reflections. It shone in each piece of glass.

'Nice place.' He inspected the dust on his fingers. 'And that's certainly a romantic touch.'

Alessandra took a vase from the alcove behind them. 'I've always thought glass is remarkable.'

She turned the vase in her hand, admiring its curvature. A sliver of light rolled across its surface. 'You shape it with heat. Make it molten, pliable. And glass has a memory. It knows it can change. It remembers. Just like water.'

She brought her other hand towards the vase. The tips of her fingers slipped straight through it. She smiled and pulled them out again. The glass clung to her hand like saliva. Alessandra stretched the glistening strands and then shook them from her fingers. The vase became solid again.

Winter was astonished. 'How the hell did you do that?'

She returned the vase to the alcove. 'Some things are easier in Venice. It has a fluidity, shall we say. Water and glass. The world has a different consistency in this city.'

Winter thought he detected movement in the room. He glanced to his left. Each vase now held the image of a face. He saw eyes and mouths, caught in glass like

136

specimen slides. The large mirror at the rear of the room also contained faces, thrust against the silvered surface as if searching for entrance.

'And some parts of this city are more pliable than others. This room, for instance.'

'What's going on?' asked Winter, uncomfortable now.

'Ombretta for the lady,' said Franco, placing a glass in front of Alessandra. 'Whiskey and ginger for her discerning British acquaintance. And for you, sir?'

'Yes, how awfully amusing,' sighed a new voice.

Winter turned. There was someone else at the table now. Not that they were entirely there, not in any real physical sense. It was as if particles of dust and glimmers of light had conspired to create a man.

'Hello, Gideon,' said Alessandra, raising her glass of wine.

Gideon Jukes – or some kind of spectral approximation of him, at least – appeared to be in his thirties, with a spill of ash-blond hair across a broad forehead. He wore a tan summer suit, though the colour had paled, just like his flesh tone, and it was cut in an old-fashioned style, the collars rounded, the buttons high on the jacket. A rumpled wing-tip shirt was open at his throat.

'I take it you're a ghost,' said Winter, surprising himself by quite how conversational that sounded.

'Please,' said Jukes. 'I prefer shade. It has a certain elegance to it, at least. I'll even accept wraith, if I'm in a forgiving mood. But ghost? Dear God, man, you might as well call me a spook. It's just a bit vulgar, don't you think?'

'I've met... people like you before,' said Winter.

'Have you really?' replied Jukes, unimpressed. 'Good for you. There's a lot of us about. The dead, you know. We do tend to accumulate.'

Winter struggled to focus on the apparition and not the chair. It was like trying to keep his eyes on vapour.

'So how do you two actually know each other?'

'She killed me,' said Jukes, casually. 'That creates rather a bond.'

'You were trying to kill me,' added Alessandra. 'Wasn't that your great heroic quest, Gideon? To tear the accursed black heart from my body?'

'You overdramatise, as ever. But yes, that was the general thrust of our relationship.'

Alessandra turned to Winter. 'Gideon hunted me for many years, across continents. He saw himself as a Christian knight. A slayer of darkness. The scourge of demons...'

'Oh, you do make it sound like a sixpenny shocker, Alessandra. I'll admit I considered you an abomination against God's work...'

Alessandra's eyes glittered. 'I think you were just a little besotted with me.'

Jukes considered this. 'Well, you may have a point there.' He allowed himself a smile, and it was a fond one.

Winter sipped his whiskey and ginger, watching as dust motes moved in Jukes's face. 'When was this?'

'I died in 1913. She killed me here, in Venice. I missed the war, at least.'

'1913?' Winter glanced at Alessandra, taken aback. 'How old are you, for God's sake?'

'She's as old as sin, dear boy,' said Jukes, expansively. 'Are you her latest fancy, then? Believe me, it won't end well. Her kind don't really do happy endings. Everlasting damnation's more their game.'

'Perhaps a starter?' enquired Franco, still hovering by the table. 'I recommend the ricotta…'

Winter dismissed him. 'What happened to you?' he asked Jukes.

'Locked in glass for all eternity, just like these desperate souls.' He indicated the mirror, still filled with imploring eyes. 'It's an old demon's curse. First recorded in Mesopotamia, some three thousand years before Christ. They've had a while to practise this particular parlour trick.'

'She trapped you in a glass? Like a jar? A bottle?'

'The medium of glass,' Jukes corrected him. 'All glass, everywhere. Banished, but free to move within that medium. You'll catch us sometimes. A glint in a pane, perhaps. A chink of light on a brandy tumbler. So like a face, just for a moment. And then we're gone. It's no life.'

'I gave you a living death,' said Alessandra. 'Because I liked you.'

'Forgive me if I don't consider myself living *la dolce vita*.' Jukes shot a jealous glance at Winter's drink. 'I could murder that bloody whiskey, for a start…'

Alessandra leaned across the table. 'We need to find a house in Venice.'

Jukes didn't blink. 'Do I look like an estate agent?'

'You know this city. You know its history. We need to

find a house known as Il Portone. Have you heard of it?'

Jukes mulled the name. 'Yes, I know it. Cannaregio district. It was Franzeri's place.'

'Franzeri?' pressed Winter.

'Eugenio Franzeri. A student of the occult. This city's always attracted them. The Comte de Saint-Germain, Guillaume Postel... even Casanova was inclined, though Lord knows how he found the time. There's a structural weakness in the soul of Venice, you see. It allows things through.'

He nodded to Alessandra. 'It's how her lot had their fun in the seventeenth century. *Il Carnevale*? That was a pact with the Venetians. The people surrendered their bodies for weeks on end. They allowed themselves to be possessed, their faces hidden by masks. They became willing avatars for higher forces. The demons savoured the experience of the flesh, the people persuaded themselves they weren't responsible for their actions. It was a mutually beneficial party.'

'It was glorious,' smiled Alessandra.

'I knew Franzeri,' Jukes continued. 'He dabbled in demon hunting. Bit of a dilettante, to be honest. The undead were his true calling. *Vampiri*.'

'Could he still be alive?' asked Winter.

'I doubt it. He was getting on when I knew him. I imagine 1913 is quite some time ago, isn't it?'

Winter nodded. 'I'm afraid so. Can you remember the address?'

Jukes delved into his jacket pocket, extracting a

goatskin wallet. 'I've got his card here somewhere. Yes, here we go…'

He made to hand the card to Winter, then caught himself, aware that it was as insubstantial as he was. 'On second thoughts you'd better just write it down, old man.'

Winter squinted at the ghost of the card. He pulled out a ballpoint and began scribbling on a napkin. The spirit of Gideon Jukes turned to Alessandra. There was affection in his voice. 'I suppose there are worse fates than this.'

Alessandra reached through his chest and took the vase from the alcove. 'Believe me, I considered them.'

'Back in the box I go, then. What larks.'

She rolled the vase in her hand, seeing the faces turn. And then she hurled it at the tiled floor, letting it shatter.

Jukes was no longer there. The mirror was empty. An eye lingered in a splinter of glass, then that too was gone.

10

It was dark by the time they reached Cannaregio, the sky like oil above the old wharves. Now the quays were lit by a hundred boundary lights. The reflections of waterside lamps twisted across the canal as sea birds hunted.

Winter and Alessandra stepped from the vaporetto, its deck lurching as a handful of passengers disembarked. This was the northernmost district of Venice and it had a mournful, abandoned air. San Michele, the city's island cemetery, lay beyond its edge, and to Winter this faded quayside felt like a staging post to the dead. It belonged to the funeral barges, taking their cargo to the grave.

A solitary gondola was lashed to a mooring post by a briny hank of rope. The boat's bow scraped against the bricks, lulled by the sway of the lagoon. The owner made a half-hearted appeal for business before returning to the private pleasure of his cigarette. The canal continued to lap the jetty, unconcerned. The smell of salt and diesel drifted downwind, blending with the sulphurous rot of vegetation from the mudflats.

Nowhere in the world sounded quite like Venice.

With no cars there was none of the background drone of a modern city. Other sounds became amplified, especially after dark: the steady clasp and retreat of water, the shuttering of windows, footsteps. And always the bells, like a rumour through the backstreets.

They left the water's edge and followed a long, dim alley, its walls converging to a slit of light that led to another, equally tight street beyond. Il Portone stood four doors down. Like all the palazzi in Venice its more elegant side faced the Grand Canal, built to be shown off. The landward approach was plainer, at least by Venetian standards.

Winter gazed up at the home of Eugenio Franzeri. Three storeys of pale Istrian stone were stacked, cake-like, upon one another, the façade flaking where centuries of rain and sun had passed across the exterior. There was an abundance of windows, narrow and arched, Palladian style. Some of the frames were smashed, the remaining glass revealing only darkness inside. The house had clearly been abandoned for some time. Its emptiness felt solid.

He knew this building. At least for a second. And then that clear stab of recognition was gone.

He was about to move forward when he sensed Alessandra's hand on his arm.

'There's magecraft here.'

Winter's eyes searched the broken windows. 'Somehow I don't think Signor Franzeri is at home.'

'Listen to me. Magic leaves a mark on the world. This building is wrapped in scar tissue. I can sense it. It lingers, even in a city as enchanted as this one.'

Winter considered this. 'If there's trouble all I'm really qualified to do is shoot at it.'

Alessandra sighed in sudden frustration. 'God, I miss the man you used to be. He had imagination.'

Winter took the gun from his holster. 'Good for him. Here's my redeeming quality.'

A thin pathway led to the door. There were weeds between the cracked parade of flagstones. It took Winter the length of the path to realise what was so odd about them. They were growing away from the light, craving the long shadow of the house instead.

He looked up, studying the carvings in the stone above the porch. A king's head, crowned in fire. The moon, broken in two, the twin fragments held by a woman's hands. Foliage, intricately sculpted. And there were chimera, too. Impossible animals peered down at him in a silent, frozen bestiary. A lion with a serpent's body, its jaw chipped away by age. A hollow-eyed bird with a panther's paws. Something that looked like a winged goat.

Winter was about to test the lock when he noticed that the weed had also insinuated itself into the doorframe. It crept out of the breaks in the wood, clinging to the arch in a scrawny tangle. Up close it looked black and brittle, as if long dead, but when Winter took it between his fingers it refused to break. In fact he was convinced he could feel it pulse.

Grimacing, he tried the door, twisting a pewter handle decorated with a mermaid. The figure curved in a perfect, spine-defying circle, the tail chasing the head. To

Winter's surprise he felt the old wood shift on its hinges. The door allowed an inch of darkness.

He stepped back and put his shoulder to it, grunting as he slammed into the mullion. On a second attempt the door swung from its latch. With the heel of his shoe he kicked it wide.

The light from the street fell upon an interior courtyard, broader than the entrance to the house suggested. The floor was studded with a Moorish array of precious stones. The majority of them had been dulled by the passing years but a few still glinted here and there. They formed complex, inscrutable patterns that Winter instinctively knew were occult geometries.

He hovered by the door, Alessandra at his shoulder. He was certain that the weed in the jamb had just twitched.

'You're right,' he said. 'There's something here. Even I can sense it.'

'Of course you can, darling. Bone is memory. Blood is memory.'

Winter bristled. 'Not now.'

He knew she was smiling at the back of his head.

They stepped inside. More of the weed infested the courtyard, reaching through cracks in the jewelled slabs and opening into serrated black petals. It grew taller and thicker in the corners, as if it had fed on shadows, not sunlight. The weed was everywhere they looked, climbing walls and twining around columns. Its taproot had clearly sunk into the foundations of the building, deep into the mudflats below.

'Do you know how houses like this get their power?' asked Alessandra, casually, as they crossed the gemstone sigils.

Winter had his gun raised now. 'No idea. Do tell.'

'People used to believe it brought luck to brick up an animal in a house. If they were alive at the time, all the better.'

'That's just superstitious cruelty.'

'Some magicians took the tradition a step further. They'd steal a house from another sorcerer. A rival magician. And that's who they would brick up. Alive, preferably. But even in death the corpse of a magician confers power on a property.'

Winter kept his eyes ahead of him. 'You really have a gift for small talk.'

A switchback staircase joined the courtyard to an upper floor. Winter and Alessandra began to climb it, their shoes echoing on the naked stone. Just enough light fell through the high windows to guide the way. There were tattered, sagging silks on the walls, looking as though they might tear from their hooks at any moment. The fabric was singed at the edges and Winter began to suspect a fire had gutted this place.

They made their way up, stepping around the black weed that had already claimed the stairs. It had a wet, glassy texture and stole its way from step to step, its branches splitting like fingers, knotting through cracks and rising again. It seemed to sense their approach, tensing with each footstep.

Winter noted the way Alessandra moved through the infestation. There was too much confidence in her, not enough caution. He had seen it in certain field agents. The absolute assurance of their knowledge, their skills. Too often it was a flaw, and a treacherous one.

'Don't take it so fast,' he hissed.

She sighed and slowed her steps, allowing him to catch up.

The staircase took them to a small landing and then twisted again, leading to a narrow hallway and a choice of rooms. The black weed had reached this level, too. It clasped the walls of the corridor and slid around half-opened doors, threading its way into the shadows. Winter saw that it was moving, fractionally, each dankly sweating strand probing a little deeper into the house.

'What the hell is this stuff?' he asked, eyeing it with a mix of disgust and wariness. 'It's all over the place.'

'It's hexweed. I haven't seen it in centuries. Somebody's conjured it. Somebody very talented.'

'What's it doing here?'

'I imagine it's guarding the house. You really don't remember anything, do you?'

'Just keep re-educating me.'

Winter followed the thickest of the strands as it curled around a door. They found themselves in the *piano nobile*, the grand floor, a vast, high-ceilinged space that had once been used to entertain visitors. Now it was empty, bare and dark, its furthest corners hidden, untouched by the finger of light from the doorway. Shattered Moroccan lamps stood in the gloom, their jewelled remains tarnished and grimy. There was the taste of dust in the air, bitter on their tongues.

The body of a man lay on the floor.

Winter approached the pile of awkwardly angled limbs. The man must have been in his early thirties, his features hard and Slavic. There was no obvious indication of violence but the skin had a bruised, bluish tint, like spoiled ham, and the flesh had already begun to sink against the contours of the bones.

It was a recent death, perhaps a day at most.

Winter eased the arm from where it had locked against the chest. It thumped to the floor, still tethered by spirals of black weed that had looped themselves around the man's wrist, tight enough to choke the flow of blood. The weed also encircled his ankles.

There was a passport in the jacket. Winter slid it from the inner pocket. It bore the letters CCCP, the iconography of hammer and sickle embossed in chipped gold leaf. He skimmed through the ink-stamped pages to the ID.

Ladislas Stefanovich Volyntsev. Born 3rd December 1931, Novosibirsk.

Winter strained his gaze against the Cyrillic script, summoning his functional knowledge of Russian, untouched for the past two years. Volyntsev, it appeared, was a manager of statistics at the Ministry of Fish Industry, Moscow.

Winter tossed the passport to one side. He pulled a slim wallet from the same pocket and quickly fingered through its contents, finding bundles of roubles and lira. Then he paused, tracing the outline of a small, flat object secreted within the wallet's lining. He broke the stitching, extracting a laminated rectangle of card that declared its owner to be Yevgeni Ilyich Chaika, employee of the Komitet Gosudarstvennoy Bezopasnosti.

'KGB,' said Winter. 'They're ahead of us.'

'Really?' said Alessandra. 'We're the ones who are still alive.'

Remembering a detail of Soviet tradecraft, Winter unbuckled the man's watch, recoiling as he made contact with the stiff, cold flesh. He took a Festival of Britain pen-knife from his pocket, extracted the miniature blade and slit the strap. Inside the sweat-stained length of leather was the tip of a strip of paper, tissue-thin and tightly pleated. Winter pinched the end and prised it free.

It unfolded into a sheet of notes, a seemingly disconnected scrawl of letters and numbers that Winter instinctively recognised as the lingua franca of field work. Place names and timings and tiny, inscrutable symbols that spoke in private code. One word stood out from the others, circled for emphasis. Winter attempted to make sense of the hasty, slanting strokes.

Zerbinati. He stared at the word as if the sheer intensity of his scrutiny might unlock it. But it meant nothing to him. *Zerbinati*. It was every damn possibility in the world.

'Do you know what this means? *Zerbinati?*'

150

Alessandra shook her head. 'I can't place it.'

Winter slipped the sheet into his own wallet then stepped from the Soviet agent's corpse and headed deeper into the shadows. Seconds later the tip of his shoe connected with something weighty and metallic. The object skittered across the floor. He knelt to retrieve it. It was a gun, and a familiar one. Webley & Scott. Standard British Intelligence issue. He had been given one himself.

He checked the clip. Empty. Whoever had owned the gun had used every last bullet before the weapon was abandoned.

Winter put the revolver back on the floor and straightened up. His eyes had begun to calibrate to the gloom. The darkness in the far corner was more than just the shadows. It was a mass of black weed. He could see its tendrils extending across the hardwood floor. They had a stealthy, predatory quiver.

Something else caught his eye, perhaps ten feet from where he had kicked the gun. At first he could make no sense of the shape in the half-light. Then, as he stepped closer, he recognised it. He reached down to retrieve the fallen object.

It was a cap. A peaked, checkerboard-patterned cap. Winter turned it in his hand, seeing the Mary Quant label on the rim inside. There was no blood on it, at least.

He tossed it back to the ground then walked towards the clump of weed.

'Winter!' warned Alessandra, hanging back.

The tendrils reared and slapped the floor as Winter

approached, like an animal making a defensive display, carving out territory. He ignored them, even as other, lower strands slithered around his feet.

There was a woman entangled in the weed, right in the heart of it. He could see her face through the black cradle. Her eyes were closed and in the near-dark he couldn't tell if she was dead or simply unconscious. The weed had raised her from the ground, suspending her from the wall, and she hung like a trophy in the shadows.

It was Libby Cracknell.

'There's somebody in here,' he called to Alessandra. 'I'm getting her out.'

Winter reached into the thick snarl of weed. The black strands were unnaturally cold to the touch and left a slick, clammy residue on his hands. It was an effort to crack them apart but he managed to prise an opening, freeing some space around Libby's body, enough for him to slip his arms around her. Her wrists and ankles were bound, lashed by the vines.

The weed clung to the girl as Winter attempted to wrench her free. The tendrils coiling at his feet mounted his shoes. He booted them away, leaving them to flex in indignation on the floor. Eventually the black weed loosened its lockhold. Winter ripped Libby's body from the thicket and laid her gently on the floor. Alessandra was already there, kneeling beside her. She put her fingers to the girl's throat, searching for life.

'There's a pulse. She's breathing.'

'I know her,' said Winter. 'She's one of mine.'

'SIS?'

Winter nodded. 'God knows what she's doing here…'

He felt a sudden, scoring pain. A tendril had seized his wrist, claiming blood as it tightened like wire around the bone. The gun was squeezed from his hand. A second vine clasped his left wrist. Another thin black whip closed around his legs. There was strength in the weed, enough to twist his limbs around, turning him to face the throng of vegetation.

The weed was seething now. The spidery heap of vines thrashed against the air. Winter struggled against its grip but he found himself hauled forward. The strands that had curled around his ankles now lifted him from the floor, raising him until he was level with the densest part of the growth.

'Don't fight it!' urged Alessandra. 'Don't let it think you're a threat!'

Winter faced the hexweed, forcing his muscles to relax. He peered into the cracks between the strands and saw something stir at the core. A single stem, capped with a black flower head. It moved with a questing, inquisitive motion, worming its way through the shadows.

The stem emerged from the vines. It was segmented and it glistened dewily. Silky black petals encircled a stigma that looked uncannily like a cluster of flies' eyes.

The black flower head swayed in front of Winter. It trembled against his left cheek, close enough to brush the skin, trailing shivers where it touched him. The weed moved down his body, tracing his jawline, skimming his throat, lingering against his torso. It pulled away for a moment.

And then it made a rapid, snapping movement, targeting his chest.

11

Winter felt his ribcage shudder. The stem had entered him.

He looked down. There was no blood, no break in the skin, but the stem was inside him nevertheless, spearing through his shirt and embedding itself in his chest cavity. He could sense it threading through tissue, navigating veins. It was searching, hunting.

He screamed. The petals had closed like a fist. Now they were tearing a part of him out. It felt like his heart at first. But it was something else, something buried in bone and blood, beyond the flesh, somehow deeper than his physical body. The petals had it in their grasp and they were determined to take it. Winter kicked in agony as whatever they had found was plucked from his chest.

The stem slid out of him. Again there was no visible trace of the violation – his shirt was intact, his skin too. Winter gathered his breath and blinked to clear his vision. The flower head hovered in front of his face, the petals splayed to reveal their prize.

It was a small, round object, roughly the size of an

apple. The orb was as black as the weed and it had a glossy, inky sheen. He had no idea how such a thing could possibly have been inside him but he instinctively knew he had carried it for some time.

'What the hell am I even looking at?'

Alessandra stepped away from Libby, her eyes on the orb. There was a trace of awe in her voice. 'It's your thaumaturgic imprimatur.'

This wasn't enlightening. 'It's my bloody what?'

'Every magician has one. It's accumulated from every act of magic you've ever done. I've never seen one before. It's fascinating.'

Winter stared at the dark, wet ball as it nestled in the petals. He wasn't fascinated. He was repelled. It was part of Tobias Hart.

'How can that thing have been inside me? It doesn't belong to me. It's his...'

'It's dead magic. Just like dead skin. It has no power. But it's enough to identify you. I think that's what the hexweed is doing.'

The petals tremored as they held the orb. So the thing was some kind of signature, thought Winter. Given what Alessandra had just said he imagined the weed was weighing it, testing its authenticity. Finally the petals closed. The stem withdrew into the thicket, taking the shiny black sphere.

Winter instantly felt the vines loosen, slipping from his wrists and ankles. With no support he fell. As he tumbled to the floor he saw the hexweed retreating. And not just the vines in front of him. Every piece of black vegetation in the room was peeling from the walls, extracting itself from the floorboards, stealing out of woodworm holes. Moving with a collective impulse it snaked to the furthest corner, unravelling into the shadows. Moments later even the shadows had gone.

Light was filling the *piano nobile*. Winter stared at the floor as he got to his feet. All around him fragments of jewelled glass were coalescing from swirls of dust. As quickly as they appeared the pieces spat themselves to the corners, locking against each other with a hard, chinking sound. The shattered Moroccan lamps were repairing themselves. In moments they were blazing, alive with colour.

A different room had been revealed. The dimensions were the same – the height, the width, the essential geography – but everything had changed. The filthy silk brocade on the walls now glimmered with gold thread. Ornamental rugs sprawled across the floorboards. There were cupboards and cabinets and alcoves, mahogany chairs and cedarwood caskets, Etruscan bronzes and framed Phoenician maps. Winter saw tables swimming with papers, clippings, card-covered files, leather-backed journals. Bookshelves scraped the ceiling, stacked with thick, gilt-edged volumes, their spines cracked from centuries of use. An alabaster sarcophagus stood against the wall, riddled with hieroglyphs.

The room shuddered, phasing in and out of Winter's vision, light wrestling with shadow. It was as if the ghost of the empty, gloomy space that had been there only moments before was fighting for dominance. And then everything settled, and was still. The new room had won.

Winter steadied himself. He turned to Alessandra, open-mouthed. 'What just happened?'

She smiled as she took in their surroundings. 'I think you happened.'

'How can…?'

She trailed a hand over a newly materialised marble bust, feeling its solidity. 'There was a glamour on this house.'

'Glamour? What do you mean?'

'It's an older word than you imagine. A witch word, before this century stole it. A glamour is a hex. A spell of illusion. Concealment.' She waved a hand at the display of objects around them. 'All this? It's the life's work of Eugenio Franzeri. Someone really didn't want it to be found.'

'You mean it was here all the time? Just hidden from view?'

'Sì,' she said, patiently. 'That is how a glamour works.'

'And what does this have to do with me?'

She stepped close to him, the teasing smile still on her lips. 'It's a powerful enchantment. The work of a truly gifted magus. Whoever cast it also conjured the hexweed to protect the house. Again, impressive.'

Alessandra was relishing this.

'Now,' she continued, casually, 'seeing as the hexweed vanished as soon as it knew who you were… and given that the glamour faded, too… well, I'd say it's obvious who's responsible, wouldn't you?'

Winter stared at her. 'You mean Tobias Hart did this?'

'You really were very good, you know. A natural. No wonder I liked you.'

'This house was waiting for me to return?'

She put a hand to his chin, her eyes dancing. 'Tell me, darling. Am I explaining all this too quickly for you? Should I start with card tricks instead?'

Winter pushed past her, unamused. He went to kneel by Libby. She was stirring now, her eyelids batting back the sudden brightness in the room. He loosened the collar of her blouse, allowing air to circulate around her throat.

'Cracknell. It's me. It's Winter.'

Her eyes opened at the sound of his voice. They strained to focus on his face, the pupils shying from the light of the lamps.

'Winter,' she repeated, muzzily.

'Are you injured?'

Her eyes moved from his face to take in the room. They darted, confused by what they saw.

'Where am I?'

Winter put an arm behind her shoulder as he helped her to sit up. 'The house in Venice.'

'This isn't where I was. Not this room...'

Winter felt her flinch, as if the memory of the weed had just caught up with her. 'It's okay, Cracknell. It's okay. You're fine. Don't expect it to make sense just yet.'

'What are you doing here?' asked Alessandra, bluntly.

Winter shot her a cautioning look then returned his attention to Libby. 'This is Alessandra Moltini. I got her out of Budapest. There were some unexpected developments during the mission. So tell me, did Faulkner send you?'

Libby took her eyes away.

'I need to know,' said Winter, more firmly now. 'Did Faulkner send you to Venice?'

The girl met his gaze again. 'I've got orders.'

'So I imagine. Were you ordered to follow me?'

Libby managed to conjure a gap-toothed grin. 'I got here before you, Mr Winter. Strictly speaking, that's not following.'

Alessandra raised an eyebrow. 'The child is spirited, at least.'

'How did you get in?' pressed Winter. 'The door was still locked when we got here.'

'Who uses the bloody door? Window, mate. First floor.'

Winter shook his head, breath escaping between his teeth. 'They don't trust me, do they? That's why London sent you after me.'

'You left the service,' said Libby. 'Once you've strayed they'll never trust you again. Bit like cheating on your wife, isn't it?'

'I wouldn't know. How did they even know this place existed?'

Again Libby lapsed into silence.

'Look,' said Winter. 'They clearly don't trust me. But you need to. Because we're in the field now. And that's how we stay alive out here. That bond of trust. It's everything. So I'm asking you again. How did they know about this house?'

Libby took a moment before replying. 'I was shown

a dossier,' she said at last. 'Not all of it, but enough. Something big from back in the forties.'

'Operation Paragon.'

Libby nodded. 'I was only allowed to see a few pages, and some of that had been black-lined. But they knew exactly where this house was. There was a report attached. It was in your handwriting.'

Winter's expression gave away nothing. 'What's so important about this house?'

'There's intelligence here. Something you went and buried, Mr Winter. A long time ago.'

'Do you know what it is?'

'On my wages?'

'It has to be something in the collection,' said Alessandra. 'Something that Franzeri found.'

Winter took in the towers of books, the tables strewn with papers. The room was overwhelming. 'And where do you suggest we start?'

'I don't know. I'm not the one who buried it.'

Buried. The word prompted a thought. 'You told me it was traditional to brick up rival magicians. You said it conferred power on a property.'

'It did. They were a resource, even in death.'

'So that's where it's going to be. Knowledge is power, right?'

Winter picked up his gun and threw the checkerboard cap to Libby. She got to her feet and the three of them left the *piano nobile* and made their way to the ground floor of the palazzo.

As with all former merchants' homes the level that faced the street had once been a warren of store rooms and offices, used for trade. The chambers were functional, barely furnished, very different to the ostentatious spaces above. One of them housed an array of hanging tools and ironmongery. Winter selected a pickaxe. He inspected its curving steel head then laid it over his shoulder.

They moved through the gloomy ramble of rooms, the damp making the shadows cool as stone. The water outside felt like a presence, even here. Winter imagined he could hear it through the walls, lapping against the underbelly of the house. Moonlight illuminated this part of the passageway, falling through a high, recessed window.

A turning to the left confronted them with a solid wall of brick. There was no reason for it to be there. Why would it be closing off the corridor instead of offering another door?

Winter trailed a hand along its cold, pitted surface, disturbing gauzy remnants of web. 'This is it, if it's anywhere. Stand yourselves back.'

He swung the pickaxe. It scraped the bricks with a brief flicker of sparks. Winter heaved the thick wooden handle again. This time the tip of the axe head rooted itself in the wall. He wrenched it free and sliced it through the air once more. The brick he was targeting began to splinter and crumble.

Winter kept swinging the pickaxe, sweating now. Brick dust billowed from the wall with each strike of the steel head. The Venetian damp had loosened the mortar but it was punishing work, and soon he was in rolled shirtsleeves.

Eventually an entire tier of brick collapsed. Winter waved the dust away and peered through the breach in the wall. The skull of Eugenio Franzeri glared back at him. The eyes were gone but something accusatory endured in the hollows.

'Found him,' breathed Winter, wiping sweat from his face. He renewed his efforts, smashing the pickaxe into the brickwork until finally the gap was big enough to step through. Winter kicked at the loose bricks below, sending them tumbling into the rest of the rubble.

He flung the axe aside and entered the chamber. Libby had struck a lighter and he encouraged her to bring it closer. The flame played over Franzeri's remains.

The body should have been buried long ago. It was propped on a plain wooden chair, the pelvis twisted, protesting, as if frozen in the instant of death. Threads of hair trailed from the skull, touching the collar of the stiff grey suit that still held the carcass. Whatever skin was left hung like rags from the tobacco-coloured bones. Leather straps had been drawn tight around the wrists and the ankles. The flesh had decayed around them.

Something moved in Winter's veins in the presence of the bones. Something quick, and hungering.

He stared at the body. What an end Franzeri must have faced, all alone. The patient horror of it turned Winter's stomach. Tied to that chair, having to watch as his own death was assembled, brick by brick. Winter wondered how long the air could have lasted in that final, desperate darkness.

'Admiring your handicraft?' asked Alessandra.

'That's hardly fair.'

'It troubles you?'

'Of course it does.' The guilt had come like a punch.

'Poor sod,' said Libby, waving her lighter over the sightless head. 'Christmas must have been really tough.'

'Keep the flame still,' said Winter, firmly. 'Bring it into the corners.'

He peered into the depths of the chamber. All he saw was bricks and cracked flagstones. The room was empty.

'There has to be something in here. Something I didn't want anybody to find.'

'You never buried things,' said Alessandra. 'You acquired things. You would have taken it, whatever it was.'

'Maybe I had a very compelling reason to leave it here.'

Winter eased a fob watch from Franzeri's waistcoat pocket. The silver felt cold in his hand. He flipped the case apart. The hours were marked in thin Roman numerals, orbiting a knot of cogs and gears. The watch had stopped at seven minutes to five. He turned it over. There was an inscription etched on the back.

Eugenio! All our possibilities, all our lives! Tobias

Winter tucked the timepiece back in the waistcoat. Then he patted the jacket, moving across the pockets. A hard, slender shape protruded to the left of Franzeri's chest. Something was concealed in the inside pocket. Grimacing as he brushed the dead man's ribs, Winter

164

slipped his fingers inside the suit and carefully extracted the object.

It was an antique Venetian fan, folded between whalebone blades.

Winter spread the silk leaves, shaking off a scurry of beetles that had found their way into the jacket. The pleats were hand-painted and depicted a sunset on the Grand Canal, black funeral barges cresting the water. The fan was studded with seven gemstones, arranged in a curiously asymmetrical pattern. They glittered as Libby's lighter played over them.

'Very decorative,' said Alessandra, unimpressed.

Libby peered at it. 'Bit morbid for a souvenir, isn't it?'

Winter slanted the fan. There was a detail within the silk that wasn't visible at first glance. The glow of the lighter exposed it: a fine thread, like a vein in a leaf, linking the gemstones.

He left the chamber, stepping through the bricks and back into the passageway. Finding a spot beneath the high window, he held the unfurled fan to the moonlight, tilting it until the leaves cast a shadow on the opposite wall. The silk left a pale, phantom image on the stone but the tracery of thread was magnified and accentuated by the light. It ran in a ragged, winding line, the gemstones dotted like markers.

'What is this? Some kind of coastline?' The shadow map trembled on the wall.

'Where exactly are we looking at?' asked Libby.

'God knows,' said Winter. 'I don't recognise it.'

There was a snapping sound from the chamber. Winter turned and saw Alessandra returning. There was a skeletal finger in her hand, freshly plucked. She offered it to Winter.

'You used to be so wonderful at bone magic,' she said, with the expectant look of a cat gifting a dead bird. 'Franzeri's bones will remember. I'll show you how to do the ritual. The girl can spare her blood.'

Libby stared at her. 'Back off, mate.'

'Don't be difficult,' said Alessandra. 'It will only require a cupful. Two at most.'

'We're going to get this to London,' said Libby, emphatically. 'This is a British Intelligence operation. I'm not here for the voodoo.'

'It's not voodoo, you ignorant child,' sighed Alessandra. 'That's an entirely different genus of magic.'

'Yeah, well, whatever you say, Lady Macbeth.'

Winter raised a hand. He had heard something. Pocketing the fan, he determined the direction of the sound. Then he eased his gun from its holster and started to walk, taking care to step softly along the flagstones. The others followed him, retracing the path through the huddle of basement rooms.

The passage took them to the edge of the interior courtyard. Winter pressed himself against the nearest wall and slid the catch of the semi-automatic. Still in shadow, he peered around the corner.

The house had other visitors now.

It was a man and a woman. They stood on the jewelled marble of the hallway, framed by the open door.

166

The pair were motionless, calm as mannequins.

'Please, no drama, Mr Winter,' said the woman, breaking her stillness. Her voice had a familiar silken quality. 'It will only embarrass us all.'

Winter stepped around the wall, the gun in his hand and fixed upon her.

'I don't embarrass easily, believe me.'

'Oh. Are you quite sure you're British?'

He knew her. The silver-blonde hair was loose now, and she wore a white woollen dress, not a business suit, but the dark eyes and engorged pupils were just as he remembered. And just the same as Alessandra's.

'We're pretty far from Scratch Hill Junction,' said Winter, keeping the gun level. 'I hope you haven't come all this way for your money.'

The succubus smiled. 'Money is rarely a concern.'

She looked past Winter. 'Alessandra,' she said, without much warmth. 'It has been quite a while. I hope this world is rewarding you.'

Alessandra nodded, her response equally measured. 'Fabienne. Likewise.'

Libby had also stepped into the courtyard. She steadied a gun that Winter knew was empty.

'As you see, we are unarmed,' said the woman, indicating the impassive, black-clad companion that Winter recognised as her chauffeur from London. 'You can put your weapon down, my exquisite girl.'

'Yes, I know I can, darling,' said Libby, keeping the gun upon her.

'Why are you here?' demanded Winter, gesturing with his own weapon.

Fabienne paused, the answer taking shape on her lips. 'It's in the manner of a business proposition.'

12

The speedboat powered across the black sweep of the Adriatic, its prow cleaving the water. Behind the craft was a wake of foam and beyond that the increasingly distant lights of Venice, the oil refinery at Porto Marghera burning against the night, a beacon of fire and steel.

Winter sat in the back of the Riva, feeling its engine thrum in his gut. The hull lurched as it fought the waves, rearing out of the sea then smashing back down again, hurling spray either side of the boat. Fabienne's silent chauffeur was at the wheel, keeping the speed somewhere, Winter estimated, in the region of fifty knots. The wind felt cold and sleek against his face.

They were passing tiny, glittering islands, strung like lanterns through the saltwater lagoon that surrounded the city. Over the years they had been home to everything from asylums to leper colonies to wartime munitions dumps. Now they were tourist traps, peddling lace and glass and postcard-friendly Benedictine monasteries. Fishing boats staked out the spaces between them, their nets flung on the water, hunting squid and cuttlefish under a high moon.

Winter turned in his seat. Alessandra was next to him. She was staring at Libby, who had one arm over the side of the luxury runabout. The girl had momentarily closed her eyes, savouring the chill of sea spray on her skin.

Alessandra watched her in quiet fascination. She put a hand to Libby's cheek, the tips of her fingers stopping just short of contact.

Libby opened her eyes, instantly suspicious. 'What are you doing?'

'I wish to touch your face,' said Alessandra, with a persuasive smile.

Libby blinked. 'My face?'

Alessandra nodded, her eyes fixed on the beads of water that clung to Libby's cheek. 'You looked so content. This experience has meaning for you. I'd like to share it.'

Libby remained wary. 'My grandad had a boat. Up in Folkestone. I spent my summers there.'

'And you were happy?'

'I was a kid. Of course I was. Why am I even telling you this?'

'And that memory returned to you through your skin?'

Libby shrugged. 'Suppose. That's not unusual, though, is it? Everybody remembers stuff like that.'

Alessandra's smile faded. There was a hunger in her expression now. 'Tactile memory is succulent. Let me consume that moment.'

Libby shifted in her seat, studying the eager black eyes

looking back at her. 'You're a bit weird, luv, aren't you?'

Alessandra turned to Winter. 'Must this child accompany us?'

If Winter had heard the question he didn't acknowledge it. He was staring across the water.

A vast bank of cloud sat on the horizon, eclipsing the stars, stark and white against the darkness. Winter was reminded of photos he had seen of an A-bomb test; it was just like one of those apocalyptic blooms, captured in monochrome. The cloud extended along the line of the sea, its edges curling back into its swollen, billowing heart. The boat was gunning straight for it.

Fabienne addressed them from the front of the craft. 'We're almost there.'

The Riva pierced the cloud. In seconds all sign of the sky was gone, replaced by a thick, damp blankness. It was all around them, obscuring everything but their faces. Winter watched the white vapour drift between the seats, its texture like woodsmoke.

The boat began to lose speed, the engine falling from a full-throated roar to a muted rumble. Now they were gliding through the water, clearly following some pre-ordained path. Reeds rattled against the hull as they entered a shallow. There was land ahead.

The motor dwindled. The Riva slid to a halt, clasped by marsh. A floodlight burned through the cloud, illuminating a jetty nestling among cedar trees. Fabienne gestured for them to leave the boat.

The shrill drone of cicada filled the cedars. There

171

was no sign of the stars through the branches, only the colourless drift of cloud. This had to be another of the outlying islands, thought Winter, perhaps the furthest from the city. The cloud had utterly shrouded it. He wondered if it even graced a map.

'What is this place?' he asked, the speedboat swaying in the water as he disembarked.

It was Alessandra who answered. 'Let's call it a retreat.'

Winter looked around him, trying to grasp the geography of the shadows. 'Does it have a name?'

'Why would it have a name? It doesn't exist.'

'Feels pretty solid to me,' said Libby, stepping onto the stone walkway that led from the jetty.

Alessandra smirked. 'Everything's solid to your kind. It must be so crushing after a while, all that concrete reality getting in the way of the world.'

'We get by.'

'There's no need to tease them,' said Fabienne, with a trace of condescension. 'It's unfair.'

'I'm amazed you can resist, Fabienne.'

'Just take us where we're meant to go,' said Winter, cutting in impatiently. 'Our little human egos can bruise later.'

Fabienne turned and led them through the trees. The cicada continued their relentless chitter, the sound filling the night. The cedars gave the air a thick, woodsy perfume that made the darkness strangely heady.

In a matter of minutes the path had broadened, bringing them to the edge of a vast lawn. The parallel swathes of grass were divided by a strip of gleaming black stone. Someone had made their home on this hidden island. Someone with considerable resources, clearly. Great squares of electric light were mounted either side of the lawn. They were dazzling, too bright to look at directly. The hot glare of the floodlights picked out a series of statues positioned at intervals along the path. The figures were giant nudes, their cool marble limbs entwining, their faces fixed in ecstasy. To Winter they looked like the couplings of gods.

The marble appeared to be in motion, its surface running like liquid. It took Winter a moment to realise that the statues were actually teeming with ants. He saw the creatures swarm across the frozen bodies, surging in black streams. One trail of ants followed the contours of a man's face, marching over the ridges of the blind eyes.

He saw something else, then, in the shadows behind the statues. A glimpse of colour, a fleeting shape. He narrowed his eyes against the brilliance of the floodlights, trying to pin down whatever he had half seen.

Again he caught a glimmer of iridescent colour. This time Winter could make out a figure. It was cowled and robed, only a sliver of face on show. A dark, wary eye regarded him, framed by a half-moon of metal that clung to the skin, covering the features of the onlooker. The façade glinted as it caught the light.

The silent figure wasn't alone. There were at least a dozen of them, watching from the borders of the lawn. They were draped in long, loose silks, their faces lost behind folds of fabric or concealed by shards of metal. The robes they wore were elaborately decorated, swirls of precious stone stitched into the cloth. When they moved there was a whispering jangle of chains and bracelets.

'Who are these people?' Libby asked Alessandra.

'Ignore them,' said Fabienne, cutting in. 'We have no business with them.'

'Why are they dressed like that?'

Alessandra answered her this time. 'Sometimes this world can burn us. We taste too much of it.'

Winter kept his gaze on the robed figures. They hovered like silken, tinkling wraiths, carefully maintaining their distance. 'You mean these people are your kind?'

'They are our wounded. This island is theirs.'

'What happened to them?'

'She's already told you,' said Fabienne. 'This world happened to them.'

Winter sensed her reluctance to share any more details. He pressed her regardless. 'You feed on our senses, don't you? These wounded, as you call them... they experienced more than they bargained for, is that what you're saying?'

'Sometimes sensory pleasure is a toxin,' said Alessandra, matter-of-factly. 'In too high a concentration it can poison our bodies, leave our flesh twisted, scalded. The inhabitants of this island are a reminder of that. The price of the banquet.'

'Not sure I fancy being a banquet for you lot,' murmured Libby, walking behind the others.

174

Alessandra smiled at her. 'Don't worry, child. You're more of an appetiser.'

'These abandoned souls are of no consequence to you,' insisted Fabienne. 'We are here to meet the Glorious.'

'The glorious what?' asked Winter.

Fabienne turned to him, purring now. 'The Glorious is the Glorious.'

They kept walking, the floodlights throwing their reflections along the avenue of black stone. Up ahead stood another pair of sculptures. Two towering marble hands reared out of the ground, cupping a curving glass tunnel. It was the entrance to a starkly modern building, as incongruous as anything else Winter had seen on this island. The cloud drifted over its tiers of windows and whitewashed concrete.

Fabienne led the way. Winter noted that there was no security presence at the tunnel's entrance. In fact there wasn't even a door, let alone a pat-down or an identity check. They simply strolled in, under the swollen glass arch. Maybe that was a demonstration of real power, he reflected. If you considered yourself truly untouchable then an open invitation was a statement.

The tunnel took them to a staircase and the staircase took them to a set of double doors. Fabienne turned a chrome handle and the doors parted. The entire interior of the building was a pristine, oppressive shade of white, but the room they now entered was so bright it hurt. It was hot, too, the air burning with the light of a half-dozen Klieg lamps mounted on tripods. Their carbon arc bulbs had been angled to face the doors, confronting visitors with an intense and disorientating battery of light.

Winter blinked, trying to clear the afterimage of the lamps from his eyes. He could just about see a desk at the far end of the room. There were two figures sat at it, conspiratorially close. As Fabienne led them deeper into the immaculate white space he saw that they were a man and a woman. Two more brutally bright lamps were positioned behind the seated figures, the combined glare obscuring the details of their faces.

'I have delivered the British agent, my Glorious,' said Fabienne. She sounded eager to impress.

'Is he aware of our proposal?' asked the woman, with a voice that melted on her tongue. There was a trace of accent there but Winter couldn't quite pin the nationality.

'Outlined in the broadest terms.'

Winter took a step towards the desk, ignoring the unspoken boundary Fabienne had established.

'How did you people know I was in Venice?'

The faces remained maddeningly vague. Winter only had the most general impression of the woman's features, blurring behind the imprint of light on his retinas.

'The Crown can barely contain its secrets.' This time the man had spoken. His voice was equally glossy, the accent just as unplaceable. 'Given the recent revelation of your nation's infidelities with the Soviet Union – Philby, wasn't that the traitor's name? – I'd say it was open season on British Intelligence, wouldn't you?'

Winter gave a grudging nod of understanding. 'You

intercepted my communication to London. Must be a weak link in Century House. No doubt someone who enjoys the kind of rewards you specialise in.'

The woman picked up the conversation again. 'There are a number of things you should realise. One, our presence is greater than you imagine.'

'And two,' said the man, seamlessly, as though the pair had shared a single thought, 'we have been operating in this world for some considerable time. Millennia, in fact. We plundered the secrets of Babylon. We stole star maps from the pharaohs and looted the sacred scriptures of the Xia dynasty. Your Elizabethan spymasters were upstarts in comparison.'

The woman spoke again, her words blending with the man's. For a moment Winter was convinced they were talking in unison. 'The countries you cling to are so small a concept. You squabble for knowledge and try to cage it within your borders. But there are empires within shadow of which you are utterly unaware. Entire frontiers concealed in the wind. We pass across your nations and you suspect nothing.'

'Maybe you do,' said Winter. 'But I know one thing. I've seen those people outside. The ones in the robes. You may have an empire, as you call it, but this world can burn you.'

'We are all at risk of that,' said the man behind the desk, evenly. 'You yourself have been burnt. By magic, was it not? You reached for that particular sun. And you paid the price.'

Winter stared into the light, determined to find a face. 'Well, if you're looking to hire Tobias Hart, you're in for a disappointment. My name is Christopher Winter. If you want to do a deal you deal with me.'

'Oh, we're well aware of your circumstances,' said the woman, her tone just as measured. 'And as you may see, we're very partial to duality.'

The pair of them rose from their seats, their movement perfectly synchronised. In fact they had an uncanny symmetry, their bodies mirroring one another so precisely they genuinely looked like reflections.

Winter watched as they circled the desk. He saw two heads, two arms and two legs and it felt as though he was staring at a calculation that refused to add up. Then he realised. They were conjoined twins. A male and a female, genetically impossible as that was. The pair were fused at the hip, their torsos twisting like rival roots where the flesh merged. They were dressed in a black collarless suit, tailored to encompass both their bodies.

'What are you?' he asked, bluntly.

The two of them chimed together. 'Are we not glorious?'

13

They were beautiful, as beautiful as each other. But it was an eerie kind of beauty, the caramel skin smooth and flawless, the bone structure geometrically ideal, as if the planes of their faces had been designed, not formed. There was something arid and inhuman in their perfection, like mannequins or magazine adverts given the spark of life.

And then there were the eyes. Winter could see them clearly now. The pupils were grey, the irises gold, what should have been the whites an oily black. The eyes made no attempt to pass for human.

'An incubus. And a succubus. In one.' Winter gave a half-smile. 'I'm amazed you didn't burn up years ago.'

Fabienne and Alessandra both shot him a cautioning look.

The two faces of the Glorious tilted imperiously. Their voices blended again, their thoughts combining. 'We are the firstborn of Lilith, the Great and Fallen Mother. Our exquisite form is remarkably resilient.'

'If you're so remarkable why do you need me?'

The woman gave the answer. 'You are a resourceful, experienced man, flesh and bone though you may be. Your work with British Intelligence has demonstrated a certain prowess when it comes to carrying out, shall we say, expediencies.'

Winter didn't hide his distaste for that kind of euphemism. 'Killing people, you mean?'

'Necessary acts of termination.'

'Yes, I've killed. Each kill was in the interests of national security. I don't exactly do requests.'

The man nodded. 'Of course. But at least hear *our* request. You may find it just as easy to justify.'

He motioned with the hand that belonged to his side of the shared body. There was the subtlest shift in the air, a sense of electrons rearranging themselves, as if bidden. Immediately the lamps softened, losing their glare to reveal the finer details of the room. Ironically there was little to be seen. It was minimally decorated in the modern aesthetic, the furniture as surgically white as the walls. The kind of room that made Winter recoil from the future.

The Glorious returned behind the desk. There was a glossy stack of prints on the flawless plastic surface. The woman's hand passed the first of the pile to Winter.

'The target.'

It was a charcoal sketch, a likeness captured in broad but efficient strokes. It showed a man, probably in his late sixties, Winter guessed, with a crest of white hair that crowned tall, imposing temples. The shock of hair had been tamed into a mane, long enough to trail on the collar of the man's suit. A snowy moustache framed a stern, thin-lipped mouth. The pale eyes were equally uncompromising. Whoever this was had the cruel, entitled air of Mediterranean aristocracy, the bloodline of a conquistador or a Caesar.

'Am I meant to recognise this person?' asked Winter, studying the portrait as Libby looked over his shoulder.

'Hardly. Don Zerbinati is famed for his reclusiveness.'

Zerbinati. Winter saw the word in his mind, circled on that slip of paper concealed on the corpse of the Soviet agent, the one they had discovered in the palazzo. *Zerbinati*. So it was the name of a man, then. He kept his facial muscles taut, hiding his reaction.

'You couldn't get a photograph? What is he, camera shy?'

'He cannot be photographed.'

'No one's that reclusive.'

'He cannot be photographed,' reiterated the Glorious, together.

Winter was handed another print. This one was an altogether more elegant piece of artwork, detailed in fine scratches of India ink. It seemed to be an illustration from a Victorian journal, probably a penny dreadful, judging by its lurid subject matter. The gothic vignette showed a woman in a nightgown, one arm raised in music-hall terror against an advancing figure.

'But as you can see,' continued the Glorious, 'he can, at least, be captured by art. And the human imagination.'

Winter peered at the other figure in the picture, the

181

one looming over the woman. It was a man, thin and ragged, dressed in a threadbare frock coat, string-belted trousers and dilapidated boots. A vagabond, perhaps, or a labourer. He shared the regal sweep of hair with the man in the charcoal sketch but there was something disturbingly animalistic in the face, the lips bared to reveal serrated teeth. There were words beneath the illustration, set in neat type. *Black of purpose and animated by intent most foul, the dread revenant sought its ungodly sustenance.*

Winter glanced up. 'Seriously?'

'Oh, he has quite a history, if you know where to look. No doubt his origins would embarrass such a self-made man.'

A third print was passed to Winter. This one was a reproduction of a medieval woodcut. Cruder in style, it depicted a rural, moonlit crossroads. A smiling monk held a Bible as a wormy figure in black rags fell to its knees, cowering. Light blazed from the holy book.

'You're telling me this is the same man? They're all meant to be Don Zerbinati?'

The male half of the Glorious addressed him. 'He left his original name on a wooden cross in a village cemetery in the Valle dei Mulini. The name could be buried but not the man. He endures, let us say.'

'A vampire,' murmured Winter, remembering the files he had seen in Budapest. 'But they can be photographed. I've seen pictures of their bones.'

Fabienne spoke up. 'It's a quirk of their physiology. They are susceptible to X-rays but no other medium has been

182

able to hold their likeness. Only art. Their flesh does not photograph. No mirrors or shadows mark their presence.'

Alessandra nodded. 'The undead are nothing if not elusive.'

So Zerbinati was one of those hellish creatures, the ones whose bones held the secret that Operation Paragon had attempted to uncover. No wonder the Russians were interested in him.

Winter returned to the first picture, the charcoal portrait. 'So what is this, a courtroom sketch?'

'In 1952 the Italian authorities attempted to prosecute him for immoral earnings,' said the female side of the Glorious. 'The trial barely lasted a day. Some legal technicality, or at least that's what the record states. Don Zerbinati is an extremely influential man. Influential to the point of untouchable.'

Winter stared at the pale eyes in the picture. They were only strokes of charcoal but there was something fearless in that gaze. 'Who is he? What does he do?'

'He rules Naples.'

'Unelected, I take it?'

The two faces of the Glorious smiled in perfect, queasy unison. 'He is above politicians, above officials. Above even the mobsters of the Camorra. The underworld is in his pocket. Every corruption, every crime, every vice in the city… all at his door. Don Zerbinati is clan leader of *I Senz'Ombr*. The Shadowless.'

'Can't say I've ever heard of them.'

'Of course not. And that is why they retain true

power. They are a whisper at the heart of a storm.'

'They consider themselves the highest caste of vampire,' said Fabienne, 'and it's true that they possess certain genetic superiorities. They can enter holy ground and move freely in the day. It's said that even the ones they turn can walk in the light. A touch of royal blood makes all the difference. And this is the king. The fount of that blood.'

'Why would you want him dead?' Winter caught himself, recalculated his words. 'Or at least less… undead?'

'Don Zerbinati has more than local ambition. He wants to unite his kind. Since the great Christian purges of the sixteenth century the vampiric empire has been splintered. Disarrayed. They retreated to the very shadows they cannot cast. A thousand independent dynasties, embedded in a thousand cities. They have power but it is diffuse.'

'Surely this is a territorial squabble between you and the vampires? I know there's precious little love lost between you lot.'

'There are implications beyond our eternal quarrel,' continued the male half of the Glorious. 'Now Don Zerbinati seeks to give structure and purpose to these scattered houses of the undead. Unchecked, he will forge a new superpower for this world, bigger than America or Russia or Red China. A shadow nation, global in scale, one that will operate from a position of darkness and stealth, as untouchable as its ruler.'

'He's called a summit of the clans,' said Fabienne. 'It is happening in Naples in October, on the Feast of the

Precious Torn. A special day for their kind. You could almost call it holy.'

'Thank you, Fabienne,' acknowledged the Glorious, tartly, before returning their attention to Winter. 'Naturally it would be advantageous if Don Zerbinati was removed from our concern before then.'

'And just how do you intend to kill him? I imagine he doesn't die all that easily.'

The Glorious paused. 'It would require a very special bullet.'

The conjoined bodies turned as one. They walked to the rear of the room. Only now did Winter realise that there was a door set into the furthest wall, its hinges all but invisible, masked by the gleam of the lights. It slid sideways with a ripple of casters, revealing an antechamber beyond. In contrast to the white room this was a gloomier space, lit by a single standing lamp.

A parchment map was suspended from the ceiling. Its edges swayed as Winter and the others filled the hidden recess. It was an old map, an Ottoman map, the colours water-pale now but the lines that marked the national borders still vividly defined. Each nation was identified in curls of Arabic script. Winter recognised the coastlines of Europe.

The eyes of the Glorious focused on him alone, the four golden irises bright and penetrating. 'We trust you found the information you were seeking at the home of Signore Franzeri. If you did, now is the time to share it.'

Winter hesitated, aware that Libby's eyes were also

upon him, a watchful reminder of Faulkner and London and a sense of duty that felt increasingly less vital to him. His professional reflex was to hold on to intelligence. But he had no idea what he had just acquired from Franzeri's remains and, to judge by this whole extraordinary setup, these people did. This time curiosity overruled instinct. He reached inside his jacket and handed over the fan.

The Glorious took it with a look that approached reverence. The man's fingers moved with the woman's, spreading the whalebone blades until the painted scene of the canal extended to the fan's full width. Marvelling at what they held, the Glorious walked to the standing lamp and tilted its bulb directly at the map. Then they placed the fan in front of the beam.

The silk cast a shadow on the parchment, turning the countries pale grey. The thread that had been inserted between the folds made a darker, more distinct shadow. It threw a ragged line upon the English Channel.

It was a map upon a map.

The Glorious adjusted the position of the fan. Now the shadow of the thread moved across the sea, gaining in size. Finally it aligned with the coast of Northern France, locking precisely into place. It matched the topography exactly, its peaks and dips echoing the contours of peninsulas and inlets. Winter assumed that the seven gems studding the silk had to be markers of some kind, denoting specific locations in the French countryside.

'Signore Franzeri acquired quite a keepsake for his collection,' said the Glorious. 'This fan was the property of

Pope Clement XIV. It vanished from the Vatican archive in 1773. It was later rumoured to be in the possession of the Marquis de Montferrat. Some say he intended it as a gift for Lilith herself. It is fitting you have brought it to us, Mr Winter.'

'What am I looking at?'

The woman answered him. 'Folklore insists that vampires can be killed in a multiplicity of ways. A stake through the heart. Contact with holy water. Direct exposure to sunlight.'

'Garlic,' said Libby, with a smirk that faded as the rest of the room turned to her. 'Just saying. I've heard about the garlic thing. Probably bollocks.'

'These are peasant defences against the lowest caste of the undead,' said Alessandra. 'The ones who are barely more than vermin.'

'Right,' said Libby, with a chippy hint of North London. 'I guess I know my place, then.'

The incubus continued. 'The higher vampire – the king, the queen – cannot be eliminated so easily. Their physiologies are considerably more robust. To kill them you need the holiest of armaments. Sacred objects. True relics. The thorns of Golgotha, for instance.'

Winter took a moment to place the reference. 'You're talking about Christ? The crown of thorns? That's two thousand years ago.'

'They endured. The thorns were preserved by an alchemical procedure and guarded for centuries by a sect of Gnostic Christians. They were venerated, for they contained the very matter of Christ. His blood. His sweat. The remnants of his pierced flesh. In time they came into the possession of the Church. And as the vampiric dynasties expanded the Church made use of them.'

Winter was curious now. 'How?'

'The burial of a vampire is a perfunctory business. They are never in the soil for long. You can see it as a perversion of the divine resurrection, if you like. But those who hunted the royal vampires knew it could be permanent.'

The woman continued seamlessly. 'They would separate the hearts from the bodies. A traditional defence against vampires but rarely one that lasts. And yet a single thorn of Golgotha, placed in an undead heart, would ensure that its owner would never rise again. Once this was done, the hearts were sealed in obsidian jars and placed far from the bones.'

'It was a very effective form of pest control,' added Fabienne, with a dark little smile.

Winter began to make sense of the past few weeks. 'So that's what we were trading in London. A vampire's heart. No wonder the bloody thing was still beating.'

Fabienne nodded. 'They are extremely sought after and there are many who are scouring Europe for them. But not every heart contains a thorn. Much of the time we are chasing rumour or superstition. The heart Jack Creadley was selling belonged to the Vicomte de Frontenac. A high-born vampire, yes, but not necessarily one who was worthy of a thorn of Christ. Still, we take an interest in every heart that appears on the market. We must pursue every possibility, however slim.'

Winter gestured at the map, indicating the ragged shadow that hugged the French coastline. 'And these gemstones mark the location of the true hearts? The ones that were originally buried with the thorns?'

'Exactly,' said the Glorious, in harmony. 'Once we finally possess a thorn of Golgotha we shall embed it in a bullet. A holy bullet, with a holy purpose. One that will remove a significant darkness from this world.'

'That's the contract you're offering me?' asked Winter, bluntly. 'Find the thorn? Kill the man?'

'What we're offering you is one million pounds. In cash.'

Winter considered the proposal. *One million pounds.* It was an insane sum, enough to ensure he would never find himself slumming with gutter life like Jack Creadley ever again. Never be scraping by on the fringes, sliding from one sordid, illicit job to the next. He could leave that shabby hole in Battersea, escape London, escape it all, before the desperation hardened into something unbreakable. *One million pounds.* It sounded like a chance at life.

But there was another consideration, beyond the blood money. This contract would place him directly into the orbit of Don Zerbinati. The Russians already had a bead on him, that much was certain. He was clearly part of the agenda of the reactivated Operation Paragon. What did Soviet Intelligence want with him? This path promised to bring him closer to the answer – and if it didn't, a timely kill would at least rob the Russians of their prize.

He looked up to see Libby's cautioning hazel eyes.

'You're British Intelligence, Mr Winter. Let's get back to London. Put this all together.'

'Faulkner hired me for one job,' Winter reminded her. He pointed a thumb at Alessandra. 'Get this woman out of Budapest. That's what I've done.'

'You know this isn't over.'

'They sent you to Venice to intercept whatever I was chasing. They don't trust me. That's obvious. I don't owe them anything anymore. You can tell that to Faulkner.'

Libby shook her head. 'I'll tell him later. For now I'm sticking with you.'

'I don't need you to play guardian angel, Miss Cracknell.'

Libby held his gaze. 'I've got a job of my own to do, mate. I was assigned to keep tabs on you. And by the sound of it this Don Zerbinati is worth a dossier. Even if it's an obituary.'

'I'm not doing this in the name of British Intelligence,' insisted Winter. 'I'm working alone.'

'No, you're working with me,' said Alessandra, decisively. 'We began this together and we shall end it together. I shall help you to kill this bastard Zerbinati.'

Winter turned to the Glorious. He saw two expectant sets of eyes, grey pupils ringed by gold. They were waiting for his decision.

'In cash, you say?'

14

The cliffs of the Côte d'Albâtre stood like chalk battlements against the sea. Gannets wheeled above them, snatches of motion against the grey weight of Atlantic sky.

Winter looked across the headland as the car clung to the coastal road. It was barely dawn but morning was already carving through the dark. The shingle beaches seized the silver light for themselves, swarms of quartz glittering beneath the rugged crests of rock. Everything else was held in shadow: the inlets, the harbours, the outlines of gun emplacements left from the last war, as much a part of the Normandy landscape now as the neat crosses of the D-Day cemeteries. Light and shadow, caught negotiating; it was as if the day was sketching itself into being.

They had followed the coastal road from Étretat, some 32 kilometres north-east of Le Havre. The Falaise d'Aval was still visible behind them, the grand arch of rock rearing out of the waves. The sea smashed against it, casting great arcs of spray through the hollow of the cliff.

Winter returned his attention to the road, watching as the headlights of the hired Citroën DS 21 cut into the early-morning murk. Libby was at the wheel of the shark-sleek, low-slung convertible, her checkerboard cap hugging her fringe and a pair of matching black-and-white driving gloves keeping the chill from her fingers. The needle on the speedometer danced just a little too high for Winter's taste, and had done for most of the journey.

Libby's tongue played between her teeth as she coaxed a little more velocity from the engine, taking the twists of the road so quickly that Winter felt sure the wheels were skimming the cusp of the cliff. He remembered how she had torn through the empty streets of London, that morning Faulkner had persuaded him to come back to all this. Perhaps she had a death wish, as only the young and invincible could.

Finally he cracked, and felt as old as God as he did so. 'Slow it down, will you?'

Libby sighed and let the speedometer dip. 'Just seeing what she's got.'

Winter wondered if she meant the car or herself. He had met kids like her before. They all had something to prove and would push their limits to do so. Operating in the field soon knocked that out of you. Adrenalin, you quickly learned, was a tool, not a drug.

'I think we know what she's got by now.'

'Pity,' said a voice from behind them. 'I imagine it must be an exhilarating sensation.'

Alessandra sat in the back of the open-top four-seater, her black bob whipped into a state of disarray by the coastal wind. Strands of hair clung to her cheek, fixed by the damp, briny air.

'You're not missing much,' said Winter. 'Just an imminent heart attack.'

'The speed and the wind,' said Alessandra, with genuine curiosity in her voice. 'How does it make you feel?'

'Alive,' said Libby, a little too glibly. 'Absolutely bloody alive. You should try it sometime.'

'Perhaps you would allow me to share it. Sometime.'

'Maybe I will. If you're not too weird about it.'

Alessandra beamed in the rear-view mirror. 'I would very much like that, Miss Cracknell.'

'You really can't feel it?' asked Libby, more thoughtfully. 'None of it?'

Alessandra brushed a stray lock of hair from her mouth. 'Oh, I feel it. I just don't experience it in the way that you do. But then I imagine your tiny lifespan makes it all the sweeter.'

'Sweet as a nut, darling.'

Winter saw the speed gauge begin to climb again. 'Keep it steady,' he cautioned.

Libby switched on the radio, summoning a crackly Johnny Hallyday, the long-wave signal stuttering as it reached across the French coast. It was too loud for Winter's liking and he immediately switched it off again.

'Wanker,' said Libby, not quite beneath her breath.

The car sped into a waiting tunnel, one that had been bored through a chunk of cliffside rock. It was sporadically lit, and for long stretches the only illumination came from the determined beam of the Citroën's headlights. The walls of the tunnel were wet and black and the tiny coin of light in the distance took an age to grow in size, despite the speed they were travelling.

Finally they emerged. The car continued to climb the coastal road for another couple of miles before veering away from the cliff and onto a rougher track. The wheels spat stones as Libby cut into wilder countryside. Here the grass clung to swollen slopes, rippling as the early-morning wind bladed through it. The sky was still a heavy gunmetal grey but Winter could see a sliver of pink through the Atlantic clouds, far out to sea. The day was coming.

They parked by a wooden signpost that had been hammered into the soil. Pointing the way to Étretat and the surrounding villages, it stood at a crooked angle, as if bent by a storm and never corrected. The whole area felt abandoned, with no proof of human occupation to break the rolling banks of grass.

Winter swung his legs from the car and walked to the boot. Libby was already there. She handed him a shovel then took one for herself. Alessandra received a torch, and managed to look simultaneously relieved and disdainful.

Ahead of them rose a small hill. Piled upon the summit were stacks of stones, assembled as rudimentary burial markers. To Winter there was something primally forbidding about these crude mounds of granite. They looked more like warnings than memorials, markers for the living to keep their distance. This was a cemetery, but one with no sense of ceremony or ostentation, clearly just a dumping ground for the dead.

'The plague reached Normandy in 1348,' said Alessandra, as they climbed the incline. 'That year they called it the Black Spring. This is where the village of Saint-Bénézet buried its taken.'

Libby scanned the wind-hardened terrain. It was empty as far as the horizon. 'What village would that be, then?'

Alessandra gave a grim, pinched smile. 'In the end I imagine there was no one left to bury the dead. In time there was no village left either. But the land will remember.'

This was the third location they had explored in the past two days, following the trail of gemstones on the coastal map. They had searched the crypt of the church of Saint Aignan in Trévières and, equally fruitlessly, disturbed the ancestral home of an aristocrat in Deauville, rumoured to have hunted vampires for sport in the eighteenth century. There was no trace of the buried hearts, let alone the thorns, and Winter was beginning to suspect they were chasing fables.

'Are you sure this is the right place?' he asked Alessandra, the shovel already feeling like a waste of time in his hand. 'It's utterly godforsaken.'

'Forsaken by man, perhaps. I'm sure your God plays a longer game.'

The earth lay at a tilt, the stone markers packed around a central hump. There were forty or more of them, pitted by centuries of wind and decay.

'Where do we even begin?' Winter wondered aloud.

Alessandra moved the torch over the rough-hewn memorials, creating a crush of shadows on the grass. The light settled on a marker that was different from the rest. It was a solid hunk of granite and there was an elementary skull carved upon it, two axes crossed beneath the jaw. A Latin motto was etched upon the stone, the letters like ghosts now. Winter could just about read them by torchlight.

'*A solis ortu usque ad occasum.*' He was long out of practice but he managed to piece the meaning together. 'From sunrise to sunset. Odd thing to have on your grave.'

'How come it's the only one that gets an inscription?' asked Libby, looking across the haphazard cluster of memorial stones. The wind had tightened over the hill and she tugged her cap against it. There was something watchful about the bleak grey countryside.

'This must be where they interred the village priest,' said Alessandra. 'The poor would have been buried as quickly as possible but they would have made an effort, at least, for the Lord's representative.'

'You think they buried the heart with him?' asked Winter. 'Why here, of all places?'

Alessandra kept the torchlight on the carved skull. It had a primitive, childlike quality, two coarsely chiselled holes for the eyes, three sunken indentations for the teeth.

'A graveyard for peasants. It would be an insult to a higher-caste vampire. I approve.'

Winter stuck the edge of his shovel into the ground, directly in the shadow of the stone marker. Libby did likewise. The soil was impacted and refused to break at first but a few more strikes saw it crack into thick, dry clumps. The shovels flung the earth onto the hillside. Alessandra moved the torch to illuminate the digging.

'There'll be a coffin, right?' asked Libby. 'First to hit it buys breakfast. I fancy chips.'

'There are no coffins here,' said Alessandra, patiently. 'You will strike bone. Perhaps not even the bones you are looking for. This is a mass grave, girl. There may even be animals.'

Libby paused to consider this. With a sour expression she carried on digging.

Sure enough there were skeletal remains in the dirt; segments of fingers and ribs, corners of skulls, poking like bright fossils through the crumble of soil. Winter suspected there were more bodies huddled here than the number of markers gave away. They had been tipped close to the surface too, suggesting burial had been a hasty, indiscriminate business. He wondered who had been left that spring to consecrate the body of the priest.

The tip of his shovel struck something hard and broad, concealed in the earth. Probably a skull, he imagined, as he raised a hand to tell Libby to stop digging. Tossing the shovel he moved closer to the ground, using his fingers to scoop away the dirt. The powdery soil crammed itself under his nails and caked his skin.

'I've got something...'

He traced the embedded outline. It felt too smooth, too regular, to be a skull. There were no pits or hollows, just a glassy, unbroken surface. The hearts had been sealed in obsidian jars, wasn't that what the Glorious had said? Winter moved his hands down, continuing to follow the shape of the buried object.

His fingers touched what were unmistakably lumps of bone. The torch revealed them to be white knots of knuckle, poking like tiny arches through the soil. He scoured away the last of the dirt. It was a jar alright, and it was held by the fleshless hands of a long-dead village priest. Winter did his best to shake the image of Franzeri's remains, back in that house in Venice. Again something stirred in his veins. Something quick, and hungering.

'This has got to be it,' he said, reaching down to prise the jar from the bones.

The jar slid from the grip of the skeletal fingers.

And then the skeletal fingers snatched it back.

Winter stared, unblinking, at the bone hands. They were still now as they cradled the jar once more. Motionless, they could almost convince him they had lain like that for centuries. But he knew he had just seen them move, felt an impossible tremor of strength in them.

He didn't take his eyes from the bones as he spoke to the others. 'Did you see that?'

'Get the jar,' said Alessandra, crisply. 'Get the jar and we'll go.'

'They bloody moved.'

'Clearly it has a guardian. Someone buried the heart of a high-born with the lowest of its kind. An even greater insult.'

'These are the bones of a vampire? Protecting something as holy as the thorn?'

'It's loyal to the heart of its king. An ingenious defence, matching that loyalty to the power of the thing that imprisons it. The thorn is encased in obsidian but it still has the power to keep this creature in the earth.'

Winter understood the implication. 'And we're removing it.'

'We'll have time,' said Alessandra, assuredly. 'It's slept for six centuries, after all.'

Winter reached down again. This time the bones clung to the jar, retreating an inch into the soil. Winter tried to break their grip but they tightened possessively across the smooth black surface, closing in a crab–like lock.

Winter saw one of the fingers uncurl. Quivering, it reared with life and struck the side of the jar. And then it repeated the movement, faster now. Faster and louder. It was creating a rhythm against the obsidian shell.

Tap-tap. Tap-tap. Tap-tap. Tap-tap.

The pattern quickly found a pace.

Tap-tap. Tap-tap. Tap-tap. Tap-tap.

He remembered the cave in Gellért Hill. The blind creature in the chair. The one that had found his heartbeat.

Tap-tap. Tap-tap.

'Jesus,' he whispered, before giving a shout. 'Move!'

The ground shuddered beneath them, dislodging other remains. Chunks of bone broke through the soil, caught in the sudden churn of earth. The stone markers began to tumble. Something was stirring in the burial pile, rising through the tightly packed dead.

Tossing away the torch, Alessandra stepped into the pit. Impatiently she ripped the jar from the priest's hands then stamped on the maddened bones. The fingers flexed uselessly, curling like pincers.

There was a disdainful confidence in her voice. 'You just need to be firm with them...'

'Go!' said Winter, turning to follow Libby, who was already backing away, the shovel slipping from her hand. He had glimpsed a shape – human but incomplete – thrusting its way out of the pit. A bone-sketch of a man, rising through a hail of dirt that drizzled from its empty sockets and poured through its open ribs.

They scrambled down the hill, making for the car. Alessandra held the black jar in both hands, pressing it tight against her chest, as if determined to keep it from the entire world. She was just behind the others.

Light was breaking to the east. Libby was in front, her sights set on the Citroën. Winter reached the foot of the hill then spun to check on Alessandra. The shape was behind her, a blur of bone and rag, its burial shroud rippling like torn flags in the wind.

It had closed the distance without her realising. The thing had no shadow but the raw crack of its bones signalled it was upon her.

'Winter!'

His name cut through the air, the last word she would ever say.

She threw the jar to him.

He caught it, feeling its hard, icy bulk slam against his fingers.

Her eyes held his. And then they widened in shock, the whites expanding around the irises.

A fist of bones erupted through Alessandra's chest, savagely fast.

It held something, something it had taken from her. The knuckles squeezed and blood streamed between them, staining the shreds of fabric snagged in their cracks.

The hand opened, revealing its prize. Alessandra's heart, plucked and crushed like fruit, payback for the one she had stolen.

Winter looked on, horrified, his eyes rising to meet hers again. He thought he caught something in her gaze, just as her pupils turned glassy and lightless. It wasn't just the realisation of her death. It was the realisation that she actually could die.

The hand withdrew with a gasp of flesh. Alessandra's body pitched forward. She slammed into the ground.

A moment later her heart joined her, discarded.

The revenant faced Winter, the coastal wind whipping its shroud. It stood unsteadily, the bones tottering, as if animated by a half-memory of life. In the absence of a face Winter imagined he saw everything from fury to triumph in the blank stare of the skull.

There were no plague victims buried on this hill, that much was certain. The village had experienced an altogether different kind of visitation.

The skull tilted on the vertebrae, locking its empty

gaze on the black jar. Winter began to edge back, fighting the urge to hurl himself at the thing that had killed Alessandra. She had died entrusting him with the jar. He had to get it away from this place. Where was Cracknell? She must have reached the car by now.

The creature ran with a gallop of bones. In seconds it was on him. They smashed to the ground together, the revenant at his throat, its fingers locking around his windpipe, charged with a preternatural strength.

The skull reared in his vision. The last of the soil drizzled from the sockets, spattering Winter's face.

Tasting earth, he stared at the arm pressing down on him. It was clothing itself in flesh and muscle. New veins laced their way along the yellowed bones, threading through sinew that had burst from the pits and the grooves. A sheath of skin began to crawl across the limb, wrapping the newly formed tissue. The priest's body was reassembling itself.

Winter kept the jar tight against his chest and jammed his free hand against the dead thing's jaw. As he tried to heave it away he could feel the new flesh forming. It was tacky and warm.

The skull was half-skin now. And there were eyes in the sockets, clear and startlingly blue, like a newborn's.

The mouth parted. Winter saw thin, keen teeth descending. The revenant twisted his head to meet them. The thing was a vampire. And it was thirsting.

A shriek filled his ears, raw and sudden, torn from new lungs. He heard something else, too, below the scream. A thud of something heavy, impacting against the creature's body and shattering bone.

Winter's chest was wet. Blood was pouring onto his shirt. There was a sharp object nestling against his skin, close to his sternum. It had pierced the priest and almost cut into his own body.

He rolled aside, fighting for breath, the black jar still in his grasp. The revenant collapsed next to him. It shuddered, then stiffened, finally becoming still. The wind toyed with the grey shreds of its burial shroud.

A slender length of wood had speared the thing. Winter saw the pole rising into the dawn sky, topped by a pointed slat that declared it was 4km to Étretat.

Libby was standing over him, her eyes cold with resolve.

She kept both hands on the signpost and worked it deeper into the priest's torso, grinding the makeshift stake. The wood scraped against the smashed ribcage.

'Bloody hell,' she breathed, disbelieving. 'That actually works.'

The vampire was already crumbling, its resurrected flesh sliding from the bones.

Winter picked himself up. Libby looked to him for an acknowledgement but he kept walking, half stumbling, his eyes on Alessandra alone.

She lay there, staring sightlessly up at him. He kept his gaze away from the monstrous wound in her chest, the blood that trailed beneath her, darkening the soil. A random strand of hair was caught in her lips. Winter coiled it over the curve of her ear, the gesture tender, unhurried. He searched her face but there was nothing now, no trace of the spirit that had animated those muscles, danced beneath that skin. It was as if she had been emptied.

'Let's go, Mr Winter.'

Libby smacked earth from her palms. She spoke again, colder and brisker this time.

'Leave her, mate. We need to go.'

The urgency in her voice made him look up. He saw movement on the hill. More of the undead were wresting their way out of the burial mound. They were no more than bones and cloth; thin, threadbare silhouettes, like crude pencil sketches against the light.

Winter instinctively knew they were hunting the jar.

Abandoning Alessandra's body they ran for the Citroën. The doors slammed and the engine stirred into life on Libby's first, insistent twist of the ignition key. The convertible lurched, its exhaust smoking.

The car leapt for the coastal road with a surge of hydraulic fluid. Winter turned in the passenger seat, stealing a glance over his shoulder. 'Drive!'

Two revenants were keeping pace, moving on all fours with a loping, bestial gait, skeletal knuckles striking the ground. Their speed was astonishing.

The closest of the creatures sprang for the back of the car. Its fingers clawed the steel bodywork, fighting for a hold. The metal screeched beneath the grasping bone.

Libby dug her boot against the accelerator. The needle on the dashboard swung but the revenant clung on. The second creature scrambled over the spine of the first, clutching at the folded roof that encircled the rear seats. The Citroën tilted beneath their weight.

Winter stashed the jar in the glove compartment. Then he rose to his feet as the car raced, one hand gripping the passenger door to steady himself. Cautiously, he began to turn, moving his hand to the top of the seat behind him. The wind was salt-sharp and urgent, whipping his tie into his eyes.

Swaying as the Citroën veered, he clambered between the front seats. The revenants were crouched on the boot, clinging to the furled roof. There were skeins of skin on their arms now, pale as gauze. Winter could see newly forged muscles pulsing beneath the epidermal layers. Eyes, too, had arrived in the creatures' skulls. They regarded him with an animalistic defiance.

Libby took a sharp bend and he fell sideways. Reeling, he snatched the seat belt, twisting it tight around his fingers till he reclaimed his balance.

Again the car juddered, stuttering as Libby cut between brakes and accelerator on another corner. This time Winter felt the right-side wheels scraping the brink of the cliffside road. The world shifted beneath the tyres and his gut plummeted.

Libby flung the steering wheel, battling to keep control of the car's momentum. She pulled the Citroën back into the centre of the road, pushing its high-pressure hydraulics to their limit.

Winter glimpsed a blur of sea and sky at the periphery

of his vision. The edge of the road threatened again as the cliff curved. He kept his focus on the revenants. They were grinding their jaws as they faced him, their teeth descending, cobra-like, from wet lips.

He threw a punch at the nearest creature. His fist connected with sticky new skin. The car swerved once more, changing his centre of balance, making it harder to weight a blow. He punched anyway, a clumsy uppercut that clipped the thing in the teeth. Blood flew from its gums.

The second revenant had slunk into the vehicle between the punches, snaking over the rear seats. Now it extended an arm, seizing Winter by the ankle. He kicked at its throat, almost losing his foothold as the Citroën weaved.

The nearer creature clasped his tie, hauling itself toward him by the thin strip of fabric. Its other hand found his face, closing in a vice of nails, determined to break the skin.

The car shot into the cliffside tunnel.

Libby took it too close to the wall. The wing mirror buckled as it struck the rock. There was a grinding of bodywork, the steel whining as it tore. Sparks peeled from the wall, illuminating the revenant in bright, fitful flashes.

Winter felt the creature's hand contract. There was an extra edge to its strength now.

It was the dark, he realised. Somehow the gloom of the tunnel had enhanced it, given it power.

He peered sideways, through the crush of fingers.

The tunnel's exit was a distant ball of light. But it was there.

'Faster!' he yelled, fighting to be heard through the hand. 'Get to the light!'

Libby stamped the accelerator. The Citroën responded with a fresh leap of speed, enough to make the chassis shake. The growl of its engine echoed as a roar, filling the black hollow of the tunnel. Again the car sliced against the wall, shredding metal.

Winter managed to jam a hand beneath the creature's jaw. He pushed upwards, forcing its head against the side of the tunnel. He felt the skull stammer against the rock and he held it there, stubbornly, until flesh ripped and spat from the bone. The thing howled, its grip on Winter's face tightening in retaliation. He felt his nerve endings blaze.

Through the pain he glimpsed the second creature. It was moving toward the driver's seat, its limbs coiled in a predator's pose.

'Libby!'

The Citroën burst from the tunnel, slamming into light. Libby swung the car from the cliff's edge. It skidded to the left with a protest of tyre rubber.

Dawn had broken over the coast. The sunrise bloomed on the water and filled the clouds, a vivid red hue shattering the grey. There was warmth in the wind now.

The vampire's hand fell from Winter's face, its strength stolen by the sudden arrival of daybreak. The skin curled from the bone, trailing veins and ganglia. And then the bones themselves crumbled, reduced to a dust that streamed into the sky like cinders.

The burial rags followed the revenant's remains, tugged aloft with a flap of cloth. Soon the coastal wind had taken all trace of both creatures.

The Citroën skidded to a halt. Winter slid into the passenger seat, saying nothing. He stared impassively at the slate-coloured tumble of the English Channel. And then he slammed his hands against the dashboard, and kept slamming them until his skin burned.

Finally he turned to Libby. She looked back at him, concerned and just a little unnerved by the rawness of what he had just shown.

His breathing steadied. 'You're going back to London.'

'Shut up,' she replied, more incredulous than angry.

'You're going back to London. There's no argument.'

She tried a conciliatory smile. 'This is a bloody argument.'

'To hell with that. It's too dangerous for you. You're inexperienced.'

'Don't be so bloody patronising.'

'Don't be so damn young.'

Libby was furious now. 'You think I'm going to die too, like her? Is that it?'

'You can go and die in London if you like. It won't be my problem.'

'I'm trained. I'm qualified. I'm good. You saw what I just did. Do I have to prove it again?'

He shook his head, fixing his eyes on the sea once more. The waves still held the sunrise. 'No guardian angels, Cracknell. Go home. I'm doing this alone.'

15

The Moon dominated the Bay of Naples, caught at the midpoint of an eclipse. It looked huge tonight, so close to the city it felt like an occupying force in wartime.

Winter studied the totality from his seafront hotel, hunched over the guard rail that bordered the balcony of his room. He was in a cotton shirt, the sleeves rolled to his elbows, starched white cuffs curling with perspiration in the sultry air. The bright wink of a Woodbine flared between his lips. It was his fourth so far and tasted like the tenth.

The umbra, the innermost part of Earth's shadow, had obscured the face of the lunar surface. A veil of dust and volcanic ash in the atmosphere gave the satellite a coppery, blood-bruised hue. It burned sullenly above the dark Tyrrhenian Sea.

The Moon governed the waves, Winter knew. Tonight he could believe it commanded imaginations too, especially here, in Naples, where the streets were saturated with superstition. It was all about the signs and omens, his taxi driver had told him, a plastic Madonna dancing on a beaded chain that hung from the rear-view mirror. God knew the man needed faith to take on the carnage of traffic that led from Capodichino airport.

Winter took his eyes from the Moon and followed the curve of the bay, past the marina and the fat, twinkling cruise ships idling on the water. To the south he could see the rugged arc of the Sorrentine Peninsula. The islands of Ischia and Capri looked hazier on the horizon, almost insubstantial, as if not quite committing to being there.

His eyes were drawn, inevitably, to Vesuvius. The great lava-blackened hump brooded over the coastline, an ever-present reminder of death and fire, forces that would never negotiate with faith. Naples sat at the foot of the slumbering volcano, not quite cowering but always wary. That plastic Madonna would blister in its flames but people still clung to these trinkets as if arming themselves against fate itself.

What kind of trinkets did Winter have? Maybe he wore his experiences like objects of faith. All those years in the field, everything he had learned, everything that yes, he clung to, even now, taking the coin of a demon.

He had been sent to this city to kill a man. An undead man, perhaps, but that detail was a wrinkle, as was the fact he was doing this for money and not out of duty. A kill was a kill, he told himself. And he wanted this to be a neat, clean job, just like all those bullets he had placed in the name of the Crown. The majority of them, at least.

He thought of London, then, more fleetingly than

he once might have imagined possible. There would be anger at Century House over his refusal to return for a debrief. He savoured that knowledge, pictured every livid vein on Faulkner's temples, because it made him feel free. No doubt someone would be assigned to bring him home. He wished them luck. Naples, he sensed, knew how to hide you.

Winter turned from the bay and gazed up at the lights piled on the hills behind the Grand Hotel Vesuvio. *Where were you tonight, Don Zerbinati? I Senz'Ombr.* The Shadowless. Did anyone in this world really leave no shadow? Where the hell would they hide if not the shadows?

A night wind ruffled the groves above the city. The trees swayed in a dark, rhythmic mass.

He glanced down. A small green lizard had crept onto the iron rail, its attention held by the glow of his cigarette. Winter inhaled and the Woodbine glimmered again. He released a mouthful of smoke in a lazy circle. The creature regarded it, unimpressed.

'Oh, you want proper magic, I take it? I think you've got the wrong man.'

The lizard blinked, tilted its head. And then it scampered for a clump of bougainvillea. Winter flicked his cigarette over the edge of the balcony.

'*Arrivederci* to you too.'

He stepped back inside the room. His leather holdall lay on the floor, unzipped. Three identical white shirts already hung in the half-open wardrobe, creased from travel. His grey linen jacket was equally rumpled, flung across the solitary chair. A toothbrush and razor stood in a tumbler by the sink. The gun waited on the bed.

Winter sat on the edge of the mattress and examined the weapon once again. It had been there when he arrived, propped against the wall, parcelled up to suggest a delivery of golf clubs. He had identified it as a customised Carcano, a bolt-action sniper rifle, lean and compact. Italian army surplus, he guessed. An older gun, but one with a reputation for precision. A modern telescopic sight was aligned along its length, the metal mount screwed into the wood.

He cradled the rifle, assessing its weight and balance, appraising its possibilities. And then he swung it at the balcony, one eye peering through the tactical scope. A tweak of the focus and the bloodshot moon resolved itself, the Sea of Tranquility framed by cross hairs. Winter let his finger meet the trigger. He had a muscle memory of what it was like to kill from a distance.

He placed the gun back on the bed. The bullet rested on the pillow, where a complimentary chocolate might have been. He picked it up. 8x56Rmm calibre. Winter turned the smooth copper casing between his fingers. It felt warm to the touch in that hot room.

The bullet had been delivered by hand, of course. Fabienne had met him in the car park of Capodichino, smiling through the shadow of a wide-brimmed hat, her eyes hidden behind tortoiseshell sunglasses. The exchange had been as brief as her smile. No chat, no pleasantries. No complication.

The Glorious had engaged an expert weaponsmith in Rome to create the bullet, a reclusive figure who went by the name of L'Artigiano, the Craftsman. Winter was told he had considerable history in this line of work. Apparently he had once forged a dagger from the shin bone of a fourteenth-century Pope. An exorcist had used it to despatch the ghost of a fallen saint in Quartiere San Lorenzo, back in '55. No doubt his latest commission had been even more of a professional honour.

The bullet gleamed in his hand, reflecting the bulb slung from the ceiling. Winter continued to turn it, picturing the holy thorn embedded inside, the one that had been prised from the withered scrap of heart locked in the black jar. Had it really pierced the flesh of Christ two thousand years ago? Or was it just another trinket, another object of faith?

A tinny throb of bossa nova music infiltrated the room, just loud enough to irritate him. Somebody on an adjoining balcony had switched on a transistor radio. Winter got up from the bed. He had left the terrace door open, hoping to cool the room with some night air. As he drew the door shut he saw the red moon shimmer on the rectangle of glass. He paused as he held the handle.

'Are you there?'

He had addressed the glass. Naturally he felt ridiculous. But he had to try, just this once, when no one else was around.

He spoke again, just as softly. 'Alessandra...'

He remembered the crystalline dazzle of that

basement room in Venice, the magic she had shown him. The power to trap people's souls inside glass. Ever since Normandy Winter had wondered if she could save herself that way, preserve her spirit as she had imprisoned others. This was the first time he had dared to ask. Was it even possible? Or was he just wishing into the dark, anything to ease the horror of her death?

He had so many questions for her. So much he needed to know about the man he had been.

There was no reply. He stared hard into the glass, willing her face to form. All it gave back was his own reflection. The eyes that met him had that tired look he knew from mirrors but somehow he seemed younger, as if an alchemy of glass and moonlight had erased the lines, smoothed the features, taken the years away. It could have been his face from twenty years ago.

It would have been the face of Tobias Hart, he realised.

For a moment he was back in that ruined Bavarian basilica, confronting his younger self, transfixed and repelled by what he saw. Hart had stood in front of him, burning with an unholy light, burning with magic, bright and terrifying as an angel.

That warlock bastard would have known what to do.

Winter felt a pulse in his forehead. A flicker of wire beneath the skin, steady, insistent. At first he imagined it was a trapped nerve or the first warning of a migraine. Maybe he should throw some pills at it, he thought, lob a couple of Anadin down his throat. But as the pulse persisted it began to feel familiar. A rhythm he had once known, natural as a heartbeat.

'Flesh is memory,' Alessandra had whispered. 'Bone is memory. Blood is memory.'

She had put magic inside him again. It had saved his life. He could sense it in his body, waiting in the veins, impatient to be used. It was like a hunger in his cells.

Winter raised his left hand and placed it on the glass. He regarded the pale, lean fingers that reached for him, matching his own. The Tyrrhenian Sea seemed to move in the reflected flesh.

He felt a droplet on his skin. He assumed it was sweat or condensation but as it trailed across his knuckles he saw it was the colour of ink. There was liquid running from the window frame. It was also black, as black as the waves in the bay.

Instinctively he pushed at the glass. The texture had changed. It was soft, gauzy.

The pulse beat above his eyes.

Winter took his hand from the window, suddenly unsure. And then, still wary, he teased the glass again, testing its consistency. This time his fingers slipped right through it. He could feel the night air on his skin.

'My God,' he murmured.

The window clung to his wrist. He turned his hand and saw the entire pane swirl, as if the molecules themselves were shifting, kaleidoscoping. His heart was beating fast. This craving in his veins? It made sense to him now.

Winter smiled to himself. The glass ran like rain between his fingers.

16

There was another London, one that was rarely recorded on maps.

It was a city of inconspicuous doors on unremarkable streets, blank windows in sealed buildings. This London hid in plain sight, perfectly camouflaged, knowing it would never catch anyone's eye or snag their curiosity. In South Kensington no one heard the hot hum of telexes behind the façade of the Commission for Generational Expenditure. On Euston Road no one saw the wink of switchboards inside a shuttered piano repair shop. Within these unexceptional places telephones rang and ink-stamped pages turned and Britain was defended.

The geography of this city was drawn with cable and wire, threading beneath concrete, weaving under tarmac. Its gazetteer was written in passcodes and disinformation. The boundaries shifted like evening light. Try to jab a pin on this private map and it would evade you. Place a compass next to it and the needle would tilt, inevitably, into shadow.

Libby Cracknell loved to keep this unseen A–Z in

her head. Sometimes she would piece it together, just for fun, sketching a mental image of how it all connected. The knowledge made her feel connected too, part of something special, beyond the everyday. It made her feel like she belonged.

Libby had left the MGB on Cursitor Street, stowing the last of her chips beneath the passenger seat, next to that morning's crumpled speeding ticket. Now she stood on the east side of Furnival Street, facing a drab expanse of brick and soot-smeared tile. A ventilation shaft and metal-mesh fire escape rose above a padlocked goods entrance. NO PARKING stated the sign bolted to the double doors.

There was another entrance to the left. This was a single door, ostensibly a fire exit. It also had a grimy veneer of disuse, though there was no padlock on this one. DO NOT OBSTRUCT declared white letters on a sheet of red metal that looked hot to the touch in the London sun.

Libby sucked the tips of her fingers, the tang of vinegar on her tongue. Then she pressed the discreet button at the edge of the doorframe, putting her face to the tiny, vigilant lens concealed in a rivet above.

There was a hiss of static as the building greeted her.

'Drink to me only with thine eyes,' she told the intercom, reciting that day's passcode with the rote rhythm of a kid at school. 'And I will pledge with mine.'

The door opened with a shudder of alternating current and the thud of a mortise bolt. Libby stepped from July sunlight into gloom, entering a space that could, if it came to it, defy an atom bomb.

Chancery Lane Deep Shelter had been built as a fortified warren in 1942. Designed to hold crucial government personnel in the event of siege, its network of tunnels extended beneath the traffic-snarled thoroughfare of High Holborn, all the way to Leather Lane.

The Inter-Services Research Bureau had maintained a presence here at the tail end of the war, helping its resistance contacts tidy up Europe in the aftermath of Allied victory. Now it was another outpost of the GPO – or so the official line insisted, the one reinforced to the press by a D-Notice. While it was true that Chancery Lane housed a chattering nexus of telecommunications equipment – Kennedy and Khrushchev had flashed through its wires during the missile crisis in '62 – its primary purpose was to listen to the world's voices, not add to them. The intelligence service had never moved out, simply retreated deeper into shadow.

Libby took the stairs, as ever. The sluggish creak of the goods lift had never suited her.

The corridor ahead was bright with strip lighting. She could hear the steady growl of the filter that kept a welcome chill in these tunnels while recycling the same stale, nylon-tasting air. Water pumped through the overhead pipes, carried from the artesian well that supplied the bunkers. And there, in the walls and the floors, the cabling and the fuseboxes, the drone of the generator, the pulse that kept this subterranean fiefdom self-sufficient.

The staff canteen was at the end of the corridor. Plates clattered through service hatches and smoke rose to stain the low ceiling, past the mock windows with their photographic murals of tropical gardens. Good for the soul, the psychologists claimed. Libby would have cracked within a week.

She felt the stares, as she always did. The looks from the secretaries clustered around the plastic-topped tables, cups of tea in hand, putting service gossip on hold as she walked past. Whenever she made eye contact she inevitably saw something hard and resentful. One of the younger women smiled, but the Revlon-coated lips didn't quite part. Libby returned her best gap-toothed grin.

She belonged, she told herself. She was a part of this. Yes, she had escaped the gravitational pull of the typing pool. She would never have to negotiate the patronising remarks and the attention of the tweed-suited wolves, itching to add another pair of knickers to their pub boasts – not that they would have got far, given she only bedded women. She was a field agent, and a good one. She had earned that status. No one needed to resent her.

Something had always set her apart. At teenage parties she had sat on the stairs as other girls sobbed their hearts out over boys. Libby had provided a shoulder to them while wondering how anything so meaningless could hurt so much. That same ache of isolation had given her focus and drive, a determination to prove herself in any world, male or female. She could have let it sit like shrapnel inside her. Instead she used it as a bullet.

The thought of Winter still made her furious. The way that scrawny, snake-eyed sod had sent her back to London, dismissed like unwanted baggage. His refusal to trust her skills, his need to bundle her out of harm's way. God, she resented him for that, as she still resented every teacher who ever ignored her potential, imagining she'd be content with a slow death of dictated memos and a spinning Rolodex.

She had been recruited a year earlier, just out of an exasperating finishing school and hungry for purpose. Family connections, of a particularly bleak kind. Her grandparents had fled the brutal pogrom of Minsk in 1919. Exiled to London they had built a respectable role for themselves in the rag trade, embracing their newfound working-class status as a badge of honour. Her grandmother had insisted she learn Russian – as much to preserve a connection to the homeland as anything – and Libby had discovered a facility for languages. Naturally British Intelligence had seized on that talent.

'We can use you,' they had told her, and it sounded like a promise. 'Smashing,' she had said.

Libby bought an apple, pocketed it, then continued to make her way through the bright, humming corridors. Finally she came to a solid wooden door whose wartime signage still declared CENTRAL BRIEFING ROOM in scuffed bronze. The man standing outside gave the briefest acknowledgement and nodded her in.

Black-and-white images of London filled the room. They flickered against the far wall, conjured by a rattling projector. A shaft of light cut through the dark, cluttered with dust.

Libby recognised the streets of Camden. Jack Creadley's gang were walking in lockstep, all suits and tiepins and attitude, kings of the borough. Winter was among them but somehow apart, his body language not quite in synch with the others. The camera fought to keep the men in focus, the picture blurring into grain. This was surveillance footage, snatched from a window above a laundry on Chalk Farm Road. She had taken it herself, two months ago.

For a moment all she heard was the threading of the reel.

'Is he dead?'

The presence in the briefing room had made itself known. Lord Auberon Gallard sat at the desk, the shuddering images playing over his lean, austere features. His voice was calm and precise, as if the question had been posed forensically, with all the emotional engagement of a scalpel.

'He's still alive.' She felt the muscles in her throat tighten.

Gallard considered this in silence. His eyes were hard to read behind the quiver of film.

'You were ordered to kill him.'

Again the words were detached, impassive. It was a statement of fact, unequivocal.

'I know, sir.'

'*I* ordered you to kill him.'

And there it was. The spider-bite of anger on that

first syllable. She had been waiting for it ever since she entered the room.

'I had no chance, sir.'

'We make chances.'

'There were circumstances…'

'We shape circumstances. I've taught you that.'

'I didn't have an opportunity.' The words were hot and fast and she wanted to take them back immediately. They made her feel stupidly young.

'You are opportunity. Every moment you're in the field. You must be opportunity incarnate.'

The camera closed on Winter's face, playing over Gallard's own. Libby peered through the projected image, trying to keep her focus on the man in the room.

'He's not exactly a sitting target.' She was showing her resentment now. She could feel it burning through her skin and she hated herself for it. *Be cooler*, she thought, *for Christ's sake*.

Gallard's slender fingers moved on the baize-topped desk, repositioning a fountain pen until it aligned perfectly with a paper knife.

'Oh, he's certainly skilled. Malcolm Hands had quite the protégé in Christopher Winter, just as I have in you. No, I simply question whether you have it in you, Miss Cracknell. The ability to kill him. Not the opportunity but the backbone. He would be your first kill, wouldn't he?'

She thought of that undead thing in Normandy. It didn't count. It couldn't.

'I was given a surveillance job. Faulkner told me to keep tabs on him.'

'Situations change. So do our needs. Life has a way of surprising us.' He gave a disarmingly gentle smile, the skin tightening over hollow cheeks and creating a shell-burst of wrinkles.

'I didn't expect to have to kill him.'

'We must be flexible.'

'He was one of us for years. I've seen the man's record. He's a threat now?'

'A liability. A potential faultline. One we must not allow to go uncorrected. Not after what you found in Venice.'

'I take it Faulkner knows? He's the one who sent Winter to Budapest.'

A cufflink caught the projector's light. There was a discreet glimmer of pearl. 'Ultimately you report to me, not Sir Crispin. The line of command is quite clear.'

'If I'm going to kill him I'd like to know why.'

'I'm sure you would. But ultimately you're an extension of my will. A muscle may as well enquire of a nerve, "Why are you doing this?"'

'He's taken a contract. They want him to kill Don Zerbinati. He'll use a thorn. A holy thorn.'

There was silence as Gallard considered her words.

'You will report nothing of this to Faulkner. The involvement of the SIS will only complicate matters. Naturally they'll try and take him back. We must pursue our own course, our own timescale.'

Gallard swept a fastidious hand across the baize,

brushing away some imagined dust. He kept his eyes on the desk as he spoke.

'So tell me, Miss Cracknell. Are you ready to prove yourself? Or should I reassign you to a task more befitting your sex?'

Libby let her face go blank, burying everything that might betray her. The tone of her voice was resolute. 'Don't doubt me, sir.'

The man in the chair looked up. The hot white beam of the projector found his eyes.

'I'm glad to hear it. I have every confidence my faith in you will be rewarded.'

The footage reached the end of the reel. Gallard sat there, perfectly still as it ran to black.

17

Chaos was the pulse of Naples.

The city was frantic, packed with altogether too much noise and motion for its streets to contain. Car horns competed against the racket of motor scooters. Radios blared and hawkers shouted their wares above the slap and thud of kids playing street football. It was a loud, brutally busy crush.

Centro Storico was the heart of it all. To Winter this quarter felt like a souk, a ramshackle maze jammed with bright flashes of colour and pockets of deep shadow. Tiers of apartments rose above the thin, winding thoroughfares, their balconies lashed together with washing. The light came in patches but it was clean and strong when you found it, picking out a scruffy little chapel or pinpointing a fruit stall. Market tables stood piled with skinned rabbit, fresh octopus and clouded jars of sulphuric water from the slopes of Vesuvius.

For all the life in these streets the dead were ever present. Naples had an almost cultish fascination with the deceased. Winter spotted shrines to lost souls dotted among the dingy stairwells and crumbling sepia walls; the statues were frozen in flame, trapped in purgatory. Votive candles flickered beside them, the faith strong but the flames weak in the sunlight.

There was something porous about this city. Its nooks and crevices had absorbed countless cultures over the centuries, from the Greeks to the French to the flash American servicemen stationed here during the war. Somehow it had absorbed the idea of death, too, taken it into its walls and doors and shadows and never let it go.

A moped rumbled past, weighed down by an entire family. A small, honey-skinned girl was perched above the rear wheel. She regarded Winter with a curious stare, her face terribly serious. The bike was quickly lost to the weaving traffic.

Winter followed the blackened stone arches of a medieval arcade, pushing past people gorging on gelato in the midday heat. The sirocco wind carried a taste of sand and kept the air punishingly humid. It was easy to forget how close the sea was, as if these streets had folded in on themselves, retreating from the coastal sun.

He kept one eye on the crowd as he walked. There was a lawless edge to this place; Winter sensed it instinctively. It wasn't just the black-market cigarettes being openly traded next to the busts of saints, cellophane-wrapped cartons stacked on tablecloths for quick removal if the police chose to show an interest. More the hint of something sharp and vicious behind the frenzy. This city watched you with a pickpocket's gaze.

Winter had been in Naples for three days now. He had spent that time listening to the streets but he was still no closer to his target. There was a mob presence, of course. Men in good Italian suits and imported American sunglasses, moving among the people with a sense of entitlement in their stride. But if the Camorra were respected like princes, feared but so embedded in the city they rarely needed to be acknowledged, then *I Senz'Ombr*, the Shadowless, were barely even a murmur.

Maybe that was real power, thought Winter. Maybe you could be so hidden, so invisible, that not even rumour could nail you down. But the Glorious had shown him that courtroom sketch from '52. Don Zerbinati existed, or at least he had done, a decade before. He had to be here somewhere in this sun-beaten sprawl.

Winter had gone from harbourside bars to cellar dives in the Quartieri Spagnoli. An Englishman touting for work, the kind of work that bypassed visas and permits. A little hired muscle, perhaps. A driver for hire – the city was a tangle but he was a quick learner – and one who was good with a gun. He had taken care not to push his questions further than they needed to go but the Neapolitan underworld was understandably wary of a stranger, especially one with a voice like his.

'Come back Tuesday,' a stevedore had told him in La Sanità, his eyes cautious over a glass of Lacryma Christi. 'There might be some work in the docks.' Then again, the wind might shift, the stars might change, God may have other plans for you.

229

The more he probed the more the Shadowless felt like mercury escaping into the cracks. Don Zerbinati was as elusive as his brotherhood. A drunk in Mergellina claimed to have seen him two years earlier, stepping from a black-windowed limousine in Via San Biagio Dei Librai. 'The oldest eyes I have ever seen,' the man had insisted, again and again, the words eventually slurring into incoherence. 'Eyes as old as a stone saint. Just as cold.'

In an after-hours club in Forcella a sullen hostess had told him to leave the city. 'You've said his name,' she declared, too quietly for the room, almost too quietly for Winter to hear. 'Now he has your scent.' She had fingered the thin cross at her throat, her nails scraping at the silver. Winter had thanked her for the insight and handed over a roll of notes for her company. 'You're a very stupid man,' she had called after him, in a molten Sicilian accent. 'I never met you, OK?'

Today's lunch was a slice of what the Neapolitans called pizza. It had recently arrived in Britain but to Winter it was still a deeply peculiar thing. A triangle of crusted bread topped with a greasy blend of cheese and tomato and studded, improbably, with olives. It took him a moment to realise he was approaching it from the wrong end. An urchin kid in the street was still laughing.

Wiping a smear of sauce from his lips, Winter carried on walking, heading along the Via dei Tribunali, the old Roman street that bisected Centro Storico. He felt increasingly aimless in the heat. Aimless and just a little dispirited. He couldn't shake the feeling he had come to Naples to kill a whisper.

It was then that he saw the church.

It stood across the road, half in shadow, the sun barely touching the bronze skulls perched on plinths outside it. They stared at him through a parade of iron railings. Above the skulls wild green leaves sprouted from cracked gobbets of masonry. The walls of the building were a cool moon-grey. It was a still, quiet place, all the more extraordinary among the riot of the city centre. It was as if the dead had claimed it for their own.

The sight of the church transfixed him. As he gazed at the skulls he felt a shudder in his blood. It was an ache, he realised. A longing.

He had to get closer. His blood wanted him closer.

Winter crossed the street, past a fruit stall, crushing the tiny Piennolo tomatoes that had tumbled into the gutter. The door of the church was ahead of him, solid mahogany garlanded with a bright fist of flowers. He pushed at the old wood and stepped into the nave. The shade of the interior took the heat of the day away.

A woman in a violet shawl was leaving, an embroidered handkerchief clutched in her hand. As she edged out of the nave Winter caught sight of a painting, its gilt frame flanked by marble skulls. He had no idea about art but he imagined it had to be Renaissance. Bodies were ascending to Heaven, pulled into the light by angels while the Madonna and child looked on, wrapped in a swirl of blue cloth.

A noticeboard held the name of the place he had just

entered. This was the Church of Santa Maria delle Anime del Purgatorio ad Arco. The Church of Saint Mary of the Souls in Purgatory.

There were others in the church, kneeling in prayer before the altar. Winter ignored them, his attention taken by an open trapdoor at the rear of the nave. A flutter of light escaped from it, and the sound of voices, also in prayer.

He followed a set of stairs, down into a basement crypt. The space he found was a replica of the nave above, but it was thick with dust and its walls were cracked and unadorned. The air tasted stale as centuries.

A twitch of candlelight lit the room. The underground chapel was littered with bones. Winter saw skulls propped in corners. Genuine human skulls, not marble or bronze. There were flowers surrounding them, some withered, some fresh. Tacky plastic trinkets hung like rosaries. Notes had been wedged next to each skull, scrawled on scraps of lined paper or written in faded ink on squares of card decorated with cats and roses.

He glanced down. There were grilles among the flagstones. Through the gaps he saw bleached bones, piled like trash in the dark. Paupers' graves, no doubt.

Again he felt an ache in his blood.

The steady murmur of prayer filled the sepulchral gloom. A man knelt in the far corner, his eyes tightly closed as he pushed his forehead against the wall. He was rocking on his haunches, telling the contents of his heart to cold stone. A skull sat above him, encircled by sepia photographs. There was a young woman in one of the pictures, smiling into bright sunlight. Winter imagined she might have been the man's teenage sweetheart, taken by war.

He began to understand. This was a place where people prayed to the nameless departed. They should have been calling on saints or apostles or the Virgin but they had chosen to venerate the lost, all those abandoned, anonymous souls trapped in Purgatory. They prayed on behalf of these unburied bones to ease their passage into Heaven – and in return, he guessed, they asked for help in this life, or guarantees that their own loved ones had made it into Paradise. It seemed to be a mutually beneficial arrangement between the living and the dead.

There was another skull on show, one that was clearly special.

It looked almost pampered as it rested on a plump cushion. But it was broken, incomplete. The lower half was gone, leaving only the deep, concave hollows of the eyes, their shattered edges sinking into velvet. The skull wore a lace veil, just like a bride's, and it was crowned with a tiara that sparkled fitfully in the candlelight. A shrine of photographs and flowers enclosed it.

Two women knelt before the memorial. One was young, the other considerably older. The girl's grandmother, perhaps. The younger woman had her head bowed and was whispering a torrent of prayer. Winter imagined she was a bride to be, petitioning the grim remains for good fortune on her wedding day.

He took his place next to the women, the dank stone floor chilling his knees. Neither acknowledged his presence but the older one stole a glance.

Winter met the cavernous gaze of the skull. His blood surged in response, quickening at the pulses and making his heart thud beneath his shirt. Despite the cool of the crypt he felt a prickle of sweat across his chest. It coursed through the scar tissue, stinging the skin.

The more he stared at the skull, the more he lingered among these bones, the more he sensed something stir inside him. It felt like a kind of energy, unlocking itself. It was embedded in the relics, he realised, and he was drawing it into his body, as unconsciously as his lungs took oxygen from the air, or nicotine from a cigarette.

Alessandra would have explained it. Karina too. He missed their knowledge, their voices, the way they had made sense of everything, decoding the madness. They had guided him through this world and lit its shadows. He realised he felt very alone without them.

Tobias Hart had practised bone magic. That much Winter knew. And perhaps that was what he was experiencing. A muscle memory of the man he had been, nothing more. The stitch of magic that Alessandra had placed inside him was reacting to the bones. That had to be it.

And there were so many bones in this place. Old bones, to be sure, chipped and cracked, but saturated with centuries of belief. Powerful bones, Winter assumed.

He stared hard into the sockets, trying to imagine the eyes that had once filled them. All he saw were twin voids, retreating into the skull like infinite whorls of ink.

He had made glass run like water, back in that hotel room. What else was he capable of?

Winter's breathing deepened, became heavy in his mouth. There was a sweetness in his blood now. And it unsettled him, because he knew he wanted more. He could feel it, black honey in his veins.

He reached out. He had to touch the skull. The ache in his blood compelled him.

The old woman gave a cry. Winter turned and saw that she had cast a gesture against him. One tiny, sun-crinkled hand was extended, the index and little finger pointing in parallel at the ground. The sign of the horns. The traditional Neapolitan hex against anyone with the evil eye.

'*Malocchio!*' she spat, keeping her fist firm. '*Malocchio!*'

She had broken the hush of the basement. Now people were turning to look, the sound of prayer replaced by a murmur of disquiet. Winter saw the younger woman's eyes. They were wide and afraid. '*Jettatura,*' she trembled, unbelieving, as if Winter's presence had tainted everything, her wedding day included. '*Jettatura…*'

The crypt felt small and oppressive. There were too many eyes on him, not enough air. Winter rose and made for the exit, pushing past worshippers, his feet colliding with wooden boxes that rattled with still more human remains.

'*Malocchio!*' the old woman shouted, louder and braver now that he was leaving. '*Malocchio!*'

What had she sensed inside him?

Winter didn't look back. He hauled himself up the stairs, through the nave and out into the heat and clamour of the street again. Naturally he reached for a cigarette.

There was the sound of music on Via dei Tribunali. It was pounding and insistent, more rhythm than melody, overpowering the transistor radios that bled from cafés and shops. Curious, and just a little dazed from his experience in the crypt, Winter began to follow it. He had no better idea of what to do just then.

A band was playing in a nearby square, touting for coins among crumbling walls plastered with movie posters. The noise they made was driving, hypnotic, a stampede of drums and tambourines, broken by shrill whistles. A crowd had gathered around them, clapping and cheering in time.

A high sun shone through washing strung between balconies. The clothes cast pools of coloured light, turquoise and purple and lime, spotlighting a girl dancing for money, an upturned hat at her feet.

Winter watched her. She must have been eighteen or nineteen, so pale that he doubted she was a local, despite her Mediterranean looks. She wore a thin grey rag of a dress and there was a matching ribbon tied at her throat. As she danced the Tarantella, the spider dance, her long black hair was a storm, lashing in front of her eyes.

Barefoot on hot paving, the girl spun and writhed, seemingly possessed by the music. The rhythm of the drums matched her, provoked her, became even more frenzied, so forceful that Winter could feel its volley in his chest. The girl appeared to be in a state of delirium. Her hair whirled and her hips shook.

Winter's eyes went to the ribbon at her throat. It was darkening on one side. Two distinct blooms had formed, perhaps an inch apart. It had to be blood, soaking into the fabric. She must have agitated a pair of wounds with her exertions.

They were bite marks, he realised coldly. Someone had driven their teeth into her throat, and quite recently.

The drums echoed and the girl was a blur of hair.

'You like my sister, *signore*? You take her for dinner?'

Winter looked down. A teenage boy was at his side. The kid had a cocky smile and keen, bright eyes in a face bronzed and toughened by street living.

'What did you say?'

'My sister, *signore*. I introduce you. A special introduction. No charge.'

He was one of the *scugnizzo*, the urchins who thrived on their wits in this frantic city. There was an American naval insignia stitched to his fraying baseball jacket, no doubt a wartime souvenir that had been handed down – or, more plausibly, stolen.

Winter smiled, in spite of himself. 'Are you sure she's your sister?'

A flash of cola-stained teeth. 'Every girl in Naples is my sister.'

'I feel sorry for your mother.'

'What can I say? Mama loved Papa very much.'

The kid wasn't going away. He dipped a hand inside

his jacket, retrieving a stash of tattered postcards. They were hand-tinted nudes, surprisingly chaste. The models had Betty Grable haircuts, twenty years out of fashion.

'These are the best views in Naples, *signore.*'

'No thank you.'

The kid switched to another pocket. He fanned another selection of postcards. This time the models were men, equally vintage. 'Perhaps you prefer pancetta?'

'I think it's time you got lost now.'

'I can get you anything. Cigarettes. Pills. Company. Whatever you need for a good time in our beautiful city. I work for the Mayor.'

Winter nodded. 'Is that so. Well, I'll tell you what I do need, you little shit, and that's my wallet back.'

The boy was about to bolt. Winter seized him by the arm and applied just enough pressure to hurt. With a grimace the brat handed over the wallet he had so effortlessly lifted a minute earlier.

Winter slid a clutch of notes from its leather folds. 'One more thing I need…'

He moved his eyes to the dancer. Breathless now, she struck an extravagant final pose as the drums smashed to a climax. The ribbon at her throat was dark as wine.

'Information. I'm sure the Mayor would approve.'

18

The heat that had all but cremated the city finally broke, a month after Winter's arrival.

Tonight he was glad of his jacket, even if it was summer linen. The wind skimming the water was keen, strong enough to slap the tide against the timber posts that staked the harbourside. As the August sky darkened he watched as squat tugboats manoeuvred sturdier ships through the network of jetties and piers. International vessels filled the docks, come to collect or disgorge their cargo. Horns blared, flags stirred and wet shanks of rope smacked against rust-scarred hulls.

This port was the engine of Naples, an ugly, functional stretch that stank of tar and salt. There was little casual conversation to be heard among these wharves. Conversation required questions and questions were inadvisable. The black economy was greased with a sense of discretion that would shame Whitehall.

Winter checked his watch. He had bought it from a street vendor on Via dei Tribunali, a belated replacement for the one he had left in that hotel in Pest, the night he had met Alessandra. It was a cheap, practical thing and he was pleased to find it was still ticking.

The hour hand teased ten o'clock. 'Almost time.'

The man at the water's edge grunted. It was the most vocal he had been all evening.

'The weather's certainly changed,' said Winter, lightly.

Another grunt, even less engaged than the last.

'It's almost British, this weather. Could be Portsmouth.'

The Italian known as Luca kept his eyes on the sea. Black curls, fashionably long but thinning, strayed over the collar of his leather blouson. He tried to stand like a much younger man but the paunch and the twist in his spine betrayed him. Still, Winter imagined he could hold his own in a fight. He had the grizzled aura of a fast, dirty brawler, all knuckles and temper.

The two of them had been on lookout duty for an hour now. It was the outer circle of trust for any gang, but in the Camorra even this kind of casual employment had a gleam of prestige. Such a position was proof you had won a certain acceptance in the brotherhood. Perhaps you could graduate to hired muscle, if your face and fists found favour. The turnover was high, after all.

Luca maintained his silence for another minute. And then, clearing his throat with a swill of phlegm, he grudgingly formed a sentence.

'Sometimes they come from the sea.'

There was a blue spark of lightning, at the far edge of the bay. It briefly illuminated the hump of Vesuvius.

'Who do?' asked Winter.

Another flash split the clouds. The outline of Capri was momentarily defined.

He pressed the question. 'You mean the police?'

Luca shook his head, watching the neon-bright twitch of light on the horizon. His next words were given as reluctantly as the last.

'Not the police. This city has a different law.'

And with that the Italian fell back into silence. To Winter it didn't feel quite the same as before. This was heavier. This was the silence of something withheld.

His eyes were drawn to the man's hand. It was holding a silver chain, the links entwined around his scabbed knuckles. A skinny crucifix dangled below the palm. A moment later Luca closed his fist around it, perhaps embarrassed that it had been seen.

The truck arrived promptly at ten o'clock. Jack Creadley would have approved. In Winter's experience criminal activity was the most punctual in the world.

The vehicle rolled across the quayside, headlights playing over greasy tarmac flecked with cigarette stubs. As the engine cut two men stepped from the cab, acknowledging Winter and Luca with sharp, succinct nods.

'Bring the goods,' said the shorter of the men, flexing his leather-gloved hands in a bid to shake driver's cramp. The other man flanked him, his face partially obscured by the brim of a fisherman's cap. Winter imagined he was the muscle, though both men had a solid physical presence that suggested the demarcation of duty might not be so clear.

They walked to the back of the truck. There was rain in the air now, fine as thread. It picked at the oil that pooled beneath their feet, caught in the pitted tarmac. Winter glanced at the sky. The clouds had darkened against nightfall. Now they were the colour of the sea.

The man in the gloves unlocked the rear doors with a busy clatter of keys. Winter peered into the back and saw three wooden freight containers. The lids were nailed shut and labelled with shipping instructions. The top crate had a cargo manifest attached, encased in plastic. Forged, no doubt. It was fairly obvious the truck's contents had bypassed customs completely.

Winter and Luca heaved the first of the crates from the pile. It was lighter than Winter was expecting, surprising his muscles. Some kind of contraband, he assumed. Cigarettes, perhaps. That would explain the weight. The thought left him with an itch for a Woodbine.

They carried the crate to a scruffy, half-lit warehouse, set back from the edge of the quay. Winter sensed the eyes of the man in the cap scrutinising him as he walked. Luca was clearly a known quantity to the Camorra, a fixture in the city's shadows. As a newcomer Winter was more of a risk, for all that he had played up his underworld connections in London. A manageable risk, to be sure. If the Camorra had entertained serious suspicions they would have removed him from Naples, and permanently so.

The crate hit the floor of the warehouse, indistinguishable from the other hammered-down boxes that filled the building. Bare bulbs hovered over these stacks of cargo, suspended on lengths of flex and swaying as the wind entered with the men. The light they gave was sketchy and Winter had to squint to see the details stencilled on the surrounding freight. He read the names of foreign ports – Rotterdam, Jakarta, Singapore – and hyphenated chains of numbers, meaningless to him.

Looking up, he saw the warehouse had two tiers. There was an upper gallery, accessible by a steep flight of wooden steps, more a glorified ladder than a staircase. He imagined this area had to be some kind of administrative space. He certainly couldn't imagine anyone hauling crates up there. The gallery was lined with windows, a number of them cracked. They held the night in their frames, the glass dingy and speckled with rain.

Winter and Luca returned to the truck, collecting the next of the crates. The other two men also carried a crate between them. As the four of them shuffled back to the building Winter noticed that the trajectory of the rain had changed. Now it was aimed at the warehouse, slanting against its walls. He could feel its touch on his face, cold and intent. The odd thing was the direction of the wind hadn't shifted at all. If anything the rain was straining against it.

They placed the last of the boxes on the floor, slamming up dust. Luca picked a splinter from his thumb and once again Winter saw the crucifix in his hand, catching the light from an overhead bulb.

The man in the gloves pulled a billfold from his jeans. He began to count through a fistful of grubby lira.

'And there were no questions?' he asked. 'No officials came?'

'No one,' said Winter, receiving his half of the cut.

The rain had hardened. It was insistent against the high ceiling of the warehouse, pecking at the shadowed timber.

'All clean, no problem,' agreed Luca, pocketing the remaining half.

'You will stay here,' instructed the man in the cap. 'At six o'clock the crew of the *Ananke* will arrive. They will take the crates. You will take the money. The money will come to us. Intact, you understand?'

'Of course,' said Winter, taking care to filter the disdain from his voice.

The gloom of the warehouse quivered like firelight. The hanging bulbs had momentarily dimmed. Winter glanced at the nearest light fitting. A solitary bead of rain slid the length of the flex. It crawled to the bulb and clung to the glass, trembling before it finally struck the floor.

'Do we get to know what's in the crates?'

The man in the cap eyed him, suspicion moving beneath his skin. 'I thought you had experience?'

'Sorry. I'm just curious.'

The man unzipped his jacket. A semi-automatic crouched in a holster, strapped against his chest. 'This is how we cure curiosity.'

Winter tried an appeasing smile. 'Home remedies are always best.'

Rain cascaded from the other lights. It raced down the undulating cables to spatter the floorboards, filling the warehouse with a terse, drumming rhythm. The bulbs fizzled as water met electricity. In seconds every last light had died. The tapping of the rain persisted.

Winter lifted his eyes. The upper tier of the building was dark now. A solid, emphatic dark. The windows that lined the gallery were impossible to make out. There was only shadow there and it was absolute.

He brought his eyes down again. The lower tier retained just enough illumination to see by. The warehouse doors had been left open, allowing a finger of light from the quayside, sodium-yellow and bristling with vapour.

The gloved man turned to his colleague. 'A fuse has blown. We need to fix the lights.'

There was a sound from the upper tier. A violent sound, like a door slamming in the wind. It jolted Winter, made a blade of his nerves.

The man in the cap eased his gun from its holster. The gloved man slid his own weapon from a jeans pocket. Their eyes tightened, searching for any hint of movement upstairs.

'I'll check it out,' said the gloved man. His counterpart nodded.

The Camorrista climbed to the gallery, gun in hand. He moved stiffly, his steps cautious. Winter saw him pause at the top of the stairs before entering the darkness. Then he was gone from sight.

The dead bulbs swung in perfect synchronisation. Their shadows rotated and merged.

Winter decided it was time to arm himself too. He

reached for his gun. The man in the cap noted this and nodded.

The rain's rhythm quickened on the floorboards. *Tap-tap. Tap-tap. Tap-tap.*

There was a cry from the upper tier, out of the dark. A broken cry, severed before it had a chance to be a scream.

Winter released the safety catch. There was sweat on the metal.

The body thudded to the ground in a shudder of dust. 'Christ...'

Winter stared at what was left of the man. The angle of the fall had bent the limbs into a haphazard heap. The head lay twisted, exposing a savage gash across the throat, deep enough to reveal the epiglottis. The flap of cartilage glistened beneath mucus and muscle. Blood spouted from the ruptured jugular even as life faded from the man's eyes.

This wasn't the plan, thought Winter. *This wasn't the agreement.*

Luca clutched his tiny cross, the chain scoring his skin. He was whispering what had to be a prayer, low and urgent.

The man in the cap moved forward. Winter reached for his elbow, trying to pull him back, but the remaining Camorrista was determined.

'Show yourself, you animal!' he shouted into the dark. 'A true man kills in the light!'

He began to climb the ladder, the wood creaking beneath his boots. 'Come on, you godless filth! Show me your face!'

Tap-tap. Tap-tap. Tap-tap. The rain echoed among the crates, nearly concealing another sound: the click of a fingernail against a hard wooden surface. It originated from somewhere inside the gallery. The rhythm was subtly altering, adjusting, switching to the pace of a heartbeat.

The man in the cap came to the top of the stairs. Now he faced the bank of shadow. His stance was full of pride and machismo, the gun jutting ahead of him.

'I said show me your face! Or has the grave made you ugly?'

This time Winter glimpsed the shape that took him. He had a fleeting impression of teeth and hands. A blur of something predatory, primal.

A gunshot joined with a scream.

More gunshots. Louder and closer, cracking the air at Winter's side. Luca had a snub-nosed revolver in his hand and was firing indiscriminately at the gallery, the shots panicked and wild.

The flashes of gunfire strobed the darkness, creating a stuttering tableau. The Camorrista was held in the jaws of another man, anchored by the throat. The body swung, helpless, the strip of flesh that was caught in its assailant's teeth tearing to breaking point. The cap fell and then its owner tumbled after it. The body rolled across the floorboards, more a wound than a man now. Behind it a figure stepped back into shadow.

Luca fired again, the bullet striking a joist and scraping the roof.

'Put your gun down!' Winter hissed.

The gun squeezed out another shot, directionless as the last. Winter took hold of Luca's arm and wrenched it down.

'Stop bloody firing!'

The Italian's eyes were huge with fear, the pupils fit to burst. 'This is my city! I know what these things are!'

'You need to stop firing!'

'They will kill us!'

Luca fought Winter's grip, trying to lift the weapon. He had leathery, obstinate old muscles but Winter kept the gun arm in a lockhold.

'Listen to me. Listen to me! We need to go upstairs.'

Luca was so thrown by this statement that he stopped struggling. 'Are you crazy?'

'If you don't come upstairs with me right now, you will die.'

'*Maniaco!*'

'I've made a deal. They won't kill me. If we're lucky they won't kill you.'

Luca moved back, his eyes narrowing. When he spoke there was disgust in his voice. 'You've made a deal? With them?'

Winter nodded. 'Follow me, Luca, and we'll both walk out of here.'

He tossed his gun away. Then he turned, spreading his hands in a show of appeasement to whatever waited in the upper tier. He glanced back at Luca, encouraging him to drop his gun as well. A moment later the snub-nosed revolver smacked the floor. It had doubtlessly been emptied of bullets in any case.

248

The two of them climbed the stairs, Winter leading the way. As they entered the gallery they stepped over the bloodied body of the second Camorrista. He was still alive, or at least on the very edge of life, his eyes pleading for an ending.

The rain had intensified against the warehouse. Winter could hear it striking glass, though he couldn't see the windows it battered.

A man waited in the dark, the details of his presence revealing themselves as Winter and Luca approached. They saw gleaming shoes, a black suit and a tie stabbed with a silver pin. He was wiping a gob of blood from a trim beard, almost preening as he did so.

'We have an agreement,' said Winter, with confidence.

The man shrugged, offering only a red smear of a smile. And then he lunged.

Winter blocked a fist. Then he took a hook punch to the jaw. The impact flung him against a table, scattering tools and papers. His face burned from the blow, bone-deep.

The man in the suit advanced, baring his lips, declaring his teeth. The canines were gleaming spikes, grotesquely extended. Spittle and blood shone on the enamel.

Winter caught sight of a long, flat-blade screwdriver. It had rolled alongside him. He snatched it from the table and went for the man's heart.

The pair of them barrelled backwards, toppling a set of stools. Winter kneed his opponent in the crotch, eliciting a raw, wounded groan. A thought flashed through his head.

Good. Something in common with these undead bastards, at least.

Winter was on top now. He pressed his advantage, urging the screwdriver closer, targeting the heart.

Killing this man would change the entire plan. But he had no choice. He had seen how the others had died.

Matching him, the man seized his wrist, forcing the tool away, making it shake in the air. Their muscles locked, straining in stalemate.

Lightning lit the harbour, flaring through the tall windows that lined the upper floor. Winter turned, just a fraction. In that moment of all-encompassing brightness he saw the pattern of the rain as it hit the glass. It was dark against the panes, narrow and focused. A thousand insistent pellets, forming themselves into silhouettes.

The rain had taken the shape of men. Each one filled a frame.

The windows shattered. Winter shielded his eyes. When he looked again there were three figures standing among the strewn glass, the wind from the docks gusting around them. They had matching suits, handsomely cut, and they faced him, confident as knives.

'*Signore,*' said their obvious leader.

Winter stared at the man. He had seen the stern mouth and tall, imposing temples before, captured in a courtroom sketch.

The newcomer spoke again, insistent now. '*Signore,* if you please.'

Winter tossed the screwdriver to the floor. He rose to his feet, keeping his eyes on the man.

Was this Don Zerbinati himself? If it was, he had shed the years. The hair was a deep black and glistened with wax. The moustache was gone while the olive skin was unlined, the lips a little fuller than Winter remembered from the picture. He looked to be in his early twenties, at most. Did these creatures possess that power? Could they actually make themselves young again? Alessandra would have known.

'Salvatore!' snapped the man. Winter's opponent gathered himself, adjusting his jacket, righting his tie.

'The crates are here,' said Winter, attempting to steady his breath. 'Just as I told your contact. The Camorra are doing business with the crew of the SS *Ananke*. They're coming at six.'

The man he assumed to be Zerbinati nodded, his eyes sweeping the warehouse. 'Your information was useful. I choose not to claim your throat tonight. A deal, my friend?'

Winter dabbed at his split lip. He saw Zerbinati eyeing the blood, his tongue flickering at the edge of his teeth. 'I wasn't expecting you or your men. That wasn't the arrangement.'

'We have a new arrangement, Englishman. One where you get to live. Savour it. It's sweet.'

The newcomer's gaze settled on Luca. 'I've spared you before, haven't I?'

'Yes, Signore Zerbinati.' The Italian struggled to keep eye contact. The cross was concealed in his hand, the chain gathered against his palm.

'Do you remember I told you to convey a message?

A warning to your brothers? To give them word that our rule of this city was total and not to be challenged?'

Sweat gathered on Luca's scalp. 'I told them, Signore Zerbinati. I swear by the Virgin, I told them.'

Zerbinati regarded the bodies of the Camorristi. 'You were clearly not as persuasive as I wished. I wonder why I even spared you.'

'Signore Zerbinati, the Camorra are proud…'

'The Camorra are dead. Was it a proud death?'

Luca's mouth opened, wordless. Zerbinati closed the space between them.

'I asked you, was it a proud death? Did you witness it?'

Luca nodded, then vigorously shook his head, desperate to give the right response. 'It was dark… I saw nothing…'

Zerbinati took another, final step. 'But you would have heard if they screamed? Did they scream like children, these proud Camorra? Or did they die like men?'

'They screamed…'

'Of course they screamed. As you all scream. You are all children to us. Your lives are soft and warm and brief. It's your tragedy that you will never be men.'

Luca raised the cross. It seemed pitiably small between his thick, weathered fingers.

Confronted by the sight of the crucifix, Zerbinati flung his hand against his face. The gesture was mocking, theatrical.

'No! Not the pendant! Spare me the pendant! It burns!'

He lowered his hand, a smirk on his lips. 'Or would you call it a necklace?'

252

Luca kept the cross steady in his fist, though his arm was trembling. He thrust the trinket at the vampire, channelling every ounce of his faith.

Zerbinati casually took the cross from his hand. 'Is this pewter? Are you threatening me with pewter? What, you can't afford silver?' He turned to the other men. 'Can you believe this guy? It's an insult! Does he think I'm some lower-caste tomb rat?'

There was an amused murmur from the shadows.

Luca stared as the vampire revolved the cross. The faith had gone from his eyes, replaced by pure apprehension.

'You seem to have trouble hearing my questions,' observed Zerbinati. 'So I shall ask again, and I shall keep it simple. Is this pewter?'

Luca stayed silent. Zerbinati held the cross in front of his face, letting it twirl and twist on the chain. 'Taste it for me.'

The Italian's eyes narrowed, uncomprehending.

'I said taste it!'

Zerbinati crammed the cross into Luca's mouth. Then he clamped a hand to the man's face, holding it there as Luca frothed against his palm, choking on the talisman.

'He's with me,' said Winter, quickly. 'You don't need to do this.'

Zerbinati ignored him. He kept his hand in place, his grip tightening, forcing the cross into Luca's throat until the tongue spasmed and the neck muscles hardened in protest. Luca fought for air, gagging as the reflex action hauled the crucifix into his windpipe.

'Spare him,' said Winter. 'Come on.'

Zerbinati removed his fingers. He observed Luca for a moment. And then he smacked his hand upwards, swatting the Italian down the stairs. Luca landed in a broken heap.

'Show me the cargo,' said Zerbinati.

Winter led the way down the steps, the four men following. He was the only one who cast a shadow on the warehouse floor.

Luca stared at him as he stepped past. His eyes were accusing, even as the whites darkened with burst blood vessels. Winter looked away but the guilt found him.

They came to the crates. Zerbinati studied the shipping manifest then put his nails to the box on top. Winter saw them elongate, tapering like diamonds. They scored through the lid, spraying splinters and wood dust.

The lid was flung aside. Inside the crate were stacks of white cartons, only differentiated by the chains of numbers stamped upon them. They had the bland, practical look of pharmaceutical goods.

Zerbinati opened the nearest carton, sliding a sheet of foil from the card container. It held eight caplets, each containing a crimson fluid. Winter could only imagine it was blood.

Zerbinati cracked the caplet with his teeth. He let the fluid trickle on his tongue. His lips crinkled. He was clearly unimpressed.

'Chemical swill,' he declared. 'No connoisseur would be satisfied.'

'I imagine it's not intended for connoisseurs,' said Winter, hoping to tease some detail on the contents of the crates.

Zerbinati gave him an austere look, his face set at a regal tilt. 'A true connoisseur would kill for their thirst. This substitute is for cowards. Those we have turned who have no stomach for claiming a throat. They're weak, but their ache is strong, like an animal's need.'

'Are there many of them, these cowards?'

'Believe me, it's an expanding market. There's always a thirst to be satisfied. And there's always *mucho scharole* to be made from a craving.' Zerbinati kissed the tips of his fingers, a gold ring in the shape of a salamander glinting in the half-light.

'Capitalism in action. No wonder the Camorra wanted a piece of it.'

'We control the flow of Scarlatto in the Mediterranean. We won't tolerate competition. The Camorra filth will be reminded of this, yet again. But you are so full of opinions, Englishman...'

Winter met the undead gaze. 'Think of it as a job interview. It would be an honour to serve you, Don Zerbinati. I trust there's a position going?'

The man Winter had assumed to be Don Zerbinati reacted with surprise. A surprise that became delight. He gave a sting of a smile, tight and sharp.

'Allow me to correct you, my friend. I am Cesare Zerbinati. Son and heir.'

19

The next evening Winter kept an appointment at La Salamandra. The club was located in Chiaia, among the march of nightlife that met the shoreline in the shadow of the hills. It was an affluent, luminous part of Naples, where the elite of the new jet age congregated, drawn like gilded insects to the throb and glitter of the city.

He pushed through the doors. The pair of gem-studded salamanders etched on the glass shimmered as they caught the last of the day's light. The hat-check girl smiled, though it had the look of professional obligation, and a set of stairs brought him to the blue-smoke haze of the dance floor. The sound of Astrud Gilberto played among the palms and mirrors, the louche thump of bossa nova soundtracking the black-skirted waitresses walking trays of drinks to patrons.

Winter cut through the dancing couples, breathing in a potent fug of perfume, cologne and perspiration. Bracelets and belly-chains jangled around him, the girls embracing the rhythm. The men tried to match them but their high-buttoned suits left them looking stiff and cautious.

Cesare Zerbinati sat at a table in the corner. It was the only booth in the room not to be surrounded by mirrors. Two chic, assured women stood up and left as Winter approached, as if by prior agreement. They slid past him, leaving no shadows on the lacquered floor. He could feel his skin cool in their presence, like the chill of a whiskey tumbler loaded with ice.

'My brides,' said Cesare, as Winter joined him.

There was a beat as Winter considered a diplomatic response. 'Then you're a lucky man. Twice over.'

Cesare broke into an unexpectedly impish grin. He reclined against the velvet-lined seat, a monarch supremely confident in his low-lit kingdom. Two of his men were positioned some distance away. 'I'm kidding you, Englishman. Can you imagine the misery? The jealousy? The demands? The movies are useful propaganda for my kind but you mustn't take their lies too seriously.'

'I'll try to remember that.'

'Those girls are my daughters.'

Winter nodded blankly, unsure if this was another joke.

'So tell me,' said Cesare, plucking an olive from a dish. 'What's your name?'

'Anthony Prestwick.'

The olive split between the immaculate teeth. 'Names are such easy currency in Naples. Can you prove who you are?'

Winter took the passport from his pocket, the one the service had prepared for the mission in Budapest.

'I've been working with the Creadley Gang in London. Jack Creadley.'

'Wow.'

'You've heard of him?'

Cesare flipped through the pale blue pages. 'No. Should I have?'

'In my city he had a certain notoriety.'

'Alas his legend has yet to reach this city.' The shreds of the olive turned on Cesare's tongue. 'Why do you use the past tense for this man?'

'He's dead now.' Winter presented this as a flat fact.

'Did you kill him?'

Winter found himself smiling at the suggestion. 'No. No, of course I didn't kill him.'

Cesare lingered on Winter's photograph, the rather glum portrait taken in a Piccadilly Circus photo booth, his face as characterless as he could make it, another suburban businessman caught in the unforgiving flash. 'Ambition is nothing to be embarrassed by. I might even applaud it. Tell me, what do you do?'

'I tend to be useful.'

'What use would I have for you?'

Winter shrugged. 'I can handle myself. And a gun. Well, most things, really. Anything that comes to hand.'

Cesare nodded, closing and returning the passport, the dance-floor light catching the coiling gold of his salamander ring. 'I saw how you dealt with Salvatore, back in the warehouse. A screwdriver, of all things. Were you confident you could kill him, my Salvatore?'

'I can kill anybody, circumstances permitting.'

'Could you kill me?'

The question hung between them, the thump of the music seeming louder than before.

Winter didn't flinch. 'Circumstances permitting. But I must think of my job prospects.'

Cesare beamed, though the smile was given to the waitress leaning in to collect the abandoned glasses. '*Grazie*,' he said, his gaze lingering as she left the table.

He met Winter's eyes once more. The charm was gone from his face.

'I can do more than kill you, Mr Prestwick. I can turn you, claim your throat, take your shadow. I can make you understand that this shallow thing you have now is only the briefest echo of a true life. I can introduce you to the great, sweet thirst. And once you have tasted blood, and want to taste so much more in the endless years to come, I can steal that gift back, with a stake or a blade, and kill you so that it really hurts.'

Winter nodded respectfully. 'You're a powerful man, Signore Zerbinati. I imagine your father must be very proud.'

Cesare scrutinised Winter's face, searching for any ghost of a smile, any hint that the last sentence had been less than sincere. 'And what would you know of my father, Englishman?'

'He's the reason I came to Naples.'

Cesare was curious now. 'Tell me what you mean.'

'Power is something I respect. Clearly you have it. I can

see that. But I didn't hear stories about you, Cesare. I never found myself wondering if you were real or just a rumour that could make even London's gangland shit itself. It was your father they spoke about in my city. Not you. Maybe you've never heard of Jack Creadley. Fair enough. But I'm pretty certain the late Jack Creadley had never heard of you, either. Frankly you're not the stuff of legend.'

For a moment Winter wondered if he had gone too far with the provocation. He had been trained to evaluate facial response – to judge if a tightening of the lips or a muscle moving beneath the skin might be a cue for retaliation. Cesare's composure was intact but there was something brittle and defensive in his eyes, something he couldn't quite conceal. Winter knew he had chanced upon a faultline.

'You came to this city to stand closer to power,' observed Cesare. 'To stand closer to my father?'

'I had to get out of London. They're cracking down on the gangs. No place for a career. There's opportunity here in Naples.'

'You betrayed three men. To impress me. To prove your allegiance. They died in that warehouse because of you.'

This was harder for Winter to internalise. But he managed it.

'Some people are born to be collateral.'

Cesare reached for another plump olive. 'You impress me, Mr Prestwick. You can fight. You have ambition. And most of all you're unafraid. It's a quality I rarely encounter. You're arrogant, too, but I can beat that out of you, if need be.'

'So I have a job?'

'I'm prepared to see how useful you can be. Report here to Salvatore tomorrow morning. There will be work for you in my city, Englishman, of that you can be assured. One day you may even be the stuff of legend.'

Winter extended a hand across the table. Cesare took it, and his skin felt cool and smooth as a stone beneath water.

'I'm grateful,' said Winter. 'I appreciate your faith in me.'

'It's not faith. Faith is what your kind use to kill mine. I make investments.'

With a nod Cesare indicated that the interview was concluded.

Winter rose from his seat, the mutual silence between the men as much a seal on the deal as the handshake. He turned and began to cross the dance floor, threading between the couples as the beat of the music pulsed through his shoes. Distracted, he nearly collided with a waitress as she made her way to the tables. Winter spun, dodging the cocktail tray in her hands. As she steadied the tall glasses the girl offered a gap-toothed grin.

'I never had you down as a dancer, mate.'

He was looking at Libby Cracknell.

Winter kept his expression neutral, though he knew his face had already betrayed him. Cesare's men had them in their line of sight. Cesare too, potentially. He stole a glance at the corner tables. The glare of the overhead lights and the nicotine veil of the room gave them a fractional cover. He edged behind a dancing couple, grateful for the man's ungainly moves.

262

'What are you doing?' he demanded, keeping his voice as low as he could against the syncopated thud.

Libby took a square of cloth from her blouse pocket. She dipped it in a glass of mineral water then attended to an imaginary spill on Winter's jacket.

'Tidying up. You can't be too careful with a Brandy Alexander. It's the crème de cacao. Tends to stain.'

'Why are you here? I told you to get back to London.'

Libby pressed the cloth against his chest, kneading the fabric. 'I went back to London.'

'I don't need your help.'

'That's not why I'm here.'

'I'm not going back for a debrief. I told you to tell that to Faulkner.'

'I told him.'

'Get out of Naples,' Winter hissed.

One of Cesare's men had broken from the wall at the far end of the dance floor. He was walking towards them.

'Make a pass at me,' said Libby, urgently. 'Clumsier the better. Do it now.'

Winter leaned in, one hand reaching for her hip. She delivered a slap to his face, authentically hard.

'*Inglese*,' she said to Cesare's man, who was already smiling. 'I know his type.'

The lackey nodded in sympathy to Winter, as if she wasn't there. 'Don't waste your time, *signore*. This one goes with no man.'

'So I see.'

Winter walked away, his cheek still smarting and

his thoughts furious. Damn the girl for being here. Her presence could risk everything, compromise the plan he had set in motion, a plan tailored to his involvement alone. Was she keeping a watch on him for London? No, he was an incidental detail now. She was here, in this club, undercover. Faulkner had assigned her to investigate Zerbinati. The Russians were chasing the ghosts of Operation Paragon. Cracknell was a countermeasure.

Reaching the edge of the dance floor he glanced over his shoulder as casually as he could. Libby was watching him leave. Their eyes locked, only for a second. Her gaze was hard and determined and the chill of it unsettled him. It was as if he had caught her with the mask gone.

Winter had seen that look before, he realised. In Normandy, just before dawn, as she had stood over that undead creature, a makeshift stake in her hands. She had killed with those eyes.

20

Tiring of the bell, Salvatore put his heel to the door. The impact of the boot splintered wood and sent flakes of paint to the pavement. The door, already precarious, swung inwards on rust-eaten hinges, its lock shattered.

'Benedetta!' he called into the hot gloom of the house. 'Are you home?'

Winter glanced at the street, feeling the crush of buildings in this skyless corner of the Quartieri Spagnoli. A crowd had assembled around them. Old women, their faces tanned and creased like Bible bindings, baskets of ham and fish in their arms. Teenage boys, some shirtless, taking a crack at macho stances but keeping a cautious distance just the same. Everyone watching clearly knew who they were, the power they represented.

Two men had come to this neighbourhood. Only one of them threw a shadow across the sun-scorched tarmac. No wonder these people were wary. Winter could sense a crackle of emotions in the crowd. Fear, resentment and an obvious fascination, even from the onlookers who held their sculpted Madonnas and murmured prayers of protection.

Salvatore entered the hallway. 'Benedetta!' he cried again. There was still no reply from inside the house.

Winter followed him in, grateful to escape the throng. He imagined it must have amused Cesare to pair the two of them together, given their confrontation in the warehouse. But then Cesare struck him as someone who'd trap two wasps in an upturned glass out of pure, malevolent boredom. Salvatore was far from easy company – any small talk between them felt spiky and sour – but a fortnight had passed without them trying to kill one another. That had to count as reasonably convivial.

The golden salamander was on his finger, as it had been for the last few days. All the Shadowless wore them – at least those closest to the inner circle – and it had given Winter a certain satisfaction to slide the ring over his knuckle. It had made him feel just that bit nearer to Don Zerbinati, though the leader of *I Senz'Ombr* remained elusive, off-limits even as a subject for conversation, as Winter had soon learned.

That bullet would need to wait.

Salvatore called again, a darkly playful edge to his voice now. 'Benedetta! Are you thirsty, pretty girl?'

The hallway was narrow and dominated by a convex mirror, the pregnant bulge of the glass surrounded by gilt angels. There was dust on the mirror's surface and more dust in the votive niches of the wall, where potted candles had burned away to their wicks, leaving only smears of wax. A clock hung above them, the dogged shudder of its second hand the only sound in the house.

Tick. Tick.

It was stifling in this cramped, half-lit space and Winter was aware he was sweating. There was something oppressive about the concentrated heat and hush and stillness. Something oddly unnerving, too. This little home felt wounded.

'Benedetta! I know you're here, girl!'

Salvatore passed by the mirror. As ever he left no reflection. Winter glanced at the glass, as if trying to catch the secret of a magic trick. As he did so he noticed a faint handprint in the dust. It was a child's hand, and it had trailed down the mirror, as if dragged from it.

A room waited. The door was closed. Salvatore twisted the handle.

'Don't hide from me, *bella*!'

The carcass of the dog was the first thing Winter saw.

The animal lay on the threadbare carpet. Its throat was torn. The gash went deep and blood matted the clumps of fur that remained. The dog's eyes were wide and still, its legs rigid. It stank like spoilt meat.

Winter spotted the girl next.

She was harder to see – the curtains in the room were pulled against the sun – but her body was wrapped in a rug and lay on a lumpen sofa pushed into the furthest corner. Her face was lost beneath a heap of black hair.

Salvatore walked towards the body. He was about to speak when Winter put a hand to his sleeve. Salvatore shrugged and let Winter approach the sofa before him.

One of the girl's arms had fallen free of the rug. Her nails scraped the carpet, long and tattered at the tips. The fingers were soiled with blood, dried to a dark brown.

Winter lifted the tangle of hair away. Her throat was also bloodied. A pair of parallel scabs marked the side of the neck. They had recently been agitated, judging by how angry the wounds were.

To his surprise Winter saw she was still breathing. He watched the swell and fall of her throat. And then his eyes moved to her face and he realised he had seen this girl before. It was the Tarantella dancer from the street. The one in the grey dress and the ribbon that had barely concealed these terrible lesions.

There was a crusting of blood around her mouth.

'Smile for me, Benedetta!' said Salvatore, bullyingly upbeat.

Her eyes reacted to the sound of his voice, shifting beneath the lids. The lashes parted. Benedetta looked up, flinching at either the minimal light in the room or Salvatore's presence.

She looked like she wanted to stay in dreams.

'Good girl,' said Salvatore, encouragingly. 'Good baby girl.'

The crust of blood broke as her lips opened. She whimpered, the sound barely loud enough to leave her mouth. And then she found her voice, even if she couldn't find words. With a sudden, agonised cry seized from her lungs she put her hands to her own throat. Her fingers clawed at the scabs, the movement frenzied and desperate.

Winter took her by the wrists. 'Hey, it's okay. Listen to me. It's okay.'

She fought his grip, determined to bring her fingers to her mouth. Her tongue was extended now, quivering between the teeth, and Winter realised she was attempting to lap her own blood, the blood she had scratched from the wound. Her hunger was terrifying.

He stared at the coagulated blood on her chin. There was animal fur caught in the dark streaks. She must have killed the dog, trying to sate this craving.

Queasy in the heat of the room, he turned to Salvatore. 'We need to get this girl to a hospital.'

Salvatore laughed. 'She's no problem.'

'I'm telling you we need to take her away from this place.'

'Relax. She just needs a fix.'

Salvatore had taken a packet of Scarlatto from his pocket. He broke three of the caplets from the foil and let them roll on his palm. The crimson fluid turned inside the tiny plastic shells.

He put them in front of the girl. 'Here you go, *bella* baby. Sweet, yes?'

Benedetta's eyes widened at the sight of the caplets. She made a soft, imploring sound. Winter still had hold of her wrists and could feel her muscles relax, no longer reaching for her throat. A moment later they flexed again, trying to push her arms closer to the red pills.

'You want these?' teased Salvatore. '*Molto Scarlatto per bella?*'

269

She was crying now. Crying with the pain of pure thirst.

Salvatore snatched the pills away, closing his fist around them. 'You owe us *molti soldi*. You cry because you are broke? You are always broke, little dancer.'

Winter was sickened by all of this. 'Give her the pills, for God's sake. Give her the pills or get her to a hospital. She needs help.'

'For God's sake?' Salvatore was openly contemptuous. 'You don't impress me as a businessman, *signore*.'

Winter watched as the girl snatched at the air. This was a business, that much was clear. The Shadowless had a neat little operation here in Naples. Claim a throat, pass on the blood lust, spread the thirst. Satisfy that craving with the chemical fix of Scarlatto, because no one in their right mind wanted to murder or maim for the real thing. Once they were hooked they would have no choice but to pay for it; unchecked, the urge would burn the sanity from their minds. And if they did put their teeth into flesh they were simply creating more victims, more customers, more demand, *more business*.

Salvatore opened his hand, revealing the caplets again to Benedetta. 'But I like your dancing, princess of the streets. I want you to dance some more in the sun. Please the people. So I give you a gift, just this once. Get me the money by next week. And I give you more of these.'

He let the pills drop into her mouth. She gulped them down, nearly choking.

Winter looked away. His eyes fell on a framed

photograph, mounted on a side table. A family portrait in hand-tinted colour. Benedetta, her parents, a grandmother and two younger children, all rather serious. A thought occurred to him then. A girl her age wouldn't live alone, not in this city.

He remembered the child's handprint on the mirror. The one that looked as though it had been torn away.

Salvatore had also seen the photograph. A smile had just broken on his face and it was one the bastard clearly relished.

'Shall we look upstairs, *signore*?'

In the small, quiet house the clock in the hall persisted.

The days that followed paid well but needed to be rinsed off each night with a fierce shower. The money was an improvement on Jack Creadley's wages – a fat packet of virgin lira rather than a wrinkled roll of ten-shilling notes – but the work left Winter feeling just as stained beneath the skin as his time in the London underworld.

In Santa Lucia he had stood there as Salvatore repeatedly put a fist to the face of a hotel manager, persuading him of the benefits of insurance. Winter had watched as blood hit the wall, grateful that his presence, and the simple threat of doubling the violence, was enough. The next day, in Vomero, an elderly café owner greeted them with too many teeth. He kept smiling even as he emptied his own till with shaking hands. The espressos were on the house. Winter had sipped his coffee as the voice of

271

Tony Bennett drifted from the wall-mounted speaker, reminding them that this was 'The Good Life'.

Salvatore walked the city with an easy confidence, opening any door he wished. The women of the brothel on Via Terracina were clearly terrified of him, even as he danced with them across the cracked tiles of their kitchen, forcing sweet wine to their mouths until it ran down their dresses. Beneath the underpass of Via Emanuele Gianturco he dispensed American cigarettes to a giggling swarm of boys. They raced behind him, thrilled and fascinated by his lack of a shadow. *Vampiro! Vampiro! I Senz'Ombr!*

In a harbourside bar in Centro Storico Winter had found himself adding muscle to a territorial dispute with representatives of the Camorra. Salvatore had flung one of the men against a jukebox, cracking the glass and sending the needle screeching across the vinyl. Then he had plunged his teeth into the man's face, wrenching ribbons of skin from the cheek until a chink of bone was exposed. Somehow the fine suit he wore made Salvatore seem even more feral as he reared over the Camorrista, a wet mess of blood on his lips. He had smiled then, sated and triumphant, as if this truly was 'The Good Life'.

Each night Winter returned to his hotel and exorcised himself beneath the showerhead until his flesh stung and steam filled the tiny bathroom.

Some nights, as the bay glittered, he would practise magic into the early hours. He felt the itch of it and he was curious to see what he might be capable of. So far he had failed to replicate the stunt with the glass – maybe he was trying too hard, he imagined; it had just *happened* before, like the physics of a dream, the ones you never questioned – but one night a liquid very like ink had dripped from his fingers, trembling through the pores until it spattered yesterday's newspaper. As it soaked through the newsprint pages it pierced them, like the tip of a knife.

He had felt a rush in his blood as he watched that happen.

Don Zerbinati was another, more insistent itch. Yes, Winter had embedded himself in Naples, in the heart of Zerbinati's empire, but for all he was winning the trust of his men he may as well have been back in Camden. Was the man he hunted even in this city? Winter began to wonder if Zerbinati was no more than a name, a myth wielded by the Shadowless to keep their power intact. The Erovores were convinced he existed – convinced enough to pay a million to end that existence – but if Don Zerbinati were real, and not just a higher class of bogeyman, he remained profoundly out of reach.

It wasn't until the last week of August that Winter found himself closing in on the man he had come to kill.

'We're going to the house,' said Salvatore, as if there was only one house in Naples.

'The house?'

'Villa Tramonto.'

They were stood outside La Salamandra, the bonnet of Salvatore's Alfa Romeo a dazzle of metal in the morning sun. Salvatore passed a package to Winter, one he had just collected from Cesare. It was roughly the size of a football.

'Keep this in your hands at all times.'

'What is this?' asked Winter.

'The head of a saint.'

Winter nodded, staring at the brown paper bundle. 'Right. The head of a saint.' He looked up, nonplussed. 'An actual saint's head?'

'Yes. Eleventh century. It's rare. So don't be a *pene* and drop it.'

'Who wants the head of a saint?'

Salvatore's patience was already exhausted. 'Don Zerbinati. Get in the car.'

Winter tried not to let the name's significance register on his face.

'What the hell does he want with it?'

'He collects them. It's his passion. The remains of Christian martyrs. Now get in the car. We don't keep a man like him waiting.'

Winter settled himself in the passenger seat, the sun-warmed leather already sticky to the touch. The Alfa Romeo took them out of Chiaia and into the hills, heading west at speed. They climbed the coastal road to the green and rocky promontory of Posillipo. It was a moneyed, exclusive quarter of Naples, peppered with villas that commanded envious views of the bay. The sun pounded the headland, playing over the sprawl of coves and caves and private docks, picking at a sea that was diamond bright. Winter winched down the window, breathing in hot road and bougainvillea.

'So this is Don Zerbinati's place we're going to?' He made the question as casual as he could.

Salvatore grunted, lowering his sun-shield against the shining blue of the bay. He cast no reflection in the small, rectangular mirror.

Winter decided to chance another question. 'So it doesn't bother you? Any of you? The sun, I mean. The Italian coast is the last place I'd expect to find your kind.'

'My kind?'

'You know what I mean.'

'You can call us by what we are. It's not an insult.'

'*Vampiri*, then.'

Salvatore adjusted the gear stick as the road rose, ever steeper. 'One thing you need to respect. And I will tell you this now, so you don't end up losing your life through your stupid mouth. There are many castes of *vampiri*. Some tremble at the cross, some turn to dust in the sun. These are vermin, no more than common filth. We of the Shadowless are the highest of the undead.'

'So I gather.'

'We walk in the light. We step on sacred ground. We eat, we drink, just as you do. Your folklore is inadequate, insulting. Compare my brothers to the lower orders and one of us with even more temper than me will most certainly kill you.'

Winter nodded. 'Consider me briefed.' He glanced again at the mirror in the sun-shield. 'So even the highest order of vampires has no reflection?'

Salvatore laughed. 'Mirrors are for those who look for imperfections. Why the hell would we need mirrors, man?'

Winter returned a wry smile, mainly to himself. 'You should have met Tommy the Face.'

Villa Tramonto rose against the cloudless sky. It perched at the very edge of the headland and made a monumental silhouette, a solid black outline imposed on a seamless blue horizon. Sunlight flared around its edges, so blindingly that at first the house appeared to be built entirely from an absence of light. Only as the car neared the gate did the details reveal themselves: cool, sand-coloured walls, shuttered windows, a gracefully angled terracotta roof.

The more Winter saw of the finer touches the more incongruous the villa seemed in the Italian countryside. There was a disparate mix of influences at work, something Persian or Moorish in the glazed tiles and gleaming mosaics that dotted the sides of the building. He found himself wondering how long Don Zerbinati had lived – and just where in the world he had walked through those centuries.

The intercom on the gate granted them entry. The Alfa Romeo curved into the driveway, purring over concrete and sliding to a halt next to a gleaming Maserati Berlinetta. Salvatore cut the engine and took the package from Winter. 'Stay here,' he instructed.

'I'm not coming in?'

'That's what I mean by stay here.'

Winter watched Salvatore cross the driveway and step

into the house, met by a maid. Then he opened the car door and got out, lighting a cigarette as an excuse. He propped his elbows on the Alfa Romeo's roof, determined to absorb every detail of Villa Tramonto's geography in the minutes available to him.

So this was where his target was concealed. Here, in an elegant eyrie at the edge of a cliff, gazing down on the city he ruled. It made sense. He should have realised there was no way a man like Don Zerbinati would have lived among the hot chaos of the streets. The king of the vampires required a castle. He wouldn't slum it with the peasants.

Winter calculated opportunities and trajectories, the breeze from the bay cooling his skin.

A perimeter wall enclosed the house and surrounding gardens. Made of concrete, it was around ten feet high – tall enough to block the view from the road, smooth enough to prevent climbing – and topped with wire that had been knotted into vicious spools. There was no evidence of closed-circuit cameras. That was lucky, at least.

Beyond the walls stood a squat throng of olive trees, part of an orchard. The highest of them offered a potential angle on the house, though the foliage was thin and would make a risky place of concealment. God alone knew what kind of vantage point it might provide. It was hard to see much of the rear of the residence from the driveway, though an undulating shimmer of light between the edge of a wall and an outbuilding suggested the presence of a pool.

One bullet. One chance. It demanded a clean, clear shot.

Winter clocked a motion to his left. One of Zerbinati's men was emerging from the shadows of the olive trees. There was an assault rifle slung over his shoulder, hanging from a strap. Winter noted the way his feet moved, halfway between a march and a trudge. He was patrolling the perimeter, on a circuit that was just long and repetitive enough to make his duty a bit of a bore. He kept his gaze ahead of him, ignoring the branches above.

Winter factored this in too, adding it to the walls and the wire, the trees and the pool. All that was missing from the equation was the target himself. Don Zerbinati; the bloody great blank at the heart of everything.

He nodded to the guard. The man regarded him in return, sunlight bouncing on the lenses of his horn-rimmed Wayfarers. No words were exchanged and the guard continued his patrol as Winter exhaled smoke between his teeth.

Salvatore stepped from the house and began to walk to the car, the head of the saint delivered to its new owner. Winter tossed the stub of his cigarette to the ground. It sparked against the wheels of the Alfa Romeo.

He would come back to this place. He would come back and he would take that shot. And the bullet – the only bullet like it in the world – would find the undead heart of Don Zerbinati.

21

Winter wiped a smear of sweat from his forehead. It had been pooling for a while, threatening to trickle into his line of sight.

He screwed his right eye to the scope again, feeling the tiny rubber cup press against the socket. The telescopic lens was fixed on the rear of Villa Tramonto, as it had been since just after dawn. Winter let the cross hairs prowl, moving over whitewashed tiles and elegant outdoor furniture and the bright, chemical blue of the pool. And then he paused, lingering on the cover of a magazine, a copy of *Tempo* left on a sun lounger. For a moment Brigitte Bardot was framed in his sights, her face coming into focus, incandescent as a frame of celluloid. He chose to let her live, but then he had always liked her smile.

The morning light played through the silver-green leaves of the olive tree, dappling his hands as he held the gun. He had placed himself on a thick, serpentine branch that twisted out of the trunk, rising at an angle that gave a degree of concealment from the perimeter path below.

The air was tart and woody, scented by the bitter fruit that hung from the limbs of the tree. The smaller of the branches swayed around him, stirred by the breeze from the headland.

He had risen at three o'clock, short of sleep but focused. Shaving at that hour had felt strangely ritualistic, an act of calm, steady preparation and not just a blade scraping across stubble. The car he had hired was waiting outside the hotel. A drab Fiat 500 that was usefully anonymous. He had abandoned it along the coastal road, on the winding climb to Posillipo. Grateful for the moonless, leather-black sky, he had cut through the trees that led to the villa, edging between the great gnarled trunks, hugging their shadows, the rifle weighing on his shoulder.

He had watched the house for hours now, through the last of the dark and the red bruise of sunrise and into the new day. At first a handful of lights had burned against the night, and he had found himself wondering if Don Zerbinati was awake and pacing the hallways of the villa. Did creatures like that actually sleep? Or was it just another myth that they retreated to their tombs and their crypts and their coffins, snuggling into the ancestral soil?

At shortly after six o'clock a maid had stepped from the doors that flanked the pool. She had enjoyed a brief cigarette, her eyes on the ripening sky, her thoughts unknown. And then she had brushed ash from her pinafore and returned inside, all the time unaware of the sights that had tracked her every movement, monitored the trail of smoke from her cigarette.

The first patrol came at seven o'clock. Winter had glimpsed the approaching guard from a distance, counting himself lucky that his eye wasn't pressed to the scope at that moment. He had shouldered the gun and edged back against the bark, holding his breath as Zerbinati's man passed below, close enough for Winter to see the shine of perspiration above his shirt collar. The guard had stepped past the tree, oblivious. There was a walkie-talkie clipped to his jacket pocket, a casually slung rifle rumpling the cut of his suit.

The patrol was on a half-hour cycle, and Winter soon learned its rhythm, sensing when to lean back into the branches. If there was to be any chance of a shot at Don Zerbinati, any chance at all, it had to come when the guard was on the other side of the grounds. And that, he knew, might be too neat a piece of timing to wish for.

The hours passed in heat and stillness, the monotony tripwired with anticipation. By eleven o'clock Winter was parched but he only allowed himself the briefest of sips from the flask of tepid water in his pocket. He was already aching for a slash, and there was no possibility of that.

The breeze moved on the surface of the pool, rippling the water. It was the only motion to be seen and it was strangely lulling. Winter had to blink to keep his concentration crisp.

And then, shortly after noon, his target was there, filling the sights like a promise fulfilled.

At first Winter saw only a flash of light, the glass of the poolside doors catching the sun as they swung open.

Someone stepped from the villa then, casting no shadow on the whitewashed tiles. Winter lifted the scope, moving from the shoes to the suit to the head. The face was tilted away from the lens but the snowy crest of hair and the high temples were unmistakable. The man carried himself like a king.

Don Zerbinati.

Winter felt a flood of adrenalin. It sharpened the moment, shut out the past and the future, locked the world into present tense.

He kept the rifle absolutely steady. The cross hairs clung to Zerbinati, binding the gun to its mark. The mounted lens stalked the man as he strode to the edge of the pool. The regal head remained fixed in the centre of the scope.

Winter slid a finger inside the trigger–guard, closing around the curl of steel that would free the bullet. The shot was waiting, simply a squeeze away. His mouth tasted like dust at the thought.

But Don Zerbinati was not alone. Someone had joined him in the sunlight.

Winter moved the lens a fraction to the left, hesitant to leave the target but too curious to ignore the new figure that had also stepped from the villa.

He knew this man, he realised.

Soviet Intelligence. High-ranking. They had crossed paths twice before, the first time in Dortmund in the spring of '61. Winter had left him beneath a railway bridge, struggling to hold together the bullet-smashed brains of a fellow KGB operative. The next encounter had been in Vienna, less than two years ago, at that fateful party at das Krabbehaus, mansion of the late occultist Emil Harzner. Now the name came back to him. *Kulganek.* Arkadi Kulganek. What was it the Russian had said that night? '*We waltz with devils.*' And here the bastard was in Naples, still dancing.

Winter returned the cross hairs to Zerbinati. They settled on the chest, framing the heart. Yes, that felt right. Not a head shot. Not this one. It had to be the heart.

He hesitated even as his finger tightened around the trigger.

The KGB had found Zerbinati. What terms had they offered? What deal would they make? What intelligence would they take away?

Take the shot, he told himself. *Ignore the questions.* This was London in his head, and he wasn't London, not anymore. He had another obligation now, a contract to fulfil.

Then he caught sight of a third figure, following Zerbinati and Kulganek to the pool. Winter nudged the scope sideways, tweaking the focus until the tall, nebulous shape resolved itself.

Again he felt the shudder of recognition. There was no mistaking the vein-riddled cranium or the wormy skin that looked so incongruous in the blazing Italian sun. It was the man in the midnight-blue suit, the one he had encountered at Scratch Hill Junction, the night they had traded the heart. The creature with the teeth in its hand.

For a moment Winter was convinced his target knew he was being watched. The man in the blue suit paused, tilting his head as if sensing the sights upon him. Sweat glistened like a larval trail across his hollow cheek. He searched the air, his quartz-clear eyes never quite straying to the trees, then carried on walking.

Winter kept his eye to the scope and his finger to the trigger. He tried to make sense of what he was seeing, decode the body language of the three men. Zerbinati and Kulganek were engaged in conversation and looked reasonably relaxed. Their smiles were easy, their hand gestures broad and expansive. The cadaverous figure that had joined them appeared to be shadowing the Russian, keeping the kind of discreet but umbilical distance Winter associated with professional bodyguards.

What did this mean? How did Soviet Intelligence and Zerbinati's empire intersect? Did the Reds have a damned vampire in their ranks?

He focused once more on Zerbinati, irritated at himself for being intrigued. He owed nothing to London, nothing to Faulkner, nothing to the machinery that had used him for so many years, keeping him numb and ignorant, withholding the truth of his past, the truth of the man he had been. He simply had to pull the trigger to pocket the fortune that waited for him. Cracknell had been assigned to Naples. She could take care of the intelligence implications. This wasn't his concern anymore.

Zerbinati's chest filled the lens. Winter lowered the sights a fraction, past an immaculately folded pocket square of white silk. The cross hairs framed the heart. In that moment the fine wires in the lens reminded him irresistibly of a crucifix.

His finger closed, a tremor of pressure against the trigger. He could sense the bullet, thirsting for release, for fulfilment.

Operation Paragon.

The words itched, insistent as a wound. And there were other words inside him. Words that he heard in the voice of Bernard Gately, facing that gun on a hill in Budapest. *'You killed one of our own.'*

Who had he killed? A decent man?

Winter tried to block the thought. Any thought, any distraction. He was the gun and he was the bullet and he was the money and he was the moment. This was just some vestigial rattle of duty. A ghost trace of Christopher Winter, SIS officer. *Ignore it. Take the shot.*

The wind from the headland stirred the leaves of the olive tree.

Operation Paragon was ongoing, he realised. It was playing out here and now, not at the dark edges of the last war but in the hot sun of 1965. Don Zerbinati was part of it. Kulganek was part of it. And Winter, in spite of himself, was part of it.

The heart waited for the bullet. The bullet that Alessandra had given her life for.

'You killed one of our own.'

It was the optimum moment to shoot.

Winter exhaled and took his eye from the scope. As

285

he did so a fresh rush of adrenalin electrified his veins. There was a flicker of movement below, through the cradle of branches.

A second guard was walking the perimeter path. He was advancing from the right. An anti-clockwise patrol, doubling back on the first guard's beat. They must have stepped up security for the Russian delegation. Winter had been concentrating so hard on the shot he hadn't even registered the man's approach.

Without breathing he drew the rifle tight against his chest. The barrel was warm and slick with his own sweat and he fought to keep a grip on it.

The man was right beneath him now.

Winter put his back to the trunk, leaning as far out of sight as he could. As the seconds passed he could hear fallen twigs cracking beneath the man's shoes.

A bird broke through the leaves, a blue–black flap of wings.

The guard turned, hunting the source of the sound. He slanted his head, looking upwards.

Winter locked eyes with the man. They held each other's gaze. For a moment it felt like they would hold it forever.

The guard tore the walkie-talkie from his lapel. There was an urgent crackle of static.

Winter sprang from the tree. The ground slammed into his knees. Back on his feet he swung the rifle by the barrel, smashing the radio from the man's hand. The device spun into the grass, still hissing on an open channel.

Winter brandished the butt of the gun again. This time he punched it into the man's throat, sending him reeling.

He moved in, exploiting his advantage. Now he swung the hilt of the weapon into the guard's face, smacking wood into bone.

Zerbinati's man spat blood and barrelled forward. His chest hit like a juggernaut. The impact threw Winter to the earth and the gun from his hands.

A voice sputtered from the walkie-talkie, lying only an arm's reach away. *'Vincenzo? Vincenzo?'*

The man was on top of him now. His thumbs were moving to the eyes, the flat wedges of flesh already filling Winter's vision.

'Vincenzo? Rispondi!'

Winter crashed his knee into his opponent's groin. The two of them twisted around the roots of the tree, struggling for leverage, for dominance. The rifle strapped to the guard's shoulder tumbled into Winter's face, clouting him across the bridge of the nose. His eyes sparked with stars.

He thrust one hand against the guard's jaw, twisting it away. With the other he reached for his own belt. His fingers shuddered, fighting to release the buckle catch.

'Rispondi! Vincenzo! *Rispondi!'*

Winter head-butted Vincenzo, his skull striking the soft cartilage beneath the eyes. Blinking back the spray of blood he whipped the belt free from the hoops of fabric. As Vincenzo swayed, disorientated, he lashed the length of leather around the man's throat.

The guard's fingers groped for the walkie-talkie, grasping blindly through the grass. It was only inches away.

Winter drew the belt tight. And then, gathering the spare leather into his fist, he tore it tighter still. A desperate retching came from Vincenzo's throat, even as his fingers found the edge of the two-way radio, his nails scraping its side. Winter urged the belt until the veins in the man's neck stood a rigid blue against the skin. He watched as Vincenzo's tongue lolled between his teeth.

Finally he saw the eyes roll white.

Winter laid the dead man's head on the ground. He took a moment to gather himself, hearing only the shallow rasp of his own breathing. Then, curious, he lifted Vincenzo's upper lip, as high as the gum line. The teeth were normal. He had killed a man, he realised, a taste of guilt swilling with the sense of relief. But of course he had. The body beneath him threw a shadow, merging with the black outline of the tree's own.

The voice from the villa crackled through the grass again, demanding a reply. Winter stared at the walkie-talkie, weighing whether to pick it up and bluff some kind of response.

A rhythmic wailing shattered the hot green hush.

An alarm had been sounded. Someone had spotted the fight. Winter could already see men scrambling in the grounds of the house. He scooped the rifle from the grass and began to run.

Keeping his head low he weaved between the olive trees, batting away branches, the ground falling away beneath him as he clung to the line of the hill. He tried to retrace the path he had taken in the dark but he knew he was trusting instinct over direction. If he could just find the car he could be on the coastal road in minutes.

A gunshot echoed through the orchard. The bullet thudded into a tree just ahead of him. Where had the shot come from? The perimeter ridge? No, he sensed it was closer than that.

Someone else was among the trees now. Winter could hear their feet on the twig-littered earth, moving in pursuit.

He kept running, his heart cannoning against his chest. The car couldn't be far now.

Another bullet. This one cracked the air beside him. It had been inches from a head wound. Too close. The next shot would shatter his skull.

Winter turned, swinging the gun around. He saw himself mirrored in a pair of horn-rimmed Wayfarers. It was the first guard, the one keeping to the clockwise patrol.

The two men stared at each other, their rifles levelled, perfectly matched.

Winter had one bullet, he knew. One precious, sacred, impossible bullet. And he couldn't waste it on the living.

With no other choice he flung the gun to the ground and raised his hands.

'*Mi arrendo…*'

He watched Zerbinati's man approach, directing him to his knees. As he did so a bastard of a thought occurred to him.

He had wasted that bullet already.

22

The light in the locked room was a pale, undulating blue, its shadows created by aquarium glass. It made the walls seem unsteady as water. There were no windows and the heat was intense, adding to Winter's nausea. He felt like a shipwreck, something submerged.

'Who sent you to kill my father?' The question, again, from the man in the corner.

Winter took his eyes from the fist in front of him, tired of looking at his own blood. He stared instead at the tank that dominated the far wall. A brace of Moray eels twisted and thrashed behind the thick glass. They had demented dots for eyes and ugly little razor smiles and they flashed between the rocks, sleek as snakes. He watched them coil like speckled lengths of muscle. The creatures almost seemed animated by the violence in the room.

'Hit him again,' instructed Cesare. 'Loosen his teeth. His tongue will follow.'

Salvatore balled his fist and struck Winter across the mouth. The edge of the salamander ring scraped the flesh but didn't quite crack the lip.

Cesare asked once more. 'Who. Sent. You?' Each syllable was a demand.

Winter regarded the other captives in the room, distracting himself from the fresh flare of pain. It was a remarkable collection of marine life that was kept here at Villa Tramonto. One tank contained the luminous pulse of a jellyfish, its translucent ghost of a body suspended in the water. In another he saw a squirming, engorged octopus, its suckers kissing like leeches against the glass. Other tanks held flickers of eyes and fins, numberless fish darting behind chinks of reflected light.

Salvatore readied his fist again but this time Cesare stopped him. Winter felt a smooth, cool hand on his jaw, wresting his gaze away from the bubbling tanks. He found himself looking into Cesare's eyes, bright in the grotto-like gloom. They were so much older than his face.

'It's a simple question, Englishman. And I have all the time I need to go on asking it.'

Winter's mouth had been numbed by Salvatore's fist. He could barely feel himself forming words. But he gave the reply he needed to.

'I was sent to assassinate the Russian.'

It was the lie he had been saving for this moment. He had taken so many punches to earn it. Only now, when he could finally pass for being broken by the beating, did it stand a chance of sounding halfway persuasive. 'The KGB man. That's who I'm here for.'

Cesare shook his head, unimpressed. 'Impossible.'

'I had a target. But it wasn't your father.'

292

'Bullshit. You know it.'

'I'm telling you. Kulganek was the kill.'

Cesare kept Winter's chin in his hand. He tightened his grip, puckering the skin. 'You came to Naples. You infiltrated the brotherhood of *I Senz'Ombr*. You won my trust. All for a chance at killing a man you cannot possibly have known would come to my father's house?'

Winter struggled to reply through the lockhold. The words hissed through his teeth. 'We had good intelligence.'

Cesare considered this, relaxing his grip just enough to let Winter take a lungful of air.

'You're lying, Englishman. And that's as insulting to the house of Zerbinati as the fact you came to our home with a gun in your hand. What were you thinking?'

Winter returned a sour smile through the shifting blue light of the aquarium room. 'I couldn't kill your father with a bullet, Cesare. We both know that.'

'So either your masters are very stupid or the bullet is very special. One of these things we will soon establish.'

Cesare took his hand away. Now the lean, bloodless fingers hovered in front of Winter's face. The nails extended an inch, sliding like glass blades from the grooves of flesh.

'My dear father has many enemies. Shall we begin to narrow them down?'

Behind him the eels spun and writhed in their tank, as if maddened with anticipation.

✦

The shadows at Villa Tramonto were cast by the dead.

Winter contemplated their outlines as he paced the marble walkway. The last of the day's light had flung them across the elegant paving, long and black and scrawny. None of the bodies appeared to be intact and so the shadows were a jumble of parts: limbs, torsos, the occasional severed head, one of which, Winter imagined, had to belong to that luckless eleventh-century saint.

The remains were preserved in glass cases that perfectly mapped their contours, wrapping around the relics like gleaming sheaths of skin. These were mounted on poles placed at intervals in the marble, marching to the furthest part of the walkway, where the edge of the villa balanced on the rocky lip of the headland. Winter was reminded of the grisly displays favoured by medieval tyrants, the ones who would exhibit the corpses of their fallen enemies as exercises in propaganda.

He took a drag on his cigarette and looked up to see a shrivelled husk of a head. This one had a chest attached to it, or at least the torn remains of one. The eyes were closed beneath the glass, the lids fused by the passing centuries, and the desiccated skin looked as if it might explode into dust if the air as much as touched it. It was a grim bit of decoration to be sure but somehow it made sense here, high above a city so morbidly obsessed by death.

Dusk hung over the Bay of Naples, the sun scissoring through blue-grey banks of cloud. There were hydrofoils on the water and a couple of racing speedboats clearly reluctant to return to shore. The lights of the coast already burned in a bright strip of traffic and nightlife along the Sorrentine Peninsula. Winter thought of all those people out there enjoying their freedom tonight in the summer heat. Those simple lives were so easy to take for granted.

Zerbinati's men hadn't taken their eyes off him for the past hour. They carried small-bore rifles and he had heard the safety catches being unlocked as they escorted him from the aquarium. They stood vigilantly either side of the pool. The water was calm now, barely stirring as the day faded.

Why were they allowing him this sunset, Winter pondered. He had survived the interrogation, keeping to the Kulganek story even as Cesare's nails had lingered around his eyes, threatening to scrape the truth out of him. Cesare could have gone further but Winter sensed his patience had been exhausted. Little wonder. It had to be tedious hearing the same response spat back at you, over and over. No wonder the best interrogators had a twist of sadism in their psyche, taking their victim's defiance as a licence to play. Then again, by the end perhaps Cesare had simply bought the bullshit.

They were keeping him alive. Maybe they planned to hand him to the Russians. A gift from the Shadowless, greasing whatever deal they were making with Moscow. Given he had insisted he was here to kill an officer of the First Chief Directorate of the Committee for State Security, Winter imagined this wouldn't exactly be an improvement in his situation.

He decided to savour this warm, still dusk as best he

could. He stopped at the furthest edge of the walkway and looked out across the sea, never less than aware of the guns at his back.

'There is considerable debate as to whether the great white shark hunts in these waters.'

The voice was calm and cultured. An Italian accent, seasoned by age. At first Winter found it impossible to place where it was coming from. It whispered against his ear, almost as close as his own thoughts, then a second later it seemed to recede, becoming a murmur and then an echo.

'Some insist the currents of the Tyrrhenian are altogether too temperate for the beast.'

The man was closing behind him, his footsteps as measured as his words. Winter didn't turn but he glanced down. There was no trace of shadow moving across the marble.

'But every sea has a pulse. Every great body of water holds the promise of blood. And where there is blood there is inevitably a predator.'

The air itself had changed with the man's presence. The dusk carried a chill now, though there was only the thinnest breeze across the headland, barely enough to stir the orchids that lined the wall at the edge of the cliff.

'An apex predator is especially determined. Do you regard yourself as an apex predator, *signore*?'

The man was at his side. The temperature had sharpened again, dropping another couple of degrees. Winter saw that the orchids were suddenly crawling with aphids, the tiny, lime-bright insects feasting on the leaves.

'Is that why you came to my city? To prove yourself? To claim your status?'

Winter finally turned. Don Zerbinati looked back at him, his eyes cool and ancient.

Winter spoke. 'I wasn't sent here to kill you. I had another target.'

Zerbinati waved away the lie. 'Please, *signore*. Respect me.'

'I respect you enough not to put a bullet in you. I was here to kill the Russian.'

'Were you, now?'

Zerbinati reached inside his jacket pocket. When his hand returned Winter's bullet was balanced on the palm. The skin around it was a vicious red, inflamed like a fresh burn and blistering even as Zerbinati displayed the projectile. It had to be the power of the thorn. Just the act of holding it was clearly an ordeal for the vampire, though his face gave nothing away. Winter could only imagine what a direct hit might have done to the heart.

Zerbinati smiled, and it wasn't without charm. 'Such an ostentatious bullet to waste on a KGB man, wouldn't you say?'

Winter didn't reply. He looked out to Vesuvius, which was wreathed in low cloud.

Zerbinati casually pocketed the bullet. 'The Russians told me there was a trade in the hearts of kings. They have intercepted such transactions, in places beyond even my influence. The Eastern Bloc, at least, wants to keep me alive.'

Winter remembered Scratch Hill Junction. So that had been a Soviet operation. His instinct today had been right; that creature was in the employ of Kulganek.

'Naturally I wondered who wanted me dead,' Zerbinati continued. 'There was an embarrassment of possibilities. But I should have known it was British Intelligence. You betrayed us all in the war. Operation Paragon was a disgrace to the Crown. A stain on your nation.'

There was an edge to his voice now. Winter turned, catching something hard and unforgiving in Zerbinati's gaze. This was an old, deep wound, that much was obvious.

'But you were the last man I thought they would send to kill me.'

Winter's surprise betrayed him. 'You know me?'

'Of course I know you, Signore Hart. Though I confess I imagined you were dead.'

Christ, thought Winter, hotly. His past would never let him go. It would keep him roped to that damned warlock forever.

He stubbed his cigarette against the wall, the tip turning to sparks and ash in the blue gloom.

'That man is dead,' he stated, evenly. 'He died quite a while ago, in fact.'

'So I see. That man was *un bastardo* but he had a certain code of honour that you clearly lack. I had heard he disappeared after the war, somewhere in Africa. And so I wonder who is standing before me now, unwilling to recognise me. You have the face of the man I knew but none of his spirit. Just a hitman for his government who couldn't even put a bullet in me.'

'So why are you keeping me alive?'

Zerbinati teased a smile at the edges of his mouth. 'Oh, we're not keeping you alive, *signore*.'

'Go on.'

'Within the hour my men will come for you. You will be executed and in darkness your body will be taken to the sea and thrown to the waves. You may even provide sustenance for the predators whose presence in these waters is so debated.'

Winter felt his blood turn cold. Zerbinati had made it all sound so plausible, so inevitable. There was a certain vertigo when you heard the facts of your own death set out. The odds were against him, he knew. But he wouldn't react. He could win this moment at least if he showed he wasn't afraid.

'I thought I might become part of your collection,' he smiled, indicating the glass-encased remains that lined the walkway, their shadows shrinking now as the sun met the horizon.

Zerbinati turned to regard the parade of body parts. 'My saints?' he asked, amused. 'I don't think you're quite qualified to join their number.'

'It's a remarkable hobby. Or is it some kind of death fixation?'

'Not at all. I collect these martyrs not to celebrate death but to remind myself there is mortality in this world. I so rarely encounter it.'

'I find that hard to believe. You didn't build your

empire by keeping people alive.'

Zerbinati considered this. 'True. But I have given life, too, of a kind. Over the centuries I'm sure it all balances.'

'Maybe you've lived too long, Signore Zerbinati. All that perspective can't be good for you.'

The undead man allowed himself the broadest of smiles. 'Oh, I see. Your bullet was meant as a gift. Very well. This final sunset is my gift to you, or at least the man I knew. Savour it. I have no doubt it will feel exquisite. I'm told mortality sweetens everything.'

He turned, the night air warming a fraction as he walked away. Winter heard the footsteps retreat across the marble but kept his eyes on the dark swell of the bay. There was no trace of sun on the water now. If there were sharks in the Tyrrhenian, chasing blood, they remained hidden in its cool black depths.

He waited for the men to come for him.

The tunnel was intermittently lit. A succession of electric torches had been hammered into volcanic sandstone, drawing power from lengths of copper cable. Every twenty feet or so the light threatened to dissolve completely before the next bulb picked up the trail. The torches passed illumination to one another like a baton relay.

The path threaded through cliffside rock, connecting a cellar trapdoor in Villa Tramonto to what Winter could only imagine was private access to the sea, some rocky inlet where a boat was doubtlessly waiting for his body. He could feel the ground beginning to level, losing the incline that had marked the journey so far. The stale air had a salt bite to it now, suggesting they were approaching water. *The cavern's mouth must open directly onto the beach,* he realised.

The men marched him ahead, keeping the pace brisk. Three men, two shadows. Salvatore and a pair of heavies assigned to security detail at the villa. Two of the men – the ones whose names he didn't know – had guns in their hands. That narrowed the options for his death considerably.

A bullet, then. Would they kill him on the beach? There was minimal chance of witnesses from the headland but maybe that was a risk they weren't prepared to take. No, that bullet waited for him in this tunnel, any moment now. He was convinced of it.

Again he tried to clear his mind, close his thoughts to everything, even the prospect of his own execution. He gathered his fists as he walked. There was fresh sweat on his palms. His breathing slowed as he focused. He had to remember how to do this. It would be his only chance.

Flesh is memory. Bone is memory. Blood is memory.

Winter heard the words in Alessandra's voice and his own. As he did so he conjured the images he needed, as vivid as he could make them: the skeleton of Eugenio Franzeri, perched upon a chair in that house in Venice; the bones piled in a Normandy burial mound; the broken skull in its bridal veil, the one he had seen in the church on Via dei Tribunali. He made himself remember how those bones had made him feel. That surge of possibility in his veins, like the ink that had swirled on that Rorschach test in London, promising the gift of magic. Hart's gift. The one he had tried to deny.

'Keep walking.'

Salvatore shoved him between the shoulders, pushing him through spills of cave water that rippled with electric light. The Italian's initial fury at Winter's betrayal of the brotherhood had soon turned to relish when he realised the kill would be his.

'I said keep walking!'

There was sea mist in the tunnel now, drifting past them, waist-high. The exit to the beach was close.

Winter remembered his hand in that hotel room, twisting the glass as if it was molten. He saw the black liquid that had dripped from his fingers, burning through newspaper. He had magic inside him, buried in his body. All he had to do was summon it, command it, just as Hart had done.

He heard the sound of waves. The crash of the water echoed through the cavern.

What were those words that Alessandra had used, in that hotel in Pest?

'You could have killed her at any moment, Hart, we both know that. All you had to do was cast a blood hex or summon a shadow scythe or…'

A shadow scythe. He knew these words. They were part of him.

Winter heard another sound. He placed it instantly.

The hungry click of a switchblade, directly behind him. It had to be in Salvatore's hand. A knife, then, not a bullet. He had seconds now, he guessed. A minute at most.

He opened his fists and looked down. The sweat on his palms was the colour of ink.

Salvatore placed a hand on his right shoulder. 'You can stop walking now, *signore.*'

Winter closed his eyes. A nerve began to beat on his brow, insistent against the skin.

Magic is memory.

He spun as the blade came flashing in Salvatore's hand.

The magic tore out of him, ripping itself from his pores.

It was black and it was whip-fast and it was entirely without mercy, a vicious, sinuous, scissoring thing that cut the men to pieces. Winter watched in horror as it carved through the bodies, cleaving flesh, dicing bone. He couldn't pin a shape to it. Whatever he had unleashed was pure, razor-edged darkness, tall as a man.

He backed away from it, from everything, from the strewn limbs and the scattered heads and the rock walls that were running with blood. He had to fight the urge to vomit.

A shadow scythe. Christ, he had expected it to be the size of a knife, something he could take in his hand and use. How could he be capable of a thing like this?

It waited above the men's remains, pulsing and seething, a locus of unearthly energy. Winter stared at the glinting, spidery mass but it was impossible to comprehend, its angles pivoting and twisting out of kilter, as if it couldn't quite map itself onto the geometries of this world. It didn't belong here, Winter knew that much. He had wrenched it from some kind of hell.

There was something else, too. He sensed that the thing was intelligent. A malign, animalistic intelligence that had relished killing those men. Hart could have stopped it; Winter had no chance.

He took a step forward, not daring to take his eyes from it. The presence quivered as he approached, spitting black sparks, tiny shreds of shadow. Winter could tell the thing resented him, knew that this wasn't its true master.

He had to get rid of it. He couldn't leave it here in this city to kill again.

'Come to me.'

He had found the words instinctively. They felt like a muscle memory on his tongue.

'I said come to me.' This time it was a command.

The thing flinched from him at first. It sputtered and hissed, reluctant to leave the bodies. And then it shifted in the air like a swarm.

Winter took a breath and shut his eyes tight as the entity approached. He felt magic clustering on his skin. It was oily and it was hot and it seeped inside him, finding its way back into his bones. He shuddered as his flesh absorbed it, every impulse in his body screaming to cast it out again.

He waited to open his eyes, concentrating on the sound of the sea, trying to match his breathing to the crash of the tide. His heartbeat finally began to slow.

His eyelids flickered open. The ungodly thing he had summoned was gone. He was alone.

He glanced at his palms. His sweat was clear again.

Winter took a final look at what was left of the men. He was startled to see Salvatore's eyes were still moving in his severed head, furiously tracking him. The vampire's mouth was set in a rictus, the canines extended, blood sloshing between the lips. There was no throat to give it a voice.

Winter turned and sprinted through the rest of the passage. The end of the cavern was just ahead and he could already see the lights of the bay beyond the maw of rock.

He exited onto a secluded strip of beach, far below Villa Tramonto. The quiet cove nestled in the base of the cliff, hidden from the coastal road. In front of him a wooden jetty led to the water. There was a speedboat tethered to it, the streamlined hull rising with the waves. It was the boat that had been waiting for his corpse. It would also be his means of escape, he decided.

The keys. He needed the keys.

With a sigh Winter ran back into the cave mouth. He ransacked the men's pockets, his fingers not quite quick enough to escape his revulsion at searching body parts. Salvatore's eyes burned at him, a good five feet away from where his torso had fallen.

Locating the keys Winter raced to the jetty, untethered the coupling line and jumped into the speedboat. Edging behind the wheel he slid the key into the ignition and pumped the shift lever. As he gunned the throttle the engine responded with a roar that vibrated through the entire chassis.

Winter tilted the wheel. Gaining speed the boat tore across the bay, cutting a white trail in the dark water.

23

Winter knew he had to get out of Naples.

He was operating on pure survival instinct now, one that overruled any need to find answers to Operation Paragon. The Shadowless controlled this city, every street of it, every nook in its crumbling, mazy slums. Once they discovered the fate of Salvatore and the other men they would come for him, and they would find him – and this time they would take his life. It had become a question of honour. A blood vengeance.

Britain would be the safer option, at least for the moment. Don Zerbinati had said that London was beyond his reach – but now he had all the motivation he needed to infiltrate the capital, hunting down his failed assassin. And he would turn the city over, that much was certain. Winter would have to go to ground elsewhere. Keep his head down in Cornwall or the Lake District. Maybe even Wales. He anticipated he would be watching over his shoulder for the rest of his days.

He had ditched the boat in the rocky shallows that ran alongside Via Francesco Caracciolo. His money and his passport – everything he needed to escape Naples – waited in the small steel safe in his room at the Grand Hotel Vesuvio. He would discard everything else and flag a taxi to Capodichino airport, catching the next plane to England. Flight or fight response, they called it. He chose flight, at twenty thousand feet.

Another thought struck him as he crossed the promenade, weaving between the waterfront traffic and triggering a blare of horns. The Erovores would not be happy. He had failed them, wasted and lost that precious bullet, all to pursue a private agenda that even now he was abandoning to save his own skin. The Glorious, he assumed, would find that exceptionally hard to forgive. And more than that, he was walking evidence of a plot to kill the leader of *I Senz'Ombr*. They'd be minded to erase him, just as a precaution.

Christ. He had manoeuvred himself into a crossfire between two of the most powerful and resourceful criminal factions on the planet. And both sides would be coming for him now.

And then there was British Intelligence. London wouldn't let him go that easily either, not now that Paragon was reactivated. He had royally screwed this up.

There were rats in the gutters tonight. Winter caught them darting between the wheels of parked cars, nimble flashes of grease and fur. He had never seen them in this street before but for a moment he felt a kinship with the verminous little sods.

He reached the cool, cream-and-honey frontage

of the hotel and crossed reception, taking the stairs to the fifth floor, two at a time. He would simply remove what he needed from the room and disappear. No time to check out. The moment he cleared passport control at Gatwick, Anthony Robert St John Prestwick would cease to exist, the identity shed like so much dead skin.

He hovered outside the door to 503. Cesare had seen that passport, cast his eyes over that name and number. Given the reach of the Shadowless there was every chance he had tracked down this room already, had known its location for weeks, in fact. Winter calculated the distance from Villa Tramonto, estimating how soon they might have discovered his escape. The timing and the geography tipped in his favour. There was no chance they could have reached this room before him. But he would have to be quick.

Winter twisted the key in the lock, lingering in the corridor as the door swung against the wall. He wouldn't put a hand to the light switch, not yet.

He peered inside. The maid had been and gone; the bed was a temple of starched linen, fresh pillows neat against the headboard. The glass door that led to the balcony was open a fraction, just as he left it every morning, hoping to cool the heat that made any locked room in Naples unendurable. The tall muslin blinds swayed in the night breeze. There was a dim mutter of traffic from the promenade, broken by the sudden, exhibitionist roar of a motor scooter.

Winter turned on the light and made for the

wardrobe that housed the safe. As he did so he glanced at the bathroom door. The maid had left it ajar.

He looked closer. Something had snagged at the very edge of his vision. The tiniest glint of light, catching a reflective surface. The mirror, maybe, or the blade of his razor.

He nudged the door an inch wider. Instinct almost made him reach for the pistol that had been taken back at the villa.

A familiar, quartz-like eye stared back at him out of the shadows.

Winter had no time to brace. The man in the midnight-blue suit came cannoning out of the room. The impact threw him against the wall, smashing the breath from his chest.

A pair of lean, bloodless hands lifted him by the lapels. He felt his feet surrender the ground. And then there was a crunch of bone on glass as his head was slammed backwards. Winter's scalp was suddenly wet with blood. The shattered frame of a painting fell in pieces to the floor.

His opponent gave a smile like a mouthful of needles. The translucent eyes narrowed, relishing the moment. The creature clearly remembered their encounter at Scratch Hill Junction.

Winter was flung across the room. He had been aimed at a rosewood table and it cracked in half as his body hit it, sending a vase of wax flowers tumbling to the ground.

Winter seized the vase even as he struggled to drag air into his lungs. Twisting across the carpet he struck it against the wall. Now he held a jagged rim, sharp enough to inflict some damage. He scrambled to his feet as the man in the midnight-blue suit loomed over him.

He took a swing with the broken vase, targeting the eyes. He barely scraped the face. A cold, moist fist clamped itself around his wrist and squeezed until the carpal bones threatened to shatter. Winter dropped the vase, his fingers shuddering in agony.

Again he was hurled across the room. This time his face smacked into hard plaster. For a moment all he could see was a volley of stars, exploding on his retinas.

He tried to rip the magic out of his body again, willing the nerve above his eyes to start beating. But he had no time, no chance to focus. His assailant had already snatched the back of his jacket. Still dazed, Winter found himself hauled into the bathroom, seeing his own blood spattering the carpet beneath him.

His head collided with the sink. He was granted half a breath and then the man rammed him against the marble a second time, deadening Winter's senses until a numb, black nothing filled his mind.

The image of a skull swam out of the darkness. He tried to lock onto it but it was gone.

His opponent spun him around by the shoulders, forcing his head backwards into the sink so that now they faced one another. Winter's vision returned to him, vague outlines hardening into detail. He saw the man's smile widen as their eyes met, the teeth altogether too large for the mouth.

He shut his eyes tight and tried to summon the image of the skull again, make it burn bright and white in his mind. It flickered tantalisingly against his eyelids, elusive as a fading signal.

Two fists plunged down upon his breastbone, making it impossible to take more than halting snatches of air.

'Flesh is memory...' Winter was forcing the words between his teeth, using all the breath he had left. 'Bone is memory...'

The pressure on his chest eased. He opened his eyes and saw the man raise and unclench his fists. Both palms were presented to him, the fingers fanning apart. As Winter watched the skin cracked open, revealing stacks of tiny, razored teeth, gleaming wetly.

He couldn't see the skull now. All he could see were the teeth, grinding and hungering in the hands.

There was a gunshot and a sudden jet of matter and fluid, hot against his face.

Winter stared, incredulous. The man in the midnight-blue suit swayed above him. The edge of his head was gone, leaving a ruptured shell. Blood poured from the wound, dark and generous, running down the wormy skin. Whatever life had been in the quartz eyes was vanishing fast, even as the pupils fought to fix on Winter.

The man teetered then pitched backwards, thudding into the tiles.

'So yeah, that was a headshot, Mr Winter. I hope it met with your approval.'

Libby Cracknell stood framed in the doorway,

gripping her service-issue revolver with both hands.

Winter wiped the stinging mess from his eyes, grimacing as it clung to his fingers. He took a moment to breathe, to steady himself.

Finally he acknowledged her. 'I told you to get out of Naples.'

She gave a grunt of disbelief. 'Do you ever run out of charm, mate?'

Winter picked himself up, coldly furious as he straightened his suit. 'You just don't listen, do you? I told you to leave me alone.'

She kept her eyes on him. The gun remained in her hands. 'You're such a prick.'

'You want me to thank you for what you just did?'

'It might make you less of a prick.'

'So thank you,' said Winter, brittly. 'I appreciate the gesture. But your duty's done.'

'You reckon?'

'No more guardian angel. I keep telling you that.'

She shrugged. 'I'm not exactly here as your guardian angel, mate.'

Winter only half heard her, his eyes on the dead man. 'I don't need London on my case. I'm finished with it. All of it. You can tell Faulkner that from me.'

Libby said nothing, watching as Winter began to drag the body from the bathroom floor. The corpse was heavy and he struggled with it but he pointedly didn't ask for her help.

Eventually he managed to wrestle it into the main

room, heaving its dead weight by the arms. Crouching, he examined the head wound, his mouth curling in distaste at the crater of brain and bone.

'I thought these things couldn't be killed with bullets,' said Libby.

Winter examined the creature's skin. It was the colour of spoilt milk and greasy to the touch, the kind of flesh that belonged somewhere sunless and deep. He knew he should leave this room. Escape this city while he still could. But his curiosity was winning.

'You used a standard lead bullet, I take it? Nothing special from armaments branch?'

She nodded. And she continued to grip the gun between her hands.

'So how is it dead?' he muttered, mostly to himself. 'What are we dealing with?'

Libby watched as he rifled through the pockets of the man's suit. 'We saw this thing in London. Was it working for Zerbinati?'

'Soviet Intelligence. Looks like the Reds are recruiting beyond the grave now.'

Winter lifted the left wrist and unbuckled the watch strap, hoping there might be intelligence secreted inside, just as he had found on that KGB agent in the house in Venice. He took his Festival of Britain pen-knife from his pocket and was about to slit the leather when he paused. There was a tattoo stamped on the pallid skin. A simple black arrowhead, with a row of Cyrillic numbers inscribed beneath it. He took a moment to place the symbol.

Oymyakon.

It was a notorious gulag, located in the ice-encrusted extremity of Russia's Sakha Republic. As Winter recalled Stalin had created the labour camp specifically for disgraced Soviet military personnel. The cowards and the thieves and the insubordinates that infested any army. Deserters, of course, had been shot on sight, which might have been an act of mercy, given Oymyakon's brutal reputation.

Now he began to piece it together. This man had been human, once. A prisoner at Oymyakon, selected, he imagined, for experimentation. Wasn't that what the Russians were up to? Searching for a way to fuse the DNA of the undead with their own soldiers? The dream of Operation Paragon, the one that Britain had chased too. And at Oymyakon they would have found a plentiful supply of test subjects, men already discarded and erased by the state, their lives now raw matter for research.

So that's what this creature was. Some kind of gruesome hybrid. It was an unsettling thought. Soviet science was evidently more advanced than Western intelligence suggested.

And yet this thing – this man – had been taken down by a single shot. It wasn't the deathless battlefield warrior that Moscow desired. Clearly it was a prototype of some kind. But if the Russians really were in an alliance with Don Zerbinati then it was purely a matter of time before they perfected their process.

Winter glanced at Libby, expecting another question. He was irritated to see that she still had the gun in her hands. It was pointed midway between him and the body on the floor.

'And for God's sake, stand down,' he told her.

He turned away once more. He was about to strike the pen-knife against the watch strap when intuition made him pause. He returned his gaze to her.

The small dark mouth of the barrel was levelled directly between his eyes.

24

Winter stared at the weapon then shifted his eyes to Libby. 'What are you doing?'

The gun remained trained on him. The girl's double-handed grip was absolutely level, absolutely certain.

'Cracknell…'

'Stay on your knees,' she instructed. 'Put your hands to your head.'

There was a distance in her eyes now. Something cold and pragmatic. Winter recognised it. This was the moment you shut down everything of yourself except duty.

'I know the ritual,' he said, dismissively. 'I want to know why London wants me dead. You are London, I take it?'

Libby's expression hardened. 'Stop talking, mate.'

'So I'm a liability. I was just getting used to being an asset.'

Her mouth was set, determined. The gun was steady. Winter sensed she could do this.

'I told you to stop talking.'

'So take the shot. Or I'll keep talking.'

'You think I couldn't kill you?'

'Are you out to prove you can?'

He caught a rogue emotion in her eyes then, just for an instant. A flash of something hot and defensive. Winter took it as a cue to keep pushing her.

'It's your first kill on orders, isn't it? Your very first kill where you don't know why. And that's always the hardest, believe me. London will claim a little bit of your soul the moment you pull that trigger.'

'I can spare a little soul, mate. What have you got left?'

'Not much. You've read the file.'

'I've read enough.'

He smiled now. 'Faulkner doesn't think you can do this, does he?'

'And what do you reckon?'

A vein began to beat against his brow.

'Oh, I think you can do it, no question. But I also think you should pull that trigger as quickly as you can.'

Her eyes narrowed, searching to make sense of what he had just said. 'Why's that then, Mr Winter?'

He felt the magic stir in him, the intoxicating, bone-bright promise of power.

'Because there's something inside me that will kill you, given the opportunity. Something terrible. It's part of me now. And I don't know that I can stop it. Not if I don't really try.'

She considered this, her expression neutral. 'You could take my life? That easily?'

'Not easily.' He saw the shadow scythe slicing through the men in the cavern. 'I don't want to kill you, Libby, but I can. So go on. Put the bullet in me before I have a chance to do it.'

The vein was drumming. It was a pulse now, and there was something seductive in its solid, unwavering rhythm, loud as the thud of blood in his temples. It would be so easy to surrender to it, to let the power flood through him, sweet and dark and thrilling.

Libby raised the gun a fraction, precisely targeting the vein.

'So kill me, Mr Winter. Show me you can do it.'

Winter locked his eyes with hers. She stared back, unblinking. The girl and the gun waited, as still as the room.

'Go on,' she said, calmly. 'Make me believe in magic.'

The moment was held.

Winter shook his head, and as he did so the tremor between his eyes began to subside. He felt the rush in his veins retreating, melting back into his bones.

'No. This is your move, Miss Cracknell. Your career prospects, after all.'

She let the trigger quiver beneath her finger. And then, at last, she lowered the gun, the sour ghost of a smile on her lips. 'You're a prick, mate, but I'm not going to kill you.'

Winter kept his gaze on the weapon, watching as it came to rest against her thigh. 'Why not?'

'Because you won't kill me. And that's not the man they sent me to take down.'

She indicated with a nod that he could get to his feet. Winter walked to the bed, never removing his eyes from the gun. He sat on the edge of it, facing her, the watch and the pen-knife still in his hands.

'What did Faulkner tell you?'

'Never said it was Faulkner.'

'It has to be Faulkner. I know the command structure, for Christ's sake.'

'I don't report to Faulkner. Not ultimately.'

'What are you talking about? You took me to see him. That's how this began, back in London!'

Her mouth moved to form an answer but she hesitated, discarding whatever words had been waiting there.

'It's not that simple.'

'Make it simple,' said Winter, his voice gentler now.

She was silent again, her eyes on the wall as she wrestled with a response. She suddenly seemed very young to him.

'Tell me,' Winter urged her. 'Believe me, I know what it's like to be in the field and not trust the line of command.'

'Chancery Lane Deep Shelter.' The words had tumbled from her.

Winter's mouth creased quizzically. 'That's just a communications hub…'

'No. It's more than that. I report there. Have done for the last year.'

'But it's not a command centre,' Winter insisted. 'Least it wasn't in '63.'

'It's a command centre. Has been for some time. Look, Faulkner hired me, but he's not the one who gave me the real chances. He's not the one who trusted me with the proper jobs.'

'So who are we talking about? Give me a name.'

Again the words seemed to fall out of her. 'Gallard. Lord Auberon Gallard.'

Winter shrugged. The revelation meant nothing to him. 'He's not SIS. What is he, Whitehall?'

'He's British Intelligence. A part of it that's above the SIS.'

Winter found himself smiling at the idea. 'No such thing.'

'It exists, mate. It's called the Sovereign Executive. It's the top tier.'

'Oh, come on, this is fantasy. The kind of paranoid horseshit I used to hear from Carl Hatherly in the Old Star and Crown on a Friday night...'

'I'm telling you this is the way it is. Faulkner assigned me to watch you. Gallard gave me other orders. He's the one who sent me to kill you.'

'And you accepted those orders? Even though you're SIS?'

She nodded, perfectly prepared to justify herself. 'You really have no idea what it's like, do you? It's an old boys' club. Wear the right tie, know the right handshakes. Make sure you have a dick or you end up doing the tea and the typing. The likes of me don't get given chances in this game. Gallard changed that. I owe him.'

Winter's tone was cold. 'You owe your loyalty to the SIS. To Faulkner.'

'The SIS screwed you over. What do you care?'

'I care when someone puts my name on a bullet. Why does Gallard want me dead?'

'He knows you. He knows the man you were. The things you did, back in the war.'

Winter weighed this. 'Then he should have killed me when I deserved it. He was part of Operation Paragon, wasn't he?'

Libby nodded. 'I think so. I think he's part of all of this.'

Winter rotated the pen-knife, watching as the enamel handle caught the electric flicker of the ceiling light. His mind was turning through the possibilities. The past was a snare, he realised, something inescapable. A coil of razor wire that was beginning to tighten around him. And he had walked straight into it, oblivious.

He placed the knife and the watch on the blanket. And then he rose from the bed and walked to the safe. There were finger-sized indentations in the steel. They had clearly been made by a hand that possessed preternatural strength.

Winter glanced at the body on the floor. The man in the midnight-blue suit had been on an intelligence sweep for the Russians. He must have been attempting to break open the safe when Winter had put the key in the hotel room door. So Zerbinati had told Kulganek of the failed assassination attempt – and informed him it was a British operation, no doubt. *Wonderful.* This entire cyclone of shit was expanding exponentially.

The combination lock spun. Winter took his passport and plane ticket and crammed them into his jacket pocket. He knew what he had to do now.

Libby watched him. 'You're getting out of Naples, aren't you?'

'No. I'm getting out of this room. And then I'm going to sort this mess out. Because if I don't it's never going to let me go.'

'Let me help you.'

'And disobey a direct order?'

'I've disobeyed it already. You're still breathing, mate.'

Winter regarded her wordlessly. Then he nodded. Returning to the bed he slit the watch strap and peeled back the leather, pinching his fingers to extract the sliver of paper he expected to find within. Some fragment of information that might supply an insight into the Soviet presence in the city. A name, a word, a scrawl of numbers...

There was nothing inside.

He tossed the pen-knife to the bed with a sigh. A second later a sheaf of shiny black-and-white prints landed beside him.

'Good job I took these, then, isn't it?' said Libby.

Winter picked up the white-bordered squares. He recognised the prints as coming from a Minox subminiature camera, service issue, sometimes camouflaged as a cigarette lighter or a compact. The images had the telltale grain that suggested they had been snatched in low light but they were adequately detailed just the same.

'Where did you take these?'

'La Salamandra. Cesare's office at the back of the club. I was doing a little unpaid overtime, let's say.'

They were photographs of a map, portions of cartography in close-up. They showed the familiar, twisting arteries of central Naples. One area had been circled with a swathe of ink.

'What am I looking at here?'

'The Avvocata district. There's some kind of excavation project going on. They're digging beneath the city. Look at the last photo.'

Winter stared at a shot of headed notepaper and an itemised budget, counter-signed by Cesare. He knew the logo. He had seen it on the streets. 'This is the gas company, right?'

'They've made a deal with the Shadowless. Cesare's hiring vehicles and equipment. It's a big, pricey operation. And he's hiding it in plain sight.'

'What's he looking for?'

'Something buried under Naples, that's all I know. You've infiltrated them. You didn't pick up on this?'

There was a cheeky hint of competition in her voice. Winter ignored the bait.

'They know I came here to kill Don Zerbinati.'

'You took the shot?'

'I wasted the shot.'

Libby absorbed this. And then she reached inside

her white cord jacket and pulled out another print. It skimmed into Winter's lap. 'Well, then. Someone's going to want their money back.'

He examined the photograph. It showed a bank statement, the transactions stacked in tight rows of letters and digits.

'Cesare's account?'

'Look for the biggest number on the page.'

Winter spotted it. He quickly calculated its worth in sterling.

'One million pounds?'

'Paid to a Swiss account. I followed the money trail. Traced it all the way back to Venice.'

Winter heard the words but it took a moment for the implication to hit him. He looked up from the photograph. If it was true it changed everything.

'Are you sure about this?' he asked, astonished.

Libby nodded. 'No mistake. He bankrolled the hit. Looks like Cesare's the one who wants dear old daddy dead.'

25

There was an uncharacteristic stillness to the Spanish quarter at four in the morning.

The mad throb of the place had retreated with the day's heat. Alleyways that had roared and clattered in sunlight were muted now. Only a handful of windows burned in buildings whose dark, crumbling façades might otherwise have been taken for derelict. Outside the market stalls crates of unwanted flowers had been left to wilt. Across the cobbles fish lay piled on half-melted slabs of ice, ready to rot by dawn.

Deep in shadow, Winter and Libby stood in a doorway in the Avvocata district, just above the gilded sweep of Via Roma. There was a plaster Madonna nailed to the flaking masonry, the pale face of the Virgin regarding them above a stack of buzzers and nameplates. Another of the city's legion of watchful spirits, and one of the big guns, too. Winter wished he had the faith to be grateful for her presence.

They had an optimum view of the street. The far end was cordoned off with strips of luminous yellow tape that swayed as the breeze stirred. Within these flimsy plastic barriers was a workman's tent, a tall rectangle of canvas staking out a sizable chunk of road. Each side of the tent bore the logo of the city's gas company.

An hour earlier two men in overalls had emerged from a slit in the canvas. A lighter had flared and the pair had shared cigarettes. Winter and Libby had watched from the doorway, too far from the men to catch their conversation. Judging by their easy body language and occasional laughter it was no more than banter. Minutes later the cigarettes were flicked, discarded, to the gutter and the men had returned inside the tent.

Shortly after that the ground shook.

Winter took it for an earth tremor at first. He felt the street shudder, a spasm of vibration, approaching and passing at speed, rolling towards Via Roma. It coursed beneath the cobbles as if a pulse of pure energy was punching through the stratum. The kinetic surge was enough to scatter a mob of birds, picking at bags of spoilt meat on the kerbside.

The coast was tripwired, he knew. This entire region rested on a cradle of faultlines and volcanic triggers. But he had a feeling this was no tectonic shift. The buildings around them had stayed stable and no aftershocks had chased that first judder.

It was a detonation charge. He was sure of it. A controlled explosion, deep underground.

Winter exchanged a look with Libby as the shockwave receded. They had shared the same thought. Cesare's project was progressing, whatever the hell he might be hunting beneath the pavements of Naples.

Now Winter tilted his watch, angling the face out of the shadows. It was five past four. The van was late. The others had hit the hour mark precisely. This ad-hoc surveillance operation had begun shortly before midnight and in that time no less than four vans had come and gone, some carrying men, others equipment, all of them punctual.

Ten minutes later a vehicle bearing gas-company branding turned into the road. Winter detached himself from the doorway, leaving Libby concealed. He stepped casually in front of the cream-coloured Lancia van, persuading it to halt.

Framed by the headlights, Winter peered through the windscreen. He knew the man behind the wheel. One of the foot soldiers of *I Senz'Ombr*. This was either a very useful or a very dangerous thing, depending on how far news of his betrayal had travelled through the ranks of the Shadowless.

Winter smiled blandly as he tried to evaluate the man's expression. The eyes that met him through the glass were innately distrustful but there was none of the telltale tightening of the facial muscles that signalled hostility. He was also relieved to see a faint reflection against the windscreen, cast from inside the van. This wasn't one of those undead bastards, at least.

Winter motioned for the man to winch down the window. '*Buongiorno.*'

The driver acknowledged him with a blunt nod. 'What do you need?'

The back of the van was empty, save for some boxes. Good. The man was alone. This was purely an equipment run.

'Change of plan. Just been told. They want you underground. You bring them the tools. I'll take the van back to base.'

The eyes hardened. 'No tools. This is cable. You should know the schedule.'

Winter shrugged, hiding his irritation at the slip he'd made. 'So many van runs. Too little sleep. You know what it's like, *amico*.'

He had made the words as matey as he could, one drone to another. The driver's expression remained sceptical. Winter had never done chumminess terribly well.

'I don't see you here before,' said the man at the wheel. There was a sharpness to this observation. 'Since when were you part of the Avvocata operation?'

Winter had the lipstick ready in his hand, the slim plastic cylinder pressed against his palm.

'They keep moving me around. All over this city. It's crazy, isn't it? I don't think they know what to do with an Englishman.'

He had loosened the cap with a tiny click. Now he slid the shaft free.

'Why would they need me in the tunnels?' the driver demanded, as tired as he was suspicious. His eyes were red-rimmed in the early hours.

Winter leaned into the open window, catching a tang of spirits on the man's breath. 'Quite frankly, they tell me shit all. But look, you're late already. Don't be in any more trouble.'

The van continued to growl on the cobblestones. Winter's hands were hidden below the door now. He palmed the cap and twisted the base of the lipstick, letting the camouflaged blade uncoil.

He indicated the radio unit fixed to the dashboard. 'Listen, why don't you give them a call? They'll confirm what I've told you. But do it quickly. You're already wasting their time.'

Considering this, the driver moved his gaze to the radio, breaking eye contact. As he reached to open the channel Winter thrust the compact blade to the side of the man's throat, urging its edge against the skin. He spoke quickly and quietly.

'Understand this. If I sever your carotid arteries you'll be dead within minutes. And that's me being merciful. I've inflicted this wound before. Unconsciousness precedes fatal blood loss. You'll be in pain but not for long.'

The pulse in the man's throat brought his skin closer to the bite of the knife.

'I don't particularly need to kill you. I imagine you're in no great rush to die. And to be honest I don't have the patience to clean that much blood from this van. We're both tired. Let's make this easy.'

The man was too mindful of the knife to nod, or make any move that might goad it to draw blood. There was a whine from the back of his throat that Winter took for acquiescence.

'Good man.'

Winter removed the blade. And then he seized the driver's head and smashed it against the dash, concussing him.

Capping the knife he tossed the lipstick to Libby. 'Standard Sovereign Executive field issue? Amazed you didn't use it on me.'

She caught it as she stepped from the doorway. 'Temptation's a terrible thing, mate.'

They moved quickly. The driver was bound with cable and stashed in the back of the van, another length of flex fixed tight between his teeth, gagging him. Winter took the remaining reel of cable. As he locked the rear doors he saw that Libby was screwing a silencer to her Webley & Scott revolver.

'Give me your gun.'

She made a final twist to the aluminium baffle. 'Why would I do that?'

'Because I don't have a gun anymore.'

'So?'

'I need a gun.'

'So do I.'

Winter held out his hand. 'Just give me the bloody gun.'

'Because you're a bloke?'

'Because I'm going in first.'

Libby flashed an urchin grin. 'Then I'll cover you, won't I? Don't try and pull rank on me, Mr Winter. You're not exactly in line for a service pension anymore.'

Exasperated, Winter walked away from the van. The

girl was right. He was in no position to demand her gun. But going into this unarmed made him edgy. There was a reassurance verging on dependency in the feel of a gun in your hand or strapped to your chest. Every field agent knew that sacred union of body and weapon.

Then again bullets would be all but useless against Cesare and the other undead of the Shadowless. This had to be a reconnaissance mission; no confrontation. Slip in, slip out. Get the intelligence on the ground and let London unravel the mess. Faulkner, at least, could still be trusted. Winter surprised himself with that glimmer of loyalty.

They stooped beneath the plastic barriers at the far end of the street. Libby hung back as Winter pushed through the canvas of the workman's tent, carrying the cable that would buy him at least a moment of plausibility with anyone he encountered inside.

The tent was empty. Only a portable stove and a trestle table, bearing a tatty copy of *L'Europeo* and two mugs of coffee dregs. Winter put his hand to the mugs. The ceramic was cool to the touch. They had sat there for some time.

He flung the cable to one side and stepped to the edge of the hole ringed by the canvas. The crater in front of him crowned a vast, sepulchral wound in the earth, the shaft receding to a half-lit gloom below, far in the foundations of the city. The rock had been drilled to a depth, Winter estimated, of fifty feet. A rope ladder was bolted to the lip of the crevice, its rungs tumbling into the dank hollow.

He whispered Libby's name. She joined him at the

crater's edge and peered into the mouth of the pit. The base of the excavation had been rigged with electric light, enough to disclose that it adjoined a tunnel, branching to the left.

'How far do you think this whole operation extends?' she asked. The chasm gave her voice a hint of echo.

'God knows. That detonation we felt could have been miles from here. This is only the keyhole to whatever's down there…'

'We're going in, I take it?'

Winter smiled despite himself. She had said it so brightly. Christ, she was painfully young. 'You're too bloody keen for this job, girl.'

'Give me time. I'm sure I'll be a narky old git like you eventually.'

'Might even keep you alive.'

Libby adjusted her cap with a smirk. 'Do keep passing on the wisdom of the ancients, mate. But I'm the one with the gun.'

Winter placed a foot on the rope ladder, testing it for support. The ladder sagged but held his weight. He began to make his way down, the wooden rungs swaying as they passed through his hands. Soon he was eye level with dark, porous rock. The air in the shaft was cool against his face, already laced with a subterranean chill.

Libby watched from the edge of the crater, ready to follow the moment he dropped to the ground.

Winter glanced down, in time to see a man in overalls emerge from the tunnel's entrance.

He froze, a hanging target, the boiler-suited figure framed between his shoes.

'*Parola d'ordine!*' the man called up, the voice booming through the shaft.

He was demanding a password.

'*Parola d'ordine!*'

Winter rummaged for words. 'I…'

Again, even more insistently. '*Parola d'ordine!*'

The shot came quicker than Winter anticipated.

He twisted the rung the moment he saw the gun. Kicking at the wall he wrenched the rope away, evading the angle of fire as best he could. The ladder spun in the shaft. The bullet scraped the rock with a fleeting match-head glow.

The man was aiming again. Winter fought to keep the ladder spinning. But the rope was tangling, suspending him in place. The second bullet barely missed him, its sparks leaping for his eyes.

There was a soft, pneumatic hiss. Winter knew it at once. The kiss of a silencer. It was a strangely kind sound.

The man slumped, Libby's bullet embedded in a lung. So much for a simple reconnaissance, no confrontation.

Winter let the ladder untwine then shinned down the rest of the rungs. He leapt the last few feet, landing on the hard layer of volcanic rock at the base of the shaft. The fallen figure in the overalls stared up at him, half-catatonic as blood thickened on his chest. He was still breathing but clearly not for long. Winter picked up the fallen gun, taking it for his own.

He checked the chamber. The weapon was empty. Winter threw it back to the ground.

'So where's his mate?' asked Libby, landing beside him, gun in hand. 'There were two of them earlier.'

Winter eyed the tunnel entrance. It was old, its sandstone walls chipped and eroded, the gloom beyond receding beneath a crush of rock. This passage had to date back centuries. 'Keep close,' he told her.

Together they stepped into the underworld, into the chill and the half-dark.

26

It was a shadow city, a buried metropolis, an echo of Naples entombed in the earth.

The Greeks had carved it from the core of volcanic rock beneath their streets. The compacted ash – as sturdy as it was workable – had been hollowed into a honeycomb of cavities and passageways. Winter could still see the pick-mark scars in the walls, left by the slave labourers, quarrying rock for the temples and villas of their masters. Muscle and blood had built this silent kingdom.

The tunnel they had entered was cramped and icily moist. Libby took the lead, keeping her gun levelled as the passage broadened. Ahead of them stood a series of arches, a succession of stonework maws retreating into the distance. These archways were tiled with chunks of brick, overlapping like unkempt teeth. It gave the waiting path a hungry aspect.

The air was stale but breathable. Winter imagined there had to be cracks in the vast arteries of rock, allowing oxygen to infiltrate the lower levels. More than anything he was struck by the absolute stillness of this hidden world.

It was tangible, a weight against the senses, something cold and hushed and heavy as the accumulated centuries.

They followed the trail of electric light. Soon the gradient began to deepen. The further they explored the more the ancient infrastructure revealed itself. Civilisation had existed here, in this dead, discarded maze. The ghost-lines of its geography could still be glimpsed. This was the imprint of another, infinitely older Naples, preserved in all its sprawl and emptiness. It was a place possessed by its own past.

The Romans had taken this quarried-out labyrinth and turned it into a remarkable water system. Winter remembered that these tunnels had once functioned as an elaborate network of aqueducts and cisterns, serving the city above. No wonder the passages were so constricted – the tighter the tunnel the faster the flow of water through these subterranean veins. A cholera epidemic in the late nineteenth century had seen the tunnels sealed but the memory of water, the dark surge of its power, seemed to haunt these glistening, echoing spaces.

'Take a look at this...'

Libby kept her voice to a whisper but Winter could still hear it echo through the arcade of rock. He looked to where she was gesturing with her gun. Heaped against the sandstone wall was an incongruous assortment of objects. A portable stove, some pans, a grime-blackened doll in an equally filthy strawberry-print dress. Scattered a little further along were toy cars and a sewing machine. The jumble of items seemed absurdly domestic in

338

the context of the tunnel but there was an unsettling melancholy to them too. It was evidence that people had tried to live down here, to survive, somehow, in the dark and the bone-deep damp.

'They must have used this as a shelter,' said Winter, crouching as he spoke. 'They found a way down here, when the bombs ripped the streets apart...'

The Allied bombardment, he knew, had been remorseless. British and American forces had targeted the ports and industrial centres, scouring the city with fire. It was a war he had no personal memory of but Hart had been a part of it, and his legacy felt like one of those spiked mines still drifting in the shipping lanes, twenty years after peace had been declared. Right now that mine felt terribly close on the tide.

Winter put his hand to the wall, tracing a series of markings on the mustard-coloured rock. It was a child's picture, crudely scratched in chalk but recognisable as a portrait of Mussolini. Il Duce was crumpling planes in his oversized fists. Allied bombers, no doubt. Next to him was a single word, the letters boldly drawn. *Vittoria*. Victory. It must have been a kid's prayer.

They headed deeper into the warren of sandstone. Soon they were navigating a long, low passageway, some ancient pipeline that had once sent water swilling between the cisterns. There was a promise of more electric light at the end of it but the tunnel felt oppressive, its walls a fist of rock around them, the air thick and rank in their throats.

The tunnel opened onto a wooden walkway that

straddled an abyss, all that was left of an underground reservoir, long empty. A squat lamp blazed at the edge of this chasm, the kind usually found at roadsides. It gave the rock a harsh yellow cast and hardened the shadows of the pit. A cable trailed across the bridge, connecting the lamp to a generator on the other side, marked with the branding of the gas company.

Winter and Libby paused at the tunnel's edge, wary of the light's unflinching brightness. As they strained their ears they could hear the sound of movement and voices. It was faint but distinct, echoing out of the aperture that lay at the opposite end of the walkway.

Cesare's operation had to be close now.

Chancing it, they crossed the wooden slats, their shadows huge and fleeting against the cavern's ceiling.

The air had thickened with dust. And there was a sharp smell of almonds, one that Winter always associated with freshly detonated gelignite.

The next tunnel opened onto a lip of rock, a crescent of sandstone perched above another yawning hollow in the earth. This void was even deeper than the one they had just crossed. The sheer magnitude of its emptiness hit like a gut punch. It was visceral, that sense of immense timelessness, a mass of history trapped with nowhere to go.

They hunched as close to the edge as they could risk, a few feet from where a ladder connected the slab of rock to the ground below. There was a pack of men in the cavern – seven, Winter counted, including the one who had been in the workman's tent – and they were standing among a tumble of rubble. A fresh fall, judging by the haze of dust that blurred the light from the assembled lamps.

Winter immediately spotted that the debris didn't match the surrounding sandstone. The colour and texture were different. It was granite, great, craggy chunks of it, torn apart by explosive.

The remnants of a wall rose from the bed of the dried-out reservoir. A ragged outline of granite – all that was left of this barricade – clung to a pair of pillars that reached to the roof of the cavern. Beyond the wall's remains lay some kind of antechamber. Whatever it contained was just out of view but Winter caught a gleam of something pearl-bright, reflecting the glare of the lamps.

There was a soft click at his ear. He turned and saw that Libby had a subminiature Minox camera pressed to her eye. She was taking reconnaissance shots, capturing the scene for London. Again the camera clicked, the sound barely registering against the deadening silence of this space.

Then Winter caught another noise, almost as soft. It had come from behind them, he was certain. He turned to look back at the tunnel.

It came again. The sound of rock striking rock, no more than the briefest scratch of impact.

He stared into the passageway. It looked like a black wound. The walls, he swore, had tightened, squeezing the light into nothing.

He rose to his feet and stepped cautiously into the mouth of the tunnel. The chill inside had intensified, just as the darkness had deepened.

The sound multiplied as he stood there. In seconds it had become a steady, brittle patter. It wasn't quite loud enough to attract the attention of the men below but the volume was building with each echo.

Winter peered into the opening. Fragments of sandstone spat like hail from the shadows, as if shaken free by the earth itself. Was it an aftershock of the detonation that had levelled the wall? No, the ground was too steady for that. But the tunnel was crumbling just the same.

Winter turned to look at Libby. She had pocketed her camera and was moving to join him. He raised a hand, directing her to stay where she was.

Winter's eyes moved across the surface of the rock. It had the texture of skin, pitted and porous, a lattice of veins chasing through it. He could almost see musculature in the contours of the wall, places where the sandstone bulged like a twist of limbs, folded upon themselves.

There was silence in the passage now. The patter of rock had stopped.

A shape very like a man erupted from the tunnel wall.

It tore itself free, its hands breaking through the crumble of compacted ash, the entombed torso following with a hard, wrenching movement. As Winter stared through a tumult of dust he saw desiccated flesh, husk-dry and tight against the bone. The face of the thing was paralysed in torment but the eyes had an awful stillness, black and emptied, as if time had burnt the life from them.

He saw the mouth, then. It was crisscrossed with twine. The lips had been stitched shut.

More rock shattered behind him. Another buried body, shrugging away the sandstone like a chrysalis. Just like its counterpart it was swathed in grimy strips of cloth, tied like a toga.

They were the ancient dead, barely lit with existence.

Winter backed out of the tunnel as the cadaverous forms advanced. Libby was at his side now.

'Sodding hell,' she breathed, equally transfixed.

They both knew there was only so much precipice left behind them.

In unison the creatures flexed their jaws, traces of wasted muscle shifting beneath the ash-spattered flesh. The lips struggled against their stitches. Slowly the mouths began to peel open. The withered twine strained to contain them, drawn taut across the widening slits. Finally the stitches snapped and the teeth were revealed, filthy but knife-sharp.

They were vampires, and they had the thirst of centuries.

A punch of white light hit the revenants. The creatures recoiled, flinching at the sudden brightness. As the spotlight struck them Winter saw the faintest spark of sentience in their calcified eyes.

'Stay where you are!' demanded a voice from the cavern floor. It rumbled around the high rock walls, the words echoing and echoing.

'Not much in the way of choice, mate,' retorted Libby.

Cautiously, Winter took his gaze from the creatures.

He looked over his shoulder, his eyes pinching against the brilliance of the light. One of the lamps on the ground was tilted upwards, targeting the ledge. The men of the Shadowless stood behind it, some with guns in their hands.

Cesare was with them. He spoke again.

'So you dare to come here, do you, Englishman? I truly wonder if it's courage or ignorance that compels you.'

Winter traded a glance with Libby. Her gun was hidden in her jacket. They both knew it wouldn't be enough.

'We should talk, Cesare.'

For a moment the only reply was his own voice, reverberating through the cavern. And then a dry, dismissive laugh chased after it.

'Oxygen is precious down here,' Cesare taunted. 'No sense wasting it on conversation with a man I fully intend to kill.'

'Shame. We have so much more to discuss. As a businessman you should be open to possibilities.'

'My friend, at this moment you have no possibilities.'

Winter pushed the only advantage he had. 'We could talk money, Cesare. Contracts, perhaps. Maybe discuss the elimination of the competition. Every businessman's dream, isn't it?'

Libby gave a private smile, knowing the game he was playing.

This time there was a beat before Cesare replied. If he was rattled by Winter's knowledge he took care to conceal it from his men.

'With respect, Englishman, you are hardly in a position to make me an offer.'

'Oh, but I so nearly was, Cesare. One million pounds could have bought us both a lot of possibilities. I'm sure you'd have considered it an investment. You might even have made a killing.'

Winter's final words became a diminishing echo, trailing away beneath the dome of rock. For a moment silence held the cavern. And then, at last, Cesare spoke.

'Get down from there. Both of you.'

Winter eyed the revenants. They seemed less wary of the light now. He saw ribs scrape against skin as their chests heaved, clutching air into their exhumed lungs. The teeth of the creatures slid against withered lips, hungering.

'You might want to call your boys off,' he shouted down. 'Assuming these are your boys.'

Cesare cast his voice past Winter and Libby. The words he used were guttural, impenetrable, seemingly remnants of some long-dead language. They were also clearly a command. Hearing them the figures in the tunnel retreated, dragging their parched and atrophied limbs away.

As Winter watched they pressed their bodies against the walls, as if surrendering to the rock. Moments later pieces of sandstone tore from the ground in an upwards hail. They spattered against the undead things, encrusting them. The walls were restoring themselves, sealing and entombing their occupants once more. Soon only hints of the creatures remained, embedded in the protrusions of the tunnel's sides.

Winter walked to the lip of the ledge, the cavern yawning precipitously beneath him. Turning around he grabbed the rails of the ladder and began to descend, rung by wooden rung. Libby followed him down.

The men met them with a raft of raised guns. Cesare dismissed the weapons, stepping through the pack with an easy confidence in his own invincibility.

'They were the first of my kind in this city,' he said, expansively. 'The Romans brought slaves here from every outpost of their empire. Hispania. Gaul. The deserts of North Africa. Every race and creed. Among them were the undead, those who craved the sweetness of a stranger's blood as much as their freedom. Their seed took hold. In time they would claim Naples for their own.'

'They're guarding this place,' said Winter, his eyes straying to the antechamber, its contents still just out of sight. 'Is that it?'

Cesare nodded. 'They are of the lowest caste, mindless but loyal. Even those who ruled this city feared their thirst. They bound their lips before sinking their bodies deep in sanctified land, far to the north. Centuries later they were disinterred and brought here, given a new purpose, a new duty, protecting this precious place.'

Cesare switched his attention to Libby, recognition in his eyes. 'I have seen you before.'

She met his gaze and said nothing.

'Of course,' Cesare continued, placing her. 'The club. La Salamandra.'

He kept his eyes on her face but directed his next words to Winter, puzzlement and distaste in his voice.

'Why have you brought a waitress with you?'

Libby glared back at him. 'You can go to hell.'

Cesare took her chin in his hand, thrusting her head back. He smiled as he spoke. 'You weren't born to be a waitress, *piccolina*. Who would tip you with that attitude?'

He flung her jacket open and tore the gun from the inside pocket. 'Webley and Scott,' he stated, examining the weapon. 'British Intelligence, then. Is the Crown so desperate that it arms a girl?'

Libby shook her face free from his grip. 'I'll let you know, mate. Once I've killed you.'

Cesare thrust the gun into her hand. 'Keep it. I insist. It's entirely useless against me but it's Her Majesty's property, after all.'

Libby received the gun with a glower. 'I can still kill your men.'

'I can buy more men. This is Naples.'

Cesare moved to Winter, peeling aside a lapel to expose the empty shoulder holster.

'One gun between the pair of you. And I thought the British economy was improving.'

'We can't all pay a million for a hit, Cesare. Or were you using Daddy's money?'

There was a flare in Cesare's eyes then, something hot and sharp that was checked as quickly as it surfaced.

'You imagine you have power over me, Englishman. But this knowledge you possess means nothing to me, or my men. Look around you. They are loyal to me, not my father. You, on the other hand, are a failed assassin. Is there anything less worthy of respect in this world?'

'I'm pretty sure patricide comes close.'

Cesare stepped away, turning his back. He took a few measured paces and then pivoted to face them again. He wore a bitch of a smile now.

'Let me show you my inheritance. It will enrich your final minutes. It may even give them meaning.'

He led them through the rubble, to where the remnants of the wall stood, reduced to blackened lumps of granite. The almond tang of gelignite was strong and tufts of smoke still drifted between the chunks of rock. As they approached the shattered entrance Winter began to glimpse what waited for them in the antechamber.

At first it was no more than a mirroring of light, the blaze of the lamps striking a reflective surface and bouncing back into his eyes. And then, as he squinted, the light appeared to solidify, hardening into bright, glistening objects. A multitude of them, scattered haphazardly across the cavern floor.

It was a sea of bones.

They lay in fossilised drifts, skeletal remains that glinted cold and white as if freshly skinned. There were great, shining tangles of them, bones enmeshed with bones, interlocking, embracing. Some reached from the burial mound with a clawing of fingers, fixed in the moment of their demise. They were immaculately preserved.

This was a necropolis.

Winter forced himself to look away. The presence of so many bones left him sick with craving. He could feel magic stirring inside him, empowered by the remains. These bones, he knew, were potent. They had to be more than human. It made the ache in his veins unbearably keen.

He raised his eyes. A statue towered over the frozen swarm. It was some kind of holy figure, a man in robes, arms spread as though dispensing benediction. The blind marble eyes were compassionate even as wine-dark smears trailed down the cheeks. Stains of the same colour streaked the fingers. It took Winter a moment to realise that he was looking at dried blood, the residue of stigmata.

The outstretched arms cast a crucifix shadow across the gleaming remains.

'San Gennaro,' said Cesare, gazing up alongside him. There was a reverence, almost a tenderness, to the way he said the saint's name, lingering on the syllables. 'Martyred at Pozzuoli in AD 305 under the purges of Diocletian. He is the city's saint, the saviour and protector of Naples. His blood is a miracle to my kind.'

Winter took his eyes from the statue and swept the chamber. He saw long-faded frescoes and crumbling mosaics on the rear walls, depictions of what he took to be pagan rites, acts of worship for the old, abandoned gods, Mithras or Demeter or Dionysus. This sunken chamber had obviously been a place of sacrament for some time.

To his left was a gallery of tall hollows carved into the sandstone. Each niche held a single skeleton, positioned in a semi-foetal crouch. Above the bones were a succession of stone masks, imprints of faces, the eyelids closed, the features lean and aristocratic. Winter instinctively knew that these were the high-born of Cesare's race.

Now he understood the purpose of the icy, echoing space he was standing in. This was an elephant's graveyard of the undead.

No, he caught himself. *The dead.* Somehow these creatures had found an end here, in this cathedral of bone and rock, entombed beneath the city.

'They came here to die?'

Cesare nodded. 'The blood of San Gennaro confers that gift. The statue weeps for my kind. Tears of sacred blood. For some this endless thirst, these centuries of need, is too much to endure. They would hear of this place. The Mortal Sepulchre, as we call it. The promise of death, at last. And they would come here, the old and undying of every land. Pilgrims in search of oblivion.'

Winter returned to the saint's face, drawn to the rust-coloured tracks beneath the eyes. 'What are you saying? The blood from this statue has the power to kill your people?'

'God's mercy, I imagine. He made us, but I doubt we are in his image. Perhaps the Almighty knows guilt. Perhaps this is compensation. It removes the weak from our ranks, at least. Natural selection, you could say.'

'This chamber was sealed,' said Libby. 'You're not meant to be here.'

Cesare regarded her, still amused by her spirit. 'My father's choice. At the war's end he was aware that these bones would soon be a significant resource. The military of many nations desired them, wished to unlock their secrets. He trusted your country, *piccolina*, and he was betrayed. And so he saw to it that no one would find them. Not my people. Not yours.'

'I saw Russian Intelligence at the villa,' said Winter. 'I take it your father's changed his mind?'

'The Soviet consulate has been making overtures of late. But he doesn't need their money. And he's certainly not persuaded by their ideology.'

'So it's your deal, then? You're a pretty unlikely communist, Cesare. The heir to a crime cartel. Tell me, where exactly do you stand on the distribution of wealth?'

Cesare cast his eyes across the bones, indifferent to the jab. 'It's not about wealth. I have wealth.'

Winter began to sense the reach of his ambition. The contract on his father had only been a prelude. 'You're not in this with the Russians. This is part of your deal with the Erovores, isn't it?'

Cesare stepped into the shadow of San Gennaro. 'Two great empires divided by an ancient enmity. Centuries of pissing matches over territory and status. One day you realise… what a waste of possibility.'

He plucked a femur from the sprawl of bones. 'DNA, they named it. Our biological heritage. All that makes us what we are. We have science on our side, just like you. If we can unlock our own secrets then we can unlock the secrets of demons, too. Incubi. Succubi. Even the sons and daughters of Lilith have genetic code tattooed in their bodies.'

The bone turned in his hand, the fissures gleaming as they caught the arc of the lamp.

'Nature has always insisted on our separation, forbidden procreation between our species. Maybe now science can unite us. Find a way to entwine our DNA with theirs. That would be a template for true power in this world, don't you think?'

'My God,' said Libby, understanding. 'You want to breed with them...'

'A hybrid race, part Erovore, part vampire. Its thirst alone would be phenomenal. They would tax the blood of humanity and feast on its senses, too. True apex predators. Just imagine their hunger. How could they not rule?'

'So why do you need these bones? Why not just use the DNA of the living?'

'The *living*...' Cesare spoke the word with contempt. 'The very language you use... It's another facet of our physiology. Just as we cannot be reflected or photographed our genetic code cannot be recorded. It exists in flux, ever shifting. Only in the state of death does it stabilise.'

'The Russians have already found bones. I've seen the creature they've created. What makes these bones so crucial?'

'These are the remains of the high-born. The ultimate incarnation of our kind. The paragon, if you will.'

Cesare lobbed the bone back onto the pile, then smacked the dust from his hands. 'This graveyard is my inheritance. And the Mortal Sepulchre will bring the Glorious and I dominion over your species. I imagine you'll wish my father had cut a deal with the Russians.'

'Don Zerbinati's still alive,' said Winter. 'I'm a failed assassin, remember? You're not inheriting this, Cesare. You're stealing it from under him. That's quite a risk you're taking.'

Cesare walked back from the bones, his body language assured.

'It would have been easier if you'd killed him. But he's abandoned this place. I can still take what I need. I'll deal with him soon enough. Believe me, I'm impatient for my empire.'

'You really think he'll be that easy to depose? A vampire king?'

'Tomorrow's on my side, Englishman. I'll find the bullet I need. And a more reliable assassin.'

He gave an imperious snap of his fingers, summoning the nearest of the Shadowless.

'Take them outside. Kill them in the tunnels. Their blood doesn't belong here.'

Two of the men moved forward, revolvers in hand, ready to march them out. As they did so Libby levelled her gun at Cesare.

'What about your blood, mate? Good enough for this place, do you reckon?'

Cesare regarded the weapon with disdain. 'Don't embarrass yourself, waitress. That's useless against me. I've told you.'

Libby kept the gun tight in her hand, aiming it squarely at Cesare's chest. 'Well, that all depends on the bullet, now doesn't it?'

Winter stared at her. She held her aim with the same unflinching poise he remembered from the hotel room.

Cesare gave a flicker of a smile, more out of reflex than amusement. It didn't linger.

'You don't possess such a bullet.'

Libby's gaze was resolute, hard as glass. 'You think there's only one of them out there? I saw the map Franzeri made. I know where the thorns are located. All of them. And so does British Intelligence. Trust me, mate, there's another bullet. And this one isn't for your father.'

Winter's eyes moved from the gun to her face. There was no crack in her composure, no giveaway shift of muscle beneath the skin, no trace of sweat. If this was a bluff she was utterly committed to it.

Libby allowed him a fleeting sideways glance as she kept the gun steady. 'I didn't come to Naples for you, Mr Winter. You were just a complication. He's the reason I'm here. That's my assignment, see? Infiltrate his business. Work out what he's up to. Put this bullet in him. So no, I couldn't exactly give you my bloody gun, now could I?'

Winter knew she had already fired the gun. That shot by the tunnel entrance. Had she reloaded without him seeing?

Cesare's men took aim at her. Once more he coolly waved the weapons down.

'Relax. She's lying. I know she's lying.'

Libby raised her chin, baiting him. 'Go on then, little prince. Gamble it. Because I'm not backing down.'

Cesare took a step, no more, toward her. 'Say you put

354

this bullet in me. This make-believe bullet. What then? The pair of you will be dead in seconds. My men won't let you leave this chamber alive.'

'It's a make-believe bullet, you prick. What do you care?'

With her free hand Libby reached inside her jacket, extricating the photos she had shown Winter in his room. She pressed the stack of surveillance shots into his palm, keeping her eyes fixed on Cesare.

'Get out of here. And get these to London.'

'I'm not going anywhere,' said Winter. The glossy prints were sticky against his flesh. It felt like he was already holding her death sentence.

'Go,' Libby insisted, the word escaping between her teeth, hot and urgent.

'Give me the gun, Cracknell. You get yourself out of here. And take these pictures with you.'

She shook her head, still targeting Cesare's heart. 'This is my mission, not yours. So shut up and for God's sake go.'

'Give me the gun!'

'You've already wasted one of these bullets, Mr Winter. Don't waste another. Go. Go now. Make this count.'

She had the bullet. Winter was so nearly certain of it. He took a step away from her, and then another, hating what he had to do. As he pocketed the prints he turned and saw Cesare spread his arms, as if mocking the pose of San Gennaro. There was absolute confidence in his stance.

'Take that shot, then,' taunted Cesare. 'Take it with your make-believe bullet.'

He nodded to one of his men, who aimed his revolver at Winter. There was the snap of a safety catch being disengaged.

'Take it now, girl. Before I instruct Giancarlo to shoot the Englishman in the head.'

Winter stopped moving.

Cesare took another step forward, determined to break Libby's resolve. His shirt strained across his chest as he extended his arms in sacrificial fashion. He was offering his heart as a target, daring her to fire.

Another step, closer still.

'Are you lying to me, *piccolina*? Or just too gutless to shoot?'

Libby faced him, expressionless.

He advanced on her again, placing a patent leather shoe in the dust. This time Libby pulled the trigger. The force of the shot sent Cesare reeling. He stumbled, fighting for balance, body buckling at the impact. There was a sudden surge of blood on his shirt. He threw his arms across his ribs, the fists tightening as if clasping the pain.

Winter's eyes flashed to the man with the gun on him. He was staring at his leader, unsure of what he had just witnessed.

Winter looked back at Libby. There was a tremble in her gun hand now but her face remained hard.

Slowly Cesare gathered himself. He gave a smile like smashed glass as he raised his head from his chest. A bullethole had burnt his suit, precisely above his heart. A

356

tiny curl of smoke drifted from the blackened fabric.

'Oh, you crazy girl,' he said, straightening up. 'I almost believed you.'

He closed the gap between them and ripped the gun from her hand. Then he walked away, weighing the weapon. 'Yes, Webley and Scott. A classic.'

He turned and shot her in the heart.

27

It was a terribly ordinary bullet that tore through Libby Cracknell.

Nothing sacred, nothing magical, nothing in the least bit remarkable. Just a plain lump of lead, jacketed in copper, shipped from a Royal Ordnance Factory in a box of a thousand, perfectly matching. For all that a single bullet could steal a life or spark a war or tilt history on its axis they tended to be dull, practical things. And this one, in this moment, was no exception.

The bullet carved through Libby's chest. Its punch was enough to knock her from her feet, slamming her body backwards. Blood sprayed from the exit wound in a bright, insistent arc. As the cartridge escaped her it struck the cavern wall with a screech of copper on rock.

Winter ran to her as she collapsed.

Cesare threw the gun to the ground, clearly having no further use for the thing. He regarded her fallen body, lying among the bones. 'Consider that a tip, little waitress.'

Winter crouched by Libby, hearing her raw, shuddering breaths as her lungs struggled for air. There was blood in her mouth and it streamed between her teeth. Her eyes were fixed on his, the pupils huge and intense, fighting for a connection.

'Keep looking at me,' he urged her. 'Don't look away.'

He threw her jacket open. The wound had drenched her blouse, spreading in a tacky, darkening smear from her ribs to her collarbone. Winter ripped the material, exposing scorched flesh that was already blistering. He peered at the point of entry, attempting to gauge the angle of the bullet and just what damage had been done.

She had taken a direct hit to the heart. If the bullet had severed the aorta then she had only minutes. If it had punctured the left ventricle then her chances were marginally higher, but he knew only immediate medical attention could hope to arrest fatal blood loss, and that was impossible, given where they were.

He pushed back his rage, determined to stay cold, to keep focused. The hole in her chest was relatively small, no bigger than a halfpenny. If the point of exit was any larger then blood could rush into the pericardium, the membrane surrounding the heart. If that occurred then the flood of liquid would throttle her heart's ability to fill and pump. He had watched a colleague die that way in Kashmir, claimed by a Red Chinese sniper. It was an excruciating way to go, a fist closing inexorably around your life.

He took his eyes from the wound and looked into her face again. 'I'm with you, Cracknell. I'm right here.'

Her eyes remained locked on him but there was a dry,

brittle wrenching in her throat. It sounded like words cracking apart before they even had a chance to be spoken.

Another memory. This one came to him like a stutter-flash of nightmare. He saw his wife, Joyce, lying on the tiles of their bathroom floor, a bullet in her chest. She was staring up at him with eyes as empty as glass. It was an image he knew well, and one he always fought to suppress, to stamp down, because the pain of it was so huge it would simply consume him. But he could never bury it. It was in the dreams that always tore him awake.

He had lost Joyce that day. He had seen her die and he had been helpless.

'Keep looking at me,' he told Libby once again. 'Breathe in and breathe out. Slowly now. That's it. We'll get you the help you need.'

He was lying to her. She was going to die, just like Joyce. It was inevitable.

Winter became aware that Cesare was pacing behind him, kicking his shoes through the dust, impatient for attention.

'Leave her be, Englishman. Or are you giving her the last rites?'

There was a murmur of amusement from the men that ringed the chamber.

'Come on, what is she to you? A crazy child. Let her die. Turn and face me.'

Winter half heard the provocation. He could summon a shadow scythe, he told himself. Take power from the bones around him, fuel the magic, unleash it on these men, on Cesare. Let that black, unholy thing have its way. Part of him craved that, craved the rush that would inevitably speed through his veins.

But Libby was still alive, still breathing, still here in front of him. He couldn't take a chance on what that thing might do to her, even in her final moments.

Could he save her with magic, as Alessandra had saved him? In that moment it felt impossible. Where in God's name did he even begin?

He forced himself to break eye contact. And then he got to his feet and turned to confront Cesare.

If he was going to die it wouldn't be as a magician.

Winter reached into his jacket pocket. The knuckle-duster was there. He slid his fingers through the rings and made a fist, feeling the cool weight of brass, tight against his skin. It was barely an advantage. But it was all that he had.

'You're going to fight me with that?' asked Cesare, incredulous. 'Maybe I should shoot you too, spare us both the embarrassment.'

Winter moved on him, his stride determined, building all the momentum he could in the meagre space between them. He swung at Cesare's face. For an opening punch it was sloppy and impulsive and Cesare easily evaded it.

A fist smashed in retort against Winter's left cheek, glancing against his eye. Cesare's salamander ring ripped the skin, vicious as a baiting hook. It drew the first blood.

Winter took a step back, shaking the blow from his head. Seconds later he traded a sharp, taut punch in return, carving upwards. This time the slab of brass connected with Cesare's jaw, striking bone. The impact of the punch rang through Winter's arm. It felt good.

One of the men watching raised a revolver. He looked to his leader, wondering if he should simply put a bullet in the Englishman. Cesare waved him down. Clearly this was a fight he meant to finish.

The pair circled each other in the dust, arms raised, shielding their faces. They exchanged a volley of punches, blocking each other's fists as fast as they were thrown. Then they broke apart again, returning to their wary shuffle among the rubble and bones.

Winter's left eye was wet with blood. The vision on that side had begun to blur, halving his perception. If he closed his other eye he knew the outline of Cesare would swim in a red haze. He tried to blink the blood away, not daring to put a hand to the eye and give his opponent even the briefest moment of advantage.

The girl was dying. This preening shit had shot her and smiled.

He threw a sudden, impetuous punch, as much a surprise to him as it was to Cesare. This one found its target, straight across the mouth. Winter heard the brass scrape against the teeth.

Cesare backed away, buying some space. He lowered his head until his eyes sunk beneath his brow. They regarded Winter, dark and thirsting, fixed on the blood that was dripping from the wound above his eye.

The vampire's lips parted. The flesh peeled away from

the teeth, curling in a feral snarl, a sheen of saliva trailing on the enamel. Winter saw the brace of canines descend, locking into place. They hung above the tongue as the mouth gaped.

Cesare opened his fists. He raised his hands, displaying the fingers. The nails extended, keen as claws, sliding from the skin as if unsheathed.

'This is why your kind will never be more than prey.'

He lunged at Winter. The nails sliced the air, ready to shred flesh.

Winter met the attack with another jab to the teeth. This one sent Cesare staggering. For an instant he was off-balance, fighting to stay on his feet. His men edged aside as he stumbled back, not sure if they should intervene.

Winter pressed his advantage. Again he targeted the mouth. He put every scrap of his hate into the punch, and the next punch too, and the one that followed. All the fury and frustration he had tried to suppress, just to keep his head level. Now it consumed him, and he let it. His rage was an energy and it impelled his fist into Cesare's mouth, over and over.

Winter heard the teeth crack as he slammed the brass. He punched again. This time they shattered.

Stunned by the succession of blows, Cesare lost his footing. He tumbled to the ground, landing in a graceless sprawl among the bones. When he lifted his face there was a riot of blood on his lips.

Winter stood over him, his chest shuddering as he tried to steady his breathing. 'Get up,' he demanded.

'Get on your feet and let's finish this.'

Eyes burning with humiliation, Cesare heaved himself onto his elbows. He spat out a mouthful of blood and teeth. All that was left between his lips were ragged white shards. The canines were barely more than splinters now, studding the gums like chips of porcelain.

'You're already finished, Englishman...'

He gave an emphatic nod. The man to Winter's left levelled a black Beretta, taking aim.

Winter stared at the gun, at the blank gape of the barrel. The bullet was imminent.

He realised his last thought in this world would be of Libby Cracknell. He saw her smiling in the London sun, rocketing that MGB through the dawn streets. No more than a moment, like all of them.

The shot didn't come. The man holding the Beretta shifted his gaze. He had focused on something just over Winter's shoulder, at the entrance to the sepulchre. Cesare had seen it too, and whatever it was had shaken him.

There was a new presence in the ancient chamber. Winter could tell it was there even though his back was turned. He sensed it in his skin, in the sudden ant-crawl of the flesh above his collar. A change had occurred in the air. Something with an aura even colder than rock and bone had arrived. Something just as old. It was a presence Winter had already encountered, only hours before.

He turned, knowing exactly who he would see.

Don Zerbinati stood among the rubble, alone and immaculate in a dark grey suit, the blaze of a lamp catching a golden tiepin. His expression was impassive, his eyes intense. There was a simple hessian sack in his hand, tied with a drawstring knot. Whatever it contained strained against the sides. As the sack slowly revolved the shape of the object revealed itself. It took Winter a moment to realise it was the outline of a human head.

Another saint, no doubt, part of that grim collection displayed at the villa.

The vampire king's arrival had a visible effect on the men of the Shadowless. Their body language altered as he strode between them. They edged back, watching him pass, wary and respectful. Whatever deference they had shown to Cesare was now transferred to his father. Don Zerbinati didn't simply command their respect. He seemed to take it by divine right.

His eyes were on his son alone. 'I always knew you had ambition. I never imagined it would be quite so brazen. Here, of all places. How dare you.'

Cesare gathered himself, wiping the blood from the wreck of his mouth. 'Father…'

'We have so little that is sacred to us, Cesare. There are no churches for our kind. No crosses. This shrine is the only mercy we have ever been shown.'

He gestured to one of the sandstone hollows. It held a skeleton, the hunched bones ornamented with gold. The stone mask above it had a woman's face, the features thin and regal.

'Your own mother found an ending here. And you choose to defile it?'

Cesare was on his feet now. 'I'm defiling nothing. I'm taking what's mine.'

'I have given you so much.'

If there had been any hint of contrition on Cesare's face it was gone now. 'This shrine is my birthright. When you sealed it away from the world you sealed it away from me. I call that a disinheritance, Father. And an insult to your own blood.'

Don Zerbinati regarded his son with disdain. 'You are an insult to the blood of kings, to my dynasty, to the house of Zerbinati. This is my city. It will always be my city. I'm amazed you think it can keep secrets from me.'

He acknowledged Winter for the first time since stepping into the sepulchre. It was the briefest glance, enough to make Winter feel he was an incidental detail in this confrontation.

'You paid this man to kill me.' Zerbinati's voice was cool and even. It was more a statement than an accusation.

Cesare shook his head and gave a quick, viperish smile. 'He's nothing to do with me. It's the British who want you dead.'

'No, it's you who wants me dead, Cesare. You and the Glorious, together. I know every detail. The bullet. The contract. The plan you have for these bones, for the legacy of our people. How you wish to pervert our species. The demon children you dream of.'

'All I want are the bones. I would never want you dead, Father. Why would you believe that?'

Winter lost patience simply standing there. 'Bullshit.

367

You made the payment. One million pounds. The evidence is right here.'

He pulled the stack of prints from his pocket and offered them to Zerbinati. 'It's nothing to do with British Intelligence. This is the proof you need.'

Zerbinati dismissed the photographs. 'You think I don't have proof? That I would make this claim against my son without evidence? Without a witness?'

He lifted the hessian sack and pulled apart the drawstring knot. Then he reached inside and removed its contents.

There was a head in his hand, held by a fistful of black hair. But it wasn't a relic. It didn't belong to some long-dead medieval saint. It was the head of Salvatore, the one Winter had severed with the shadow scythe in the passage beneath the villa. And it was still animated with unholy life, just as he had left it on the tunnel floor. The shearing wound had sealed itself into an angry pulp of sundered flesh and congealed blood.

Salvatore's eyes fixed on Winter, alive with hate. His mouth opened but the click of saliva was the only sound it could summon.

'The remains of your men were discovered soon after the Englishman's escape,' Zerbinati told Cesare. 'Salvatore and I came to a mutually beneficial agreement. He was commendably loyal to you but he has no desire to endure life this way. He told me of your ambitions. I gave him the voice he needed.'

He placed his hands either side of the head, spreading his elegant fingers across the bloodless skin until they rested beneath the eyes and the mouth. When he spoke again his voice had a guttural register. Three raw syllables that sounded as though they had been ground from a man's throat.

'*Bastardo!*'

Salvatore's eyes hadn't left Winter. The word was meant for him. In the absence of lungs and vocal cords Zerbinati was channelling the thoughts trapped inside the decapitated head. A vampire monarch's gift, Winter could only imagine.

'In return for his confession I have brought him here,' declared Zerbinati, his voice regaining its characteristic silk as it resonated across the rock walls. 'He shall find mercy among the pilgrims. A finality he would otherwise have been denied. So you've done some good, at least, Cesare, by unlocking this sepulchre.'

He walked to the feet of San Gennaro, the shadow of the saint falling upon him. Reverently he placed the head among the bones.

Salvatore's eyes rolled up, staring at the outstretched arms, at their promise of an ending. The lids flickered, then closed in gratitude, waiting for the hallowed blood that would one day seep from the marble hands.

Don Zerbinati turned to his son. 'Why, Cesare? Why crave even more power than you have?'

Cesare matched his gaze. 'Is that really how you built your empire? By asking such a stupid question?'

Zerbinati belted him with the back of his hand, sending blood flying from the ruined mouth.

'I am your father. And I am your king.'

'Well, what other reason do I need?' Cesare was frothing blood as he fought to push words through broken teeth. 'You call this a dynasty. How can it be a dynasty when you will never die? My bloodline is meaningless. You know that, Father. I've been your heir for centuries. I will always be your heir. Our kind inherit nothing! So I take what is mine!'

Don Zerbinati listened, and nodded, weighing a reaction.

'You will inherit my mercy,' he said simply. 'And my regret.'

As Winter watched he delved into his suit pocket. When he opened his hand the bullet – the sacred bullet – was resting on his palm, blistering the flesh around it.

Cesare stared at the object, realising his father's intention. 'You won't end my life. I'm still your blood!'

'Then my blood is poisoned. I'm cleansing the bloodline.'

Zerbinati took his son by the back of the head, wrenching him onto his knees. Cesare tried to pull away but the older vampire had superior strength, superior will.

'This is the power of the Christ. This is why you should have learned to fear it.'

Zerbinati locked a hand to Cesare's mouth, prising the jaws apart, forcing the shattered teeth to separate. The bullet was burning in his hand, charring the skin with a hiss of heat. Winter could smell the flesh searing in the presence of the thorn.

Cesare screamed as Zerbinati put the bullet on his

tongue. His father clasped the jaws together and pulled the head back, keeping his hand firm against the lips. In seconds Cesare had the bullet in his throat. He began to choke on it, compelled to swallow it down.

Zerbinati released his grip and stepped aside.

Cesare rocked on his knees, his eyes widening.

There was a tiny ignition of light at the centre of each pupil. The smallest flame catching hold, burning out of the black circles, scorching the irises and turning them into hot red coronas. In seconds the whites of the eyes were also on fire, seared into blindness. Soon the sockets held only smoke, pouring out of the eviscerated holes.

The skin cracked and curled like bonfire leaves, crumbling against bone. Cesare reached for his face, the tips of the fingers already reduced to ash. Even the golden salamander ring ran molten in the flames.

A voracious heat consumed him. A holy heat, absolute and annihilating, blazing out of his chest, out of the bullet, out of the hallowed thorn that had drawn the blood of the Nazarene millennia before. The conflagration savaged his body, purging the flesh like a wrathful spirit.

Cesare's carcass fell to the cavern floor, charred organs and blackened entrails exposed through the rags of his suit. There was no life left in him, only the cinder sparks of the dust that had once been skin.

Winter felt the sweat cool in his pores now that the heat had passed. He was shocked almost into numbness by what he had just witnessed. He looked from Cesare's remains to Don Zerbinati. The man's face was impassive.

In that moment he seemed part of the necropolis, something old and monolithic.

'You said this was a place of mercy.'

There was a flutter of muscle beneath the mouth. Zerbinati's eyes shimmered in the light of the cavern. He was fighting tears. It was obvious now. 'Mercy is always a matter of judgement.'

Winter pushed past Cesare's men to where Libby lay. He knelt beside her, easing her hand from the wound and sliding his fingers into hers, through the warm paste of blood. Her hand briefly tightened in response, but it was clear the strength was leaving her. The girl's skin had a pebble-coolness to it now. The blood was slowing in her veins as her heart failed.

She was still breathing but the pattern had changed; a dry rasp of breath followed by no breath at all and then, after an agonisingly long pause, another halting intake of air. It was the way people died, Winter knew. The awful, fractured rhythm of the final moments, snatching at existence.

'I'm with you, Libby,' he told her again. 'I'm not going anywhere.'

He remembered taking that bullet in Budapest, how Alessandra had saved him with magic, with a demon's enchantment that had crept from a mirror and healed the damage. He had that power inside him now, and no idea how to use it, how to shape it, how to keep this girl alive. He could only will her to keep breathing. Just one more breath, and another. It was all he could do and Christ, it wouldn't be enough.

'Who is she?'

Don Zerbinati was standing over them.

Winter kept his eyes on Libby, watching as she dragged the dusty air into her mouth. 'British Intelligence. She took a chance. She was brave.'

'She was your friend?'

Winter snapped at his use of the past tense. 'She's still alive. She's right here. She's breathing.' The words were as much for her as for Zerbinati.

Seconds passed before another tortured breath broke the hush of the chamber. Libby's hand hung limp in Winter's, barely any weight at all.

'My son did this?'

Winter nodded, on the verge of exasperation. 'He shot her. He shot her in the heart.'

Zerbinati considered this in silence.

'You're quite right,' he said at last. 'This sepulchre is a place of mercy. I can ensure she lives.'

Winter looked up, searching the other man's face. 'How?'

'We must make a deal.'

'There's no time for a bloody deal!' Winter shouted the words, his composure breaking. 'If you can save her, save her! Do it now!'

'First we reach an agreement,' said Zerbinati, evenly.

Winter sighed through his teeth and turned back to Libby. 'What are you asking?'

'I ask only your discretion. Tell your people nothing of what you found in my city. This crypt, these pilgrim bones. All that is buried here. Destroy those photographs.

373

Never speak of what you discovered. This site is sacred to my kind. It is not a charnel house to be plundered. Do we have an understanding?'

Winter wasn't persuaded. 'The Erovores told me about your ambitions. You're expanding your empire. You'll end up provoking a war between my people and yours.'

'The Erovores lied to you,' Zerbinati countered, coolly insistent. 'I have all the power I require, here in this city. Why would I provoke a war? The world is exquisitely balanced and I exist within that balance. Cesare had ambition but the centuries have burnt ambition from me. Simply respect my rule. British Intelligence must stay out of Naples. Once they learn where I have concealed the bones it will only be a matter of time before Moscow knows.'

'You've met with the Russians! I saw Kulganek at the villa!'

'Paragon is a dead operation for me. Another war, another alliance. I have told the Soviets we will reach no accommodation. If they choose to pursue their research it will be without my blessing. And that is an unfortunate place for anyone to be.'

'And who says you're telling the truth?'

'You have my word. The word of a king.'

Winter knew there was no time to debate this. 'Say I agree to this deal. Just how do you intend to save her?'

Zerbinati regarded the dying girl at his feet. 'I intend to give her life. As a gift.'

Libby's eyes widened as they met Zerbinati's. She

was on the edge of consciousness but the meaning of his words had cut through her.

Winter took a moment longer to realise the implication. 'No chance...'

'This is the proposition I'm offering. Do you accept?'

'Turn her into one of you? Just what kind of life do you think you'd be giving her? You people are monsters. I've seen your gift. A girl in the Spanish quarter, killing for a fix of blood...'

'We are far from monsters. Let me prove it to you.'

'You're the undead!'

Zerbinati nodded, accepting this with good grace. 'But we are not the dead. She would know life, at least. Do we have an agreement?'

'It's not my choice,' Winter protested. 'How can you imagine it's my choice?'

Libby gripped his hand with the last of her strength. She was fighting to focus, fighting to speak, determined to push the words from her throat. Winter leaned in, placing his head closer to hers.

'I want to live,' said Libby. The syllables cracked as she uttered them, all but lost in a choking swill of phlegm and blood.

She might be delirious, thought Winter. Brain activity was always chaos in the last moments.

'Listen to me,' he urged her. 'Do you understand what he's saying? What he's offering you? It's not life...'

Libby's eyes flared, a flash of hazel against white. It was as if she had summoned a final, familiar spark.

Again she forced the words out, blood spilling onto her chin as she spoke. 'I want this...'

Zerbinati addressed Winter. 'Do we have an agreement?'

Winter nodded, then let his hand slip from Libby's. He rose to his feet, keeping eye contact with her as long as he could.

'Do it. Do it quickly.'

Don Zerbinati knelt beside her. His spine arched as he threw back his head, drawing down the teeth.

The bite was taken with an unexpected tenderness. There was compassion in the way he didn't linger, didn't rend or shred the skin. Winter had only ever witnessed a vampire's blood-frenzy. This was different. There was nothing savage in the way Zerbinati pierced her throat. It was precise, almost surgical. An act of mercy, just as he had promised.

Libby gave a raw, urgent gasp as the teeth sank into her neck. Her body shuddered as her hands curled into fists. It was as if a vicious, animating current was fighting to escape her. Again she gasped, a shock of cold cavern air punching into her lungs.

Zerbinati took his teeth from her, dabbing at the blood that ringed his lips. Without turning his head he gave a command to the men. '*Stiletto!*'

One of the Shadowless proffered a switchblade. Zerbinati sprung the slender length of steel and scored his palm, summoning a crescent of blood. He brought the hand to Libby's mouth.

She instinctively lapped at the skin, her tongue darting against the wetness. There was hunger – and life – in the way she drank from the wound. Her eyelids quivered, lost in the new sensation, the new desire. And then she was still, her arms falling either side of her, rolling into the dust. Zerbinati rose, the transaction of blood complete. 'She'll be taken care of at the villa. She will need time.'

Winter crouched beside Libby, looking away from the puncture wounds on her throat. Her expression was dazed but her breathing had stabilised, back to its usual rhythm.

She raised her head, her eyes finding him. For a moment all she could do was stare, disoriented. And then, with an effort, she lifted herself onto her elbows.

'Take it slow,' said Winter.

The words tumbled out of her now. 'Feels weird… Everything's bright… I can taste it…'

Winter placed an arm around her shoulder. He pulled her close, hearing her breathe, feeling the brisk, solid thump of her heart, a heart that would outlast his, might even outrace the world.

'They're going to take care of you. It's going to be alright.'

As he held her he stared at the cavern wall.

There was only one shadow on the ancient rock.

28

The car waited in the blue dusk, its engine idling, poised for the interception.

Winter had tucked it into a lay-by, among the wild hawthorn that bordered this country road, just off the A2 on the main commuter route between London and the mansions of Kent. The car's position allowed him a view of approaching vehicles. There was just enough distance – just enough time – to determine silhouettes and skim licence plates. The rural speed limit was an advantage in that regard but this would be a tight, precise manoeuvre, turning on a matter of seconds. He had rehearsed it in his head until it was nearly a muscle memory.

The engine throbbed through the chassis of the saloon. Winter could feel the wheel vibrate in his hands as he glanced at the dashboard clock. Eighteen minutes to nine.

The sun had begun to fade an hour ago and the late summer twilight felt heavy on the Kent countryside, smudging the details of trees and hop kilns. Only the occasional Morgan or Mercedes broke the stillness of the fields, headlights chasing asphalt as they passed. If some returning stockbroker spotted the Rover Mk II wedged against the hedgerow they didn't slow. A breakdown, no doubt, a job for the RAC. Or maybe it was a furtive office tryst, fogging the rear windows.

Winter had hired the car from a firm in Sevenoaks. Once again he had used the name of Anthony Prestwick, a man who had begun to feel more real with each deception. In a day or so – if this went to plan – he would post an envelope to the firm, enclosing a roll of banknotes, more than enough to cover the inevitable damage to the car. It would be a tidy, decent thing to do. He would use a postbox in Faversham or Broadstairs, or some other town he had no intention of ever visiting again.

Winter sat there, staring through the passenger-side window, the remains of a travel sweet turning on his tongue. The road was reasonably quiet at this point in the evening, the traffic sporadic. People tended to flee the city at six, or perhaps a glass of port later. But not the man he was waiting for. This man had a schedule of his own, one that Winter had mapped and anticipated over the past weeks. It was just about all he could pin down.

Winter's Ford Zephyr waited in a tree-shaded copse on the other side of a field. He had left it there that morning, knowing he would need it later, once the Rover had served its purpose.

It was gone nine o'clock when he spotted the Bentley in the dying light. There was no mistaking the imposing grille and quad headlights of the Continental Flying Spur. A glance at the licence plate confirmed the target.

It was approaching from the left at a comfortable 30 mph.

Now.

Winter put his foot to the accelerator pedal, gunning the 3-litre engine and sending the car lurching out of the lay-by with a roar.

Then he stamped on the brake, arresting the surge of speed as best he could.

A horn sounded. The Bentley had no chance to swerve. The Rover was right in its path. Winter registered the driver's face, the shock and rage in his eyes.

He shut his own eyes and turned away, keeping his head absolutely level to counter the risk of whiplash. He gripped the wheel, muscles tightening as he braced for impact.

The prow of the Bentley ploughed into the passenger doors. Winter heard a protest of metal as the cars clashed, two sets of bodywork grinding and buckling. The pulverising crunch shook his bones and knocked the breath from his body. His head hit the driver's side window, his temple juddering against the glass, but the seat belt kept him secure.

At almost two tons the Bentley had the greater heft. Its pure weight and impetus sent the Rover scraping across the asphalt, some twenty yards along the road. The tyres of the smaller car screeched as they were rammed sideways.

Locked as one, the vehicles finally slid to a halt. Winter opened his eyes, lifting his hands from the steering wheel. He tested his fingers. No breakages. He looked to his left. The passenger window was shattered, the rear one too. A mess of glass littered the leather interior, mixed with splinters of wood from the ruptured panelling. Through the wreck of the window he saw the Bentley's chauffeur, furiously pushing himself out of his seat.

A jammed horn blared through the dusk. It was a strident, hateful sound. In the aftermath of the crash Winter couldn't tell which car it was coming from. He unclipped his seat belt and stepped out of the Rover, ignoring the bruised, winded ache in his chest.

He walked to the other side of the car, grinding scattered glass beneath his shoes. 'I'm so terribly sorry, old man. All my fault. So bloody stupid.'

The driver was already in his face. 'What the hell's your game, you tool? Didn't you see us coming?'

Six foot one, estimated Winter. Ex-service bearing, all fists and shoulders. Prominent veins, hot, pinched eyes. Not the longest fuse. Too confrontational for a bodyguard but could clearly handle himself if need be.

'I can't apologise enough. It's an insurance claim, of course, but damnably inconvenient for you. I'll let you have my card.'

'This is a Bentley!' the man shouted above the insistent sneer of the horn. 'You don't do that to a Bentley!'

'Really, so sorry. Complete idiot. But we'll sort this out.'

The chauffeur turned to inspect the damage. The chrome grille was shredded, the silver-winged hood ornament knocked out of kilter. With a pained sigh he lifted the bonnet, wrenching the length of crumpled metal away from the engine. Steam hissed from the radiator in a scalding cloud.

As he leaned in to fix what he could Winter cold-cocked him with the gun he had slipped from his suit. The weapon fell in a brisk, slanting blow. Concussed, the man hit the ground, his face twisting against the asphalt.

Winter spun the weapon so that the handle sat in his palm. He stepped past the driver's unconscious body, past the gleaming olive bodywork of the Bentley. When he reached the rear door he rapped his knuckles on the window.

'Get out,' he instructed, with a curt wave of the gun.

At first there was no response from the car's remaining occupant. And then Winter heard the thump of the door's security bolt being unlocked. It was just audible over the incessant horn that still filled the road.

He reached out and opened the Bentley's door.

Lord Auberon Gallard sat among the expanse of wood and leather, his austere features given extra keenness by the half-light. He regarded Winter with cool, grey-eyed detachment.

'You know, you could have just asked my secretary to put this in the diary.'

'I told you to get out.'

Gallard swung his lean legs from the vehicle, his smartly cut camel coat sweeping over the dimpled leather. There was a black attaché case in his hand, embossed with the letters S and E in gold leaf. He held it close to his body.

The man carried the scent of sandalwood. But there was another note, too, beneath the cologne. Something sweetly bitter as old flowers.

Exiting the car he drew himself to his full height. He

383

was bony but imposing, with more presence than his thin frame might have suggested. Gallard took a moment to inhale the drowsy evening air, the hollows of his cheeks sharpening beneath the skin.

'To die in an English field, in late summer...' He turned to face Winter directly, acknowledging the gun. 'I take it you are here to kill me?'

'I'm here to get answers.'

'Of course you are. A lifetime's worth.' There was a provocation in his eyes as he said that.

Winter found the man unexpectedly familiar. Just the faintest ghost of recognition in those aquiline features, in the crisp, supercilious manner, so poisonously polite. They had met before, he felt sure of it. This was one of Hart's memories, rising inside him but not quite breaking the surface. He had a history with this man.

The horn ceased.

'I'm impressed you found me,' Gallard continued, lowering his voice to match the sudden hush of the road. 'Good work. Most diligent. You're a credit to Sir Crispin.'

'Everyone has a pattern. Even you.'

'Yes, but even so. You retrieved this intelligence from the girl, I take it?'

Winter said nothing.

Gallard gave a pursed smile. 'She went silent on us weeks ago. I rather imagined you'd killed her in Naples.'

'I did. Always a mistake to leave a potential assassin alive. Key rule in this game.'

'Pity. She had promise.'

Winter glanced at the empty road. It was time to move. Another car would be along any minute, discovering its route blocked by the conjoined heap of the Rover and the Bentley. There was no telling how long Gallard's chauffeur would remain unconscious, either.

He waved his gun, indicating the rusted gate that waited at the edge of the field, its iron bars askew, slanting into the earth.

'Start walking.'

With a louche show of obeying Winter's instruction, Gallard turned and led the way. Beyond the gate the field sprawled into fast-falling darkness. The two men stayed close to the cover of the tree-lined perimeter, walking through parched grass and crumbled earth, the shadows of branches spidering over the back of Gallard's coat. The gnat-busy air had the queasy scent of hops, drifting from the kilns that rose like castle turrets against the first stars. Rooks cawed in the oaks, the birds beginning to roost as the autumn equinox approached.

Winter kept the gun fixed on Gallard's spine.

The path took them to a solitary outbuilding. It was centuries old to judge by the ragged state of its crude slab walls. Across another field lay a farmhouse, its distant windows as bright as the building's crude, empty apertures were black.

Gallard waited for Winter to unlatch a wooden door that had been warped and scoured by the elements. And then he stepped inside, still pressing the attaché case to his chest. Winter followed him in, watchfully.

The interior was stark and stone-cool. The only light in the structure came from the high, ripe moon outside. Agricultural implements hung from hooks hammered into raw stone and there was an astringent smell of oil from the rags draped over pots and buckets.

'Stand against the wall.'

Gallard did so, placing himself halfway into a chalky arc of moonlight. His storm-grey eyes moved across Winter's face.

'I seem to recall you were rather boyish. Bit of a cherub, in fact. What happened? Was it that knife you took in Namibia? A near-death experience must be terribly aging.'

Winter knew this show of insouciance was a psychological ploy. A counter-move, designed to get under his skin. He was intrigued nonetheless.

'I knew you?'

Gallard marvelled. 'You really have no recollection, Tobias?'

'My name is Christopher Winter.'

'That was never your name. An identity the Crown assigned to a shell of a man. Not the man I knew in the war.'

'It's the name I've taken. It's who I am.'

For a moment Gallard's tongue idled against his lips. He had sensed a faultline. 'It frightens you, doesn't it? *He* frightens you. All that you were, all that you did. The man you could be again. You were so easily seduced by magic. But you were never quite sated, were you? Part of you still craves the black gift in your veins. Just like he did.'

Winter shook his head. 'He's gone,' he said,

unequivocally. 'I'm not Tobias Hart.'

Gallard indicated the gun in Winter's hand. 'I knew you'd come for me. All these years I've kept a watch on you. Intercepted your briefings, your psychological assessments. When Malcolm Hands disappeared at the same time you did I imagined you must have killed him. Reclaimed your memories. You became an active risk to me at that point.'

'So you sent the girl to kill me. She took her time.'

'Oh, first we had to find you. And then we observed you. I needed to know just how much of your past you remembered. The contacts you might renew.'

'You overplayed your hand. I don't remember you at all. You've stepped into daylight for nothing.'

'This is hardly daylight. And it's brought us together, at least. I'll be the one who kills you this evening. There's a rather lovely symmetry to that.'

Another provocation. Winter ignored it, keeping the gun steady. He nodded to the gold-stamped initials on Gallard's attaché case. 'Sovereign Executive. Just how long have you been hidden away in Chancery Lane?'

'Where else would I be?' parried Gallard. 'Those tunnels have always concealed us. Back when we operated under so many shadow names. The Joint Technical Board. The Inter-Services Research Bureau. All those bogus branches of the Admiralty or the Air Ministry. We were wrapped in dead ends and cul-de-sacs and blind alleys. Infinite loops of misdirection. We've always known how to hide among the filing.'

Winter realised what Gallard was saying. 'You're telling me you're the remnants of the SOE...?'

Special Operations Executive. Hart had worked for it, Judit Majoras had told him, back in Budapest. It had been the covert intelligence network created to back the resistance in Axis-occupied Europe. Churchill's Secret Army, they had called it, not entirely favourably. And there had been another, altogether more damning name: The Ministry of Ungentlemanly Warfare.

'You were dissolved in '46,' said Winter, disbelievingly. 'Attlee himself shut you down. That was a prime minister's direct order.'

'Oh, we'd overrule God in the name of country, believe me. The Joint Intelligence Committee was always queasy about our methods but they knew we were more effective than the SIS. Peace is fragile, war is inescapable. We were a bespoke weapon. They'd need us again. So we retreated even deeper into the labyrinth. And we've sat at the heart of it all ever since.'

Winter processed the words. 'I was part of this, wasn't I? The SOE? Back in the war?'

Gallard tapped a nail against the golden initials. 'For a while. When we could pry you from the SIS. Given we never employed gentlemen you were our supreme asset. And then you betrayed me. In the end you had all the loyalty of a switchblade. It was only ever the hand that twisted you that counted.'

Winter needed these answers more than he dared admit to himself. 'Go on.'

388

'It was an alliance of convenience,' shared Gallard. 'All of us. British. The Russians. The Shadowless. We established contact with Zerbinati in '41. He was a key player for us, and just as keen as we were to undermine fascist rule in Italy. At war's end he realised our true agenda. The necropolis beneath Naples. He severed the alliance. Sealed the bones away.'

Again Gallard rapped the attaché case, a single nail striking the metal box-frame. The sound echoed in the stone-cool air.

'I knew the Cold War was coming. Soon the Russians would be a liability. We had already shared too much research with them. I instructed you to kill every Soviet scientist that was part of Operation Paragon. You were ordered to savage their necks, bleed their bodies dry. Naturally the SIS would blame the Shadowless. But the SIS gave you a counter-order. You were to kill one man. And one man only.'

Gallard continued to tap the case as he talked. The rhythm seemed random at first, no more than an anxious tic.

'One of our own,' said Winter, ignoring the skittering nail as he focused on the man's words. 'I killed one of our own, so I've been told.'

Gallard's finger found a steady, insistent pulse.

Tap-tap. Tap-tap.

'You killed me,' he stated, dispassionately.

Now the nail had the rhythm of a heartbeat.

It had locked itself to Winter's own, matching it precisely.

Tap-tap. Tap-tap. Tap-tap. Tap-tap.

The man's skin tightened as he smiled, his eyes acknowledging Winter's instant of realisation.

Sir Auberon Gallard was undead.

Winter held the gun level; for all that he knew it was useless now, just so much scrap in his hand. He heard the nail quicken against the case, keeping pace with his heart rate.

'It was an ugly death,' Gallard continued. 'Not really worthy of your talents. A wire to the throat, for God's sake. You had no inkling of what I was and I let you believe you'd succeeded. Convenient for me, in the long run. The SIS wanted me out of the way. They thought they could preserve our relations with the Soviets. Of course they didn't have the means to kill me. Not a high-born vampire. Not a king.'

'The house in Venice,' said Winter, putting it together. 'Il Portone. I put an enchantment upon it. Your orders?'

'Zerbinati believed we were sweetening the alliance, ensuring no one would find the map to the thorns. He thought we were protecting him. But I was securing my survival. I always knew the thorns of Christ could be used against me. And then you went and broke the hex…'

Gallard took a step away from the wall. He stood directly in the moonlight, his skin silver-pale, his irises almost translucent, like coils of water. It was as if he had been bled of all colour. A true revenant, clinging to the world like an after-image.

'What did you need with the bones?' asked Winter,

buying time as he calculated whatever options he had left to defend himself. 'You're not exactly short of vampire DNA...'

He glanced at Gallard's hands as they gripped the case. They had altered shape, thinning to inhuman proportions. The fingers tapered like reeds, preternaturally long. As Winter watched, the nails slid from the quick.

'A proprietorial interest,' said Gallard. 'I had no intention of letting the Russians be part of the final experimentation. They were useful scavengers, nothing more. The bones would be held by Britain. And I would guard their secrets. Bury them, if need be.'

Gallard took another step, defying the gun aimed at his body. There was the sound of bone grinding beneath muscle. His face was shifting, elongating, the skin plucked tight against the planes of the skull. As Winter stared the hollows of the cheeks deepened into troughs while the jawline sharpened. The effect was lean and peculiarly jackal-like.

'The parasitic wasp lays its eggs in a living host. These tiny eggs become larvae, and once they have injected that protective womb with all manner of toxins and pathogens they consume their host from within. It's a cruel process. Darwin considered it proof that there could never be a beneficent God. Imagine how he would have shuddered at the existence of my kind.'

Tap-tap. Tap-tap.

'I am proof of God,' Gallard declared, the scent of brittle flowers filling the old stone building. 'At the dawn of creation he exiled a tribe of blood demons from the world. They so offended the Almighty that he banished even their reflections, cast them out of glass and mirrors, stamped out their shadows. They were his children but he wanted no reminders of his mistake.'

Winter glimpsed another face, sharing the light with Gallard's own. It seemed ancient, bestial, with the crude, dreadful blankness of an idol. The face was the colour of blood, blackened and decayed. It hung there, a fleeting death's head beneath the flesh. A second later it was gone.

'But parasites are the most resilient of God's works. The blood demons endured, and so did their thirst, across eternity. They took humans as their hosts. We incubated them and they claimed us from within, like larvae. But they were generous. They let us live. Forever.'

Tap-tap. Tap-tap.

'That's what we are, the high-born ones, the monarchs of the undead. Symbiotic vessels, preserving the first of our kind. Our gods are inside us. We thirst like they do, and they sip the blood we steal.'

Gallard bared his teeth in a bright, feral smile. 'It's a very gratifying arrangement all round.'

He threw the case aside, moving in.

Winter emptied the gun. Bullet after bullet studded into Gallard, the successive impact of the shots driving him back against the wall. The barrage had no chance of wounding let alone killing him but it won Winter the seconds he needed to dive sideways.

He rolled across hard stone, hurling the gun away.

Scrambling to his feet he seized a pitchfork from the shadows. It was crowned with four brutally pointed prongs. Winter readied it as Gallard approached. The vampire was bloodied but barely winded by the bullets.

The heart, he told himself. *Aim for the heart.*

He thrust the steel through the air. Gallard weaved. The prongs missed their target, snagging only the bulletholes in the shirt, shredding the cotton as they tore free.

Winter lunged again, ramming the pitchfork at Gallard's ribs. This time it stabbed the flesh. He could feel the reach of the steel inside the body. It was embedded in tissue, scraping bone. Straining now he urged the implement deeper. It sunk another inch closer to the heart.

The two men were locked together by the length of wood and metal. Leaning in, Gallard brought his teeth to Winter's throat. The razored enamel came close enough to break the skin. Winter felt hot saliva spatter his neck. He twisted away, his veins bulging beneath the wet, distended jaws. He could hear the click of Gallard's epiglottis, close to his ear. Sweat compromised his grip on the handle but he levered a fraction of space between them, enough to escape the grasp of the teeth.

Gallard's hands closed around the head of the pitchfork. Matching his strength against Winter's he pushed down, determined to extricate the steel from his impaled flesh. Winter fought him, his mouth contorting with the effort.

Gallard had the edge. The prongs slid free with a soft sucking sound. They were running with blood.

Winter let go of the pitchfork. He backed away,

stumbling into the pots behind him. There was a threshing flail on the ground. He seized it, whirling the chained sticks at Gallard's head.

Gallard caught the flail and tore it from Winter's hand. He flung it away.

Winter retreated again. He was out of options. Any moment now he'd be backed against the opposite wall.

Flesh is memory. Bone is memory. Blood is memory.

Alessandra's words were all that he had.

Winter closed his fists. He felt the touch of his own skin as he took a deep, steadying breath. Inside him, he knew, was an enchantment of bone and muscle, its secrets stitched in a bright maze of veins. Every part of him held the memory and truth of magic. Enough to shape the world.

He shut his eyes as Gallard closed the space between them. Now his world was dense as ink. And that ink surged and seethed and spiralled with possibility. It moved like a storm across his eyelids, just as it had swirled on that Rorschach test in London. Tiny capillaries glittered in the darkness, the threads of his blood electric.

He was Christopher Winter. He was a magician.

The nerve above his eyes began an insistent beat. Winter reached inside himself and summoned a shadow scythe. And this time he shaped it, made it exactly what he needed. He was no longer afraid of it. This one he would sculpt and command.

The heart, he told himself. *Aim for the heart.*

The magic tore from his body, wrenching itself out of blood and bone.

Winter opened his eyes as Gallard screamed. A solid, lightless shard had skewered the vampire's chest, piercing the heart. It was a lance of pure shadow and Gallard reeled beneath its impact, fighting in vain to rip it free. His hands were burning at the touch of the black spear.

The scream decayed, turning to a protracted, agonised hiss. Gallard staggered and fell, his skin splitting, fracturing, reclaimed by the centuries. He hit the stone floor as a cadaver.

He was dead, for the moment.

Winter stood above the remains. The shadow scythe quivered, lodged between Gallard's ribs. The shard was impenetrably dark but Winter saw that darkness glint and coruscate. He called it back into his veins, receiving it with a soft, exhausted sigh.

He could hear rain on the stonework, infiltrating the slabs.

Winter lit a Woodbine and walked to the open door. He looked out across the countryside, the oaks and the kilns and the stillness of the harvest fields. The sudden shower had made the moonlight gauzy. A cobweb hung in the arch of the doorway, beaded by raindrops. Winter watched them run on the spider's silk as he savoured the bitter rush of the cigarette. If his hand trembled he paid it no mind.

When the Woodbine was finished he took a hammer and chisel from the wall and prepared to extract the heart of Auberon Gallard.

29

Libby hated the light at first.

She hated the way it woke her; the way it stung, hot and sharp, the instant she opened her eyes. Even on her eyelids the weight of it hurt. Confronted by mornings she would push her face into the pillow and try to dream again. Her dreams felt like protection, even the ones where she was cold and quiet and churchyard soil engulfed her bones.

She tried to dream of better things than being six foot under. Kissing smashing girls, usually, in secret corners of Chelsea clubs. But the soil would find her, filling her mouth, an inescapable reminder that she was stealing mornings never meant for her.

At least the grave didn't hurt her eyes. That was something.

During those first weeks at Villa Tramonto heavy wooden shutters had sealed away the light, preserving the room in a cool, insulating gloom. Day and night became a dim mulch of hours, broken only by simple meals and glasses of sharp, sweet apple juice, her favourite. And then one morning she woke to find the shutters had been opened an inch, and an inch again the next morning. Each day the slice of light widened across the floorboards until finally it reached the great white bed, with the ivory sheets that drowned her.

Soon the light didn't hurt quite so much anymore.

One day a maid had entered and placed a tall silver clock on the dressing table. It changed everything. Now the days had a shape, and the hours moved just that little bit faster.

Libby would lie there, alone in the sparse, pristine room, exploring how different she felt. The chill of her skin was weird, and that unsettled her. She would trace her fingers along her arm, across the curve of her shoulder blades, into the incline of her throat. The pulse in her neck would beat against the tips, the steady Morse that told her she was alive. But her skin was so cold, and that made no sense, because her blood was raw as fire inside.

Sometimes she felt like a fountain beneath a whisper.

All of it was odd. The world – and this room was the world, for now – seemed almost too real. She could see strokes of paint on the far wall, hear the movement of the clock's gears in between sweeps of the second hand. Sometimes she was convinced she could taste iron on her tongue, enough to start her salivating. They had warned her about the thirst, how keen it would feel, as keen as the world.

She had barely noticed the loss of her shadow, at least to begin with. Only when she crossed the room with her own strength did she realise how incomplete she felt. It was as if a fine layer of self had been amputated. One day she thought about it altogether too much and her balance went, leaving her clinging to the rim of the marble sink, fighting tears. She missed the reassurance of that other Libby, the silent imprint of existence she had taken for granted her entire life.

The mirror was even harder, of course. It waited for her now, as it did every morning, daring her to approach. Libby let it wait there.

A new maid brought her breakfast today. The girl was pale in spite of her Mediterranean looks, with sleek black hair that fell to her waist. Libby watched her place the tray on the bedside table, hearing ice bob and crack in a glass.

'I don't think I've seen you before, have I?'

The maid shook her head, handing over the apple juice. Libby noticed that her nails were badly chipped, though she had coated them with varnish as best she could.

'What's your name?'

A smile. 'Benedetta.'

'I'm Libby.'

The girl repeated the name like a puzzle. 'Libby…'

'Have you just started today?'

Benedetta frowned at the words. '*Mi dispiace. Non ho capito.*' She leaned in to lift the lid of the butter dish. As she did so she pushed a tumble of hair from her face, draping it across her shoulder.

Libby stared at the puncture wounds on the girl's

throat. The skin seemed to be healing but the incisions were so deep the marks looked as though they might never fade, not entirely. She wondered how vicious her own wounds looked, beneath the gauze and cotton.

'How long?' she asked, nodding to the bite marks. '*Da quanto?*'

'*Mi dispiace. Non ho capito.*'

Libby could sense the cool, still-water aura of Benedetta's body, close to hers. There were no shadows from that body on the white sheets, no glimmer of its reflection in the porcelain dish on the breakfast tray. The girl was breathing, her heart was obviously beating, and yet her presence seemed to make no impression on the room, as if she was barely more than a memory of someone.

God, thought Libby, was this how people would see her now? Halfway to a bloody ghost?

There were so many questions she wanted to ask this girl.

Benedetta placed a foil packet beside the bruschetta. It contained two caplets of a crimson liquid that caught the waking light in the room. Scarlatto, they called it. Libby would take the pills later. They eased the thirst but the queasy, salt-milk taste of them was proving to be a daily challenge.

The new maid left with an awkward curtsy. Libby savoured the apple juice for a while, watching the sunlight stretch across the floorboards. Then she threw back the ocean of sheets and walked to the waiting mirror.

The surface had been shrouded in muslin during her

first weeks at the villa. Don Zerbinati himself had held her by the arms the day the drape was removed. And he had steadied her as she recoiled.

The thought of it still made her sick, that first, searing glimpse of nothingness. It had felt like a punch, a fist to the face, to the soul. To see an empty room in the sun-struck glass and not a trace of yourself. It was an obliteration of everything that had defined her; the wayward fringe, the freckled nose, the gap in her teeth she had hated as a kid.

Some days she was convinced she could still catch a hint of herself. A vague, transparent outline, subtly altering the way the light fell on the mirror. But if she looked again the blur in the glass was gone. She was afraid it was only her imagination.

Libby picked up a Mary Quant lipstick from the dressing table. This was the one without the hidden blade, the one she wondered how she would ever apply again, now that she could never look back at herself.

She pressed her left hand against the mirror, noting how the glass didn't mist beneath her touch. And then she took the lipstick and drew around the contours of her hand, carefully tracing the dips and peaks of her fingers, the curve of her palm.

Libby took her hand away and stared at its clumsy rouge afterimage. Almost a reflection, she told herself. Almost a shadow.

Then she slashed the lipstick against the mirror in quick, determined strokes. A line for the nose, a dash for the mouth. Two round guesses where the eyes would be.

Thick, smudgy dots for freckles. Every mark she made gave her strength. It felt like she was reclaiming herself in the glass, stating her face all over again.

Taking a step back she gazed at the crude, bright likeness.

She should have been dead. But she was here, and she existed.

Would London want her back? It was all that she knew, all that she had driven herself to be. Part of her needed that continuity, the certainty of Queen and country, orders and expectations, the chance to prove herself again and again. And yet she had worked for Gallard – and who knew if the SIS could forgive that. Maybe she should follow Winter's lead and slip that world, find a new future, take the time to make sense of what she had become. But London, she knew, so rarely let you go.

Libby heard a sound from outside. The echo of feet, moving in a fast, violent rhythm. Curious, she moved to the window, peering through the shutters, her eyes flinching at the direct light.

The maid, Benedetta, was in the private part of the courtyard directly below the room. She had kicked her heels away. And she was dancing in a strip of sunlight, her hair a black cascade as she flung and whirled her limbs, so sure that no one was watching.

It was a dance that Libby recognised. It was called the Tarantella, the spider dance.

3ø

In early October Winter returned to Naples with the heart of Auberon Gallard in his hand luggage. He parcelled the stolen organ in crisp brown paper and informed the lady on the customs desk it was a gift of English ham. She smiled and assured him that Neapolitan salami was altogether superior.

Two of Zerbinati's men escorted him from the terminal at Capodichino to a waiting Lancia Flaminia. There was no conversation as the car climbed to the rocky swell of Posillipo. Winter watched the clear light play across the coves and breakwaters that clung beneath the coastal road, marvelling at how the same sun, at the same time, could be watching over a damp, leaf-cluttered London with such disdain.

Villa Tramonto awaited, like a great white bird on the edge of the headland. The gates opened, allowing the Lancia to slide past the shining sports cars hoarded in the drive. Winter was walked to the rear of the villa, where Don Zerbinati sat at a table, poolside, picking at a plate of mussels and olives, a glass of white wine casting spirals of light on his suit. His men positioned themselves at a discreet but watchful distance.

'Please, sit down,' the vampire said, dabbing a square of satin to his lips. He regarded the parcel that had just been placed on the table. 'The heart, I take it?'

Winter gave a dry smile. 'Another relic for your collection.'

'Hardly the heart of a saint.'

'I removed it as soon as I could. It wasn't the easiest job in the world.'

Zerbinati frowned at the crumpled, string-bound package. 'You were wise to separate it from the body. But as a high born of the undead I confess I find your lack of reverence distasteful. This was the heart of a king. Remember that.'

'You told me to bring it to you.'

'I anticipated a little more respect.'

'You had no idea Gallard was one of your own?' asked Winter. 'All that time you were dealing with Paragon?'

Zerbinati shook his head. 'The man was unknown to me, but then he may have worn many names over the centuries. At the time of Paragon he was embedded in London. I was embedded in Naples. We never met. I only dealt with his proxies.'

'Like me.'

'You are not the man you were in the war. That's clear to me now. Something has changed in you.'

'For the better, I trust?'

Zerbinati paused, the glass at his lips. 'I miss your fire.'

Winter squinted against the hard, clean light. He could hear the slap of pool water, stirred by a listless noon breeze. 'Of course now you have an interesting choice to make.'

The vampire took a sip of wine then skimmed his tongue across his lips. 'Tell me what you mean.'

'Two royal hearts, Don Zerbinati. One belongs to Auberon Gallard. One belongs to your son. And you only have a single sacred thorn between them. Now assuming you didn't leave Cesare's remains in the Mortal Sepulchre, which heart will you place it in? Who gets to truly stay dead?'

For a moment Zerbinati revolved the glass between his fingers, watching as it mirrored the Mediterranean sun. And then he moved his gaze to the city and the bright crush of houses piled on the hills above the bay. Vesuvius loomed like a bruising mood on the horizon.

'Naples worships the dead. I may be its king but I will never truly be part of it. Its people call us *I Senz'Ombr*, the Shadowless, because death is the shadow denied to my kind. Tear away the trinkets and superstition and what remains is one simple, absolute truth – death is the shadow that tells these people they have lived. Now my son has a shadow.'

Winter studied the other man's face. It was unreadable in the sunlight. 'So you've made your choice, then?'

Zerbinati drained the last of the wine. 'The girl is ready to meet you now.'

He rose from the chair, leaving his plate to the mosquitoes that had been circling the table, attracted

405

by the briny tang of the mussels. Winter followed him across the white sun-struck marble that bordered the walls of the villa.

'How's she coping?'

'The first weeks weren't easy. But she's strong. Resilient. I've been impressed by her spirit. She will need time to find her place in this world.'

'What should I know?'

Zerbinati kept walking but took a moment to choose his words. 'You should know that she wanted this.'

'I was there. I remember.'

'Yes, you were. But you must go on remembering. She will doubt herself in the years ahead.'

Libby Cracknell waited by the main door in a lemon-yellow sundress, her eyes shielded by a pair of round amber-tinted glasses. Her skin looked snow-pale in the sharp light and she was thinner than Winter remembered. Only as he approached did she break into a smile.

'Alright, you wanker?'

They embraced in an awkward, English way, exchanging equally awkward pleasantries. Winter was startled by the chill of her body but said nothing.

Stepping back he glanced at the maid who hovered at Libby's side. He placed her at once, though there was no sign that she remembered him. It was the dancer from the street, the one they had found in that grim house in the Spanish quarter. The name came to him a second later. *Benedetta.* Don Zerbinati must have taken her on after Cesare's death. There was kindness in the man, it seemed. What was it he had said, back in the Mortal Sepulchre? *'We are far from monsters.'* Winter began to suspect that might be true.

Zerbinati also embraced Libby. His hug was more robust. He leaned in and told her something that Winter couldn't quite catch, words that clearly belonged to the undead alone.

Libby nodded, understanding whatever private truth had passed between them.

She said her goodbyes to the maid, who passed her a small suitcase. Then she crossed the drive to a gleaming, smoke-grey Maserati Berlinetta that was parked between a pair of vintage Ferraris. Don Zerbinati flung her a set of car keys. She caught them with ease.

'You're driving?' asked Winter, as she stowed the suitcase in the boot.

'Of course I'm driving.'

They settled into the hot leather seats, the gates of Villa Tramonto breaking open before them.

'Where are you heading?'

Libby twisted the key in the ignition, relishing the snarl of the waking engine. 'Home. Eventually. How about you?'

Winter realised he had no idea, not anymore. 'Pretty sure somewhere will occur to me along the way.'

The Maserati swung onto the coastal road, gathering speed as if ready to outrace the sea itself. The needle rose and the asphalt began to blur. With the engine roaring they shot past the azure glitter of the Tyrrhenian. As the car carved into the hills a flash of gold filled the rear-view mirror, catching Winter's gaze. No doubt it was just the sun hitting the glass but he wanted it to be Alessandra's eyes, watching as they tore into the day, and all the days beyond.

He looked across at Libby. She was smiling as she gripped the wheel, the heat and the wind in her face.

If the sunlight hurt her she didn't let it show.

ACKNOWLEDGEMENTS

Louise Blain, who discussed the finer points of undead lore with me on a bench by Bath Abbey; Ella Bowman and the Great Unknown Neapolitan Waiter; Bob Erskine for a little local knowledge.

Cat Camacho and Joanna Harwood, my insightful and meticulous editors at Titan Books; Natasha MacKenzie for another magical cover.

Julie Crisp, my fabulous, not-so-secret agent. Dana Spector at CAA, for championing Mr Winter.

Dad, my family and all my friends. You keep the vampires from my door.

ABOUT THE AUTHOR

Nick Setchfield is a contributing editor to *SFX*, Britain's best-selling magazine of genre entertainment in film, TV and books. A regular writer to *Total Film*, he's also been a movie reviewer for the BBC and a scriptwriter for ITV's *Spitting Image*. He lives in Bath.

DARK INK
Gary Kemble

Freelance journalist Harry Hendrick is working on a story about a paedophile ring preying on boys at one of the city's most prestigious schools, and probing rumours of a union official who's blowing members' dues on an exclusive professional dominatrix. Those investigations lead him into the web of Mistress Hel, who plies her dark arts from her luxurious suburban lair. Harry believes she's driven by a desire for vengeance, until rumours reach him of clients under a supernatural thrall, of demonic visions, and something dark and infernal which is spreading out into the world.

PRAISE FOR THE AUTHOR

"Offers more than a passing nod to John Birmingham and Stephen King" *Books + Publishing*

"Has the crucial ingredients of the best of the genre (cracking pace, intricate plotting, irresistible intrigue) while largely evading the cheesy, overblown language of its cheaper examples" *The Saturday Paper*

"Keeps you guessing until the end" *Weekly Times*

THE PLAGUE STONES

James Brogden

SHE'S WAITED CENTURIES FOR REVENGE...

After a brutal break-in leaves her family traumatised, Trish Feenan jumps at the chance of a fresh start in a charming historic community. But in the back garden of her new cottage sits an unsettling reminder of past wrongs: a standing stone, once one of the markers that kept plague sufferers outside the village bounds, its 'powers' renewed every year in a ritual that seems to be more than just local oddity.

As the Feenans settle in, they experience unexplained accidents, accompanied by sightings of a girl who vanishes into thin air. Soon, it becomes obvious that there is a reason traditions must not slip, and that all acts of betrayal, even those committed centuries ago, have consequences...

PRAISE FOR THE AUTHOR

"Nicely done" *Daily Mail*

"Brogden keeps up a steady supply of shocks and chills" *SciFi Now*

"Something special and unique" Risingshadow

For more fantastic fiction, author events, competitions,
limited editions and more

VISIT OUR WEBSITE
titanbooks.com

LIKE US ON FACEBOOK
facebook.com/titanbooks

FOLLOW US ON TWITTER
@TitanBooks

EMAIL US
readerfeedback@titanemail.com